Atlantean Secrets

Volume 2

Forever Love, White Eagle

Samuel Sagan

Clairvision™

PO Box 33, Roseville NSW 2069, Australia
www.clairvision.org
info@clairvision.org

By the same author:

* **Atlantean Secrets, Volume 1 – Sleeper Awaken!**

* **Atlantean Secrets, Volume 3 – The Gods are Wise**

* **Atlantean Secrets, Volume 4 – The Return of the Flying Dragon**

* **Bleeding Sun – Discover the Future of Virtual Reality**

* **Awakening the Third Eye**

* **Entities, Parasites of the Body of Energy**
  (published in the US as Entity Possession)

* **Regression, Past Life Therapy for Here and Now Freedom**

* **Planetary Forces, Alchemy and Healing**

* **Clairvision Astrology Manual**

* **Clairvision Knowledge Tracks, correspondence courses in meditation and esoteric knowledge including audio-cassettes, videos, printed material and electronic texts.**

Visit the Clairvision Website for book excerpts, free books, Atlantean Secrets music, and a full concordance of the *Atlantean Secrets* saga:

www.clairvision.org

Book cover by Michael Smith

Copyright © 1999 by Clairvision School Foundation
Published in Sydney, Australia, by Clairvision
PO Box 33, Roseville NSW 2069, Australia
E-mail: info@clairvision.org
Website: www.clairvision.org

ISBN 0-9586700-8-0

Atlantean Secrets

The Tetralogy

ACKNOWLEDGEMENTS

First and foremost to Lord Gana, whose flow of inspiration was the driving force to begin, carry on, and complete this epic novel.

Then to the people who edited, proofed and illustrated *Atlantean Secrets*: Avril Carruthers, Catherine Ross, Debianne Gosper, Eva Pascoe, Gilda Ogawa, Michael Smith, Oonagh Sherrard, Orna Lankry, Philip Joseph, Ros Watson, Rosa Droescher, Ruth Camden, Tobi Langmo and Wilhelmina von Buellen.

Last, but certainly not least, to Gervin extraordinaire, friend and master in Thunder. Without him, none of this would ever have happened. *All glory to the teacher!*

A note on the use of italics

Italics have been used to indicate the following:

1) Quotes from the Law of Melchisedek, for example:

One of the most misunderstood of all verses of the Law was *"One Law, one way. Praise the Lord Melchisedek!"*

2) Discourses of gods, angels, and Flying Dragons:

The White Eagle responded,
"Soul of Highness,
Child of eternity,
Angel of the human hierarchy,
I have waited for you since earlier than time.
And here you come, shining,
Punctual for the cosmic appointment,
Making the Mother of the Light proud of her seed."

3) Discourses engaged in by human beings while raised to the level of consciousness of gods, angels, and Flying Dragons (therefore including communications through the power of the Point). For example,

"Gervin!" I Point-called. *"Please do something! Quick!"*

4) At times, italics have been used to emphasize a particular word in a sentence, for example:

"Gervin," Teyani said, "if it wasn't coming from you, I would *never* believe this story!"

From Volume 3 onwards, however, due to the marked increase in conversations with angels, gods and Flying Dragons (categories 2 and 3), common expression from the Law of Melchisedek have been left unitalicised.

Volume 2

Contents

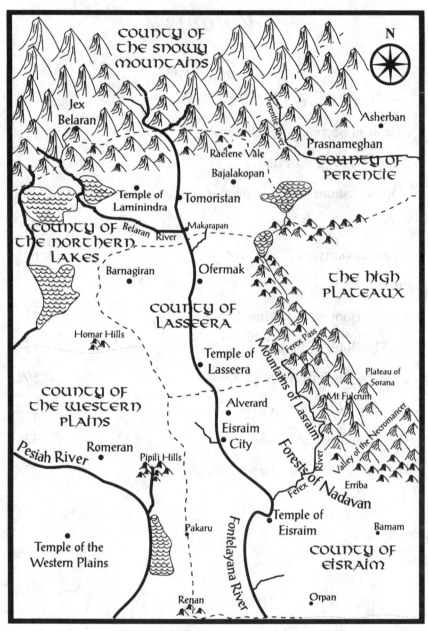

The Counties of the Centre North

Foreword

The twenty-two books which constitute the four volumes of *Atlantean Secrets* follow a carefully arranged sequence, designed to take you through a succession of spaces of consciousness and realisations. To enjoy the effects woven behind the lines, it is therefore essential to start from the beginning of Volume 1, *Sleeper Awaken!*

At the end of *Forever Love, White Eagle*, you will find a large map of the temple of Eisraim. For a map of the counties surrounding Eisraim, see p. 4. For a diagrammatic representation of the different worlds where this story will take you, see the cosmological ladder p. 325.

A glossary of the main names and terms used in *Atlantean Secrets* can be found at the end of *Sleeper Awaken!* For a more comprehensive study, see the saga's concordance, *From Eisraim to Philadelphia*, which can be obtained from the Clairvision School's Internet site.

Like Flying Dragons, the *Atlantean Secrets* epic is musical in essence. Characters, gods, angels and worlds each have their themes, and a number of scenes are accompanied by musical scores. This music, which forms an important part of the epic, can be heard in full at the Clairvision site:

www.clairvision.org

The prelude of *Forever Love, White Eagle* is set in the future. Virginia and Hiram have just died during a gigantic space battle – a story told in the novel *Bleeding Sun*. Arriving in the Fields of Peace they join Master Barkhan Seer, who shows them Archive records of the ancient continent, Atlantis. The whole saga of *Atlantean Secrets* unfolds in front of them.

Now, to the Archive halls, where Barkhan Seer's secrets are waiting.

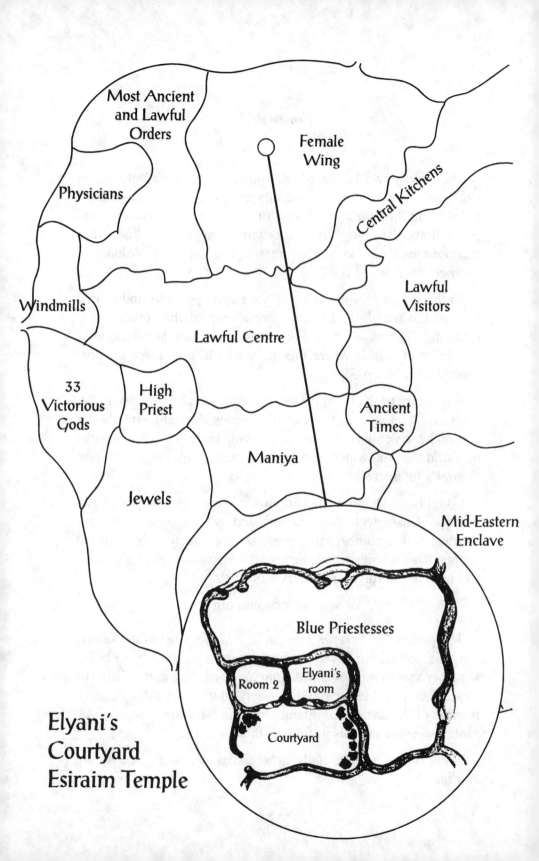

Most Ancient
and Lawful
Orders

Female
Wing

Central Kitchens

Physicians

Windmills

Lawful Centre

Lawful
Visitors

33
Victorious
Gods

High
Priest

Ancient
Times

Maniya

Jewels

Mid-Eastern
Enclave

Blue Priestesses

Room 2

Elyani's
room

Courtyard

Elyani's
Courtyard
Esiraim Temple

Prelude

Fields of Peace, Archive Hall Five, Space Age

"Enter!" Master Barkhan Seer invited.[1]

Virginia Serah and Hiram the Unstoppable walked into the fluid darkness of Archive Hall Five, their faces lit by the silvery starlight that peered through the dome-shaped ceiling. Their appearance was the same as a few days earlier, when they still lived in physical bodies in the Philadelphias: young adults, not even eighteen years of age, matured early by the war. Virginia, the beautiful daughter of Elyani Serah (flight-alias Panther), still looked grey, defeated, beaten, heavy with twelve years of sorrow and the black filth of the Rex. Hiram, the lost child who had conquered the powers of Revelation Sky and triumphed twice over Ahriman, was glowing, his disharmonious features softened by the River of Remembrance, his eyes lit with the calm assurance of an initiate who can be anything, do anything.

As they walked, Virginia kept her almond-shaped eyes fixed on the floor. Hiram looked skywards, fascinated by the stars. Since he had arrived in the Fields of Peace he had discovered a passion for gazing at the night sky. The stars whispered ancient mysteries to his soul, touching him with their rays in a surprisingly tactile way. For the stars of the Fields of Peace are no ordinary stars, but mighty breaths of Spirit filled with the archetypal magic wisdom of Revelation Sky. Their light is Life, their colours pure Cosmic Fire.

Pulling himself from the stars' magic, Hiram joyfully greeted his master, "Praise the Great Apollo, Master Barkhan Seer, Prince of Thunder!"

Clad in the brown gown of the Masters of Thunder, Master Barkhan Seer was standing directly beneath the dome's vertex. He echoed Hiram's buoyant voice, "Praise the Great Apollo, Hiram, Knight of the Apocalypse and Descender! And welcome to you, Virginia of the last hour. Are you better today?"

---

[1] Pronounced 'Barkhan Zair'.

Virginia didn't speak, she kept staring at the floor. She was still stunned, not from her violent death but from years spent detained on Philadelphia 6, swamped by the Rex's venom.

Standing by her side, Hiram answered for her, "Much better already. Since we last spoke to you we have spent a whole night and a whole day by the River of Remembrance, listening to the songs of time, letting the river's feelings flow through us. We found many ways of speaking without words. Today we kept eye contact many times. Words will come soon, the River of Remembrance told me. Tomorrow we will go back to the chambers of healing. But we have come to ask a favour, Master Barkhan Seer. What Virginia needs now is to hear about her parents. I am convinced it would help her find herself. So we thought perhaps you could show us some of the Archive material about Serah and the Panther?"

Virginia had been separated from her parents at the age of five, when Philadelphia 6 was invaded by the troops of the Rex. From then on her life had turned grey. As she became entangled in the Rex's virtual reality, even the images of Elyani and Serah gradually became lost. She could hardly remember their names. All that remained was a devastating emptiness, a world without hope, a masquerade of virtual puppets. Until Hiram came.

"What would you like to see?" Barkhan Seer offered.

"What are we entitled to see?" Hiram asked.

"Before leaving for the spheres of remoteness, Szar-Serah instructed me to grant you full access to his personal records. To both of you."

"To me too?" Hiram wondered.

"You saved his life only a few days ago," Barkhan Seer reminded him.

"I know, I know. But still... I am touched to learn that Serah gave me as much access as he gave to his own daughter."

Barkhan Seer pushed his lips forward and nodded, "Szar loves you... more than you have realised, Sir Hiram. When he returns from remoteness, he will have much to tell you. For now, just tell me where you want to begin, my Archive is all yours."

Thoughtful, Hiram gazed at the field of stars again. He slowly extended his hand. Reaching Virginia's chin, he gently lifted her head so her eyes met the stars. She bent her head to the side, resting her cheek on his palm, contemplating a feast of luminous clouds – myriads of multicoloured jewels. Barkhan Seer contemplated her, Hiram, and the precious harmony of their togetherness.

"Why not start from the beginning, then?" Hiram decided. "How far back could we go?"

"As far as Atlantis, if you want. Thirteen thousand years ago." Barkhan Seer conjured a three-dimensional image of a curly-haired little girl dressed in white running along alleys covered in mists, "Elyani of the White Eagle, when she was four years old. At the temple of Eisraim."

A tall, dignified woman with long dark hair, also dressed in white, took Elyani in her arms. "Lady Teyani, Grand Master of the order of the White

Eagle," Barkhan Seer provided the commentary. "She wasn't yet the grand master of the female wing of the temple of Eisraim."

Hearing the name Teyani, Virginia lowered her gaze to watch the Archive images.

Another little girl dressed in white was running to Teyani. "This one was Alcibyadi," Barkhan Seer said.[1] Teyani, a strong woman with wide hips and a slim waist, took her in her arms, still carrying Elyani against her left breast. One child in each arm, she entered a small empty chapel made of what seemed like red basalt. She sat cross-legged in the centre of a large circle carved in the floor. Soon both children fell asleep on her lap, and she entered a state of deep meditation.

"Beautiful like a fecundity goddess!" Hiram exclaimed, moved. "Was this in the temple of Eisraim?"

Barkhan Seer nodded, "The chapel of the White Eagle."

"And where was Szar at the time?"

Barkhan Seer conjured an image of a blond little boy dressed in a light-beige robe, walking in a forest. "Not yet called Szar but Orlon, son of Orlon. He was born far from Eisraim, in the county of Sheringa. On the western shores of Atlantis."

Hiram was appalled by the boy's near-emaciated face, his pale, greenish complexion and his extremely slow movements. "Was he sick?"

"No, but he wasn't exactly a physical child. A certain lack of incarnation..." Barkhan Seer continued to show images of the children as they grew up. On the right, Szar-Orlon was in a classroom with little boys all dressed in beige. They spent their days learning verses of the Law by heart.

On the left, little Elyani and Alcibyadi were practising magic rituals with Teyani. A curly-haired little boy in a brown gown, a few years older than the White Eagle apprentices, was helping.

On the right, as Orlon grew up he remained by far the skinniest of his class. His beige little friends moved terribly slowly, but Orlon seemed the slowest of the lot.

On the left Elyani and Alcibyadi, now ten years old, were taking lessons from a Brown Robe priest with a long thin face, piercing grey-green eyes, grey hair falling to his shoulders and a short grey beard. "Recognise this man?" Barkhan Seer asked. "Master Gervin of the Brown Robe.[2] From their most tender years Elyani and Alcibyadi were taught by him."

Years passed. On the right, Orlon and his friends were still spending their days repeating verses of the Law. On the left, a group of twenty-four young priestesses in the Eagle were being trained in the arts of prophecy, Voice projection, astral travelling, theurgy, healing, herbalism, and the use of soft stones. "Teyani had started recruiting her team," Barkhan Seer commented. On the right, Orlon was standing very still, slowly beating two

[1] Pronounced 'Alsibyahdee'.
[2] Pronounced 'Djervin'.

short wooden sticks against each other. "Orlon tried to learn music, but it never really worked out." Barkhan Seer stifled a smile.

As the images went on, Hiram kept glancing at Virginia, observing her reactions. As he had hoped, something in her responded to the images of Szar – an elusive but unmistakable 'ffffoooohhhh' whisper in the high end of her column of Spirit, echoes of her nature in remoteness. Using his massive Point of a Knight of the Apocalypse, Hiram held her energy high up, while surrounding her with the Eagle's boundless love. The result was instant: life in her eyes, more of her presence in the Archive hall.

Moved at the sight of so much giving, Barkhan Seer praised, "Hiram, Hiram... how right Serah was when he wanted you to be the next White Eagle of the Philadelphian Air Force! The legend lives on. Nothing can stop a White Eagle on his way to a Flying Dragon."

Light of Highness pouring into his Point, Hiram kept holding Virginia who slowly rocked her head, gathering herself.

"Because of the extraordinary circumstances in which Szar's Atlantean existence ended, we have records of *all* his memories, not just scenes that came to us through the fields of Eisraim," Barkhan Seer explained. "Watch this. It was a crucial moment, an hour of God."

Elyani's image faded. In a new scene, seventeen-year-old Orlon, son of Orlon, was beginning the final examination that was to decide his career as a public servant of the county of Sheringa. By the side of a dirt road, Master Gervin was rescuing a woman of low caste. He called for help. Hesitantly, Orlon let his friends continue the race and responded to Gervin's call. Slowly, timidly, the frail boy in beige walked towards the man in the Brown Robe.

"A destiny was sealed," Barkhan Seer's voice was grave.

After this, Orlon followed Gervin and received from him a new name: Szar. The two returned to the temple of Eisraim.

Watching images of Szar dressed in a light-pink gown, Hiram was surprised, "Wasn't he part of the Brown Robe?"

"It took years before Szar became an apprentice of the Masters of Thunder. At first he was trained by an order of priests called the Salmon Robe. Powerful ritualists, but not particularly awakened."

"Difficult to believe how slowly they walked!" Hiram was amused, contemplating pink Szar peacefully chatting with another young man in pink in one of the temple alleys.

"This was Artold, his best friend at the time," Barkhan Seer said. "And this was the first time Szar and Elyani met."

High priestess Elyani of the White Eagle, now a flourishing young woman, was walking down the same alley. Szar and Artold kept walking without taking any notice of her. Absorbed in her own inner contemplation, she didn't notice them either.

Prelude

"For years, they walked past each other without seeing one another," Barkhan Seer smiled, letting Archive images unfold. "They eventually met when Master Gervin asked Elyani to be Szar's travelling instructor."

Szar was lying unconscious in a sarcophagus. Two priests were closing the sarcophagus with a translucent slab. The priests left the room, Elyani entered. She was accompanied by another young woman clad in a long white dress. "This one was her friend Seyani of the White Eagle. One of the high priestesses who were sent to Egypt."

"So Egypt was a *real* country, not a legend?" Hiram discovered.

"Not a legend! One of the first places where civilisation reflourished after the end of Atlantis."

There followed images of Szar travelling in astral spaces, zapping from darkness visible into the fields of stars. Meanwhile, in the kingdom, he was striving to achieve 'awakening', the mysterious goal that Gervin had set, but that always seemed to elude him. He prayed late at night in the chapel of Lord Gana. He started asking Master Gervin questions, gradually realising that the life of Salmon Robe priests was spent mechanically following the rules of the Law. He strove to stop being a puppet.

"Another crucial moment," Barkhan Seer announced. In a large chapel, Hiram counted twenty-seven Salmon Robe priests. Singing spellbinding hymns of the Law, they were conducting a momentous ritual with gold and copper utensils everywhere, seeds, spices and flowers of all colours forming geometrical patterns on the floor. Shaken by a profound realisation, Szar of the Salmon Robe stood up and left his position.

Walking out of his sleeper's life.

The vision filled Archive Hall Five with vibrant spiritual presence. Touched by the Mother of the Light, Virginia turned to Hiram and established eye contact with him.

He made himself White Eagle for her.

A ffffoooohhhh breeze passed through her. She was fighting to break her shell, fighting against the accumulated weight of resignation and hopelessness.

In the Archive record, time seemed to have slowed down. The singing could no longer be heard, there was but an immense silence charged with the presence of the Mother of the Light. In slow motion, Szar was walking out of the chapel, each step bringing new meaning to the creation.

Looking deep into Hiram's eyes, Virginia said, "Yes."

Szar reached the door of the chapel, opened it, turned back to contemplate his Salmon Robe friends. They were so absorbed in the ritual that they had hardly noticed his departure.

"Hiram, I know," Virginia said. "I know who you are. What you have done."

Szar took a last look at Artold, at the flame on the altar, at Prates his teacher in the Salmon Robe. Still in slow motion, wise Prates turned to him. He remained silent but his eyes said, "Go, child. Let the Mother of the

Light take you by the hand. I know who you are, what you will do. We shall meet again in the Fields of Peace."

Szar turned away, walked through the doorway, found himself in the alley outside the chapel. A new life had begun.

"A smile?" Hiram whispered, tentatively.

Imperceptibly, Virginia's face softened into a near-smile. And she spoke to Hiram again, this time without words.

Hiram chuckled and gave a handclap, "Taken!"

They returned to the Archive visions. Szar was wearing the brown gown of the Masters of Thunder. He had been sent by Gervin to fetch a precious soft stone from a hermitage in the mountains of Lasraim. On his way back he lost the stone, and then nearly committed suicide by letting himself drown in a lake. The White Eagle sent him a vision, symbolically showing Elyani in great peril. Forgetting about suicide, Szar jumped out of the water and rushed back to Eisraim, very much in his power.

"A common trick of the gods," Hiram commented for Virginia. "When the hero is hitting rock-bottom, let him play knight in shining armour. They did it to me too, you know. And it worked just the same."

Barkhan Seer laughed. Virginia's face softened a little more.

Now Szar of the Brown Robe and Elyani of the White Eagle were sitting together on a purple lawn in a little courtyard bordered by laurel trees. She gave him a white beverage. It made him choke, flames of energy coming out of his mouth.

"What is *that*?" Szar asked, horrified.

"Dragon's milk," Elyani answered candidly. "Very secret, and totally magic."

Hiram whispered, "On arriving at Philadelphia 6, my plan was to bewitch you with Dragon's milk."

Virginia turned to him, her face lit with an intrigued smile.

Hiram shrugged, "Who knows? Another life, perhaps."

Then came the gruesome scenes of Szar's first descent into the Underworlds – mutilated corpses, rotting carcasses, screaming crowds, large-scale madness. When he saw how avidly Hiram and Virginia were drinking the images, Barkhan Seer grinned, "If these visions are too painful, perhaps we can skip them."

"No," Virginia answered, her eyes fixed on the Underworlds.

Hiram clapped his hands and marvelled when Szar picked up Vivyani in the caverns of sickness.

"No," Virginia said, having already guessed.

Soon Szar dumped the priestess by the side of the path and returned to the kingdom. Alone.

After this came the tender times of Szar's recovery, Elyani patiently looking after him. Seeing their innocence, their warmth, their playfulness, Virginia smiled again. Then Szar departed for the temple of the Dragon in Mount Lohrzen, far in the south in the county of the Red Lands. There followed the breathtaking scenes of the death in the Dragon, when insane intensities of Underworld fire rushed into Szar's body, first killing him, then resuscitating him.

Szar was reborn a Great Warrior.

"Talk about a descent!" Hiram kept commenting. Regarding Marek the indestructible, Szar's teacher in the Dragon, he inquired, "Is he the Marek I met?"

"Same!" Barkhan Seer answered. "There's only one like him."

"You bet!" For Virginia, Hiram added, "Marek is a bit of a legend. He and your father were best friends. I mean in the Philadelphian Air Force."

In the temple of the Dragon, Szar underwent a metamorphosis. His shoulders doubled in width, huge muscles coming to him straight from the Dragon's depths. His thin blond hair became thick and strong, slightly darker, curly locks falling onto his shoulders. And he started growing a beard.

Hiram recognised him at last. "This is the Szar I'm familiar with. This is how he looked when he taught me and when he was my copilot," he said, attracting another intrigued smile from Virginia. "Except that he wore his brown gown, of course," he added.

Dressed in black cloth pants and shirt, Szar, Son of the Dragon, underwent the Warriors' training in the black dance and the weapons of the lesser magic of the Earth. And he descended into the Underworlds again. But this time, nothing like the pandemonium of the caverns of sickness – only the breathtaking beauty of Underworld landscapes filled with piles of luminous gems shining like the stars of the Fields of Peace.

After eighteen months of non-stop training, Marek gave Szar a different mission: his first ritual murder of a Nephilim. Szar had been led to think the Nephilim were a race of depraved murderous giants, vicious monsters with supernatural powers, excessively dangerous. Szar carefully selected a small group of three pilgrims on their way to the cave of Verzazyel the Watcher, only a few days' walk from Mount Lohrzen. He chased them for a day, then struck.

But when Virginia saw Szar's proposed victim for the ritual murder, her mouth opened in astonishment. The Nephilim was no giant monster. She was a stunningly beautiful woman with long red hair.

"Felicia! Deep trouble!" Hiram grinned. Having heard Szar's version of the story, he couldn't wait to see what the Archive had to say.

Inspired by the clear fountain, Szar couldn't resolve himself to murder Felicia. He just took her soft-stone pendant and let her go. After this he went roaming in the canyons of the Red Lands and visited the cave of Verzazyel the Watcher. But the powerful occult forces stored in the cave made him fall asleep and dream. In the dream he was projected into a fabulous reality where Felicia was waiting for him. In fields of stars, she taught him how to dance. Enthralling and splendid, this 'dreaming' in the Watcher's mind felt far more real than reality.

On waking up and exploring Verzazyel's cave, Szar came across the same Felicia. But this time she was dying, having burnt herself while trying to conquer the power of the Watchers.

"Szar was haunted by the memory of Vivyani," Hiram elucidated for Virginia. "He couldn't just turn his back and let Felicia die."

Szar carried Felicia's body to another cave in a nearby canyon and endeavoured to heal her, using forces from the Underworlds. The healing work was monumental. Felicia's body of energy had been totally ravaged. It had to be reconstituted from scratch. Szar spent thirteen days descending deep into the Underworlds, collecting water of life and precious gem-forces, bringing them back to the surface into Felicia's body. But when Felicia finally woke, she was cold and hostile. Barkhan Seer sketched the background, "Great Warriors and Nephilim had been enemies since the early days of the kingdom of Atlantis. If Lohrzen had founded the order of the Great Warriors, it was precisely to exterminate Nephilim giants and their armies."

Nevertheless, this particular Nephilim woman and this unusual Great Warrior quickly became best friends. Watching their animated discussions in the cave in the Red Canyons, Hiram couldn't stop laughing, and Virginia ended up laughing with him.

For the first time.

"This was one of Szar's most difficult trials," Barkhan Seer emphasized. "His beloved teacher, Gervin, had sent him to Marek. Marek had ordered him to go and slaughter one of the Nephilim. But instead of killing Felicia, he had rescued her from certain death! He found himself in a terrible dilemma. He couldn't return to Mount Lohrzen without having murdered one of the Nephilim. But even though he was an over-trained warrior, the idea of killing an innocent human being was totally unacceptable to his clear fountain."

"Especially *this* human being! Can you imagine how he felt after spending three weeks in a cave with her!" Hiram laughed, immensely enjoying the sweet irony of Szar's dilemma. He and Virginia applauded when they saw how, directed by Felicia's prophetic sight, Szar descended into the caverns of sickness, located Vivyani's soul and escorted her to an Underworld cavern beneath the temple of Eisraim.

But when they saw the following scene, they stopped laughing. The beautiful Felicia announced her intention to return to Verzazyel's cave. She had decided to descend into the crypt again, and attempt – for the second time – to conquer the fire of the Watchers. Not out of character for her. But she tried to entice Szar to descend into the crypt with her.

When Szar accompanied her to the entrance of Verzazyel's cave, the Watchers made Felicia more stunning than ever. Szar joined her for a last supper just outside the cave, under the full moon. Feeding him refined dishes of Nephilim cuisine, Felicia declared her love for him in a passionate plea and revealed, "Szar, this was the meaning of the dream Verzazyel the Watcher sent you: come and dance with me in the crypt, and tonight you will receive more power than you ever believed could exist. You and I will conquer the Fire, enter the Watcher's mind, and cognise the past, the future, and the mysteries of the spheres."

When Szar hesitated, Felicia offered to activate the power of the cave and give him a vision of any event of his choice.

"What if I wanted to see how my friends of the White Eagle received Vivyani's soul after I delivered her to them?" Szar asked.

The wish brought the vision of a young woman with long dark hair, dressed in white. She was on her knees, sobbing among piles of rubble. At first, Szar didn't recognise her, and Felicia offered to interrupt the vision. But to his amazement, Szar realised the woman was Teyani of the White Eagle – more than twenty-five years younger than the Teyani he had met in Eisraim.

"Shall we see a little more?" Felicia suggested.

8 – The Book of the White Eagle

8.1 To those who can't listen...

Nineteen-year-old Teyani was searching what had once been the temple of Karlinga, now piles of plass rubble. Again and again she discovered the mutilated bodies of her friends. Sobbing and coughing, she wiped her hand across her face, smearing the milky whiteness of her skin with soot from the smouldering fires.

She finally discovered the man she had been looking for. His twisted body lay in the ruins, his eyes wide open, his cheeks covered in caked blood, his head half-crushed by a large unmelted plass block.

She fell on her knees and took his hand. "No!"

It was cold.

"Ledno... Ledno! What am I going to do without you?" Holding the fruit in her swollen belly, Teyani cried, "Our baby... what about our baby?"

She turned her head, slowly taking in the desolation of the scene.

Everything was lost.

There was nothing left to fight for, nothing to hope for.

Her world was dead.

Only one course was left – a total surrender to the Divine.

The realisation brought a different light to her face. The whisper of the wind faded. Colours changed. The world turned darker. A brighter light appeared, superimposed on the darkness.

With the dignity of a high initiate, Teyani stood up.

Through darkness visible, she sensed the presence of one of her friends. She found her way to the ruins of a staircase. It led to what had been a crypt, now a chaos of fallen walls, angular plass pieces and dust.

"Adya! Can you hear me?" she called.

"Teyani?" an uncertain voice answered.

Teyani picked her way down the steps. The ceiling of the crypt had just about collapsed. The misty greyness of winter filtered into what used to be a chapel of the White Eagle.

"I think I've broken both my legs, Teyani."

A huge chunk of plass had fallen on the young woman's legs, trapping her beneath its weight. She was covered in bruises, her white dress in tatters. Teyani reached across to her and caressed her curly brown hair.

"Have you seen the others? I can't sense anyone," Adya sounded weak.

"They are all dead," Teyani said.

"The Black Robes have killed all of them?" Adya's voice choked. "Ledno?"

Teyani was silent.

"And our sisters of the White Eagle, have you seen them?"

"All dead," Teyani repeated.

Adya started crying, bringing back the pain in her legs. It made her shake.

Teyani's voice was serene, "*Peace, my friend in the Law!* Move back again."

Adya moved back, slightly withdrawing her consciousness from her physical body, thereby disconnecting from the pain in her legs and the discomfort of the awkward position. The shaking stopped.

Teyani contemplated the bulky chunk of plass under which Adya was trapped. It had fallen from the ceiling. It was a beam-shaped fragment, more than twenty lawful feet long. It was no longer glowing, but still as solid as a rock. Four strong men wouldn't have been enough to lift it.

"You warned us, Teyani, didn't you? You said the Black Robes were coming and we should move to the east. Why didn't we listen to you!"

Teyani was standing very straight, absorbed in the Great Light of the Eagle.

A verse of the Law ran through Adya's mind: *To those who can't listen, the Lord Melchisedek can give no mercy!*

If only...

She shook her head. "Where were you hiding?"

"In the crypt of Apollo. The Black Robes didn't find it," Teyani said.

"How is your baby?" Adya asked.

Teyani's eyes were shining with tranquillity. "It does not matter, Adya. We are going to leave."

Adya raised her head and looked around, "What else could we do!"

She lay back against the piles of broken plass fragments and closed her eyes. In a flash, she remembered a prophecy that Ledno had given her: just before her twenty-fourth birthday, she was to meet love. A man from the east, a man with exceptional powers. He was to take her with him. She was to give him a child that would be the pride of the White Eagle, shine his glory high in heaven.

How could she think of such things when her White sisters were lying dead amidst the wreckage?

Yet she could not avoid regretting, "Hard luck! Such unlawful hard luck! Only three months away from my twenty-fourth birthday."

"Adya, are you ready?" Teyani called, as if already from the Light.

Adya laid her hands on her chest. "I am ready, Teyani."

Together, the two women chanted *the hymn of the departing souls*.

"Let the White Eagle take me!" said Adya.

Teyani, holding her belly, whispered, "Let the White Eagle take us!"

8.2 Teyani's ascension into the Eagle's Highness

Dead to the world of mortals, the two women left their bodies and found themselves in darkness visible. Before they even started ascending through the spheres, the White Eagle came to meet them.

A light flared in Teyani's heart, "My forever friend, here you are already!"

She moved towards the Eagle's presence. In no time the dark purple atmosphere was replaced by a blazing white light with a slight hue of blue. Teyani was no longer in darkness visible. The Eagle's power was transporting her into the spheres of Highness.

She kept walking towards the Light, chanting a hymn to her god and most treasured friend:

"Here I come, White Eagle of the gods.
This Light which many fail to recognise after they die,
I enter joyfully.
The spark of the Unborn God,
The blazing glory, brighter than all the fields of stars,
I embrace joyfully.
Free from the fetters of destiny,
Unhampered by human dreams and illusions,
Released from the burdens of life in the kingdom,
I come and give myself to you, White Eagle.
Capture me in your infinity.
Take me to this point of eternal sunrise,
Where you forever dwell.
Enchant me away from the dreaming of gods and men,
Awaken me to your glory.
Only your love I want.
Only your Ineffable Light I will marry.
Here I come, White Eagle of Highness."

Teyani kept advancing, entering ever greater intensities of Light. The Eagle's presence responded.

"O my beloved child,
My dear friend and precious lover,
Here you are, standing in your full glory!
Soul of Highness,
Child of eternity,
Angel of the Human Hierarchy,
I have waited for you since earlier than time.
And here you come, shining,
Punctual for the cosmic appointment,
Making the Mother of the Light proud of her seed.
Sweet is this instant beyond time,

Where we can meet face to face,
Having desired each other for so long.
Let your Spirit feed on my fountains.
Let your Light join with my Spirit!"

Light met Light. Teyani shone, intoxicated with the Eagle's elixirs of ecstasy. She kept advancing towards the Great Source of the Light. The Eagle spoke again.

"Beloved spark,
My sister in infinity,
Stop where you are.
Ascend no more. Stay on the edge of that which retains shape.
The time for our Great Lovers' Dance has not yet come.
More works in the kingdom are to be accomplished.
I must ask you once again to be my maid,
Tread perilous paths,
And bear the dull greyness which men have set on Earth."

Teyani replied,

"O my Lover,
O thunderbolt of my kidney,
Shall I lose you once more?
Shall I once more descend from point to line,
Line to plane,
And from plane to the kingdom?
Grey indeed is the kingdom,
And each day more empty of the Ancient Earth's magic.
What place is there for me in such a boring sphere?
The waterfalls no longer chant the glory of angels.
Sulking animals no longer talk to men.
Precious herbs are turning into weeds,
Flowers no longer carry the fairies' joy,
And the elves are losing their sense of humour.
The trees themselves are losing their spirit,
Their fruits no longer convey your Mother's infinite sweetness,
And their leaves in despair fall in the coldness of autumn.
The gnomes hide in their caves,
The salamander species is endangered,
The wind no longer speaks to the wise.
The morning dew is no longer pregnant
With the buoyant chaos from which all things arose.
Sunrise no longer tells the story of the creation's birth,
Sunset no longer holds the mysteries of pralaya.
Malchasek and the Great Angels of Highness
Are slowly withdrawing their Light,
And their breath of Highness will soon have disappeared.
O White Eagle,

The ancient glory that was Earth is fast vanishing.
The world of men is becoming a world of dwarfs,
And the blissful mists of the kingdom
Are now turning into dark threatening clouds
That will soon pour a consuming deluge
And destroy all of Atlantis."

The Eagle spoke,

"O wise woman, great magician,
Dear to the Earth and keeper of her wisdom,
I know your pain.
Great perils await the kingdom,
And from this ever greyer sphere
Where iron, like a plague, is spreading fast,
My presence soon will have to be withdrawn.
But, child of the Earth,
You must kindle the flame in your heart
And keep hope,
For the souls' dark night will be followed by a dawn.
Under giant rainbows,
A kingdom will emerge –
A renewed soil, for a new vine to be planted,
A new race, for your children to be reborn,
A new playground for the mighty and the meek.
Another dawn, another day, another night
To further prepare
The promised rendezvous with Light
Which the Architect of Hierarchies has planned for humanity.
This cosmic game
We must play and play well,
Each of us must lay his stone
To build the temple of universal destiny."

The White Eagle further raised his Voice, transferring formidable powers into Teyani.

"Stand up, child of my kidney. This is my will:
Regain the irresistible strength which you have conquered
In your former lives.
Fierce and glorious, descend into the kingdom.
Let your Voice shatter all obstacles.
Become the head of the White Eagle's order.
Go and seek Thunder the mighty.
Let him take you to the east.
In his county you will find a nest
For the White Eagle's maidens,
A place of joy and high Spirit,
The dwelling of Thunder.

There, a rainbow web is being woven
And seeds for great achievements are being sown.
There, you will give birth to a daughter.
And Adya too, the beloved soul,
Will carry a White Eagle to shine my glory
High in the heavens
And prepare the coming of the kingdom of the rainbows.
Teyani answered,
"O White Eagle, I am your servant maid.
Thy will be done."

In this Light beyond time, Teyani opened and received, and her Spirit was fortified.

Then she walked through Highness to a chamber where scenes of her past lives were waiting for her.

There she contemplated the glories of the Earth as she had known them in remote times – the Ancient Days when the Godhead's glory was awake in all things. She saw the dance of the fairies and the elves. She saw the rivers flowing with silvery waters of life, their sandy beds carpeted with specks of gold and orichalc. She saw the perfect harmony in which all beings sang the beauties of Mother Nature, accompanying her cosmic spheres' fathomless melody.

Teyani saw her past self, the great magician who commanded awesome forces and ruled like a queen over the fresh world's powers. Gnomes, salamanders and other elemental beings all fought for the privilege of being her servants. Giant trees invited her to come and hear their legends, and to gossip about the secrets of nature. Volcanoes asked her permission before erupting. The wind sang his best tunes for her, for he desired her and begged her to become his lover. He enjoyed surprising her with the cheeky kiss of a quick breeze when she stepped out of the water after bathing in the river. The ocean called her 'his special friend' and blessed her children with long lives, and when she swam he sent dolphins and big fishes to brush against her. During the night, owls looked after her sleep, sending wise dreams and premonitory inspiration. Larks sang to wake her in the morning, and came to her shoulder when she called them. She could charm any animal with her songs. Panthers and leopards turned tame at the sound of her Voice.

Laughing with joy, Teyani looked down to the spheres of Melchisedek. She saw Adya, waiting for her. So she hurried from point to line, line to plane, and from plane to the fields of stars. Arriving in darkness visible she realised she was carrying one of the White Eagle's feathers in her left hand. Placing it in her hair, she let herself fall back into her body.

8.3 Back to the kingdom

Adya opened her soft brown eyes. Finding herself back in her body, back in the piles of broken plass chunks, she sensed Teyani's presence close by and burst into sobs, "No, I don't want to be here! Why is this happening? Everyone can die if they want, why can't we? The gods have rejected us. Teyani..." Turning her face, she saw her friend sitting perfectly straight, ablaze with White Light.

Awe-struck by the brightness, Adya whispered, *"Oh my Lord Melchisedek*, what has happened to you?"

Entranced, Teyani slowly stood up. Her mouth half-open, she lowered her incandescent gaze onto the huge plass fragment that pinned Adya's legs.

The light became even brighter, making Adya wonder, "Teyani?"

Set in motion by a mighty breath of Highness, Teyani started projecting the Voice – Voice like Adya had never heard before.

A dazzling flood of light pouring out of Teyani's mouth.

Unreal, formidable, awesome.

Every piece of plass in the temple's ruins was shaking. The ceiling of the crypt creaked dangerously.

Raising both hands, palms facing Adya, Teyani further intensified the torrent of Voice.

Rolling thunder, ten thousand angels singing through her mouth. Immense and terrifying.

Adya lost touch with her body. For a few seconds the devastation was gone, the kingdom far away. There was but a gigantic White flame.

Gate to another world.

Eternity.

When Adya reopened her eyes, the Voice had stopped. An eerie silence had descended around them.

To her utter astonishment, the massive plass chunk over her legs had crumbled. All that was left were small piles of tiny crystal-like chips.

She tried to catch her breath, "Teyani..."

Fierce and radiant with the power of the Eagle, Teyani was contemplating her. Again, she raised her arms.

Again, she projected the Voice. This time onto Adya's maimed legs.

There was an explosion of Light. White flames of Life coming out of her mouth. Under the pounding, Adya began trembling like a leaf. She wondered whether she too was going to crumble. She lost all reckoning of time.

One Law, one way. Back to eternity. Nothing but Fire.

The universe, a flame.

White Eagle's sovereign might.

The creation burnt out by Highness.

When it stopped, Adya lay in one piece but stunned, unsure which world she was in.

Teyani lowered her hands slowly. Another outburst of Voice, phonation of Highness, "Stand up!"

Compelled by the Word's irresistible momentum, Adya found herself standing on her feet.

There was no pain.

Breathless, standing through the sheer power of God, she stared at Teyani.

Teyani Voice-projected, "Follow me! Now!" She turned abruptly and walked up the steps.

Adya's body started walking behind her.

Infused with the power, Teyani went straight to the crypt of Apollo, with Adya trailing behind her.

Adya walked mechanically. Was this a dream? The temple destroyed, the bodies of her friends strewn over the ground amidst a sea of broken plass fragments, her nineteen-year-old sister in the Eagle suddenly performing miracles as in the Ancient Days of the Earth.

As they entered the crypt of Apollo, Teyani Voiced, "Sit down!"

Adya instantly collapsed on the floor of the large empty crypt.

Teyani walked to the central altar, lit a flame and started chanting the opening hymns of the White Eagle's ritual.

This time, in her normal voice.

Two minutes later Adya, in shock, heard Teyani begin the hymns of the instalment ceremony for a new grand master of the order of the White Eagle.

"But Teyani..." she couldn't help intervening, "don't we already have a grand master?"

Teyani turned round, "Our grand master in the county of the Western Plains died last night. The White Eagle called her back to him."

"But how can you invest yourself with the power of the lineage?"

"The power will come to me straight from the Eagle," Teyani replied. Using the Voice, she ordered, "Sing with me!"

Together they resumed the installation hymns. Their chants were frail at first. But soon Teyani's voice became Voice again, the tonal feast of dancing angels, resonance of ancient mysteries that turned the dark space of the crypt into a field of stars and Adya's heart into a White pyre.

A pyre vast like the Eagle's Highness.

"*In the name of the thirty-three victorious gods, in the name of the Ancient of Ancients, the Lord Melchisedek, and his angels, in the name of the Mother of the Light, I, Teyani, facing Cosmic Fire, now invest myself with the powers of a grand master of the order of the White Eagle.*" Closing her eyes, Teyani Voice-thundered the secret name of God, normally handed down from grand master to grand master, today flowing into her from the White Eagle himself,

"Isha."
From Revelation Sky to the Deepest Underworlds, One Spark.
The Eagle's dance.
Edge of Highness. Whiteness eternal. Forever love.

8.4 Faith

The ceremony completed, it took a while before the light in the crypt returned to some normality.

Gradually, the kingdom became the kingdom again.

Teyani, nonetheless, was still glowing. She went to sit by Adya's side and took her hands.

Adya looked up at her, still catching her breath. "Teyani... what has happened?"

Teyani was matter of fact. "I met the Eagle in the spheres of Highness. He commanded me to return to the kingdom and take charge of our order. I followed his command. We will be moving to another temple, Adya, a place where our order will attain great fame."

"Where is that place?" Adya asked.

"I don't know. Somewhere towards the east. Thunder will take us there."

"Thunder?"

Her eyes ablaze with her faith in the Eagle, Teyani answered in near-Voice threshold, "I don't know, Adya, but I will find him. Whoever Thunder may be I will find him." She closed her eyes and paused.

A presence was approaching the temple.

"Oh, Mother of the Light... it's my boy!" Teyani exclaimed.

Adya tuned into darkness visible. "Lehrmon?"

"He is alive! Oh, Mother, Mother... thank you!" Teyani placed her hands on her heart. She ran up the stairs to the temple courtyard and called out loud, "Lehrmon! Lehrmon! Here! I'm here!"

A six-year-old boy with curly black hair appeared. From a distance he contemplated Teyani's shining aura. Then he slowly waved his hand in the particular fashion he always used to greet her.

"Come, my boy," Teyani called. "It's safe here!"

Lehrmon rushed towards her.

She sat on the ground and took him in her arms. "*Praise the Lord Melchisedek! Here is my strong man in the Law!*" She held the child tightly, rocking him in her arms. "Where were you my love?"

"Hiding. When I saw the Black Robes coming, I ran as fast as I could into the forest. No one saw me."

Teyani kissed him, "You're such a clever boy, Lehrmon."

"Lady Teyani, what has happened to all the people in the temple?" the little boy asked.

Holding him in her arms, she brought the Light of the Eagle onto him. "They have gone for the Great Journey. To the beautiful place."

"Like my parents?"

"Yes my love, just like your parents. *Gone to the place where the Sun is eternally bright*. Now come with me," she got up, "Adya is waiting for us down there."

Hand in hand, they walked down into the crypt of Apollo.

"*Praise the Lord Melchisedek, Lehrmon!*" Adya exclaimed.

"*All glory to the Lord Melchisedek, Lady Adya,*" the little boy responded, looking at her with a grave expression in his eyes.

How could this boy, an outcast, have such depth? Adya had often wondered.

The three friends exchanged a few unimportant words, before Teyani knelt down and took him in her arms again. "Lehrmon," she said in a serious voice, "I must go away for some time, to find a new place for us to live."

Lehrmon put on his most grown-up face, but tears sprang into his amber eyes.

Teyani smoothed his hair, caressing the black curls, "Lehrmon, I promise I will come back as soon as I can and take you to our new home. And I will take care of you as I always have since your parents went to the beautiful place. But for now, I want you and Adya to be strong. Adya will stay here with you, but she has hurt her legs, she cannot walk. I need you to go and get some food for her."

Lehrmon nodded his head gravely.

After discussing practicalities with Adya, Teyani went to inspect the neighbouring cellars. The Black Robes had come to kill everyone and to desecrate the temple, not to pillage its food reserves. There were still plenty of nuts, grains and roots – enough to feed her friends for a year if needed.

Teyani returned to the crypt of Apollo and gave further instructions to Adya. "If you sense anyone approaching the temple, keep the door of this crypt locked, and hide! And whatever happens, do not try to contact me through darkness visible. The Black Robes would detect you in no time."

"But where will you go, Teyani?" Adya asked.

"Towards the east. I will follow the Light of the Eagle until I find Thunder. Then I will come back here and take the two of you with me."

Adya was taken by a wave of unlawful panic at the idea of being left in the crypt with her injured legs and no one but Lehrmon to look after her.

"When the Eagle spoke to me," Teyani told her, "he prophesied you would give him a baby girl, a White Eagle who will not only shine his glory high in the heavens, but also carry out his works and prepare the coming of the kingdom of the rainbows."

"You are the mother, Teyani," Adya smiled sadly. "Your child can fulfil the prophecy."

"Have faith, Lady of the Eagle," Teyani blew a mighty breath of Spirit into her. "Have faith in the Word of our Lord! If he promised you a daughter, you will live and have a daughter." Turning to Lehrmon she smiled, "Will you marry her, *great man in the Law?*"

Lehrmon went to Teyani and snuggled into her arms.

She held him against her breast. "Good bye, my friends. Look after yourselves, and the Light will look after you."

The last image she took with her was Lehrmon, standing on the pedestal of a broken column close to the crypt of Apollo. Tears were rolling down his cheeks but with composed seriousness the curly-haired little boy stood straight, giving her his special wave as she disappeared from view.

8.5 Atlantean indifference

Teyani surrendered to the Eagle's Light and let it direct her steps. She had no idea where she was going, and she did not know what she was looking for. Yet the Eagle clearly pointed the way, and her love for him made the journey joyful. Absorbed in the contemplation of his Light she hardly saw the world around her. There was but Light walking towards the Light, and Spirit joined with Spirit.

After she had been walking for three days, Teyani began to run out of provisions. Before being pregnant she had often fasted while undertaking harsh ascetic practices. Fasting had always been a joy to her, an opportunity to celebrate her love for the Eagle. But the fruit in her belly was demanding food, and her pregnant body was starting to suffer from these unlawfully long hours of walking.

As she was passing the house of a peasant family who had been long-time friends of the temple, she decided to go and knock at their door.

A familiar female voice answered, "*Who, sent by the Lord Melchisedek, is knocking at the door?*"

"It's Teyani of the White Eagle, *by the grace of the Lord Melchisedek.*"

Inside the house another voice shouted, "Don't answer! All the people of her temple have been outlawed."

The door remained closed.

Teyani was shocked. She thought these people were her friends. She knocked again, but the household remained silent.

Her hands on her belly, Teyani turned away and kept walking.

Further on she knocked at the door of another house but the people recognised her through the window and stayed mute when she called. She tried a few more houses. Each time, as soon as people heard her name or saw her face, they became deaf to her calls.

Teyani fought hard against the ugly taste of anger that welled inside her. "Didn't these people call me their *friend in the Law?* Didn't they come to my temple when they needed healing or advice from the gods? Haven't I always served them?" Her being outlawed was an outrage. She could hardly refrain from cursing the Black Robes. But she held fast to the Light and to her love for the Eagle. Yielding to the anger would only have cut her off from the very source of the Light – and then what would have been left for her?

Further along the way she found a pear tree and feasted on its juicy fruits. Before leaving, she raised the Voice and projected a hymn to bless the tree, as wise people used to do in the Ancient Days of the Earth. And the tree was happy. On her way, streams gave her their water, and welcoming trees enveloped her with their energy at night so that she slept fast and her baby was safe.

Two days later she entered a village where no one knew her. But as she walked towards the marketplace someone soon whispered behind her back, "That woman is an outlaw!" The rumour spread like a fire in dry leaves and by the time she reached the first stall in the market, everyone was ignoring her.

Her young body was reacting strongly to the smells of food. She approached an old man who was selling wonderful dishes made of baked cereals and fruits. "*My friend in the Law, through the grace of our Lord Melchisedek, I became pregnant*. I need some food. Could I have one of your cakes?"

The man kept himself busy, as if no one had spoken to him.

"Have I become a ghost, that you neither seem to see nor hear me?" Teyani raised her voice, but with no result.

Staring at him, she almost yielded to anger again. How easy it would have been to dump a curse on him – a real curse, one that sticks and attracts nasty beings and influences, and diseases, and ill intentions from relatives, friends and neighbours. Three words were all she had to Voice, and the man would be sick for the rest of his life.

But soon she hated herself for harbouring such thoughts. "White Eagle of Highness, protect me from myself!" she uttered aloud, after again trying to get a response from people who simply blanked her out.

Following the Eagle's Light, she kept walking towards the east.

Day after day, village after village, Teyani was met with the same indifference. Finally one evening, as night was approaching, she realised her situation was becoming desperate. The very survival of her baby was at stake. She chose a wealthy-looking peasant's house and knocked at the door.

There was no answer.

Teyani projected the Voice, "Open this door!"

Compelled by the power, someone immediately came and opened the door. She was an elderly woman with grey hair, dressed in a dirty white gown. She did not say a word.

"*Woman of the Law*, I am hungry." Teyani held her belly and begged, "I need to feed my baby. Will you give me something to eat?"

The woman remained blank.

"Give me something to eat!" Teyani Voice-demanded.

The woman turned back and took Teyani to her kitchen. There a man was sitting, eating his dinner. He ignored Teyani and kept eating.

The kitchen smells penetrated every cell of Teyani's body. "O White Eagle," she whispered, "will you despise me for wanting food so much?"

The woman served her and she started eating like a glutton, but she hated herself for what she was doing. "How can I be using the holy powers of my order to behave like a thief?" Her body didn't listen. It kept eating, and she could feel the baby's joy inside her.

Before leaving she grabbed some nuts, seeds and fruits from the kitchen shelves and filled her bag with them. Then she thanked the man and the woman who continued ignoring her, and she left.

That night she sought refuge in a thick wood. She searched for a chestnut tree large enough to shelter her. She found one more than two hundred lawful feet high and collapsed on the ground under its boughs. She started sobbing, "Now I have become a thief!"

For the first time, Teyani was gripped by the insidious temptation to let herself die. Giving up would have been so easy! All she had to do was to move away from her body and let herself drift in the space. Wasn't that what all these people wanted her to do, anyway? Their rejection weighed heavily on her chest. It seemed like aeons since she had heard someone speak her name. She couldn't stop crying. She addressed the tree, "*O chestnut tree, most knowing among the spirits of the forest*, why can't you talk to me? In the Ancient Days of the Earth, you and I were the best of friends. You used to call me when I passed by. So many times I came and sat under your leafy canopy and projected my blessings. You entertained me with your tales and legends of long ago. So many times you warmed my heart with your wit. Is everything forgotten? Is everything lost? Have I become an outlaw even to you?"

The tree did not answer.

8.6 The appointment with Thunder

Two men in brown robes were walking along a rocky path.

One of them, a tall broad-shouldered man in his early thirties, stopped to pick up a stone. "Gervin, isn't this one of your favourite rocks?" he gently tossed it to his companion.

Gervin, perhaps forty years of age, looked at it with piercing grey-green eyes. "Yes, it is!" he answered, touching his beard. "This kind of red basalt is usually found close to volcanoes that became extinct quite a while before the creation of the kingdom. Melchard, we are in an area with special powers!" he threw the rock back to his friend.

"Why so?" Melchard asked, looking at the basalt.

"Because the magic forces of the Ancient Earth were awake when the volcano erupted."

"I don't follow."

"See, Melchard, some time before the creation of the kingdom, the magic powers of nature were sealed deep into the Earth and made inaccessible to human beings, probably because they had become too foolish. Now, what are volcanoes, really? Huge shafts that penetrate into the inside of the Earth. By the way, descending into them through darkness visible is a very odd experience. Have I told you about this?"

Melchard shook his head.

"Anyway," Gervin went on, "a volcano that was active long before the creation of the kingdom is like an open mouth through which the Earth still releases her ancient forces. This is why magicians are attracted to places with red basalt. But we have to keep moving, my friend."

"Yes," Melchard quickened his pace, dropping the rock. "After all that's happened in the last days, there is no guarantee we will be on time for the eklipson."

"Oh Lord Melchisedek, I hope so!" Gervin accelerated his pace even further. "I already missed one eklipson three years ago, when I was kept in Eisraim and couldn't make it to the Western Plains. This time I want to be at the appointment!"

"As long as we get to catch tonight's boat on the Pesiah river, everything will be fine. Will you explain this incredible theory about eklipsons again? Why does the sky suddenly become dark in the middle of the day?"

"Studying the Watchers' lore, especially the books of Barkayal, Tamiel and Asradel, one is led to think of the sun as a sphere of fire revolving around the kingdom."

"A sphere of fire? Has anyone ever seen it?" Melchard questioned.

"No," Gervin answered, "nothing like it. But that could well be because of the thick mists that cover the kingdom. I have heard that in the Northern Lands, when you climb to the summit of the Snowy Mountains, the sun's appearance is sometimes very odd – especially during the dry season when the mists become sparse. I am planning to go there next year and verify it myself."

"If I hadn't seen so many miracles when you and I were initiated into Thunder by Orest, I would find it difficult to believe such unlawfully stretched theories, but..."

The two men laughed.

"Now," Gervin continued, "going back to the eklipsons, suppose a huge rock was to stand between us and the sphere of fire, then suddenly the day would turn into night."

"You mean a huge rock floating in the sky?"

"*My friend in the Law*," Gervin laughed, "if you knew all the things that can be found in the Watchers' lore, you would think Orest's views were quite moderate, after all."

Melchard sunk in thought for a while. Then he asked, "Did I also hear you say that at times, there can be eklipsons of moonlight?"

Gervin stopped walking. "Can you feel it? At the upper borderline of darkness visible."

Melchard halted and tuned in. "Huge flames. What is that?"

"Someone in big trouble," Gervin said. "Someone powerful. These are mighty forces!"

His eyes closed, Melchard nodded, "I see a woman. Not far."

"Let's go and have a look," Gervin turned off the path and walked in the direction of a wood.

Melchard followed. "I see an exceptionally bright light. We have to be on guard, this woman could be dangerous."

Having arrived at an avenue of huge maple trees, they stopped to contemplate a strange scene. Teyani was lying on the ground, unconscious. She was clad in a dirty white cloak, most of her face hidden by its hood. Ten lawful feet around her body, the space was ablaze with dancing red flames of energy. In darkness visible, a shrieking vibration could be heard.

"Is this a protection shield?" Melchard frowned.

Gervin shook his head. "She could have found a cosier place to fall asleep. And look at this golden light... she's pregnant! Which could explain it. She must have triggered forces she was unable to contain because of her baby."

Melchard closed his eyes. "She is being harassed by horrible nightmares. Nasty mists from the Underworld."

"Let us stop this!" Using the Voice, Gervin projected a short, muffled sound. The red flames and the hissing sound in darkness visible instantly disappeared. Gervin walked up to Teyani and knelt on the ground. Uncovering her face, he let out an exclamation, "Look how young she is!"

"She is about to lose her child," Melchard said, his eyes still closed.

The two men carried Teyani and placed her under a generously spread maple tree. They tried to sit her up against its trunk, but as she did not wake up they had to lay her on the ground.

"This sleep isn't doing her any good," Gervin decided, projecting soft Voice sounds onto her gateways.

A few seconds later, Teyani opened her eyes.

Startled at seeing the two men so close, she immediately sat up, raised her Voice and projected onto Gervin, "Move away!" as if she was being attacked.

The force she used was nothing like a deluge from Highness. Still it was more than enough to make anyone normal retreat. But Gervin remained sitting quietly by her side. "*Peace, my young friend in the Law!*" he gave her a reassuring smile.

Teyani intensified her Voice. White flames poured from of her mouth, "Move away!"

But the flames vanished as soon as they reached Gervin's aura.

"Stop!" the Master of Thunder Voice-shouted, still as a rock. "You are going to kill your baby!"

Teyani became quiet. Disconcerted, she looked at Gervin.

"Who are you?" she asked.

Gervin took on a polite smile. "My name is Gervin, of the Brown Robe. *Meet my lawful friend*, Melchard of the Brown Robe," he pointed behind him. "We found you lying unconscious on the path."

Gervin took a closer look at her. Her long black hair was dishevelled and caked with mud. Her eyes were shining, but she was very pale and her energy felt as dry as the rocky deserts of the Red Lands.

He took a water bottle out of his bag and offered it to her.

It had been three weeks since Teyani had heard someone address her – more than enough to make Gervin's voice sound like the harmony of the spheres. She hesitated. Her stomach ached. A searing headache clouded her mind.

Gervin opened the water bottle, drank a sip, and placed it on the ground by Teyani's hand. "We didn't find any bags near you. Have you been attacked?"

Teyani nodded.

"And you used the Voice to defend yourself," Gervin added. "But perhaps you didn't know that a pregnant woman should be careful when projecting certain forces, especially when standing on an ancient volcano." He kept contemplating her, "You are very thirsty, *my young friend in the Law*, why don't you take some of our water?"

It was clear the two men could only be priests. Teyani asked, "Which temple are you from, *men of the Law*?"

In a meek voice, Gervin answered, "The temple of Eisraim, in the east."

Travellers from the east! This sounded like hope.

With the directness which, life after life, had taken her to great enlightenments – but also into great troubles – Teyani asked, "I am looking for Thunder, can you help me find him?" Then she took the bottle and she drank.

Melchard's eyes widened. Gervin twinged his beard in perplexity, watching the young woman who was avidly emptying his bottle.

Masters of Thunder do not easily reveal their identity, especially to strangers. "We are just travellers on our way to the county of the Upper Western Shores," Melchard said, while Gervin studied her intensely.

Tuning high into the White Eagle, Teyani received an unmistakable sign that told her she had nothing to fear from Gervin. "My name is Teyani," she said, and with a touch of irony in her voice, she added, "of the White Robe," for this was the lawfully polite way of not revealing the name of her caste. Dropping all protection seals, she established eye contact with Gervin and let him plunge into her energy.

"Teyani of the White Eagle!" Gervin exclaimed, surprised to see her so much a woman, when Barkhan Seer had announced a child.

But ten years had passed since the clearing of Erriba!

Teyani was puzzled by the flare in his eyes. "Who are you?"

"Your friend," Gervin answered, recalling the solemn promise made to Barkhan Seer. "Your friend!"

Turning to his companion, he said, "Melchard, I am afraid you'll have to catch this boat without me."

8.7 The Mother of the Light knows the value of a human life

Teyani and Gervin were walking together.

Teyani burst out laughing. "Gervin," she said, "if it wasn't coming from you, I would *never* believe this story!"

After ten days of Gervin's care, his wise treatments and joyful company, Teyani had regained her spark, and the golden light of her pregnancy was blossoming again.

"Nothing is more difficult to believe than the pure truth, Lady Teyani!" Gervin sighed philosophically. He resumed, "Once the fire was extinguished, I had to perform a clearing on the ass and release the stray spirit. After which the ass stopped prophesying and talking to the priests of Barradine through darkness visible. This is when it became evident that the priests of Barradine had lied to everyone."

"Do you mean it was the ass who had made all these prophecies?" Teyani kept laughing.

"Exactly! From the day of the clearing, the priests of Barradine could no longer predict anything. And his majesty the prince of Eisraim never returned to their chapel."

For a few seconds, Gervin inundated Teyani's baby with his healing presence. Then he asked, "Tell me again, what predictions did the people in your temple make about the warp of energy fields?"

Teyani's expression became grave. "Several times we prophesied to the prince that the windmills of the Law had gone wrong, and that the fields were bound to cause catastrophes in the county."

"Such as?" Gervin asked.

"Rare birds like pierra-pierras and olous would disappear, and so would the twenty-seven magic herbs of Sierra Olan, and perhaps even the herbs of madness. A long drought would shrivel the crops in the plains of Mildus. The volcanoes of Lierne, which everyone thought dead, would spout a flood of fire. And throughout the county, people would be stricken by strange diseases that the hymns of the Law would be powerless to heal."

"Uh! Oh!" Gervin exclaimed. "No wonder you brought trouble on your-selves!"

"So you think it was our predictions that caused the Black Robes to attack us?" Teyani asked.

"More than likely. Those who prophesy about looming disasters must be extremely careful these days."

"But Gervin, didn't you tell me that you yourself made similar predictions?"

"Yes, and some of them much worse than yours, in fact. But the prince of the county of Eisraim is a wise man who studied in my temple. And there is so much power in the temple of Eisraim... the king of Atlantis himself would think twice before attacking us."

"How many priests are there in your temple?" Teyani asked.

"More than twelve hundred, not counting *the lawful attendant of various castes*," Gervin answered.

"There were less than fifty men and women in the temple of Karlinga," she said.

For a split second, scenes of the devastation flashed across her mind.

"See, Teyani, the Black Robes derive all their psychic powers from the warp of fields. If the prince of your county was to listen to people like you, he would have to forbid many rituals and energy manipulations. This would mean the end of the Black Robes, and of quite a few other orders."

"But if they don't listen," Teyani shook her head in dismay, "the warp of fields will become more and more corrupt, and it will destroy us all. What good will that do the Black Robes?"

"I know, *my friend in the Law!*" Gervin answered. "*To those who can't listen, the Lord Melchisedek can give no mercy.* But tell me, Teyani, after you had warned the people in your temple that a catastrophe was looming, why didn't they listen to you?"

Teyani shrugged her shoulders, "Perhaps they didn't know what to do. Abandoning our temple and moving east seemed such an impossible enterprise!"

"And so they preferred to ignore your words. This sums up the entire tragedy of the kingdom, my dear friend. The problems are clear, but the solutions they demand are so drastic! Everyone prefers to pretend nothing out of the lawful ordinary is going on. Too many orders would lose their powers if the needed rearrangements in the fields were implemented."

The two friends walked on in silence.

"The temple is just on the other side of that hill," Teyani said. "Shall we call Adya through darkness visible?"

"Wait a bit more," Gervin cautioned, not wanting the priestess in hiding to betray her presence too soon.

"I wonder how little Lehrmon has managed," Teyani said.

"Where did you find Lehrmon, Teyani?"

"His mother abandoned him two years after he was born. The father was from a caste she was not allowed to marry."

Gervin gave one of his ironic smiles. "So you managed to get the people in your temple to accept an outcast? How magical of you, Teyani!"

"Believe it or not, Gervin, I lied!" she confessed. "I told them his parents had died. No one bothered to ask more."

Gervin chuckled.

"I was only fifteen at the time!" Teyani pleaded.

"And if you found him now, would you still lie to save his life?" Gervin asked.

The question left Teyani thoughtful. After deliberation, she quoted a hymn of the Law, "*The Mother of the Light knows the value of a human life.*"

"*And cursed is the man who goes against her will,*" Gervin completed the verse.

"Anyhow, the people of my temple never really accepted Lehrmon, they just tolerated me looking after him."

They walked on, pensive.

"Teyani, Teyani..." Gervin declared after a while, "the whole area around the temple is empty. I can only sense one soul over there – not two."

An hour later, when they arrived at the temple, the scene was still one of devastation and ruin. The corpses had disappeared. The village priests would have carried out the funeral rites.

Teyani and Gervin went straight to the crypt of Apollo. They found the door of the crypt wide open. They walked down the steps.

No one inside.

Teyani stood straight, showing no emotion.

"Someone is coming," Gervin sensed through darkness visible.

"It's Lehrmon!" the Eagle's love radiated through Teyani's smile. "Let's go and meet him." She walked up the stairs and called loudly, "Lehrmon! It's me, Teyani. I am back!"

The little boy came into view. He ran towards them, but when he saw Gervin with Teyani, he stopped and stood still. Hesitantly, he waved his right hand at her in his special way.

"Lehrmon, it's safe!" Teyani called. "This man is our friend." She went up to him, knelt by his side and rested her head on his little shoulder. "You are safe and well, my love! *Praised be the Mother of the Light!*"

Lehrmon did not answer, his grave expression hiding a thousand-year-old smile, his gaze fixed on Gervin.

Thunder-still, Gervin plunged his sight into him.

"Lehrmon, what has happened to Lady Adya?" Teyani asked.

"The soldiers came to take her."

Teyani inhaled a deep breath. "When did they come?"

"Three days ago," Lehrmon answered.

Teyani searched his face, "Did they hurt her?"

"I don't know."

She put her hand on his shoulder and they walked towards Gervin.

"*Praise the Lord Melchisedek, Lehrmon!*" Gervin spoke from high in the Light.

Too fascinated to answer, Lehrmon just drank in Gervin's presence.

Hiding her distress, Teyani sat on the ground, rocking the little boy in her arms. "I missed you, *my great man in the Law!*"

Gervin sat by their side. "Now there is no reason not to call Adya through darkness visible."

"Aren't you worried about revealing our presence?" Teyani asked.

"Fear not, White Eagle!" Barkhan Seer's mighty presence spoke through Gervin. "I can't see the Black Robes daring to attack us."

"I am not even sure if Adya has a soft stone with her," Teyani said.

"I will supply the energy for the connection," Gervin offered. "Do you want me to take care of Lehrmon?"

Teyani shook her head. Still rocking the little boy against her, she closed her eyes and rested on Gervin's energy, establishing a connection with Adya.

"She is alive," she said after one minute. "They've taken her to Tipitinan." Then she opened her eyes and turned to Gervin. Her voice was matter of fact, "She is in jail. They are about to beat her to death."

She closed her eyes again and tuned high into the Eagle's Light. "Gervin, I must go to Tipitinan immediately!"

"*No way, woman of the Law!*" Gervin's answer was no less matter of fact, "You nearly lost your child a week ago. Rushing to Tipitinan is out of the question."

A few seconds passed before Teyani again made her plea, "I have no choice. It is the Eagle's Will that Adya live. I *must* go and rescue her."

"Teyani," Gervin raised his eyes skywards and sighed loudly, "I know you are a mighty soul, but..." Making eye contact in a line of Thunder, "...you are nineteen, you are completely untrained, and moreover you are pregnant! Ten days ago I found you half-dead on the ground. Going to fight the prince's army and their Black Robe allies all on your own is simply out of the question."

"*The Mother of the Light knows the value of a human life,*" she argued.

Gervin cut the quotation short, "Very well then, let us begin by not wasting yours!"

"Gervin, please understand. I cannot disobey the Will of the Eagle."

"Is it the Will of the Eagle that you kill yourself?" Gervin's voice heated up. "Teyani, you do not stand a chance."

"I know I am nothing, Gervin, but the Eagle will be with me," her certitude was unyielding. "With his help, I can do anything."

There was a brief silence.

Realising that nothing would sway her, Gervin said in his softest voice, "Teyani, until I met you, I thought my teacher was the most stubborn soul in the kingdom." He shook his head, "I was wrong!"

"Will you let me go?" she tried with a soft voice.

"*No way, woman of the Law!*" Gervin's suddenly forceful tone took her by surprise. "Now will you please let me think for a minute."

Gervin stood up and went for a walk among the ruins.

Invoking the Eagle's Light, Teyani held Lehrmon against her. Lehrmon felt the Light and responded by snuggling into her breast and touching her belly.

Teyani smiled, "Our baby is going very well, Lehrmon. She has been moving a lot in the last days."

"What's her name going to be?" Lehrmon asked.

"A beautiful name – Alcibyadi."

8.8 Archive Hall Five, Fields of Peace

Hiram and Virginia's gazes were lit with wonder.

"So is this the vision that Verzazyel the Watcher gave to Szar," Hiram marvelled. "What a work of art!"

In the all-knowingness of the Fields of Peace, it made such perfect sense.

Through the grand workings of time, the glory of the Lords of Destiny is revealed.

Seen from the kingdom, however, this vision had been perceived as a complete enigma. Barkhan Seer showed images of Szar and Felicia sitting outside Verzazyel's cave, captivated by Teyani's story but utterly perplexed as to why it was being shown them.

Under the full moon, Szar was pulling his beard, "This must have happened at least twenty years ago!"

"Twenty-seven years," Barkhan Seer corrected for Virginia and Hiram. "Teyani was nineteen when she fell pregnant. When Szar received this vision Alcibyadi was already twenty-six."

And he let the Archive records of Szar's memories unfold.

8.9 The entrance to Verzazyel's cave, county of the Red Lands

When Teyani pronounced the name "Alcibyadi," the vision abruptly ended.

Feeling dizzy, I looked around me. Verzazyel's cave was invitingly close. Stunningly beautiful, Felicia was sitting right beside me, inundated with moonlight.

Mechanically, my hand reached for the cup of glorious sunrise in front of me. After a quick sense-smell which met with the motley vibrations of the many dishes laid on the delicate white cloth, I put the cup back without drinking.

Burning with curiosity, Felicia asked, "Why did it suddenly stop there? And what has it got to do with Vivyani? It didn't tell us what the White Eagles did with her soul after you brought it back from the caverns of sickness. Did it make sense to you?"

Perplexed, I shook my head.

"Do you know if Teyani ended up giving birth to Alcibyadi?" Felicia let one of her complicated tiers of red hair fall down her back.

"I know there is an Alcibyadi who lives in Eisraim. She is one of the priestesses of the White Eagle. I never met her, but I know she is a friend of Elyani's."

Felicia seemed even more intrigued by the vision's sudden ending than I was. "These Black Robes had nothing to do with the Great Warriors, did they?"

"No, nothing."

"And what about Adya? Do you know what happened to her? Did the Black Robes beat her to death?"

"I have no idea who Adya is. I had never heard her name before tonight," I confessed. "I really can't see any connection with Vivyani."

"Would you like to see more?" Felicia asked.

"One thing I learned in Eisraim: *asking an oracle the same question twice is dangerous folly.* The oracle's second answer is likely to be so confusing it will poison your mind."

Felicia gave an amused smile, "How lawfully true!"

"I trust Verzazyel knew exactly what he was doing when he showed us these scenes. It might even make sense to us one day," I reasoned.

"*All glory to the Watchers' omniscience!*" Felicia immediately approved, as if Verzazyel was listening. "But this vision was tantalising. I want to know what happened next!"

"I wonder how Gervin managed to talk Teyani out of going to Tipitinan," I mused.

"What makes you think he did?" Felicia questioned. "Didn't he acknowledge that Teyani was even more stubborn than he was?"

"That was an excellent tactic," the trained warrior inside me answered with a grin. "Did you notice how Teyani's voice immediately mellowed after he said it?"

Felicia chuckled playfully.

"And do you know who Lehrmon is?" she asked.

"Of course! Believe it or not, the poor little outcast has become one of Gervin's disciples in the Brown Robe – one of the most powerful men in the counties of the Centre North. Now I see what he meant when he told me that he and Gervin had clicked the very moment they met."

"This Brown Robe you are wearing, does it mean that you are part of Gervin's Thunder-caste?"

I answered with a nod. We were too close for me to play hide and seek.

Felicia became very still, her eyes fixed on the entrance to Verzazyel's cave.

I went as high in the clear fountain as I could. "Felicia, I will not go back to Mount Lohrzen," I declared. "It all became clear inside me when I heard Gervin quote these verses: *The Mother of the Light knows the value of a human life, and cursed is the man who goes against her will.* Before killing anyone I will go back to Eisraim and take instructions directly from my master."

"Does this mean you are coming with me into the cave?" Felicia asked timidly.

I stood up. Dragon below, clear fountain above, I opened to her, "I can't, Felicia! Despite all the hurt I feel at the idea of losing you, I just *cannot* go with you. I belong to Thunder, this I know in my bones. If there are such powers as the Point and the magic of the Flying Dragons, I want to receive them from Gervin and from no one else. If I were to step into Verzazyel's highest initiation, I would have to change destiny and tread the path of the Watchers – a completely different life, a completely different future."

"But didn't Gervin himself send you to receive initiations from the Sons of the Dragon? Isn't their stream of initiation different from that of Thunder?"

"Very different. But I only underwent the early stages of the Great Warriors' initiation. Gervin instructed me to stay no longer than a few times a hundred days – not twelve years, as would be needed to conquer the Warriors' highest level of power."

Felicia stood up and came very close to me, letting the warmth of her magnificently adorned body pass into me. "It would not take twelve years to awaken the Fire of the Watchers. Not even one hundred days. Only one hour." She softly touched my chest, drawing a vroofing wave from the Dragon.

Out of nowhere, images of the lake where I had once nearly committed suicide flashed back into my memory, and I knew the present moment was another crossing of destinies.

"Felicia, if I listened to my mind I would think only a fool could refuse the power you are offering me, and I would immediately take the step with you. When I listen to my heart, I feel devastated at the idea that if I am not with you to hold your energy, you may end up dying in the crypt after all. And listening to my Dragon, I feel a strong urge to come and dance in the spheres with you. But if I hold on to the clear fountain and listen to nothing else, then I know my path is with Thunder – not with the Watchers."

Felicia did not answer. Her total blue eyes just kept looking at me.

"If I were to betray the clear fountain there would be nothing left of me, Felicia."

She knew it was true, and I knew that she knew.

"Will you wait till I come out of the cave?" she asked.

I shook my head slowly.

A long silence.

"Szar, I will never forget you." She paused. "It's better if you go now. I need some time to prepare myself."

A violent pain hit me in the chest. Before I could speak, Felicia had sealed my lips with her index finger. "*Hush, man of the Law!*" she said in a gentle voice, "Just go."

I walked a few steps backwards, fixing the image in my memory – her eyes, shining through darkness visible, her complicated hairstyle, her blue dress with the pendant lit by moonlight, the white cloth laid on the ground, covered in candles and dishes. And the entrance to Verzazyel's cave right behind Felicia.

Then I turned away, Dragoned myself to the bottom of the canyon, and started walking towards the north.

Each time I felt like turning back, I held to the fountain.

"*One Law, one way! He who never sleeps, never dies!*"

8.10 Eisraim, Teyani's apartment

Alcibyadi stretched her long feline body. "I don't even feel tired!" she declared, sitting up in bed.

"Be gentle with yourself," Teyani warned. "Yesterday your body was still hibernating."

"I don't feel at all like I have just come out of three weeks of hibernation! I feel like getting up and dancing. And I'm hungry!" the young woman declared.

Elyani and Teyani exchanged a glance, turning their palms to the gods in disbelief.

Teyani closed her eyes, sensing a familiar presence, "Guess who is coming!"

Alcibyadi's face lit up, "Lehrmon!"

Two lawful minutes later, Teyani went to open the door.

The strong man in the Brown Robe stood in the doorway. He slowly waved his hand at Teyani, greeting her with his shining amber eyes.

He was carrying a large basket filled with fruits of all colours. "*Praise the Lord Melchisedek, Ladies of the Eagle!*" He put the basket on the floor and hugged Teyani.

"*All glory to the Lord Melchisedek, my great man in the Law,*" she held him in her arms.

Lehrmon walked into the room. He gave Elyani a quick kiss and went to sit on Alcibyadi's bed.

Alcibyadi had a Fields-of-Peace smile on her face, "Lehrmon," she took his hands, "Lehrmon... so beautiful that you came all the way for me."

The Master of Thunder was on the edge of tears, "Thanked be the Mother of the Light! I prayed for you, I called for her help from morning to night."

"And the Lord Melchisedek knows how long days can be in the spheres of remoteness!" Elyani rejoined.

"An unusually fast recovery," Teyani marvelled. "Alcibyadi first opened her eyes during the night, and look at her! She is already asking for food."

"You look incredibly clear!" Lehrmon rejoiced. Turning to Teyani, he asked, "Did Szar bring her back?"

"We don't know yet. Alcibyadi, do you have any recollection of who rescued you?"

"Of course I do!" she exclaimed.

"Let me guess!" Elyani said cheerfully. "A tall thin man with fair hair – light, thin hair. A small moustache and no beard. Blue-grey eyes. And a large birthmark on his left cheek."

Alcibyadi shook her head, "No, he was not at all like that! He was strongly built, with huge shoulders. And he had long curly hair, dark blond. And a beard."

Elyani forced herself to keep smiling.

Feeling the wave of disappointment, Teyani commented, "The Underworld often causes strange distortions in people's perception."

"This man was a great dancer," Alcibyadi continued with enthusiasm. "After he saved me from the caverns of sickness, he took me to a space just underneath the temple. It looked like a huge cave dug in dark-blue rock. And he started dancing in front of me. It was magical! I have never seen anyone dance like that. Just by looking at him, I could hear the music of the spheres. The coldness the Underworld had left inside me melted like snow under sunlight."

Teyani and Elyani exchanged another glance. Neither of them could imagine Szar as a great dancer – which meant there was a major problem. If Alcibyadi had not been rescued by Szar but by a stranger sent by the gods, then who would be in charge of further rescue operations? What guarantee was there that other candidates could be sent down to the Underworld safely?

But the present occasion was for celebration. The four friends kept chatting joyfully.

"Lehrmon," Alcibyadi asked, "tell us about the spheres of remoteness! These Flying Dragons that live beyond the Abyss of the Deep and the Fault of Eternity – what did they show you?"

"Incredible! I will never find words to tell you what I have seen. Whatever you may have encountered, even in the fields of stars at the very peak of the triangle, is nothing compared to the glory that the Flying Dragons have set around themselves. They have secreted their own worlds, straight out of the Light of Highness." Recollecting the feelings, Lehrmon went on, "In their lower spaces they do strange things with time, making it move sometimes forwards, sometimes backwards, so the Mother of the Light delivers hundreds and hundreds of new stars for them. Some of their spaces are so packed with stars, and the light within them is so bright, that it is impossible to distinguish them from the spheres of Highness. With the Point, they do even stranger things. They have built infinity on top of infinity, and worlds with so many dimensions that they themselves cannot always fathom their depths."

"How long does it take you to get there?" Alcibyadi asked.

"This is one of the most curious things," Lehrmon stroked his beard, "it seems to last for an infinitely long time – especially while crossing the Abyss of the Deep and the Fault of Eternity. And yet, one can go to these Flying Dragons and come back in one second."

The priestesses silently tuned into Lehrmon, catching the Point-boggling impressions and the atmosphere that accompanied his story.

The friends went on to chat about unimportant things, savouring the joy of their togetherness, until Teyani took Lehrmon for a walk in the courtyards outside her apartment.

"So, my son," she asked him, "what news do you bring with you? Have the Flying Dragons something to offer us?"

"Oh, mother," Lehrmon sighed, "the news is not good. The Flying Dragons fully support the Archive project. They are only too happy to give their backing to the gathering of Masters of Thunder who are building the temple of light in the Fields of Peace. They are even going to link Space Matrix to the Archive. But as for the growing deterioration of the warp of fields, they say there is nothing they can do. Atlantis must meet her destiny." He paused. "Did you communicate with Gervin?"

"Yes. He is still with the Spirit of the Great Ant, in the far spheres of remoteness. He says that things are even stranger over there than in the Flying Dragon spheres you just visited. But as far as the warp of fields is concerned, it seems that no solution is going to come from the Great Ant either."

"All these intelligences are offering their friendship to Thunder," Lehrmon went on. "They will support the brotherhood of the Knights, and they are ready to pour the miraculous light of their Universal Knowledge Banks into our Archive. But when it comes to rescuing Atlantis, they all say there is nothing they can do."

"I too have some grim news," Teyani held Lehrmon's arm, "two more signs that Gervin had predicted have been reported, both by the priests of the windmills of the Law and by the Field Wizards. The blue-light rituals no longer alleviate the overflow of black muck in darkness visible, and noxious elementals from the second intermediary world have started pouring through the windmills of the Law."

Lehrmon stopped walking and faced Teyani. "Then the Lord Melchisedek have mercy on us! From here on, it could all happen dreadfully fast."

"I know." Teyani turned her eyes to the gods. "Sometimes when I walk through the temple I find myself looking at all the marvels we have built, and all the people we have trained, and all the beautiful connections we have established with the gods, and I wonder, how many years before it all collapses?"

"Have you heard from Woolly how the Archive stones are progressing?"

"Ferman of the Field Wizards told me the whole project is ahead of schedule. This Woolly, by the way... each time I speak to one of his assistants, I hear amazing stories. They all talk about him as the greatest stone maker in the entire kingdom. But what a difficult man to get along with! Did he really throw a bucket of white slime in the face of the high priest of Lasseera?"

"Well," Lehrmon laughed, "I guess he did. Yes."

Taking advantage of the elusive smile on Teyani's face, Lehrmon cheered her, "Come on, we must forget all our troubles for the moment and celebrate Alcibyadi's return." He ran his hand caressingly over the bushes that bordered the alley, "Look at your laurel trees! They are more magnificent than ever." He feigned suspicion, "Teyani, I wonder what charm you have been using on them?"

Teyani's smile shone. She had always regarded Lehrmon as a gift from the gods. A gift of love.

He took her by the arm and started walking back to Alcibyadi's room. "Tell me what you think of this idea: what if I were to take all your White Eagles for a quick tour of tirthas with Alcibyadi, when she has recovered?"

"It's probably just what they all need," Teyani sighed. "Lightness, and some fun. A little hope wouldn't go astray either."

– Thus ends the Book of the White Eagle –

9

The Book of Elyani

9.1 The gods throw the daiva

Answering the call of the gods, long-haired Mareena went and sat at the cascade of blue Life and Light, where the birds of paradise, which are so rare, come to mate, and where the wise receive inspiration.

The world of the gods is no place for waiting.

The gathering was sudden and irresistible. In a split second of the gods, there they Point-were, lofty and glorious – three, and thirty-three, and three hundred and thirty-three thousand. Their fullness of Spirit shone bright and the sky, exhilarated with their immortal might, grew pregnant with lightning.

The birds of paradise became silent.

The whole creation held its breath.

In the twinkling of a third eye, from their omnidirectional sight of Thunder, the assembled gods encompassed all human horizons – past, present and eternity. They judged and decided, and their plan was mysterious and formidable, far-reaching, full of wonders.

Trillions of bells tolled. Thus spun the spindle of destiny. The gods had thrown the daiva.

Then, as suddenly as their presences had Point-gathered, they went.

And the creation breathed.

The birds of paradise resumed their song.

Long-haired Mareena understood the plan. She saw its wisdom, and she approved.

But she cried.

Looking down to the kingdom, she breathed a whisper,

"Elyani, beautiful child, will you ever forgive us?"

9.2 Welcome home, Warrior

As I was approaching the surrounds of the Eisraim temple, I took the soft-stone medallion in my hand once more, wondering whether to use it to call Elyani. The desire to hear her voice took on the proportions of a cosmic itch. But what would I tell her? When you haven't seen a dear friend for a week, you easily find all sorts of little things to tell them. When you haven't seen them for nearly two years, where do you start?

A familiar face came into view.

Uncovering my head, I ran towards the Salmon Robe priest and greeted him, *"Praise the Lord Melchisedek, Artold! How are you, my friend in the Law?"*

Sweet Dragon of the Deep, how good it felt to see this man! He had not changed at all. Yet I found him marvellous, clad in his brand new pink gown.

"All glory to the Lord Melchisedek!" Artold answered. But as he looked at me, he seemed perplexed.

I hid my hair behind my head with one hand, using the other to cover my beard. "It's me, Szar! Do you not recognise me?"

Clearly, he did not. Yet he answered politely, *"Szar, my friend in the Law, I am well indeed, thanks to the Good Lord Melchisedek! And you?"*

"Wonderful, Artold! I am so happy to see you... you simply can't imagine! The trees look so happy in the county of Eisraim."

"And how are your parents, Szar?"

Hearing him start the pre-recorded conversation made me nearly burst out laughing. But I didn't want to offend him, so I answered lawfully, *"I trust they are well, Artold, even though I have not heard from them for some time. And how are your parents, my friend in the Law?"*

I let the conversation unfold for a while, then lawfully took leave. *"Farewell, man of the Law!"*

As I watched the salmon robed sleeper disappear back through the mists, I opened my mouth to drink in the air. In the county of Eisraim the air was so much nicer than in other counties! Not to mention the grass of course, and the flowers, the people. I couldn't help running with joy.

The mists were quite thick that day. I could hardly see more than fifty lawful feet in front of me. I followed the path that led from the Holy Fontelayana river to the temple's main entrance.

When I was only a few minutes from home, I perceived an unexpected sign in darkness visible: an alarm signal, as if there was danger ahead. I ignored it and kept running.

A few seconds later, the same signal recurred. I stopped and sense-smelled the space. No Nephilim presence. But three men were coming towards me. Dangerous men, from a caste who knew how to fight. The smell indicated they were after me, ready to attack.

I couldn't believe my nostrils. "Oh my Mother the Dragon, what's this nonsense?"

The men were closing in on me. All of a sudden the Warrior's instinct took over. I found myself inspecting the terrain, searching for toxic earth lines and venomous wells. No one was coming up behind me. The path was clear, if the need for retreat presented itself.

The three men emerged out of the mists.

I sealed my energy and became still.

I did not recognise them. Two of them were tall fellows who dangerously resembled Nephilim Hunters. Yet neither their aura nor their smell showed signs of the Nephilim spice.

The one in the middle was a small man, completely bald. He shouted at me, "Who are you, *man of the Law*?"

"Szar, disciple of master Gervin of the Brown Robe. Please test for my recognition symbols," I answered, noticing the small man wore no shoes.

"We have already tested your recognition symbols," he said.

"And so? Can I come into the temple?"

"*No way, man of the Law!* There are three influences with you that do not match our record of Szar's energy."

After a moment's hesitation, I decided the best thing to do was to call Gervin through darkness visible. But as soon as I tried to activate a voice channel, all three men projected the Voice at me, "*Stop, man of the Law!*"

I had to further shield my energy to protect myself from the power they were throwing at me.

One of the fellows threatened, "If you try to infiltrate the temple through darkness visible, we will have no choice but to strike you."

This left me speechless.

"Who sent you here, *man of the Law*? What do you want?" the small man asked.

"*Men of the Law*, this is ridiculous! Can't you call Gervin?" I asked.

"Gervin is away," he answered.

"Can you call Lady Elyani, or Lady Seyani of the White Eagle?"

"They're away too."

"Then call Gana-Gerent!"

"Now then, Gana-Gerent died last year."

So my old friend was dead! I felt a bad pinch in my heart. But this was no time to be overcome by sadness. I needed some practical inspiration – fast! Stroking my beard, tuning into the clear fountain, "What about Lady Teyani?"

"Teyani is in the temple, I will communicate with her right now," one of the men said.

After a few seconds, he declared, "Sorry, *man of the Law*, but Teyani cannot warrant the influences that are on you."

"What does that mean?"

"Means that Szar never carried the kind of forces you do, so Teyani doesn't believe you are Szar."

"But... but what do you want me to do, then?" I asked.

"Wait! Teyani is on her way."

"Can I sit down?"

"Do what you want, but do not come any closer to the temple," the small man warned.

I slowly walked to the side of the path, finding a position from which I could have much better control of a line of venomous wells located between the three men and me.

The men walked backwards until they vanished in the mists.

No thoughts, just Dragon, I started singing a children's song from my school years,

"What does a madman do when his first son is born?
He dances. He dances.
What does a madman do when his second son is born?
He dances. He dances.
What does a madman do when his third son is born?
He dances. He dances..."

The situation was far too tense for me to dance, so I only moved my body a bit, keeping the presence of the three men in my peripheral awareness. Ready to activate the venomous wells any second.

It seemed to take forever. When a fourth presence finally made itself felt, I was still singing,

"What does a madman do when his wife is dying?
He dances. He dances."

Then I saw her coming out of the mists, escorted by the three men.

"Lady Teyani!" I called out. The vision at the entrance of Verzazyel's cave was still so vivid in my mind that I almost expected to see a pregnant nineteen-year-old Teyani walking towards me.

The Teyani in front of me was in her late forties. She was still beautiful, although not in the same way. But her walk was just the same.

"Szar?" she asked tentatively.

I did not move, to avoid provoking a reaction from the three men. I just looked at her, *"Praise the Lord Melchisedek, Lady Teyani."*

One of the men warned her, "Better stay where you are, Lady Teyani." As she kept advancing, he insisted, "Lady Teyani, please, don't!"

She ignored him and came right up to me. "Szar! What has happened to you?"

I didn't know what to answer. Resting on the Dragon, I kept looking at her. The three men waited behind her, ready to strike.

Teyani seemed so unlawfully surprised that I was embarrassed, not sure what to do with myself. Gazing at me, she touched my cheek where I used to have the large birthmark.

After a moment she turned to the men. "It's him, Namron!"

The smaller man spat out some black root he had been chewing. "Now then, what about the three influences?" he asked.

Perplexed, Teyani turned back to look at me again.

"It's nice to be home!" I whispered to her.

She smiled. "Namron, it's definitely him. I personally warrant for this man. He is Szar of the Masters of Thunder."

Namron didn't seem at all satisfied. He told his men to stay where they were and walked toward me.

Teyani saw in my eyes that I was ready to strike. She was taken aback. "Don't!" she put her hand on my shoulder, "Namron is a friend."

Eyes fixed on the small man, I slowly unclenched my fists.

Namron stopped ten lawful feet away. "*Listen, man of the Law*, my function is to protect this place. You carry three influences that are three good reasons for me to worry. Will you tell me where you got them and what you intend to do with them?"

I appealed to Teyani, "I have no idea what he is talking about."

Namron frowned, "Where have you come from?"

"The temple of Vulcan and the Sons of the Dragon, in the county of the Red Lands. Master Gervin sent me there to study."

"Have they initiated you into something?" Namron asked, drawing some black root from his pocket and cramming it into his mouth.

I nodded, "Great Warrior."

"Great Warrior?" Startled, Namron spat out the black root before even starting to chew, and he further sealed his energy. "That could certainly account for one of the influences. What about the other two?"

I didn't know what to say. The silence grew thick and tense.

Teyani intervened, "Szar, none of the people you are anxious to see are presently in Eisraim, but a few of them are visiting sacred tirthas only a few hours from here. I'll take you there myself. I need to talk to you, anyway." Then she turned to Namron, "By the time we come back I have no doubt we will have worked out what these mysterious influences are."

"Stay here and wait for me!" Teyani instructed me. Then she started walking back to the temple with Namron.

I didn't budge. I extended my perception to sense whether the three men were moving away. Namron was talking to Teyani, "You must be careful, *my dear friend in the Law*! If you *really* want to go with him, let me at least give you an escort. These Great Warriors are called black nightmares. They're trained to kill. It's the only thing they practise, and they do it from morning to night..."

I disconnected the perception. I didn't want to hear any more.

I went to sit on the side of the path. My forearm flexed, I contemplated my left palm, slowly clenching and unclenching my fist, resuming the nursery rhyme where I had left it,

"What does a madman do when his horse is dying?
He dances. He dances."

Looking at the ripples in my forearm muscles, I started to remember the delicate people of the Eisraim temple. I thought they were my friends, but were they, still? It began to dawn on me that perhaps I had become too different from them. What if they found me disgusting? "They'll avoid me, and call me a nightmare behind my back. That's if they allow me inside the temple at all, of course." The idea of being rejected by Elyani was too devastating to contemplate. And what if Master Gervin himself was to condemn what I had done?

The unfairness of the situation was overwhelming. Staying at Mount Lohrzen had cost me dearly. In my early months over there, I had had to tap from all my resources to resist the temptation to run back home. Yet had I left the Sons of the Dragon before they had started training me in the black dance, none of this nightmare would be happening.

And now what? Had I gone too far in the path of the Dragon? Could it be that my home was now no longer Eisraim but Mount Lohrzen? I thought of Floster and the warm brotherly welcome he would give me if I returned to the temple of Vulcan.

An ugly thought crossed my mind. At this time of the year there were still plenty of Nephilim pilgrims in the county of the Red Lands...

"What does a madman do when his house is melting?
He dances. He dances."

The need for a cosmic dance sprang from the deepest of the Dragon.

I extended my perception. The three men had gone. There was no one around, and no sign of an approaching presence. I took off my cape and stood up.

No thoughts, just Dragon, I danced my mind off.

I danced as in Verzazyel's dream, and the field of stars was my witness.

I danced to the celestial melodies, turning the mists into clouds of light.

I danced with the only companion that was still with me – my Mother the Dragon.

9.3 Lost again

A warning signal. A presence was approaching. I automatically clenched my fists and shifted from Felicia's style to the first movements of the black dance.

Sense-smelling the surrounding space... Only one presence. Not one of the Nephilim. A woman.

Teyani.

I unclenched my fists and made myself Dragon-still.

A few minutes later, the woman with the long dark hair emerged from the mists. "So you dance!" she said, a touch of amazement in her voice.

Embarrassed, I was. How long had she been watching me through darkness visible?

She came up to me. "I brought some food for you. But let us go somewhere else. This is not a very nice place." And she looked straight in the direction of the venomous wells.

Could she see the wells?

We started following the path away from the temple. All at once, the vision of nineteen-year-old Teyani in the temple of Karlinga flooded my memory.

Teyani immediately turned toward me, a curious look on her face.

I held on to the clear fountain and silenced my mind. I had forgotten that in the company of people like her or Gervin, one had better be careful with one's thoughts. So I rested on my Mother the Dragon and kept walking, *no thoughts, pure Dragon.*

"What are you doing, Szar?" Teyani asked.

"Nothing, Lady Teyani," I answered, diving further down to make my mind Dragon-still.

"It feels to me like you are pulling the strings of a subterranean charm!"

"I am just resting on the deep energies of the Earth so as not to disturb you with inappropriate thoughts, Lady Teyani."

She stopped. "Yes, this is what I can feel: music, deep inside the Earth. Nature around us is chanting."

Perplexed, I let go of my Dragon connection.

She shook her head. "No, not like that!"

I rested on my Mother the Dragon again.

"Yes! This is marvellous. It makes me feel like dancing!" she exclaimed.

My face lit up. Could it be that Teyani liked dancing?

"Did you learn to do this at the temple of Vulcan?"

I nodded.

"It's beautiful, Szar! I want to hear everything that happened to you there. But let us sit somewhere and have lunch." She looked around, "Which tree shall we choose?"

"A chestnut tree?" I suggested, remembering the vision.

Teyani frowned with surprise.

I immediately regretted my words. "No, I don't think there are any around here. How about that oak?"

As we headed over to it, I reflected, "Lady Teyani, things seem to have changed a lot in Eisraim since I left. There never used to be guardians at the entrances. What has happened?"

"Nothing has changed in Eisraim," she said.

"But no one used to ask me anything when I went in and out of the temple."

She pointed to a gnarled root of the oak. "Sit down!" she said with the natural authority of someone who has been a grand master for twenty years. "Namron and his men carefully monitor every single person who comes into the temple. Before you went away they had never sensed anything dangerous about you, so there was no reason for them to intercept you. Namron's men are remarkably discreet. There are many in the temple who don't even know they exist."

I took my head in my hands. "Dangerous..." I echoed, "this is exactly what Master Gervin asked me to become when he sent me to the south."

The irony made her smile, "Well, then, Gervin will be proud of you. You have become so dangerous that our security people hesitate before letting you into the temple!"

I did not know whether I should find this funny.

"*Cheer up, man of the Law!*" she blew a mighty light into me. "All will soon be clarified. And tonight we will be with Lehrmon, Elyani, Alcibyadi and my other priestesses of the White Eagle. I have spoken to them through darkness visible. They're all very anxious to see you."

Elyani! Three hours earlier I would have been transported with joy. Now all I could think was, "And what if she hates what I have become?"

Teyani sensed the wave of distress. She took my hand, "Szar, what is happening to you?"

"Is there something wrong with my energy, Lady Teyani? These three influences that worry Namron... I don't even know what they are!"

Teyani became mountain-still. For a moment she looked just as she was when in the temple of Karlinga, about to blow apart the plass chunk on Adya's legs. She took on a solemn voice, "Szar, I am deeply indebted to you for what you have done. I give you my word, we will find out what all this is about!"

Teyani of the White Eagle indebted to me! That was almost as comforting as being patted on the shoulder by Master Gervin. But it was her special warmth that touched me.

The Eagle's flight.

Now, at long last, I could ask the burning question. "Lady Teyani, will you tell me what you have done with Vivyani's soul?"

Teyani looked puzzled. "Vivyani?"

"Didn't you find her soul after I left her in the blue cavern under the temple of Eisraim?"

"Szar," she said after some hesitation, "we did not find Vivyani. Alcibyadi was the one we picked up."

Her words struck like lightning.

So *this* was the meaning of the vision sent by Verzazyel the Watcher! *This* was why when I had asked how Vivyani's soul had been received, I had been shown a story revolving around Alcibyadi's birth.

Vivyani was still lost in the caverns of sickness.

I leapt up, placed my two hands flat on a branch. Teeth clenched, I took a long hissing inhalation and held my breath.

Teyani got up and moved close, "Szar, I don't understand. Did you think she was Vivyani?"

I could have screamed till the depths of the caverns of sickness rose up and delivered their howling agony to the gods above.

There was nothing left but the Dragon of the Deep.

"Here is the music again!" the simple wonder in Teyani's voice reached into me.

"I can't believe I have done this! Lady Teyani... that night, the Eagle was with me. I *knew* I had the power to find Vivyani! If I hadn't been such a sleeper I would have recognised that the soul I picked up in the caverns of sickness was not hers. All I had to do was descend a second time..."

"All you had to do was descend a second time?" Teyani echoed, startled by how easy I made the descent into the Underworld sound. "Szar, do you know..." she hesitated, "do you know who Alcibyadi is?"

I answered with a nod, not knowing whether to mention the vision.

Teyani could tell something was going on. She plunged her magician's gaze into me for a moment, "You don't want any food, do you?"

I shook my head.

"Right!" she picked up her bags and took my arm. "Let us walk, *my friend in the Law*. I want you to tell me all the things that have happened to you, from the very moment you left the temple of Eisraim. Everything!"

As I began to speak, Teyani tuned into the Light of the White Eagle and shone it down on me.

9.4 The Dragon, keeper of the ancient treasures of the Earth

The mists were ablaze with sunset when Teyani and I reached the tirtha lake where Lehrmon and the White Eagles were supposed to meet us.

There was no one there.

Paradoxically, I felt quite relieved. I was becoming more and more apprehensive at the prospect of meeting Elyani.

Teyani called Lehrmon through a voice channel of darkness visible. Dropping the bags, I went to pay my respects to the lake. Smooth and serene, it stretched out as far as one could see into the mists. As the hush of sunset descended, not a murmur broke the silence. Chanting a few verses of the Law, I ritually drank a few sips of water.

When Teyani came over she told me our friends were still on their way. Lawfully paying her respects to the tirtha lake, she blessed it in a near-Voice threshold. The words were simple, the Voice was profound. Fascinated, I watched her slow movements. Nature sang through the harmony of her gestures.

When she finished, she sat and contemplated the diffuse redness of the mists reflected in the water.

I approached her. "Lady Teyani, *may the Lord Melchisedek thank you* for the Light you have poured on me all afternoon. I feel very much relieved now."

"Don't thank me, thank the White Eagle!" The warmth in her voice brought back memories of Elyani taking care of me on my return from the caverns of sickness.

Elyani... knowing she might arrive any minute was both wonderful and terrifying. Resting on my Mother the Dragon, I kept the anxiety at bay.

"I can hear music in the Earth again!" With a gesture of the hand, Teyani invited me to sit next to her. "What is it that troubles you?"

I swallowed. This woman could read my thoughts even when I wasn't thinking. "Lady Teyani, do you have any idea what the three influences are?"

"I think I do, yes. From what I saw when you were talking to me this afternoon, I can confirm what Namron detected. One of the three influences goes down deep into the Earth. It must be the power of the Dragon that the Great Warriors have awakened in you. The second influence is extraordinarily fiery. It is stored in the orichalc plate you wear on your neck. Is this the jewel that Lohrzen wore?"

I nodded.

"Fire like in the giant volcanos of the Ancient Days of the Earth!"

That fitted the image I had of Lohrzen. "What about the third influence?"

"The third is even more curious than the other two." Teyani gazed at the lake.

I waited for the verdict.

"It has to do with the centres of energy above your head, and the powers of the Flying Dragons. My guess is that you have received forces while you were in the initiation crypt where you found the Nephilim priestess."

"The cave of the Watcher was such an enigma. I could feel nothing while I was there – no forces, no presence. Yet it kept me dreaming for an entire week."

And what a dream! Far more real than reality.

"Some of these powers can be so confusing. Anyway, now I understand why you scared the Underworld out of Namron."

I kept swallowing. "Is it that bad?"

"No, not bad, just... intense!"

"Do you think Namron will let me in next time?" I asked somewhat timidly.

Teyani burst out laughing, "Of course he will let you in! *Man of the Law*, Namron is going to love you! For years I have heard him complain how few people we have to defend the temple, if ever we needed to. I don't give him two weeks before he tries to enrol you in his troops."

I was still wondering whether to mention the vision. "Lady Teyani..." I began tentatively.

"Szar!" she turned to meet me. But her eyes were caught by the soft-stone medallion around my neck. It had popped out of my shirt when I bent over to drink from the lake. *"Oh my Lord Melchisedek!"* she exclaimed. "Do you realise what you are wearing?"

I nodded, taking the pendant off my neck and putting it in her hands. "A present for Lady Elyani."

"Voof!"[1] Her fingers treasured the medallion as she contemplated it. "This thing is priceless! Only princesses wear stones like this."

"The Nephilim are the great experts in these soft stones. This one comes from one of their temples in the north, in the county of the Snowy Mountains."

"How did you catch hold of such a jewel?" she asked.

"Someone gave it to me."

"Someone..." Teyani had a curious look in her eyes as she placed the medallion back around my neck.

I could have avoided blushing by resting on the Dragon, but then she would have heard the music anyway. So I blushed.

Teyani politely turned towards the lake. "Gervin was so wise to send you to the temple of Vulcan!"

Her comment did not surprise me in the least. Still, I wondered what she was seeing.

She pre-empted my question, "Szar, tell me again, when I hear this music in the Earth, what exactly are you doing?"

"I rest on the blissful energy of my Mother the Dragon."

Teyani stood up, "Will you do it again for me?"

I jumped to my feet and vroofed a few waves from the Dragon's depths.

Slowly, Teyani began to move, as if she was about to start dancing with the vroofing waves. "This is magnificent! Do you realise what it means?"

I didn't have a clue. I began the slow movements I had learnt in the dance dream.

"Szar," she said, half-mirroring my movements, "these Dragon forces make the Earth chant as she used to in the Ancient Days, long before the birth of the kingdom. The repercussions are enormous!"

I was still mystified.

"Follow me!" the grand master started wending her way among the trees until she found a small plant whose flowers had not yet blossomed. She knelt on the ground and observed the buds. Using a gentle Voice frequency, she projected a long "booo" sound onto the buds.

I stood still, admiring the musical harmony in her Voice.

---

[1] A sophisticated Atlantean sound, difficult to render with English phonemes. Other possible transliterations would be, "Phaoof!", "Faoof!", "Fvaoovf!", "Shoof!" But this unique and vibrant ritual interjection was half-way between a spoken word and a breath, coloured by near-Voice threshold undertones, rich with the joy and enthusiasm of the White Eagle's lineage.

"Now, call on the music," she commanded.

I started a few slow dance movements, resting on my Mother the Dragon.

"Deeper!"

I praised the She-Serpent, keeper of the Furnaces of Doom.

"Good!" Teyani turned to the plant again and Voice-projected another "booo" sound.

This time, something astonishing took place. After she had been projecting the Voice for half a minute or so, three buds started opening. Teyani kept modulating the Voice-sound with soft, loving impulses.

As the "booo" sound went on, the flowers kept opening.

After two or three minutes, three little yellow flowers had blossomed.

Teyani became silent. She gently blew on the flowers.

Eyes riveted on the yellow petals, I forgot my dance.

She picked one of the flowers, placed it in her hair, and stood up. "In the Ancient Days of the Earth things like this used to happen all the time. Nature was enlivened by energies that have now completely disappeared, concealed deep inside the Earth." She started walking back towards the lake. "Do you know what elementals are?"

I followed her steps. "Little beings like gnomes, salamanders and other spirits of nature?"

"Yes, but there are many others," she said. "In reality, there are elementals behind everything that can be seen on Earth: the water of lakes and seas, the air you breathe, the fire, the winds, the mists, the soil, the grass, the precious herbs and the trees, and the rocks, the mountains. Of course, the elementals that sustain the waters of a river are very different from those found in the sea, and the elementals that come through the northern winds give a completely different feeling from those which accompany the desert winds from the south. Then, too, there are elemental beings governing the return of spring, and others in charge of snow and morning frosts. There are elemental beings in your muscles, and in your brain. The heat of your body is linked to particular elementals, and so is the redness of your blood, the strength of your hair, the vitality of your flesh."

She picked up one of her bags and invited me to sit with her close to the water. Opening the bag, she took out two large *pears of the Law* and started blowing softly on them. Wisps of silvery-white shining mist came out of her mouth and enveloped the fruits. She placed one of them in my hand, and bit into the other. As I contemplated my pear with amazement, she continued, "Even the air you breathe out carries elementals, and they are not at all the same beings, according to whether you are happy, sad, angry, or inspired by the gods."

Fascinated, I watched the shining mist slowly dissipating.

"Eat it!" Teyani ordered.

Refraining from resting on the Dragon, I promptly took a bite and swallowed.

"The taste is so pure!" I exclaimed in surprise.

"In the Ancient Days of the Earth, before the creation of the kingdom of Atlantis, all fruits tasted as pure as this. And there was music everywhere in nature. Every leaf on every tree sang, forming an immense choir."

"Was it due to the elementals?" I asked, my mouth filled with the succulence of the pear.

She nodded. "The elementals were infused with Light and Spirit coming from the highest spheres."

"Were those elementals different from the ones we have in the kingdom today?"

"No, they were the same. But in the Ancient Days they shone the wisdom they received through the Light. It made them very smart. They could do all kinds of extraordinary things. The trees talked a lot, especially the big ones. And if you were nice to them, they would tell you which of their fruits was the best, and they would give it to you."

Teyani took two more *pears of the Law* from her bag, and again blew on them. When I saw the shining silvery mist of energy coming out of her mouth, it made me want to laugh with joy. She gave me one of the fruits. This time I ate without hesitation.

"It was all so beautiful, Szar. There was Light, love and music in all things. The weather was always kind. No one ever felt pain or hunger. There was no need to grow crops, there were fruits everywhere, and they were so much more nourishing than those we have in the kingdom now. You just had to eat one or two of them and you felt satiated for the whole day – there was no such thing as indigestion. And you could talk to the animals! They understood very well what you meant, and when you asked them questions they gave you astonishingly wise answers." I had finished my fruit. Teyani grabbed two more pears from her bag. She did the blowing trick again, and this time placed both pears in my hands.

"And the wind, Szar..." her voice breathed the magic she was describing. "I *loved* the wind, he was so nice to me. He came with me wherever I went, and kept whispering flattering things to me..."

I took advantage of her pause, "Was everyone a great magician like you?"

Teyani's laughter resounded like enchanted bells. "No, not at all! Nearly everyone was blissfully asleep with their eyes wide open. They behaved wisely, but this was because wisdom permeated all things. Truly, they had little or no wisdom of their own. They were never unhappy, their heart always felt warm. But this was because there was joy and heartness in the air. They drifted carelessly among the delights of the world, not even realising how special and beautiful everything was. They thought it would all remain the same forever, if they thought at all. Little did they know."

In the stillness that followed, I bit into one of the pears still glittering with silvery light and ventured to ask, "Will you tell me the reason you think Master Gervin sent me to the temple of the Dragon?"

"As you must have heard, great clouds of darkness are sweeping through the kingdom. The energy fields are fast deteriorating. Do you understand what the fields are?"

"Not very well."

"Gervin and Lehrmon are great wizards of the fields. No doubt they will teach you. The fields are sources of astral power that everyone uses for voice channelling and for thousands of other things. But in the last decades, there have been increasing problems with the fields. They do not work as well as they used to, and they make nature sick. The elemental layer is turning into an *unlawful mess*. All the little beings of nature are going crazy. Whatever we are doing with the fields disturbs them badly. This is why rare birds are disappearing, and so are a number of precious herbs. More and more plagues are destroying our crops, and new diseases seem to be appearing every year – the kind of diseases the hymns of the Law are powerless to heal."

"Do you think that Master Gervin intends to restore the balance in nature?" I asked.

Teyani burst into laughter, "*Praise to you, my great man in the Law*, for the faith you have in your teacher. But what you are asking from Gervin is more than the gods themselves can achieve! A single man – even Master Gervin – will never be able to correct the sins of the entire kingdom."

Night had come. Teyani tuned into the energy of the water. I kept tuning into her Light.

"In our work at the temple," she went on after a silent concentration, "we are hitting more and more stumbling blocks due to the fact that the elemental layer is turning into a noxious chaos. A number of practices which in the past used to be simple and *lawfully straightforward* are now turning into sheer nightmares. If there was a chance your Dragon could help us, we would all be deeply grateful to him."

"Her," I corrected. "The Dragon of the Deep is a She-Dragon."

"How interesting!" Thoughtful, Teyani added, "I think I can relate to this. What else can you tell me about the She-Dragon?"

I rested on my Mother, this time to seek inspiration. "I can always rely on her support. She never gives up on me, even when I do stupid things. She is my joy. People have absolutely no idea how beautiful she is. They believe her fierce and terrible. Sometimes she does appear to be like that, especially in the beginning. But in reality, she is pure ecstasy. So intense an ecstasy that those who are not ready to receive it get burnt. But to those who know her and who love her, the She-Dragon of the Deep speaks softly and lovingly. Her *Voice, which is the Thunder of the Earth*, is the most magnificent force I have ever contemplated. But one must descend deep inside the Earth in order to hear her melodies."

Teyani was drawing more and more of the Eagle's Light onto us. A subtle wind of elation was wafting in the air, and I knew she understood what I was trying to convey.

Carried by a vroofing wave, I jumped to my feet. "Lady Teyani, I would like to show you something if I may."

Teyani stood up, "Show me!"

The moon had not yet risen. "We will have to walk in the dark, if you don't mind," I said.

Her laugh rang out, "O Great Warrior, Lady Teyani is not afraid of the dark." She took my arm and let me guide her.

"What I want to show you is called a gate of the Dragon," I explained as we walked. "I can sense one, located on the other side of the lake."

"What's a gate of the Dragon?" she was curious.

"A special entrance that leads to the Underworlds. Normally, those who haven't died in the Dragon cannot see them. But with you..."

She chuckled, "Are you going to test me, Great Warrior?"

I gasped, "Of course not, Lady Teyani!"

As we approached the gate I said, "Here! Just in front of us."

"Yes," she said, "I know this feeling well. How does the gate appear to you, Szar?"

"An ascending breeze. The blissful breeze of my Mother the Dragon. And there is a particular fragrance, by which the gates can be detected from a distance. Can you smell it?"

"No," she said after a careful sniff. "To me, this gate is a particular land energy that I recognise by its friendly feeling and melodious sounds. One of several types of wells through which energies from the inside of the Earth come to the surface."

"An energy well!" I exclaimed. "This is exactly how it feels to me."

"But not all energy wells are like this one," she added.

I perambulated slowly, wondering what the other wells could be. "Just beneath us," I said, "stands the full glory of the Underworlds. Nothing like the caverns of sickness and all those places of hell I saw when I first descended. The Dragon gates lead to huge caves and spaces that are so magnificent no words can describe them. This is the domain of my Mother the Dragon. The deeper you go, the more astounding it becomes."

"How tempting!" Teyani spoke from high in the Eagle's Light. "How long did it take you when you descended and rescued Alcibyadi?"

"Perhaps... thirty lawful minutes."

"Thirty minutes!" Teyani was more than a little disconcerted. She tuned into the gate and sensed its energy for a while.

This woman's hand knew so well how to caress the breeze. I carefully third-eyed her energy, wondering whether I should try to take her down with me.

Too dangerous.

Later on I walked back with her to where we had left our bags. We found a tree house for her to sleep in. They were always plentiful around tirthas. After thanking her wholeheartedly, I returned to the gate to treat myself to its breeze for the night.

I wove a protection field around the lake. Just in case. "Unnecessary?" I wondered. "Who cares?"

Never underestimate the enemy, especially when you don't know him!

9.5 The gate of reunion

It was the middle of the night. An alarm signal woke me, coming from the astral beacons of the protection field.

A presence was approaching the lake.

I automatically clenched my fists and jumped up, starting the initial movements of the black dance, sniffing the space.

Only one presence. Not one of the Nephilim. Not someone from a fighting caste. A woman.

"Mother the Dragon, have mercy on me!"

Elyani was coming.

I dropped my astral camouflage to let her sense my presence in darkness visible.

She immediately felt me. Through the space she called, "Szar?"

"Here, Elyani!"

Only two days before the new moon it was still completely dark, despite the late hour of the night. I pulled some energy from the gate's breeze and created a faint green glow in the space – a Warriors' trick to help friendly presences find their way.

I quickly tied back my hair and concealed it inside my black shirt, praising the Mother of the Endless Night for allowing me to hide in her darkness.

It didn't take long before I heard the sweet voice calling, "Szar?"

I extinguished the green glow with a gesture of the hand and stood on the Dragon. How ridiculous! Gearing myself as if to greet a trio of Nephilim Hunters.

"I am here, Elyani!" I said, calling the Great Dragon for help.

I heard her steps. She walked slowly, slowly, towards me.

She was here.

"Szar?" her voice sounded insecure.

"It's me..." was all I could answer.

She stopped just in front of me and remained still. I *knew* her eyes were closed.

I closed mine. *No thoughts, just Dragon*, I courageously reached out, touched her hand.

She lightly touched my face with her fingers.

Oh Lord, I had forgotten how soft she was. I tried to tell her, but my voice choked.

"Is something wrong?" she asked.

"Elyani... I am a bit afraid."

Small voice, "Afraid?"

"My appearance has changed, Elyani. I am not sure how you will react when you see me."

"The White Eagle said I should come to you during the night."

What would I do without the White Eagle?

"And inside, have you changed?" she asked.

I held my breath. "It's been a long journey."

She withdrew her hand.

"No, please!" I took her hand back onto my cheek. "I have missed you so much!"

I wondered if she was crying. I touched her cheek. She was.

Her hand stopped on my beard, then went down along my neck slowly, slipped under the cape, moved over the Warrior's shirt, explored my chest, my shoulder.

She felt as good as the Dragon of the Deep. I thought of telling her, but I wasn't sure she would understand it as I meant it.

"I was *so* afraid you were going to die," she whispered.

"I did!" I answered. Promptly correcting, "I mean... a few times. I mean, I didn't die." I searched for words, pulling from high up in the fountain.

No words came, but I found a thread to her heart.

Simple, silent, light.

I took her hands tight – not too tight – and started revolving around her, slowly.

"Were you the man Alcibyadi saw dancing?" she turned with me, slowly.

"Could be. When I brought her back from the Underworlds, I found myself just underneath the temple of Eisraim. I wondered where you were at that moment. And I wondered how it would feel to dance with you."

"Did you get sick after you descended to rescue her?"

"No, I no longer get sick when I descend. Elyani, the Underworlds are not at all what people think. They're magnificent."

She hesitated, "Did you go down more than once?"

"Dozens of times. When you know how, it's just as easy as travelling in the spheres. But amazingly beautiful, Elyani."

My slow revolution around her had taken me right on top of the gate. Still holding her hands tight, I remained still, letting the soft ascending breeze warm up the space of togetherness.

"Oh!" she exclaimed, "what is that?"

I dropped her hands and jumped away from the gate, worried the breeze might harm her. "Are you all right?"

"Wonderful! I can hear music everywhere!"

"Music?" I echoed, curious, resting on my Mother's unfathomable silence.

She took my hands again and came closer to me, her breast nearly touching my chest. "Does it make you feel like dancing?"

"Till the end of time!"

"It makes me feel like laughing!" she said.

I tiptoed my way back to the gate.

"Oh!" she marvelled again. "The music!"

Standing on the gate, I started spinning slowly, making her revolve around me.

She burst into a fresh laughter.

That we may fly together.

"Voof! Where does all this music come from?" she kept laughing, as if she was tasting my Mother's ecstasy. "What are you doing to me, Szar?"

I made her turn faster and faster around me. It made her energy flare into a tall flame of white light.

Remembering how I had felt after my first Dragon's dance, I pulled her a few lawful feet away from the gate. "If you do too much the first time, your head will feel as big as a pumpkin when you wake up in the morning."

She drew her warm body close to me. Taking her softest voice, "So is this what you were doing while I was consumed by anxiety for you?"

I sat down on the ground. "No, I've also learnt the most incredible cooking recipes."

Carried by the momentum of the musical melodies, Elyani completed a slow revolution around me, lightly touching my shoulders. "And what else have you learnt?"

I said nothing, wondering what Marek and his men were doing at that precise moment.

She sat by my side. "After spending the day with you, Teyani said I could never call you my brown chicken again. Is that true?"

"No, it's not true. When did you speak to her?"

"A few hours ago, when I was on my way," she said.

"You must be unlawfully tired from all this walking."

"Exhausted!" she said. "We walked all morning, then Teyani voice-channelled us at lunchtime, and we kept going all afternoon in order to meet you. The others stopped in the evening, I kept on till I found you."

The flight of the Eagle.

Touched to the core, I was. I tried to tell her. When I opened my mouth, all that came out was, "Do you need to rest?"

"I'll sleep tomorrow, when they all arrive."

"How is Alcibyadi?" I asked.

"She's beautiful. She can't wait to meet you, she talks about you all the time. You do know who she is?" Elyani asked.

"I know, I know... Teyani's daughter."

"Did Teyani tell you?"

"No, I learned it through a vision sent to me by an angel."

Harmonies. He travelled.

Hesitating, she asked, "Will you tell me what happened to you while you were away?"

"My memories are all yours, White Eagle. Just ask," I took her hand.

She held it tight.

A whisper in space, far away.

"Could we start with the vision?" she asked.

Far, far away.

"I was sitting in a canyon under the full moon, in the south of the Red Lands county," I began my story, letting subjective impressions and images flow into her body of energy. She drank my words, letting herself be transported into the sharp dryness of the Red Lands.

When I finished narrating the vision of the pregnant nineteen-year-old Teyani, there was still no moonlight. "Until yesterday," I concluded, "I still believed that the soul I had rescued was Vivyani. It was only when Teyani and I talked that I realised what had happened."

There was not much that could be spoken. The vast softness of the Eagle shone through her.

"And what about Adya?" I asked. "Have you ever heard her name?"

"Have I ever heard her name..." she took a long breath. "Adya was my mother."

Adya, Elyani's mother?

Surprised out of the Law, I was.

Looking back, Adya did have the same curly hair, the same brown eyes.

As I was trying to put the facts together, the curiosity I had felt outside Verzazyel's cave flared again. "So Adya didn't die in jail!" I exclaimed. "But how did Teyani manage to rescue her in time? The Black Robes were about to beat her to death."

Elyani didn't answer. I realised I was being as tactful as a charging bull. Remembering she had once told me off for asking about her father, I sat in front of her and took her hands. "I'm sorry, I'll never mention this again."

"No, don't say that," she had an immense softness in her voice. "I want you to know. They did beat her, but she survived. It's a beautiful story, but before I can tell you I need to ask someone's permission."

"You don't have to," I tried to offer all the sweetness of my Mother the Dragon.

"But I want to," she insisted.

I held her delicate hands, impressed by the strength behind her words – a strength of a kind I wasn't accustomed to. It had vastness, it breathed, it was light.

When silence is full, there is no need for words.

An elusive whisper. Deep blueness.

The song of a lark in the distance caught my attention. "Your body is shaking with fatigue. How about sleeping for an hour or two?" I said, partly because she was exhausted, partly because I could sense the first lights of dawn on their way.

"I don't want to sleep!"

I put my arms around her and gently pulled her to me, letting her rest on my lap. I held her in my arms to warm her up and caressed her hair. "You don't have to sleep. Just close your eyes for a minute."

She snuggled into my brown cape.

It didn't take long before I could tell from her breath that she had fallen asleep. "As soon as she wakes up," I thought, "I must tell her I love her."

What does a Great Warrior do when he is about to explode with joy? He turns to his Mother the Dragon and praises her glory.

"O wise She-Serpent, deeper than the abyss, what a wonderful creation you have unfolded for your children. Praise to you..."

I was interrupted by an approaching presence. Lady Teyani, returning from her nightly astral travelling through the spheres, was coming near us in darkness visible.

"Oh my Lord Melchisedek!" Here I was, discovered by the White Eagle's grand master, one of her priestesses sleeping in my arms. Just thoughts, no Dragon, I wondered anxiously if I was breaking the Law. What was I going to tell Teyani?

She arrived so fast I didn't have time to prepare my defence.

She stopped just in front of us, straight, shining the Eagle's Light, and spoke to me through darkness visible, *"Praise the Lord Melchisedek, Szar!"*

"All... all glory to the Lord Melchisedek, Lady Teyani!" I responded through the same voice channel.

She had all the tenderness of a mother contemplating her sleeping children. "Elyani loves you a lot, you know."

"Hum..." Where was that clear fountain?

"Szar, I have come to ask you a favour," she said.

"But... *by all lawful means*, Lady Teyani!"

"I want you to show me how to descend into the Underworlds. Can you take me down through your gate of the Dragon?"

I was blank.

"Isn't there a gate just a few lawful feet from here?" Teyani inquired patiently.

"Yes, of course!" I tuned into the blissful breeze.

"Ah!" Teyani sparked, "here is the music again."

"Descending is actually very simple," I said. "All I have to do is let myself glide down through the breeze."

"Can you do it without waking Elyani?" the grand master asked.

"Hum... but yes, of course! My Mother the Dragon can take care of my body and keep it in sitting position while I am down there."

"Show me!"

Simple. I let myself be pulled by the attractive power of the breeze. It immediately made me slip out of my body, and in one second I found myself in a superb orichalc cavern lit with reddish-golden light. At least fifteen hundred lawful feet wide. In the middle of it stood a lake of shining silvery waters – the Underworld replica of the tirtha lake on the surface.

"Ooooh!" I wriggled my nostrils to better take in the water's fragrance. "There are fishes in that lake!"

But there was no Teyani in sight. I quickly paid my respects to the holy lake by Voice-projecting, "*Praise the Great Mother!*" and I let the breeze take me back to the surface.

Teyani was waiting. "What does it look like down there?"

"A lake, but twice as large. Magnificently pure..." As I struggled to describe it, Teyani tuned into me and picked up the impressions.

"Voof!" she marvelled. "What do I need to do to go down?"

I moved to the side of the gate and said, "Come just on top of the breeze, and follow it down."

Teyani tried in vain, the breeze kept pushing her up.

After a minute of unfruitful efforts, I warned, "Lady Teyani, you must be careful. To those who haven't died in the Dragon, this breeze can prove toxic. It could make you extremely sick."

Teyani moved towards me. "And what if I tried to dive into the lake and met you down there?"

Normally that would have been impossible. But for someone like Teyani... "Certainly worth trying!" I nodded. "I'll go down and wait for you in the cavern."

She zoomed off towards the lake.

Through the everywhere-ness at the Edge of Highness, he journeyed.

I contemplated Elyani, asleep like a child in my arms, wishing she could come and discover the lake with me. Then I let myself glide down into the orichalc cavern again.

Awe-inspiring silence! Just one sniff was enough to make you vroof from toe to head. I looked longingly at the lake of water of life, very much in the mood to swim. But what if the grand master of the White Eagle found me intoxicated with water of life (just after finding me with one of her priestesses asleep in my arms)? I just dipped my hand into the fluid silveriness and sprinkled it over me.

Immediately, I felt silly. Containing myself, I resumed the nursery rhyme where I had left it, "*What does a madman do when his tooth is aching? He dances. He dances...*"

I wondered how it would feel to be dancing with Elyani in such a place. There, at the edge of the waters, I started moving my body. Just a bit. "Cautious dancing!"

A few minutes later Lady Teyani had still not appeared. I let myself glide back up to the surface.

Her long silhouette was waiting for me near the gate. "No, it doesn't work. When I dive into the lake in darkness visible, I arrive at the usual shafts that lead to the caverns of sickness."

No surprise. However great her powers might be, she hadn't died in the Dragon. I held to *lawful silence*, not knowing what to suggest.

"I should probably try to understand more about this 'death in the Dragon'. I will speak to you later," Teyani said. Without further comment, she lawfully took leave and disappeared in darkness visible.

"She is special," I nodded, pondering on the flow of forces that illuminated her aura when she let out that magic "voof!"

And by the way, hadn't she said that Elyani loved me?

In an outburst of joy, I let myself glide down into the orichalc cavern. "Voof!" I whispered as I passed through the gate.

The rendezvous will be in sight. Miss not the call.

The Dragon's joy inspired me, "Silvery quintessence for my White Eagle! Let the power of the waters make her shine." I jumped into the lake and made myself a sponge for its sparkling vitality. "Not too much, or it will make her sick!" I thought. Then I let myself glide upwards through the gate. "Voof!"

Day had arrived, the mists not as thick as the day before. I was greeted by a family of swans gliding over the lake. Elyani was still asleep in my arms.

I moved back into my body as gently as possible so as not to wake her up. I distilled the purest essence of the water of life into her energy. Together with it, I added a solid injection of life force drawn from the nearby gate, to wipe away the fatigue of the previous day.

I contemplated her, her head on my lap, her warmth mingled with mine. I had never realised her body was so caressingly soft.

"How could I be such a sleeper?"

I wondered, wishing the instant could have stretched forever.

9.6 The man who hated running

When Elyani woke up, she tucked herself into my cape. I greeted her back in the kingdom by caressing her curly hair.

"Is it already day?" she asked.

"*A beautiful morning of the Law*, with a family of swans swimming in front of us."

She hid a little further inside my cape. "I feel fantastic! As if I had been sleeping for an entire aeon."

"Oh, that's good!" I thanked my Mother the Dragon for her kind help.

"I feel like dancing!"

"Really? I love dancing in the morning," I exclaimed.

She extracted her hand from my cape and slowly passed it over my face. "I can't get up. I'm locked inside you."

"A Dragon swallowed the key!"

She kept exploring my face and my beard with her fingertips.

"If you can cope with the red eyes, the long fangs and the bone through my nose, I'm sure it will all be fine," I assured her. "We might even..."

She sat up in front of me and opened her eyes.

Leaving me paralysed.

"She *has* changed," I realised, discovering an intensity in her eyes I had never noticed before.

She plunged her gaze into me. "Blue eyes... I missed you, missed you, missed you." She caressed my hair and gently untied the curly locks, letting them fall on my shoulders.

She passed her hands over my torso. "This Dragon friend of yours... what an incredible work he has accomplished."

"She," I said in a small voice. "The Dragon is a she-friend. I mean the friend is..." I said no more.

In the islands of light, a laughing timelessness.

Elyani touched my left cheek. "While you were hibernating, Teyani and I covered your face with balms of rare herbs, trying to get rid of the birthmark. Nothing worked. You have learnt to do extraordinary things, haven't you?"

I nodded, and taking Gervin's jokingly serious attitude, looked up to the left and started twinging my beard.

She burst out laughing. "Is this how you escape each time the Dragon starts running after you?"

"The Dragon is pure sweetness, Elyani. She's my Mother. She's beautiful."

An intrigued smile lit her face.

My body became Warrior-still, "Someone is approaching. A group of people. One of them is dangerous," I announced.

Surprised at the abrupt change of tone in my voice, Elyani gently stroked my clenched fists. "It's just Lehrmon and my sisters in the Eagle."

"Are you sure?" the Warrior questioned. I sensed the surrounding terrain, searching for a particular type of venom well only found close to lakes. It worked wonders when it came to putting a group out of action.

I realised Elyani was observing me with a baffled expression on her face. Suddenly, I was afraid of losing her. I dropped the monitoring of my protective beacons and surrendered to her shining brown eyes.

"I haven't yet told her I love her," I thought.

There was not a trace of rejection on her face. "What has happened to my brown chicken who used to forget precious soft stones in the middle of the forest?" she asked in an amused voice.

"He's had a bit of training," I smiled, almost reassured. "By the way, Lady Elyani, I brought a present for you."

I took the soft-stone medallion from around my neck and placed it in her hands.

Her eyes lit up. "Voof!" she exclaimed, with just the same art as Teyani.

Hearing her, it became obvious: the 'voof' ritual cry had been revealed by the White Eagle himself and transmitted through generations of priest-esses, just like the "Ha! Ha! Ha! Ha! Ha!" of Lohrzen's lineage.

"Szar!" she said, "this is..."

"...my first present. I have never given you anything."

While she was admiring the soft-stone treasure, I deliberated, "Do you think we should go and greet Lehrmon?"

"No, let's hide in the lawful wood!"

Laughing with glee, I stood up and took her by the hand, and I started running towards the lake.

She followed, stupefied. "Szar! You are running?"

I promptly stopped. "No! Not really. I mean... not all the time!"

Her intrigued smile reappeared.

"Do you hate people who run?" I asked.

"No," she replied straight away, "not at all!"

"I used to hate running," I admitted. "I didn't hate people who ran, but I hated it when they wanted me to run with them."

Laughing, she started running again, pulling me by the hand. We traced the shoreline all the way to the tree houses. Then she let herself collapse in the grass, panting, her eyes closed. I knelt down beside her and let my hand run on the gateways of her heart, easing the flows.

My body became rock-still, sensing an approaching presence.

"Hum... *Praise the Lord Melchisedek, Lady Teyani!*"

"Mother Teyani!" Elyani exclaimed joyfully. She jumped up and ran over to her, throwing herself into her arms.

I stood up, not resting on the Dragon so as to avoid the music.

"*All glory to the Lord Melchisedek, my children in the Law!*" Teyani hugged her, immediately picking up the silvery quintessence I had poured into her. "You are glowing! Fresh like a waterfall."

Arm in arm, the two women walked towards me.

Teyani announced, "Gervin is back in Eisraim. I spoke to him. He wants you to join him, Szar."

The clear fountain tuned into me, illuminated with Gervin's presence.

"Any other news?" Elyani asked.

"Gervin has a few incredible stories to tell, as usual when he returns from the spheres of remoteness. Quite a lot seems to have happened with the Flying Dragons of the Great Ant."

I received another emergency signal from the beacons of the protective field I had woven the night before. "Someone's coming," I warned.

Startled by the energy in my voice, Teyani stopped talking and stared at me.

"Here they are!" Elyani exclaimed, as the troop emerged from the trees. Lehrmon of the Brown Robe, leading a group of women dressed in white. More than twenty of them.

Lehrmon stopped and stood still, giving Teyani the special wave of his hand, a distinct impulse travelling from him to her in darkness visible.

She shone.

Mother of the Light, so much love!

Tuning into me, Lehrmon laughed and clapped his hands, hurrying towards us.

He dropped his bags, lawfully greeted Lady Teyani and hugged Elyani, then came to me and took my hands. *"Praise the Lord Melchisedek, Szar, my brother in the Brown Robe!"*

"All glory to the Lord Melchisedek, Lehrmon!"

"You have made us all so happy!" his joy shone like a bonfire, filling the space with the unique warmth of the Masters of Thunder. Contemplating his luminous amber eyes and the tranquil strength that radiated from him, I was surprised how dense and solid his energy was. This had completely eluded me before.

Behind him, the priestesses of the White Eagle were paying their lawful respects to Teyani. But as one of them came towards me I had a shock.

Long dark hair, piercing black eyes. With her white dress she looked so much like the nineteen-year-old Teyani of my vision...

For a moment I wondered where I was.

"Praise the Lord Melchisedek, Szar of the Brown Robe!"

"Do you recognise this woman?" Lehrmon asked. "Lady Alcibyadi of the White Eagle."

I tried to smile, but I was hit by the memory of Vivyani.

The blonde Vivyani, lying on her deathbed.

Why did it have to hurt so much whenever I remembered her?

Elyani must have heard my thoughts. She rushed over to us, took Alcibyadi in her arms and started talking to her. Meanwhile Lehrmon took my arm and walked me to the lake. "Szar, brother, I owe you. Did you know that Alcibyadi and I grew up together?"

"No, I didn't. Was it in the temple?"

He nodded, "With Elyani."

"Well, I'm really glad for you, Lehrmon," I answered, trying to push Vivyani's image away.

Lehrmon gently tapped my Great Warrior's shoulders. "Looks like you have a few stories to tell, Szar!"

"Could be, *my friend in the Law*," I forced a smile through the Dragon.

"Is it true that Namron refused to let you into the temple?" he asked.

"I'm afraid so."

Lehrmon appreciated the irony, "I can already see Master Gervin laughing his clear fountain off when he hears this story."

I still found it only mildly amusing. "By the way, have you heard that Gervin is back and wants to see you?"

"I could probably be in Eisraim in two hours," I estimated, remembering all the breaks Lady Teyani and I had taken on our way to the tirtha.

"Two hours!" Lehrmon laughed, "Well, Gervin won't be able to see you until tonight. So why don't you give yourself six hours and ask Elyani to escort you?"

"What a lawfully excellent idea!" I answered, enthused. "Did you say you grew up with her?"

"The Lord Melchisedek I did! I first held her in my arms when she was three hours old."

When we returned to the White Eagles, Alcibyadi was standing apart from the group. I tried to walk towards her, but Vivyani's corpse stood in the way.

Resting on the Dragon, I emptied myself and joined the others. "*Lady Elyani of the White Eagle, would you care to escort me back to the temple of Eisraim?*" I asked in a formal voice.

A smile at the corner of her lips, she replied no less formally, "*Sir Szar of the Brown Robe, if Lady Teyani, by the grace of our Lord Melchisedek, permits me, it will be my privilege!*"

Thank the Lord Melchisedek, Lady Teyani permitted.

9.7 The gate from past to future

Elyani stopped to catch her breath. "Do you think... we could take a break?" she asked, her eyes closed.

"Again? But we're nearly there!" I said.

"Ah?" she said in a small voice. "Well, let's go on then."

I contemplated my left palm, sensing the space half a mile around us. Not one presence. I swung round towards Elyani and lifted her up in my arms.

She reopened her eyes, laughing, "Szar, what are you doing?"

Carrying her, I resumed the walk. "Giving you a break."

She put her arms around my neck, "I wonder what you are going to do in the temple to exercise!"

"I have no idea. I'm sure I will find something. Pity there are so few rocks around Eisraim. Climbing is good for the Dragon."

"By the way, there is a surprise waiting for you in the temple."

"Really?" I exclaimed. I had always hated surprises. Pulling strength from the Dragon, "I love surprises!"

"Well, Great Warrior, get ready for a lawfully big one!"

"Has it got to do with Namron and his men?" I asked cautiously.

"No, no, don't worry! He and Teyani have voice-channelled the problem through. Everything will be fine this time."

I heard the sound of a stream nearby. I thought Elyani might like to drink from it, so I turned off and entered the wood that bordered the path.

As we were sitting by the water, Elyani said, "See the energy of this little stream? Rather grey, isn't it. When I was a child, it was shining blue. The taste of the water was divine. The people of the temple used to come here to fill their jugs. Now... now, it's just water, and the crayfishes have disappeared."

"How can that be?"

"Seven years ago, the energy field that fed the elemental forces in this area collapsed."

"Can't it be fixed?"

"The problem is, it collapsed because the larger field out of which it fed had itself collapsed."

I stood up and felt my roots in my Mother the Dragon. The aura of the water remained grey.

"If we could fix the fields, do you think it would allow us to find the souls of the White Eagle's priestesses who got lost in the Underworlds?"

"Still thinking of Vivyani?" Elyani's empathy reached out to me. "I wonder what could help you forget."

I copied one of her faces. "I don't want to forget. I want to find her!"

"Szar, until I met you I thought my teacher was the most stubborn soul in the kingdom," her elbows resting on her knees bent up, she cradled her chin in her hands. "Well, I was wrong!"

The expression sounded familiar. I pursued my line of thought, "Before the fields started to deteriorate, what did people do when someone got lost in the Underworlds?"

"Well, they didn't get lost so often, for a start. And when someone did lose their way, the priests used a method called 'resonance'. It was quite simple. They just had to create a certain vibration, a bit like a musical note, which resonated specifically with the lost person. Deep in the Underworld, the person's soul was attracted by the vibration and led back to the kingdom."

"Why can't we do that any more?"

"As the energy fields became chaotic, so did the Underworld. The vibrations no longer seem to reach down there, or if they do they must get lost in the chaos of the caverns of sickness. The resonance no longer brings people back."

"When you descended and lost your way, did the resonance method help you find your way back?"

"No, my dear friend in the Law," a shadow passed over Elyani's face, "the resonance method had long stopped working."

"So how did you come back?"

She sat up as straight as Teyani. "Do you know that I was only fourteen when I went down? Gervin ordered it. At the time everyone thought he was unlawfully cruel. In reality he saved my life. He knew that the fields were deteriorating very fast and so in his wisdom, he made me descend as soon as possible."

"Still, you lost your way! Who picked you up?"

"No one. I lost my way but I never stopped walking, that's what saved me. I went on and on until I finally found a way out. It seemed to last forever, but I never forgot the commandments Teyani had been hammering into me..."

"Keep walking, hold on to your symbol! " I recited. *"Never stop on the way! Never walk back, never look back!"*

"You remember well," the smile reappeared on her face.

"If it hadn't been for these words I would still be in the caverns of sickness. But now that I have contemplated the glory of the Underworlds through the Dragon's gates, all these nightmares sound a trifle unreal."

Elyani took on her intrigued look again. "Do you think there's a chance I could peep through a Dragon gate?"

"I would love to take you down with me, but I have no idea how to do it!" I told her the story of Lady Teyani's visit the night before. Hearing how embarrassed I had been, Elyani burst out laughing.

"It's time to go. I'm sure you can walk, now," I decided.

It only took us an hour to reach the temple surrounds. I was on high-alarm mode, gearing myself for the possibility of another encounter with Namron.

"Don't worry!" Elyani kept repeating.

And she was right, Namron did not even show up. Before long we came to the familiar arch where I had first set foot in the temple with Gervin, nearly eight years before. In an outburst of joy I jumped up, but couldn't reach the top of the arch (funny I had never thought of trying before). Here were the alleys bordered by holy trees, the aspiringly-arched hallways, the friendly courtyards with the colonnades and all the statues of the gods, the people peacefully going to and fro. It all felt so familiar. No one recognised me, of course, but so what? I recognised the feeling, and it made me extremely happy.

Elyani by my side, happiness was such a natural state.

"I don't even know which quarters of the temple Gervin wants me to stay in," I said. "Where are you taking me, White Eagle?"

"To the surprise."

"Wait!" Abruptly, I clenched my fists. "I can sense Namron." I turned to the right and pointed upwards. There he was, quietly sitting on a chapel roof, his bare feet hanging in the air, observing the people passing by.

The small man with no hair on his head smiled at us and waved his hand in a friendly way.

Elyani smiled and waved back.

After a second of deliberation, I did the same. "Funny I never noticed this man before."

"Could it be that you are seeing things differently, now?" Elyani suggested in a candid voice.

"Could be. So what about the surprise?"

She grinned, "*Follow me!*" She took me to the portal of the female wing of the temple, and then through the daedal of corridors that had never failed to confound me.

"Looks like we are going to your apartment!" I construed.

"Well... we are and we are not," she riddled me.

It was the perfect comment for this headache of a maze. During my Warrior's training, I had promised myself that on my return to Eisraim I would master the labyrinth. But I was already starting to be confused. Extending my perception through darkness visible and sense-smelling the space, I tried to map every single well and earth line I could find.

"I can sense a Dragon gate not far from here," I exclaimed.

"Oh really?" the White Eagle said, far too innocently for me not to get suspicious.

I took the smell of my Mother's breeze as a reference. But instead of moving straight towards the gate, Elyani was taking me to and fro through corridors that felt to me pretty much like the bewitched maze of Verzazyel's cave. I started wondering, "Could it be that none of these hallways exist physically, and that we are travelling in an angel's mind?"

"There is Flying Dragons' magic in the air," I concluded.

Elyani chuckled, "Think so?"

I shook my head, more and more appalled, "This Flying Dragon business is *such a pain in the Law*!"

Round and round, up and down, in and out, my head in a whirl, before I knew it I was standing in front of it. "Oh my Lord Melchisedek! I just don't believe this!"

"So, how is my surprise?" the White Eagle raised her eyebrows.

I was astonished. We had arrived at Elyani's courtyard, and there, right in the middle of the lawful lawn with the little purple flowers... there it was, the Dragon gate!

"Oh my Mother of the Endless Night!" I sniffed the blissful breeze in disbelief. It instantly brought a wind of elation inside. "This is simply... out of the Dragon!"

Stroking her chin, Elyani was fully satisfied. "Gervin warned me I should watch your face carefully when you arrived back here from the temple of the Dragon."

"An ambush!" I thought. "But... but how did you know there was a gate here?" I couldn't understand.

She smiled enigmatically.

"Does Gervin know about the gates of the Dragon?" I spoke without thinking. Stupid question! How could Gervin not know about the gates, or anything else?

"Well," Elyani sat on the lawn, and I beside her, "long ago, a young man from the temple of the Sons of the Dragon came here. It must have been before I was born, or not long after, but I have heard the story several times."

"Marek!" I recalled my master in the Dragon narrating the story of his miraculous recovery after being Point-murdered by the Nephilim Hunters. "Of course! Marek the indestructible came here to be healed by Gervin!"

"Marek?" she echoed. "I am told he was one of the weirdest visitors we ever had. The priestesses of the female wing used to call him 'Sniffing Dragon', because he sniffed everything and everyone all the time. Whenever they offered him a healing drink, he would become terribly suspicious and sniff the beverage for at least a lawful minute before drinking. But the strangest thing..." her eyes, wide open, resembled Underworld jewels, "one day, he climbed onto the roof of one of the temple's chapels..." she burst out laughing loudly as the scene came back to her. Clearly, the breeze I had drawn from the gate was doing something to her. As far as I was concerned, the idea of Marek inspecting the temple's roof did not surprise me in the least. I anxiously waited for the rest of the story.

"There he was, standing on the roof, everyone watching him. He started sniffing and sniffing..." she had to pause to laugh, then tried again "...and then he began jumping from one roof to another. Below, in the alleys of the temple, everyone started following him. He went on sniffing his way from roof to roof until he arrived here. And then..." her laughter bubbled up, "he was standing on the roof, just over there..." Elyani pointed to the roughly flat roof on top of her bedroom, "...and he jumped down into the courtyard, landing right in front of an old priestess of the Purple Robe. Nefertine, her name was. She was almost completely blind. *Unlawfully shocked*, Nefertine exclaimed, 'Oh my Lord Melchisedek, what is *that?*'"

Elyani lay on the grass, holding her belly from the laughter.

I let my hand run on her gateways, helping to ease the flows. "And what happened after that?"

"He kept sniffing, probably for the gate. But old Nefertine thought he was some kind of black angel fallen from heaven, sniffing her like a beast of prey. Bravely, she started chanting a hymn of exorcism."

"What did Marek do to defend himself?"

"Nothing, he ignored her. He kept sniffing, and she kept chanting her exorcism hymns. It went on like that until the grand master of the female wing arrived."

"And then?" I asked anxiously.

It took a few seconds for Elyani to recover her voice. "Well," she sat up and let out a long sigh, "when everyone realised how important the gate was to him, they let him stay in this bedroom, which happened to be empty at the time." Elyani pointed to the room where she had taken care of me during my descent into the Underworlds. "But he never slept in the room, even when it was raining. He preferred to stay here on the lawn."

On the gate, of course.

"What about the old priestess? Was she living in your bedroom?"

"Yes. Funnily enough, the two became great friends. The oddest pair of friends one could imagine in the kingdom! They spent entire days telling each other stories and she took good care of him, as he used to have bad fits of convulsions. Before he left, he gave Nefertine a magnificent present. The temple physicians had given up on her blindness, saying it was *beyond lawful treatment*. Sniffing Dragon healed her. She fully regained her vision. After that, she lived for many years. Long enough for me to hear the story from her, and several times. She used to call him 'my black friend'. I will never forget the way she used to say, 'Oh my Lord Melchisedek, what is *that*?' when she described their first encounter."

Elyani lay back down on the grass with her eyes closed, her hands touching the leaves of her favourite laurel tree.

I stood up and walked over to the ascending breeze, paying my respects to my Mother.

"Is it a good gate?" Elyani inquired.

"The gates are *all* beautiful, my White Eagle. Each one chants the glory of my Mother the Dragon." But I was still intrigued. "When did you move into your bedroom?"

"When I was fourteen, after I returned from the Underworld."

"But what made you choose this particular place?"

"I don't think it was pure coincidence. But before I can tell you, I need to ask someone's permission."

She was probably talking about her parents. I didn't insist.

I wriggled my nostrils and inhaled deeply, filling my energy with the invigorating fragrance coming from the breeze, and I walked to the outside wall of her bedroom. I put both hands flat on the living plass substance of the wall, "So good to feel this again. Do you know there wasn't one plass wall at the temple of the Dragon!"

"Really? What kind of building was that?"

"Caves dug in the rock. There are few openings but inside the caves the walls don't glow, you need torches to see at night. And wherever you go, your shadow follows you. You can see it dancing on the walls."

"Shadows on the walls? How weird!"

"You get used to it. Listen, can you tell me something about the Law of this temple?"

"*By all lawful means!* What would you like to know?"

"Is there any provision that says one should not walk on the roofs?"

She burst out laughing again, opening her eyes as she considered this. "I have never heard anything about walking on the temple roofs. My guess would be that during *the Sublime Revelation of the Law*, no one thought of asking the gods about this point."

"It's not forbidden... then it must be lawful," I concluded.

Stepping on the asperities of the plass wall, I promptly lifted myself onto the uneven flat terrace that covered the two adjacent bedrooms.

Elyani could not believe her eyes.

From where I was, I couldn't see much. Balancing my feet on rough edges of the plass facade, I climbed up another wall.

"Watch your lawful step!" Elyani sat up. "Don't hurt yourself!"

"Oh! Is *this* where we are?" I exclaimed as I reached the second roof. "Now I understand. It's obvious!" I was discovering the temple from a completely different perspective, and it all made sense. "This tangle of corridors must be happening in the bewitched mind of some remote angel! Look at this, we're hardly three hundred and fifty lawful feet from the enclave of the *Most Ancient and Lawful Orders*," I mused, wondering which roof was the chapel of the Salmon Robe. "I could get from here to the main entrance of the temple in less than five minutes! Probably less than two, actually."

"I wonder if it was wise to tell you the story of Sniffing Dragon," Elyani murmured thoughtfully.

"Don't worry, it wouldn't have taken me long to figure this out. Can you tell me what I am standing on at the moment?"

"The roof of the chapel of the Blue Robe priestesses." [Map H, 320]

"The Blue priestesses... they're the ones who talk very, very slowly."

"It's proverbial," Elyani answered.

I surveyed my surroundings, then I climbed down to the terrace that formed the roof of Elyani's bedroom, and from there jumped back into the courtyard.

"Elyani, this opens completely new horizons for me! I wonder why I never thought of observing the temple from above before."

She was sitting by her favourite laurel tree. I came and sat in front of her, contemplating the glitter in her eyes.

It was like melting in the ocean.

Softness beyond words.

"Can you feel?" she lightly touched my hair.

"What?"

"The Light of the Eagle. It is here for you, pouring into your heart."
Beyond time, beyond spaces, the softness of the Eagle.
I opened to her love.

"Yes," she whispered, "like this."

"Whatever it is, it is magnificent. It makes you shine." The feeling of having been separated from her for so long was overwhelming. "Friend, friend... I pray Gervin never asks me to go away from you again."

Her hand found her way to my chest. "You have become so different, Szar."

I tucked my head in my shoulders, "Have I changed too much?"

"No," her voice was balm, "I didn't mean it like that."

Holding onto the clear fountain, I surrendered every fibre of myself to the limpid brown eyes.

Her fingertips moved caressingly along my chest. "You never used to say warm things to me before. When you left the temple, you didn't even hold my hand."

"I know." I remembered Szar-ka, the desperately inoffensive brown chicken. "My Dragon was completely asleep. I had no idea what love was about. I just drifted blissfully, enjoying your warmth like children do. I thought it was really nice of you to take care of me when I was sick. I had no idea what you were feeling."

"Well," Elyani declared, "I am deeply indebted to your Mother the Dragon for what she has done with you."

"I was so afraid you were going to hate me."

"But why?"

"Because of what I have become. You are a fine, delicate person. In Mount Lohrzen, everything was so harsh. The violence was wild. You have no idea the kind of things Sniffing Dragon made me do during all those months."

"Well, I find you much softer than before."

I had tears in my eyes. "Really?"

"Now when you touch me, it feels special. Sweet like Teyani's honey elixirs. It never felt like that before."

Tears were dropping into my beard, "Elyani, it's terrible... I have learnt to kill. And I have been taught so many ways to break things, demolish houses, lawful bridges even!"

She gently laid my head on her shoulder and enveloped me in her arms as if in the Eagle's wings. "Maybe it all goes together," she said. "Maybe the people who can be the most violent are also those who can be the sweetest."

"Sounds just like my Mother the Dragon." I watched a tear droplet fall into the hollow behind her clavicle. "Do you have any idea if Gervin will ask me to go back to the temple of Vulcan?"

"Gervin is always impossible to predict," she reminded me. "A few months ago when I was very sad, he promised me there would be beautiful moments between us after you came back. Some great fun. But knowing him, this could mean anything. Anyhow, you can ask him soon. He said he would join us around sunset and share dinner with us."

Gervin! Gervin at last!

"Maybe you should *get some lawful rest*. How are you feeling after so much walking and so little sleep?" I inquired.

"Flying high, like an eagle!"

Gently, I extricated myself from her wings. "We still have three or four hours before sunset. Why don't you sleep while I go and pay my respects to Lord Gana?"

She smiled, "Are you still his high priest?"

"Shame on me, I lost my thread to him. I used to feel his presence around me all the time until about a year ago. But when I started mastering the black dance there was a profound change in my energy. After that, I could never feel Lord Gana as I used to. Something happened, I don't know what. I want to go and surrender to his wisdom. Perhaps he will accept me."

"Isn't Lord Gana called the wisdom of the Dragon? And isn't he a great dancer among the gods? How could he not like a sweet dancing dragon like you?"

"I must have gone wrong somewhere, but I don't even know how it happened. Maybe he will tell me."

"*The mind of the gods transcends the wit of mortals!* Shall I take you to the portal of the female wing?"

"*No way, woman of the Law!* This time I want to find the way by myself."

"Sure?" she asked with a touch of irony.

"Dragon-sure! But if I am not back an hour after sunset," I added, "could you please have a quick look in the corridors around here?"

"*Fear not, man of the Law!* I will find you."

I looked into her eyes, letting her sweetness seep into me. Then I stood up, paid my respects to the gate, and courageously broached the hallway.

9.8 Lord Gana before and after

"*Oh my Lord Melchisedek,* save me from the magic of the Flying Dragons!" I exclaimed, as it became clear that I was lost. Completely lost.

I had been trying to keep the gate behind me as I walked, and had succeeded for at least three minutes, until I hit a circular stairway I had never seen before, and that seemed to go up forever, until finally – finally! – I reached a long, straight corridor along which I walked with the secure reference of the gate at my back, and it seemed all right for a while, except that when I arrived at the end of that corridor the gate was no longer behind me but in front of me. From then on, things went from bad to worse. And I thought Verzazyel's cave was bad!

I came to a stop in the middle of a circular hallway, so exasperated I could have jumped and sworn the Underworld's Bottom off. But an elderly, dignified-looking Ochre Robe priestess was walking towards me, so I closed my eyes as if I was in the middle of an intense spiritual concentration.

As soon as she had gone, I regretted not asking her for directions. I turned left at the next crossing. It led me to another corridor, and now I felt the gate in a direction that made even less sense. I was outraged.

"You Flying Dragons can go to Azazel and get lost!"

From then on I just kept walking without even smelling my way until I arrived at the next courtyard. Having cautiously checked that no one was watching, I quickly climbed onto the roof of the building.

"Is this where I have landed?" I was bewildered. I had gone in exactly the opposite direction from my designated target.

Concealing my energy, I jumped from roof to terrace and terrace to roof, finding my way from the female wing to the enclave of the *Most Ancient and Lawful Orders*. In many spots I didn't even have to jump – plass gangways went from one building roof to the other. It took less than three minutes to reach the domed roofs of the chapels of the windmills of the Law. They were separated from the enclave of the thirty-three victorious gods by the straight path of the Law, this long winding artery that went *from the temple's main gate to the cremation grounds in the far south* (symbolising the life journey of every priest and priestess in Eisraim). The straight path of the Law was the broadest alley in the temple but it was easy to pass over it. In the vicinity of the main entrance of the temple it was covered by several colonnades that linked the roofs of the enclave of the windmills to those of the thirty-three victorious gods.

In less than five minutes altogether I was on top of Lord Gana's chapel. Feeling Dragon-good about the ride. The maze of the female wing had been conquered. Somewhat.

I waited for the alley to empty, checking through darkness visible that no one was approaching. Then I jumped down and found myself in front of the chapel door.

Timidly, I opened it and went in. The chapel was empty.

As soon as I stepped over the threshold, I was flooded with Lord Gana's unique golden light. It came from the altar and from the fields in the plass floor, walls and ceiling. Light with presence. Ancient. Awesome, and mysterious.

Splendours of Eisraim!

As I had done so many times before, I went to sit in front of the altar and started the ritual invocation,

"*Ha! Gana! Lobatchen Zerah! Hera, Gana! Simayan ho Zerah!
Nama Gana, Nama Gana, Gana Gana, Nam Nam...*"

The light was alive. It was charged with sound. The walls were repeating the mantras with me. The light was pulsing, from the altar to the walls and from the walls to the altar. My energy expanded, filling the space of the temple and pulsing with the glow.

"*Nama Gana, Nama Gana, Gana Gana, Nam Nam...*"

The bliss of an anemone of light. A divinely peaceful practice, but...

What was it that was missing?

The *living walls* were holding me softly. The space was there, just like it used to be before I went away. The mantras were still magnificent. Why did it all feel so incomplete to me?

I started the chanting again. "*Nama Gana, Nama Gana, Gana Gana, Nam Nam...*"

A few lawful minutes later, I started feeling a certain drowsiness. I instantly stood up. "This practice takes me back to my sleeper's mind!"

I remembered the days I used to spend chanting behind this altar. It became obvious that those long hours of mantra chanting had been a way of comforting myself in my lethargy. "*Lawfully wonderful!*" I thought in horror. "I used to come here to add a flavour of Gana-dreaming to my sleep."

And I used to call it divinely inspired trance!

I walked to the entrance and stood in the doorway, watching the priests passing by in the alley.

Forever friends will meet on the forever summit of the worlds.

It crossed my mind to walk away and forget Gana's priesthood once and for all.

"*No way, man of the Law!*" I shook myself, "It was never Lord Gana's fault if I was a sleeper. There *has* to be another way!"

Walking back to the altar, I addressed the god from the highest of the clear fountain, "Oh Lord Gana, you are too important to me! Please don't let me walk away. It can't just all stop here. I want to learn an awakened way of worshipping you."

Dancing, perhaps?

I gently tapped the floor with my foot – a flat, polished floor, shining with the light of the god. The glowing plass looked like pure gold, as in a cavern of the Deep Underworlds.

I remembered one of the strongest experiences I had ever had. It was while searching for Vivyani under the guidance of the White Eagle. I had plunged deep into a Dragon's gate and merged its ascending flow with my clear fountain, creating a column of Spirit that seemed to reach forever high up in heaven.

There was no gate in Lord Gana's chapel, so I anchored myself in the depths of my Mother the Dragon, using the grounding as a resting place to call high up and invoke the god.

Using the Voice, I projected one of Gana's most powerful mantras onto the flame on the altar, "*Gang gang Gana! Gang gang Gana! Gang gang Gana!*" I started moving, slowly, letting myself be guided by the knowingness of the chapel. Strange movements flowed through my body. Somehow, I was following a thread.

But something was lacking. This sort of dance before the altar simply wasn't enough.

Finally I stopped and shook my head, contemplating the *living walls*.

"I must be missing the point!"

9.9 The storytelling night

On my way back to Elyani's courtyard, as I was passing over the chapels of the windmills of the Law, I saw Namron. He was sitting on a rooftop, on the other side of an alley.

He waved at me. *"Praise the Lord Melchisedek! How are you, Szar, my friend in the Law?"*

"All glory to the Lord Melchisedek! Very well, Namron, my friend in the Law! Strange, I never used to meet you before. Now our paths seem to cross all the time."

"Well," Namron observed, chewing his black root, "you didn't use to walk on the roofs much, before."

"Ha! Ha! Ha! Ha! Ha!"

Startled by the roaring violence of the Warriors' Voice-laugh, Namron somehow managed to keep smiling. He exhaled slowly, *"A lovely sunset of the Law, isn't it?"* and he went to spit out his black root, only to realise he had already swallowed it.

"So much nicer seen from above!" I pointed to the alley, "The people down there don't know what they are missing!"

"How true, my friend in the Law!"

I lawfully took leave and bounded across the rooftops towards Elyani's courtyard. "This time, no Flying Dragons' nonsense!" There was *no way in the seven spheres* I was going to descend into that labyrinth of corridors ever again.

Crossing the enclave of the *Most Ancient and Lawful Orders*, it didn't take long to reach the roof of the Blue priestesses' chapel. Gervin had already arrived. He was standing in the courtyard, thirty lawful feet below, talking with Elyani. As I didn't want to give them a rude surprise, I noisily climbed down onto the roof of my beloved friend's bedroom to announce my presence.

"Hum..." I cleared my throat, *"Praise the Lord Melchisedek, Master Gervin!"*

Gervin looked up and raised his eyebrows, stroking his beard. *"All glory to the Lord Melchisedek, Szar!"*

From Elyani's bedroom roof, I jumped into the courtyard as smoothly and discreetly as possible, and walked towards him.

The clear fountain clicked instantly. The space was full with his warmth.

Gervin illuminated the courtyard with his serene smile. He did not seem at all disconcerted by my physical appearance.

As I drank in the sight of him, images of the young Gervin rescuing Teyani came back to me. His piercing, awe-inspiring eyes had not changed a single bit. His grey hair was slightly shorter, no longer falling to his shoulders. His grey beard was a little longer, elongating his thin face. He shone with the light of Thunder.

Elyani invited us to sit on the lawn, close to her beloved laurel.

Gervin turned to her, "A different Szar!"

Grave, she nodded.

"And a different Elyani too!" he added with a teasing note in his voice.

A touch of embarrassment ran on the face of the White Eagle.

Gervin put his hand on my shoulder, "And so, *my friend in the Law*, how do you like this courtyard?"

"It has some very attractive sides... I mean, the gate is beautiful."

"Beautiful!" Gervin echoed wholeheartedly. "Speaking of Dragon, there is no need to worry about Marek, I sent him a message saying I had called you back urgently, which is why you couldn't return to his temple. He understood very well."

I was no longer a deserter!

I opened my mouth, but didn't know what to say. This *unlawful weight* having been lifted off my shoulders, I felt like jumping for joy.

"All glory to the teacher!" I managed to articulate. "Master Gervin, this is a wonderful present. I felt terrible at the thought of letting Marek down, after all he has done for me."

"I sent the message two days after you left his temple, so he did not worry at all," Gervin said.

I was flabbergasted. So Gervin had been following every single action of mine! And I had gone through weeks of aaa-gony for absolutely nothing! The misgivings I had had about taking care of Felicia, the doubts, the remorse, the guilt for not following Marek's order – all for nothing!

"By the lawful way," Gervin went on, "you left an excellent impression in the temple of Vulcan. Marek was most complimentary about you."

So I was no longer a traitor! Deep inside, I thanked my Mother the Dragon. "Does this mean I do not have to go back?" I held my breath.

"This I don't know," Gervin twinged his beard, smiling at Elyani. "You see, Lady Elyani seems to think this Dragon of a period has done you a lot of good. I wonder if we should try to satisfy her further by sending you back to Vulcan for a few more years?"

Elyani's mirth mingled with my immense relief.

"Tomorrow, we'll discuss what is to come next," Gervin announced. "But for now," he clapped his hands twice, "Elyani and I want to hear every single thing that happened to you while you were away."

Plates were laid on the grass and my friends started eating a frugal dinner of fruits and cereals while I began my story, "The canyons of the county of the Red Lands..."

Elyani and Gervin knew how to listen to stories well, catching all the impressions I was trying to convey, and sharing the emotions that had marked this 'Dragon of a period', as the master had rightly called it. From time to time they applauded and asked for more details. When I described my brethren the Sons of the Dragon and their eccentric customs, laughter ran lawfully wild. Only to be replaced by exclamations of wonder when Gervin and Elyani contemplated Lohrzen's orichalc plate around my neck. They asked me to demonstrate the black dance, and they enjoyed the story of Lubu and his three ugly Nephilim sisters so much that for a moment I feared they would ask me to tell it a second time.

As I talked, several parts of the story were starting to make sense to me. Being listened to in such a warm space gave new meaning to various facets of the adventure. And I discovered Elyani's side of the story: what she had been feeling, and how she and Teyani had invoked the grace of the White Eagle before I was sent to die in the Dragon. This explained my cosmic dreams of ascension into the spheres, and the shining Light that had so impressed Marek.

I didn't contain my amazement at the Flying Dragons' magic that had befooled me in Verzazyel's cave, and we all laughed at my throes of doubt and indecision when I was healing Felicia, thinking the Great Warriors would never forgive me for resuscitating one of the Nephilim pilgrims. My friends' eyes opened wide when I spoke of the incredible foods of the Nephilim, and Gervin complimented Elyani at length on the medallion I had brought back for her. He particularly enjoyed my retelling of the vision of Teyani, Adya, Lehrmon, Melchard and himself. At the end he laughed and commented that he too would have been consumed by curiosity, left in the middle of such a tense story – was Adya going to die in Tipitinan's dungeons? But he didn't say any more! For fear of embarrassing Elyani, I asked no questions, not even whether Melchard had managed to see the eklipson.

When I told them how I had declined Felicia's invitation to descend into Verzazyel's crypt and receive the fire of the Watchers, Elyani and Gervin gave me a loud ovation.

It was close to midnight when I finished. I thanked my dear friends for their listening and their warmth, and we all stood around the gate's ascending breeze as if around a bonfire.

"Master Gervin," I said, "you haven't yet told me which part of the temple you want me to stay in."

"That's right! We have to find a roof for you!" he teased me.

Caught in the elated atmosphere of the evening, Elyani burst out laughing. "Szar, tell us! What is the most beautiful roof you have seen in the temple?"

"Hum..."

"Now that Lehrmon is no longer visiting the temple of Lasseera or travelling through the spheres of remoteness, we can't let you stay in his apartment, of course," Gervin said. "Suppose you could choose *any* place you like, Szar, where would you stay? Back in the dormitory of the apprentices of the Salmon Robe, perhaps?"

The time had come to demonstrate courage. "Well," I tuned high into the fountain and took strength from resting on my Mother the Dragon, "we Warriors like to stay close to Dragon's gates whenever we can. It's part of our Law, actually."

"Well," Gervin raised his hands, "how could I go against the Law?" He turned to Elyani, "Moreover, it seems that Szar won't be creating any disturbance in the corridors, will he?"

Elyani pursed her lips and confidently shook her head.

"Of course, we will need a special dispensation from Lady Teyani, grand master of the temple's female wing. It might not be so easy to contact her at this late hour of the night."

"Actually," Elyani intervened, "I spoke to Lady Teyani earlier this evening. *As to the temple's Law, the technicalities of the case are simple due to an established and certified precedent: an identical situation involving someone from the very same caste and sub-caste, the Great Warriors' branch of the Sons of the Dragon,* who stayed in this bedroom only twenty-three years ago."

"Sounds like the doctors of the Law are on your side, Szar!" Gervin rejoiced. "By the way, have you heard the story of Marek's visit to our temple?" He wriggled his nostrils and started sniffing all around him.

I nodded gravely, and Elyani laughed again. After some more chatting, Gervin instructed me to come and visit him in the enclave of the jewels the following morning, and he took his leave.

I took a deep breath, making myself full with the fragrance of my Mother's breeze, and then let out a Dragon-extravagantly loud "Youyouy-ouyou..."

Elyani's eyes grew as big as Alohim blossoms. "Oh my Lord Melchisedek, what is *that*?" she mimicked the way Nefertine had first greeted Marek.

"*Fear not, woman of the Law!* It's just the innocent way the Warriors express their joy. All this sounds too beautiful to be lawfully true! Marek was never angry with me, Gervin doesn't want me to go back and kill Nephilim pilgrims, Lady Teyani of the White Eagle treats me like her own son, and my Mother the Dragon has manifested one of her blissful gates just in front of your bedroom. How could a man be happier?" I took another deep breath, making myself tipsy with the breeze.

"I want to know more about Felicia!" Elyani took her chance.

I took her hand and we went to sit by her favourite laurel tree. "She is an amazing person," I told her.

"And amazingly beautiful too."

"True. And so intelligent! She is nothing like a sleeper, let me tell you."

"Mm..." Elyani nodded thoughtfully.

I could guess from her voice that something was wrong, but I had no idea what. So I went high up in the fountain to seek inspiration. "At times, though, Felicia could be such a pain in the Dragon... you have no idea! And I hate to think what she would be like when she is angry. Some of these Nephilim people can be abysmally vicious."

"Oh really?" she smiled. "Do you think she will become a princess?"

"I don't even know if she is still alive!"

"Does it matter to you?"

"Of course it matters. I spent so many hours looking after her! I came to regard her as my child. It was the first time in my life I took care of someone. After all those months spent bashing sandbags and beating the Underworld out of imaginary enemies, it was such a relief. And it made me think a lot about you."

"About me?"

"Of course, you! Remember once, after you had prophesied for me, I walked out of your room without even stopping to consider what you were feeling. You came out into the courtyard and you told me off. I had no idea what you were trying to tell me, or what taking care of you could have meant." I paused. "In that cave in the red canyons, I had plenty of time to ponder on what you must have been feeling during all those weeks you were looking after me," I pointed to my new bedroom – the room where my body had been kept while I journeyed through the caverns of sickness. "I used to think it had been hell for you, and perhaps it was, but at the same time... there can be such a joy in giving! That's what I discovered when I healed Felicia. All those hours spent fixing her gateways were hard work, but my Mother was pouring so much joy and caring warmth into me... sheer delight! It was not until then that I began to thank Master Gervin for sending me to the temple of the Dragon. Before this I had never had anything to give to anyone."

"*All glory to the teacher!* You know you made Gervin very happy by rescuing Felicia, don't you," Elyani shone. "He hates the way sleepers and puppets of the Law let people die in the street without even turning their head."

"Where would we be if Gervin had not brought our good Lady Teyani back to Eisraim and..." I stopped myself before mentioning Adya's name.

"Soon, I will ask permission to tell you Adya's story," Elyani pledged.

So it was not Gervin's permission that was needed.

"Stand up, high priestess of the White Eagle! Now is not the time to ponder on the sadness of the world, but to thank the Lords of Destiny for not separating us again – no more temple of the Dragon," I took both her hands. "I want you to prophesy for me."

She replied in her prophetess' voice. "*Ask, man of the Law, and the oracle shall speak.*"

"I want to know which god I am supposed to thank for so much joy. Is it the White Eagle?"

"Wait!" she said, "there is something else to celebrate."

"Yet another present from the gods?" I asked, incredulous.

"Gervin has decided that in the coming days you are to start your training in the Eisraim style of power of the Point!"

Thoughtful, I scratched my head. "Does this mean I am going to learn how to find my way through your temple corridors?"

"It's about time! How embarrassing for Gervin if someone were to find out that his apprentice can't even find his way to his bedroom."

"If any of this has to do with Flying Dragons, I think I am going to need a lot of support in the coming weeks. Did Gervin tell you who my instructor would be?"

"Of course! Can't you guess?"

I had my suspicions. "You?"

"Yes," she bowed, "*your lawful servant!*"

9.10 The beginning of the end

Finding myself in Gervin's aquamarine chamber once again was a moving experience. What an awesome presence was held within the *living walls* of that room! For thousands of years masters of the lineage of Thunder had taught in it, among them a string of legendary names such as Takhar the Unbending, Barkhan Seer, Firen Seer, Olembinah, Semper and Orest. The air was vibrant with their Living Word. The aquamarine light was the keeper of myriads of secrets.

Gervin welcomed me with all the warmth of the Brown Robe, and invited me to sit with him. He started by inquiring after my health, then he said, "You don't get sick very often these days, do you?"

I shook my head. I had hundreds of questions on my mind, but tuning into him I understood that this was a time for him to speak.

Having asked a few unimportant questions about my journey, he began, "There has been some very sad news regarding the warp of energy fields in the last weeks. Do you understand what the fields are?"

"Only vaguely."

"Lehrmon and the Field Wizards of Ferman's team will start teaching you about them in the coming days. The fields are the foundation of so many things in the kingdom of Atlantis! And they are so ancient that most people take them for granted, as well as all that is derived from them. The holy atmospheres of the chapels and temples rest on the fields, and it is through the fields that a number of great angels can make their presence felt in the kingdom. Most rituals, through which priests link with the gods, rely on power supplied by the fields. And the active participation of the gods in human affairs is mediated through the fields. The fields make buildings grow, and they form the energetic blueprints that keep plass walls together. We use energy derived from the fields for the purpose of healing, and for controlling diseases and epidemics. The fields allow us to grow rich crops, and to eliminate pests. Anything that has to do with soft stones comes from the fields, since soft stones are receptors for the power of the fields. Without the fields, only high initiates would be able to use the voice channels of darkness visible for communication. But even more important than all of this, the clarity of mind of many wise people rests on the energy coming from the fields. People never think about this because the fields have been active for so many generations. But if the fields were to be withdrawn, their minds would be turned into chaos. They would lose their vision, their prophetic abilities, and their perception of the spiritual worlds."

Gervin looked at me with surprise. I was twinging my beard, pondering deeply on his words.

I dropped my hand onto my lap. "Hum... is it because of the degradation of the fields that new diseases are appearing, and particularly diseases that can't be controlled by the hymns of the Law?"

Gervin nodded, "As Lehrmon will explain to you, the warp of fields has secured harmony in nature and balance in the kingdom for thousands of years. It was the will of our Lord Melchisedek that the fields would radiate the order of the Law and magnificent states of consciousness for human beings to enjoy. In turn, by chanting the mantras and the hymns of the Law, human beings would feed the fields and control them.

But in the last generations, the fields have undergone a gradual deterioration. They no longer radiate the full purity of the Law. Each year new diseases appear, more and more crops are lost due to pests, and the Underworlds are completely out of control. As well as all this, the chanting of the hymns of the Law is losing its power to influence the laws of nature."

Limpid, crystalline, irresistible, he has transcended time.

Gervin paused and kept eye contact with me for a moment. Then he continued, "The most tragic thing of all is that people in the kingdom have taken a fatalistic attitude, as if the degradation was unavoidable. A number of measures could have been taken, and could still be taken, but no one dares to deviate from established rules. Sleepers hate change. And there are influential people with vested interests who oppose any change because it would mean a drastic loss of power for them. For more than twenty years I have been prophesying that the present course of events is pure folly. When I speak, people often believe what I say, but taking action would result in too much hardship. They prefer to keep sleeping and let fate overtake them – and this they will do until the very end."

As Gervin held eye contact with a *living wall*, I studied the way he was twinging his beard very carefully. When he noticed the intensity of my gaze, he dropped his hand and frowned for a second. Then he went on, "People believe that the degradation of the fields is a slow process. Every few years they realise that certain forces have weakened a little bit more. Take the soft stones, for instance. When I was a child, a decent soft stone would allow you to communicate with anyone in the kingdom, no matter how far away they were. Now, even with the marvellous medallion you brought back for Elyani, someone in the county of the Eastern Shores could never reach a friend in the Western Shores. It all happened gradually. Every so often we realised that we had to draw a little more power from the fields to voice-channel each other, and that the communications did not convey our feelings as well as they used to."

All of a sudden Gervin stood up. Drawn by his magnetism, I stood up with him. He walked to the end of the room. Resting on the Dragon, I stayed where I was.

He turned towards me. "My friend, I want to speak to you now about grave matters. These must not be discussed publicly, even with the people of our temple. The present situation is grim. In the last weeks, the Field Wizards have reported dark omens. The fields are no longer deteriorating gradually, but faster and faster. The bleak reality is, the entire warp of fields is on the verge of collapse, and so is the kingdom with it."

At the high end of the fountain, ten million suns. Gervin sees.

"Many years ago," Gervin continued, "I carefully studied how the degradation of the fields was taking place. This led me to predict a number of events that were to occur one after the other, signposting the looming disaster. I knew only too well that once some of these signs were observed, the end would be near. But what no one could predict was how long it would take for the sequence to unfold. It could have been a few dozen generations, or it could have been a few dozen years.

For more than two decades, none of the critical signs were observed. But in the last months the Field Wizards have reported that a particular ritual no longer alleviates the overflow of chaotic elemental beings in darkness visible. This, to me, indicates without a shadow of a doubt that the entire warp of fields is about to break down.

From here on, things will move fast. It may take a few years before the total collapse begins, but it could all happen within a few months. To tell you the truth, it could even happen in a few days."

Anchoring in my Mother the Dragon to withstand the shock of his words, I held onto the fountain.

"Now for the worst part. What will happen when the fields start collapsing for good? The bell will toll for the sleepers. Temples and chapels will become empty of the presence of the gods. People will be taken completely by surprise. In the middle of a prayer their deity will become silent, and all the support they used to receive from the upper spheres will vanish. They will be stricken with fear, and they will become totally blind to the spiritual worlds. Many of them will lose their mind. Some will lie prostrate and let themselves die, others will take to the streets like madmen, attacking each other for no reason.

Nature too will turn mad. The warp of fields is used to control crops, so there will be entire years during which the land will yield no grain. There will be droughts as never recorded in the kingdom before. Great shortages of food, even famines will occur in parts of the land. In other places, there will be massive floods and tidal waves.

And throughout the kingdom, buildings will start melting. Without the fields, the plass can't stay alive. In a matter of months, the *living walls* of all edifices will liquefy. The most magnificent temples will be reduced to heaps of amorphous whitish substance. Not one house will be spared. Even tree houses will become an unlawful mess of branches.

Expectably, the populace will be panic-stricken. People will flee in all directions, looking for food, but there will be no safe place to go. The king's administration will soon be overwhelmed and prove incapable of controlling the situation. The remnants of temples and villages will be ransacked by hordes of bandits. And the people who survive the massacres and the famines will be stricken by strange, terrifying diseases. There will be corpses strewn in every field. Darkness visible will be swamped by the wandering souls of the deceased, and there will be no priests to direct them. This in turn will cause an overflow of the Underworlds, and more plagues in the kingdom.

Finally, after a few decades or a few generations of mounting chaos and misery, the Lord Melchisedek will have mercy and will end the suffering of men by causing torrential rains. For months and years the rain will fall, washing away the glory that was Atlantis. Not one county will be spared. The entire kingdom will be engulfed. The savages in the remote lands, far beyond our eastern shores, may well be the only survivors. And it won't be long before they forget we even existed."

Gervin closed his speech, gazing into the void.

I felt as if the clear fountain had struck me with lightning.

When I could finally force words out, I asked, "Master Gervin, when did you say these things were going to happen?"

"Not all counties will be hit at the same time. And no one can predict the exact date of the beginning of the end. So many factors are involved. I used to think it could take up to twenty years before the situation in the county of Eisraim got really out of control. But now my guess is it will be much less than that. To be honest with you I have to tell you again, everything could collapse in a matter of months, even days. This *is* the beginning of the end."

Gervin slowly walked back towards me and sat down. I sat too, thankful to put my weight on something solid.

"Szar," he resumed, "I need your help. It concerns a very secret project, called 'Archive'. It will not prevent any of the disasters that are about to strike the kingdom, but if we succeed it will preserve a great deal of the knowledge of Eisraim, and of another temple as well. I will explain more in the coming days, when you have got a better grasp of fields, streams and soft stones. But for now there is another important thing I want to tell you." Before continuing, Gervin reinforced the eye-contact between us. "I will soon ask you to take part in the team of Field Wizards who are working hard on the completion of the Archive. In the troubled times which are coming, each of us will have to give their very best. I am personally asking you to move fast, Szar. I know you are no longer a sleeper, and I know that you have gone through great hardships in the last years. But I must ask you to awaken further – and fast. Every day counts. I need you to be very strong."

"What should I learn first?" I asked.

"The streams, with Lehrmon. If you can I would like you to learn about soft stones with the team of Field Wizards who work under our great expert, Master Woolly. The man himself is not easy to get along with, but the Field Wizards around him are quite friendly." His voice boring a hole in my third eye, Gervin hammered, "But of all things, *awakening* is the most important," and he kept eye contact with me, pouring his thunderous energy into my fountain.

"I'll have to go soon, a *lawful representative* of the prince of Eisraim is waiting for me," he announced. "Was there something you wanted to ask me?"

"Well... Master Gervin, I had come with a particular question in mind, but after hearing your words I feel ashamed to even mention it."

Gervin smiled. "Tell me, *friend in the Law.*"

"I was... I was going to ask whether the Masters of Thunder can be married. It sounds like such a futile topic to mention, now."

Gervin burst out laughing, making me wonder where he found the strength to laugh in such tragic times. He got up and came over to me, put his arm around my shoulders, and walked me to the door of the aquamarine chamber.

"Wondering how to behave with Lady Elyani?"

I nodded.

"Mm..." the Thunderbolt Bearer was quite amused, "if the situation wasn't what it is, I think I would have left you in the throes of hesitation for a few months. It would have been excellent for your spiritual development. But now," he became more serious, "I want you to be happy. Enjoy every lawful minute! Make my little Elyani as happy as you can. There is no rule saying whether the Masters of Thunder should be married or not. If we have made ourselves such a secret caste, it is precisely so we can follow our Truth, regardless of the sleepers' rules. The Masters of Thunder's only rule is to follow the integrity of the clear fountain."

9.11 Point storm

I came out of the aquamarine chamber shattered. I Dragon-dragged myself along the alley, singing mechanically, "*What does a madman do when his house is melting? He dances. He dances.*"

Lehrmon was not yet back in Eisraim, so I just walked to Lord Gana's chapel. Arriving in the enclave of the thirty-three victorious gods, I lawfully bumped into Artold.

This time he recognised me. "*Praise the Lord Melchisedek, Szar! How are you, my friend in the Law?*"

"Fine, Artold, *my friend in the Law. And you?*"

"*I am well indeed, Szar, thanks to the Good Lord Melchisedek! And how are your parents, my friend in the Law?*"

I looked up to the mists. Then I smiled at him and placed my hand on his shoulder, holding onto the heights of the fountain.

He smiled back. A lovely smile.

I lawfully took leave and kept walking. "What will happen to Artold when the bell tolls?" I thought. I looked around me – the people, the buildings. "What will be left of all this in twenty years?"

I was hit by visions of half-melted chapels.

I knew there were fields in the walls. I had never realised that without fields, all *living walls* would dissolve – even the plass of the temples, which everyone believed to be eternal. Like the Law.

So it was all an illusion?

In this enclave, the chapels had been lawfully erected tens of thousands of years ago. They were *as holy as the Heart of the Law*.

The sense of loss was overwhelming.

When I arrived at Lord Gana's chapel I wondered, "And what if it began next month, or next week?"

The chapel was empty.

The presence held by the *living walls* was sublime. As always.

I addressed the special golden light, "And what if it was tomorrow?"

"*Ha! Gana! Lobatchen Zerah! Hera, Gana! Simayan ho Zerah!*" I saluted the god and started a slow dance.

My mind was blank. I let the vroofing Dragon direct the movements and offered the clear fountain to the god.

After I had been dancing for some time – the Lord Melchisedek knows how long! – I was struck by a flash of inspiration.

It was sudden, violent, shocking.

The sky is on fire. Barkhan Seer is laughing. In Revelation Sky, Kartendranath is waiting for Hiram.

As bright as lightning. Coming from high, it shone above my head.

Awesome Golden Sun. The Sons of Apollo are planting seeds for the brotherhood of the Knights. Jinia is waiting. In the Great Ant, they know her well. That we may fly together. A thousand angels are dancing above my head. Long-haired Takhar is standing by the River of Remembrance. For ever and ever. Epochs pass, legends live. There are powers greater than sleep and oblivion.

Inside my head, I wasn't sure what this was about. Too dense to be expressed in words. But above, it was luminous.

Condensed into a point, it contained an entire program to shed sleep.

I *knew* it was the seed for the awakening I had been seeking for so long.

And I *knew* it was also the seed for a new covenant with Lord Gana.

But what exactly was it?

Child of the stars, fathom thy depth!

I sat down, trying to understand.

Infinity in one point, from Eisraim to Philadelphia.

My mind remained blank, unable to comprehend the vastness above my head. I tried to gather my thoughts, but the fabric of my mind felt totally insubstantial compared to the hyper-fast-moving denseness above.

I stood up again. "What to do?"

That was easy! Whatever was vibrating above my head had the knowing of hundreds of things I could do, and immediately.

"Where to start?"

That too was easy. I ran to the door.

I stopped myself and turned round, realising I hadn't expressed my gratitude to Lord Gana.

"*Gang, gang, Gana!* Thank you, *o great victorious god, slayer of the enemies of heaven, defeater of the armies of asuras, conqueror of the great sky,* hero among the celestials! *Gang, gang, Gana!*" I would have liked to cry with joy but there was no time! I started running again. Not even bothering to wait for the alley to empty, I lifted myself onto the top of the chapel and sped over the roofs as if I was in the middle of a war exercise with Marek.

"*Praise the Lord Melchisedek, Namron!*" I shouted as I was racing over the colonnades on top of the straight path of the Law.

"*All glory to the Lord Melchisedek...*" Namron, quietly sitting on his favourite dome in the enclave of the windmills, looked at me as if I were strange. "Is everything all right?"

"*Lawfully wonderful!*" I kept racing.

He replied something, but I was already too far to hear his words. Less than two minutes later, I reached the roof of the Blue priestesses. Elyani was just walking out of her bedroom. I whistled so as not to startle her.

She looked up.

I jumped down. "Elyani, I must talk to you!"

"Can it wait? I must lawfully hurry to a meeting."

"*No way, woman of the Law!*" I looked at her. Her long white dress showed her shoulders. A bit. She was wearing a touch of black powder on her eyelids. In the Point-storm I realised I had never noticed she wore make-up. Her skin was shining. Her eyes were shining. Her heart was shining, with my medallion on top of it.

"You are so beautiful!" I whispered.

She smiled. "What's happening, sweet Dragon?"

"I'm not sure, but I need to have a lo-o-ong conversation with you."

"Well, how about you dance for an hour or two and wait for me? It doesn't have to be on the lawn, it could be on the roof. I have to go and give instructions to Maryani, the next White Eagle to descend into the Underworld. As soon as the meeting is lawfully over, I am all yours."

"Two hours?" I exclaimed. "Impossible! Anyway Maryani doesn't need preparation. Just tell her to forget about that *keep-walking-hold-on-to-your-symbol* business. In the present state of the fields it's become a complete waste of time. Instead she should just find a nice place and wait for me. Done!"

"A nice place in the Underworld?"

"But of course! It was never my Mother's intention that people should go through an ordeal to visit her."

Elyani gave me a look, half-frowning, still smiling. Resting her consciousness on the soft-stone pendant, she called through a voice channel, "Maryani, some extremely urgent matters have come up. I must cancel our meeting. I will see you tomorrow."

From the clear fountain I drew liquid softness, "Thank you, Elyani."

She made herself profound, an ocean of Eagle-ness.

"Elyani, I don't know what's happening to me but I know I have to speak to you," the words rushed out of my mouth. "I owe you a deep and sincere apology. Until today I had never noticed that you wear black powder on your eyelids. How could I be such a sleeper?"

She became a little softer even. "I am glad I cancelled my appointment!"

"Wait! I have even more important things to tell you," I came very close to her. "I don't think I have ever told you that you are beautiful. I want to tell you that you are fantastically beautiful. Seeing you shine is a constant joy for me."

She opened her eyes wider, joyfully perplexed at this explosion of compliments.

"I also want to tell you that you are the sweetest woman I have ever met. It's true. It's just taken me a bit of time to say it, that's all."

I closed my arms around her. "And I have never *really* taken you in my arms, can you believe it? I can't!" I held her against me, letting waves of my Mother's sweetness vroof from my body to hers. "But the thing I really need to tell you is... I love you, Elyani! I love you! I love you!"

The Eagle's flight on the Edge of Highness.

She didn't answer with words but with an opening that made my Dragon weak.

Beyond the fields of stars, a deep night, an ocean of sound.

"I love you! Just having said it, I feel so much better, you can't imagine!"

"Oh, yes I can!" she murmured.

"Suppose I had died this morning. By now, I would be a soul in pain, wandering through darkness visible and asking all the other ghosts, 'Why didn't I tell her how much I loved her? Why didn't I kiss her?'"

Slowly, I moved towards her until my lips met hers.

Elyani folded her arms around my neck, enveloping me in the Eagle's wings of Light, plunging her soul into the kiss.

Vastness.

Vaster than space, beyond the birth of time.

"I love you, Szar of the Brown Robe. With all of me, I love you!"

The words had a mighty impact, but not one I would have expected. I was hit by the continuation of the revelation that had started in Lord Gana's chapel.

It was massive. All at once, a hundred thousand angels were blowing trumpets down to my clear fountain.

"What... what is *that*?" I started wobbling on my legs.

"Your Point." The White Eagle gently pulled me, making me sit on the lawn. She sat by my side. "Your Point is being awakened."

"Is this what the power of the Point is like? It's awesome!" The speed of the flow of thoughts above my head was phenomenal, as if the hundred thousand angels were all talking to me at the same time.

And yet my head was empty. "It's above, in the clear fountain. It goes far too fast. I can't put it into words."

"Don't try to!" she rested her head on my shoulder. "Let it remain above, in the Point."

I felt overwhelmed by the sheer immensity of the experience. "What should I do?"

"In this early stage, nothing. Just let it happen," Elyani advised, taking me in her arms. "A beautiful thing about the power of the Point is that it allows you to do several things at the same time." She put her lips to mine in a long, tender kiss.

The angels didn't seem to mind. They kept talking above my head as if nothing was happening.

Elyani moved her lips to my ear. "Still flowing?"

"Tremendous!" I exulted. "So different from the soft choirs of angels I sometimes hear in meditation. It's like..." I looked for words.

"*Concentrated knowingness*. The angels are explaining the laws of the Point to you."

"I have never felt anything move so fast!"

"*The mind of the angels of the Point is the swiftest of all winds.*"

"Winds?" I laughed. "You mean a hurricane! Voof!"

"No, you are not allowed to say this magic word," she protested, gently slapping my shoulder. "You haven't been initiated into the White Eagle mysteries."

An upsurge of power rushed into my clear fountain. "It's going too fast! I don't know that I can hold it much longer."

"Try to remain extremely still."

I did my best, but the experience was sliding away from me, as if I was lacking the density to retain it. "It's fading!"

"Dragon-still!" she ordered, and she pulled me by the hand, making me stand right on the gate.

Letting the clear fountain rest on the Dragon of the Deep, I made myself rock-solid. The power of the Point immediately regained its intensity.

Elyani stood in front of me, holding my gaze.

Above her head, I saw a shining star.

This triggered another explosion in the clear fountain. From all directions of space, millions of angels were speaking and singing torrents of hymns to each other. Every word counted. Every note had meaning. The creation breathed.

"Now I understand who Gana is," I whispered, "I am inside his mind!"

"He loves you," Elyani's tranquil strength shone through her smile.

"*Nama Gana, Nama Gana, Gana Gana, Nam Nam,*" every fibre of my Dragon-body chanted the mantra. And the god started dancing through my body.

Elyani danced with me.

9.12 Molten glimpses

In the little courtyard bordered by laurel trees Elyani was dancing, illumined by the blazing star above her head.

I was with her, amazed at the Eagle's Light which shone through her.

Far above, as if on the other end of the clear fountain, Lord Gana was dancing on the shore of a sea.

I was with him, amazed at the magnificence of the silvery waves.

His mind, storming silence, lighthouse of fire.

A dancing god is a universe in motion. Unstoppable.

He worships the source of all sources, his mother, the sea.

I tread the edge of nowhere-ness.

Mother of the Light, protect my way!

Remembering the wars against the asuras, when Gana uprooted the mighty mountain range of Shimegan, igniting it with his mind. The gigantic mass of fire, he threw upon his enemies, crushing the unholy city of Ohlsen, the dwelling of Beram and his titans. The decimated titans took refuge around the quiet lakes of the plains of Lorelai. By strength of Spirit, Gana dried out the lakes and the ninety rivers which fed them, forcing the titans to retreat into the Underworlds, where the armies of the gods pursued them down to the range of volcanoes which borders the Furnaces of Doom. There the battle raged for six hundred years of the gods, till Gana defeated the last of Beram's sons in one of the most ferocious duels of magic of all times.

Triumphant, Gana returned to Amaravati.

He walked to the shores of the sea, and he danced.

Surrendering his victory to his mother.

Worshipping her with his music.

Is this what music is? But it's not at all what I thought it was.

Gana dances.

Ocean of eternity. Time condensed in a drop.
Elyani dropped on the ground.
"Are you all right?"
"My love," she was panting, "I'm sorry... I just can't move any more."
The softness of sunlight showed that midafternoon had passed.
"Oh, I am so sorry!" I fell on my knees beside her. "You must be exhausted."
"Is there... something to drink?" she asked.
I ran to the bedroom and brought back a jug of water. "The beauty of this sea was breathtaking!" I marvelled as she drank.
"Especially after two hours!" she agreed, still short of breath.
"Does it have a name?"
"The Molten Sea... I'll tell you in a minute."
I let my hands run on her vital gateways. "Oh my Lord Melchisedek, you *are* exhausted!"
She laughed, "Flying high, with the Eagle."
"Last night I shouldn't have kept you awake until dawn."
She was catching her breath. "You don't sleep much since you have become a Dragon... I had a bit of rest this morning... when you were with Gervin."
"I have to take better care of you."
Ant gigantic. Spread in immense spaces. Pristine purity.
I stayed at her side, letting her recuperate. But another explosion took place above my head, just as violent as the earlier one.
"Oh, this is fierce!" I held my head in my hands, wondering how not to explode. "Is this what happens to people when their Point is being awakened?"
"No," she caressed me with her voice. "Your Point is flaring because Gervin has decided we need to move fast with you. He wants your column of Spirit awakened as soon as possible."
"Awakened..." the incandescent energy above my head was far beyond lawfully bearable limits. "Awakening is not at all what I thought it was!"
"Flarings don't last," she encouraged me.
"This fire could easily consume me!" I called on the Dragon to calm the inverted volcano that was gushing its fire into my system.
Was this what Felicia had to endure in the Watcher's crypt?
"What could we do to help you?" Elyani sat up and closed her eyes, seeking inspiration.
The liquid elixir of infinity which gave birth to Cosmic Fire.
"I have an idea!" she lay on the lawn. "Give me a healing! A loving healing," she added, putting my hand on her chest. "With all the might of your Mother the Dragon, as if my very survival depended on her sweetness."

I let my hands run on her body, sweetness flowing from Dragon to heart and heart to Dragon. Elyani made herself vast, and the magic of the touch took over.

"What are you doing to me?" I laughed, feeling myself expanding beyond the limits of the temple.

"I am the Great Sea who gave birth to the gods." Playfully, she took on her magic woman's voice, "Plunge your fire into me!"

That made sense to the Point. Guided by its superior know-how I recharged her life force, while images of the Molten Sea kept trickling down from the fountain.

Under my hands, Elyani's breath became supernaturally peaceful.

On the shore of the Molten Sea, the waves ebbed and flowed.

"The gods call this sea *the most fascinating of all things*," Elyani murmured.

"Fascinating," I echoed, my hands plunged in Elyani's fluid softness.

"She is the most sacred place in the world of the gods."

"She?"

"Yes, the hymns call her 'she', like your Mother the Dragon."

The silvery hues on the waves reflected a buoyant joy of life.

"Many of the gods were born from the Molten Sea," she said, her fresh liveliness tenderly surrendered. "*The Molten Sea created them, and they matured in the depth of her womb. And they woke up one morning – the first morning of the gods. The waves took them to the shore, and they started creating their own world.*"

"And the gods created our spheres!" I marvelled, my left hand lightly touching her belly. "If all things were fashioned by the gods, and if the gods themselves came from the Molten Sea, then..."

"*She is the source of all things,*" Elyani chanted a creation hymn. "*When the gods create, be it a new bird, a new tree or a new world, they tap from the Molten Sea's unlimited potential.* So goes the mysterious verse: *The Molten Sea is the formless' first form and its forming power.*"

"So pure!" we let ourselves be washed by the liquid images.

When the mists began to blush with the first hues of sunset, the Point-storm had passed. I was bathing in a fluid space, softly intoxicated by the enlightened touch, merged in a regenerative fullness of a Molten kind.

"Elyani!" an anxious voice called through darkness visible.

The magic woman pulled herself back into her human self. "Seyani?"

"Elyani, we need you at the controllers' chapel. We have seventeen travellers stranded at the edge of the spheres of remoteness. We need to perform a rescue ritual."

"Seventeen at once! Oh, gods! I'll be with you immediately."

9.13 Mouridji's lawfully coded message

Elyani returned with the night. I was on the Blue priestesses' roof, my aura still vibrant with the last glimmers of sunset, the fresh peacefulness of the Molten waves still mellowing the incandescence of the Point. Climbing down, I wondered why I had never *really* looked at sunsets before. They conveyed such a superior feeling of peace. Yet until now I had never realised how special they were. How could I be such a sleeper?

The White Eagle was carrying a basket. "I met Mouridji the prophetess. She gave us a basket full of food. She said she prepared it specially for you and me. And she asked me to tell you how *lawfully delighted* she was to see you back in the temple, and lodged in the female wing."

"But how does she know I moved here?" I frowned.

"Mouridji always knows these things."

"Mm..."

The Blue Lagoon. Far, far away.

She stood close to me. "The first time you kiss me welcome home," she smiled and closed her eyes, soft and fresh like the night.

I took her in my arms and conscientiously fulfilled the wish.

In the Blue Lagoon, he is waiting. He knows you will call him.

Startled, Elyani opened her eyes. "Did you hear that?"

"What?" I didn't know what she meant.

"Oh... nothing."

"How did the rescue operation go?"

"Quite uncomplicated," Elyani sat on the lawn, pulling me down with her. "The travellers are all back in their beds, safe and well. But this accident should *never* have happened. It was caused by a field disruption of a kind unknown until today."

"And why did the space controllers call you?" I was curious.

"Because until two days ago I was the leader of their team. I was nominated for the position after you left for the Temple of Vulcan."

"Chief Controller of Eisraim!" my Dragon exclaimed in awe. Since my most tender years I had looked up to the space controllers with unbounded admiration.

"Only during the day. It's a smaller team. The night team with its forty-eight controllers is twice as large."

"The controllers of our temple are much more powerful than normal controllers, aren't they?" I raved.

"They have to be. The priests and priestesses of our temple astral travel much further away than normal people."

"And why are you no longer Chief Controller, Lady Elyani?"

"When you came back, Mother Teyani relieved me from the function."

"Did I do something wrong?"

"No, no. Teyani decided I needed some time for myself, that's all."

"All glory to the teacher!" I sent a loving thought to Teyani.

When you call him in the Blue Lagoon, Elyani will be sitting by your side.

Elyani voiced the call of her stomach. "I am starving! Aren't you hungry? I haven't seen you eat once since you came back."

"I don't need to, I feed on the breeze of my Mother," I pointed to the Dragon gate. "But I'll eat to keep you company."

A white cloth was laid on the lawn, and Elyani unpacked Mouridji's delicacies: a bunch of raw celery, a small jar of osamon oil, two loaves of cereals (blue corn, it seemed), boiled vegetables, and stewed *pears of the Law*.

I sat in front of her, watching her attack the food ravenously, and trying to imagine what she was like when she directed her team of twenty-four top-level space controllers.

Between mouthfuls, Elyani gradually informed me that Lehrmon, "Would you pass me the cereal loaf, please?" had voice-channelled earlier to let us know of his return, "Now, that's really good celery. I love celery!" and had invited me to meet him the following morning, "Oho, the osamon oil is spiced with herbs of madness!" to start instructing me about stones, streams and other secrets of the Field Wizards.

"Soft stones are still a mystery to me," I cautiously sense-smelled the osamon oil from a distance. "But... wait a minute! Hasn't Mouridji of the Purple Robe put an influence in that oil?"

"Oh, nothing serious," she dipped a celery stem into the oil and handed it to me. "You know, using soft stones is trivial," she said, "it's making them that's difficult. Gervin told me he would like you to learn the art from Woolly – if you can manage to get along with the man, of course."

I took the celery, sniffing the colourful astral fumes with utmost circumspection. "I gather Master Woolly is a strange character. Have you met him?"

"Only briefly. Gervin and Lehrmon regard him as a genius. Until he joined their team of Field Wizards, the Archive project was undergoing grave difficulties. Can you pass me the other cereal loaf, please? Woolly solved problem after problem by coming up with completely new and original solutions – power of the Point, lightning-style."

So Elyani knew about the Archive.

"But Woolly has a reputation for terrible manners and an awful temper," she went on. "Have you heard of that viscous substance, like a whitish jelly? The soft stones are crystallised out of it."

I shook my head.

"Looks disgusting," she pulled an evocative face. "About a year ago, Gervin sent Woolly to help our friends at the temple of Lasseera. One evening, Woolly got so aggravated at one of the senior high priests that he threw a huge bucket of jelly in his face. And to make things worse, he refused to apologise."

I chuckled. "What happened? Did they expel him from the temple?"

One thousand aeons ago, when a cosmic night finished, he rose.

"No, they couldn't. That's the problem with Woolly, he is too precious! He saved them years of work, so they had to bear with him. But the high priests never forgave him."

He rose and filled the immensity of the spheres with his light.

After long deliberation, I decided to bite into the celery (resting firm on the Dragon). It didn't do anything particular to me.

"No, don't try to resist!" Elyani said in a little voice. "It's supposed to make you merry."

Dragon-still, I waited for the impact.

She shook her head, "But you don't understand! This dinner is a lawfully coded message sent to you by the priestesses of the female wing."

This sounded astounding. "What does the message say?"

"The dinner says, 'Welcome, Master of Thunder'. The celery says, 'We like the airy freshness of your youthful nature.' The loaves are made of blue corn, beloved of the gods, meaning, 'The gods have sent you here!' The *pears of the Law* mean, 'Little Elyani is all yours – it is already stewed! And look, we haven't spiced the osamon oil with herbs of wisdom, but with herbs of madness.'"

I moved closer to her. "What would herbs of wisdom have indicated?"

"It would have meant, 'Young man, lawfully behave yourself with our priestess,'" Elyani's voice unfolded the magic of her softness.

"Oh, gods," I sighed, melting.

Her fingers encircled my wrist, her head resting on my shoulder.

"Well, I see what I have to do, then!" I set about eating dish after dish, starting methodically with the lawful loaves of sacred corn, then mopping up the vegetables, and drinking the oil straight from the jar.

Elyani watched patiently. She no longer seemed hungry.

"Tonight, you *must* go to bed early!" I said with Dragon-authoritative certainty, a thin streak of pear syrup dripping into my beard.

"Must I?" she wiped the beard with her long white sleeve, her gaze plunging deep into me.

Liquid universe. Unbounded vastness. The fire was born from the waters.

Rediscovering the magic of the Molten Sea in her eyes, I suddenly wasn't so sure.

9.14 The missions to Aegypton

"*Who*, sent by the Lord Melchisedek, is knocking at the door?"

"Alcibyadi!"

"Come in!"

Alcibyadi crossed the twelve-lawful-feet-high doorway and walked into the geode-shaped room with sapphire-inspirited plass walls.

Rubbing his eyes, Lehrmon yawned loudly. "I worked with Woolly till unlawfully late in the night," he mumbled.

She came over to his bed and sat by his side, immersing herself in the deep blue glimmers dispensed by the *living walls*. It was this hour in the early morning when the plass wakes up and starts giving brighter light.

Seeing she was in tears, Lehrmon sat up and pulled the whole of himself into the kingdom. "Dear soul, dear soul, what is happening to you?" he smoothed her long dark hair.

Alcibyadi held his gaze, tears rolling down her cheeks, unable to speak.

Opening his alohim-sized heart, Lehrmon took her hands. "Little Alcibyadi, I am glad you came to me. It is a joy to be here for you. Will you tell me what makes you cry?"

She opened her mouth, but her voice choked. She took a long breath, gathering her courage. "This morning at the chapel, the White Eagle sent an oracle. Six priestesses are to leave the temple. I am one of them. We are to go far, very far, Lehrmon. We'll... we will never come back."

In a world where exile was worse than death, it was a cruel sacrifice the Eagle was demanding from his priestesses. Lehrmon bit his lip and tuned in high up, in those regions where clear fountain and Thunder meet. With the sleeve of his brown gown he wiped her tears. "Go where?" he asked.

"It's so far, Lehrmon! It's not even in the kingdom. Far in the east, on the other side of the ocean. A savage land, called Aegypton – a name I had never even heard."

Overwhelmed, Lehrmon called on Gervin's presence.

The warm heartness of the Masters of Thunder instantly filled the room.

"My friend," he said, "my beloved sister, we are going to have to be very strong. Who did the Eagle say should go with you?"

"Pepni, Seyani, Afani, Berni, and Maryani if she comes back from the Underworld."

Lehrmon felt his heart being ripped. Not wanting to add to Alcibyadi's distress, he held fast to Thunder and contained himself. "My friend, such dark times are coming for the kingdom that we should praise the Eagle's wisdom for this. He must have prepared a better future for you in the land of Aegypton."

"The oracle said we would be treated like goddesses, but I don't care," Alcibyadi the strong started sobbing. "Lehrmon, I love you so much, the idea of having to leave you is unbearable. When you used to go to the temple of Lasseera, or even to the Flying Dragons, I knew you would be back. But this time... it's too horrible."

Lehrmon held her hands close to his chest, "My beloved sister, you have always been my joy. Losing you would be like losing half of myself..."

"Lehrmon," she interrupted, "I don't feel like being your sister. I want to be your wife."

Lehrmon kept biting his lip.

"Lehrmon, have I only ever been a sister to you?"

Lehrmon took a deep breath. "Alcibyadi, I have known for a long time that one day you and I would be separated. You have no idea how shattered I was when I discovered this. It was when I was travelling through the abode of Thunder, while Gervin was initiating me into the Brown Robe. After that I preferred to stay away from you. I mean, I remained your brother."

There was a long silence.

Alcibyadi sat very straight, looking deep into him. "Lehrmon, I want a child from you before I go."

"But..." Lehrmon was astonished. "Alcibyadi, that is not even an option! Anyway, could you imagine yourself travelling while being pregnant?"

"And so what? My mother did it before me. And maybe the baby will be born by then. We don't know how long it will take before the Eagle sends the signal for the departure."

"But... Alcibyadi..."

"I have already asked the White Eagle's oracle for permission to have a child, and there was no objection." She gathered the will that ran through her blood, the blood she shared with Teyani. "Lehrmon, I want a child from you. I know your destiny is to join the Archive people in the Fields of Peace, and I am not asking you to come with me. But I want to take your child with me to the land of Aegypton. I want to watch him grow up, and I want him to look like you."

9.15 Waking up to the world

I woke up feeling so much joy I could have shattered the wall separating us from the Blue priestesses with the loudest "Youyouyouyou..." ever Voiced in Lohrzen's lineage. That, probably, would have been excellent for the Blue priestesses, who were badly in need of awakening. But only twelve lawful feet from me the dear White priestess was enjoying her first night of sleep after three intense days.

Still like the Mother of the Endless Night, I listened to her breath.

From the Dragon.

The breath of someone you love has profound meaning, especially when you listen to it with all your body and let it sink deep inside you. It creates mysterious melodies in your life force. It awakens strange rhythms, a dance to celebrate the Ancient Days of the Earth.

The room was lit by dim whitish glows coming from the plass walls. After nearly two years spent sleeping in caves I was rediscovering the joy of being surrounded by *living walls*. Plass wasn't just some kind of crystal, it had *life*! Tuning into the plass walls from my Dragon I could feel them breathe. I could feel their roots in the ground and how they were drawing forces from the soil, much like trees. The walls created an amazingly comfortable cocoon of life force, where one could spread one's energy and feel totally supported, nurtured and safe. In comparison, the plass-less stone walls of Mount Lohrzen were so cold, and dead!

But then of course Mount Lohrzen wouldn't melt down when the warp of fields rendered the lawful ghost.

From the Point came an irresistible impulse to be vertical. Warrior-silent, I tiptoed to the door. After quick lawful ablutions – the Point couldn't wait! – I climbed onto the roofs and found my way to a high dome of the temple's female wing.

I sat in meditation, contemplating the tinges of colour heralding the rising of the sun.

Thanks to Elyani's Molten magic, the Point-ness above my head was no longer storming. It flowed like a majestic river giving herself to the ocean. It still didn't make sense to me, but the sunrise made sense to it.

Sunrise, I discovered, like sunset, seemed to hold a key to the ocean of knowing above my head.

I sat under the vibrant power, holding its intensity from the stillness of the Dragon.

As the wash of colours began to fade, giving way to a new day, I felt Point-inspired to go and explore the roofs of the temple. I soon noticed Namron's silhouette on a roof of the enclave of the *Most Ancient and Lawful Orders*. I jumped my way towards him and saluted him. *"Praise the Lord Melchisedek, Namron, my friend in the Law! What a beautiful morning of the Law!"*

"All glory to the Lord Melchisedek, Szar, my friend in the Law! What a beautiful morning in the Law indeed. Have you heard the news about Holma, the ascending goddess?" he asked, his teeth black with the root he was chewing.

"No, *my friend in the Law*, what happened?"

"Now then, nothing good," Namron scratched his bald head and spat into the alley without looking down. "She's fallen unlawfully ill. If she were to fail the great ritual, it would be the worst possible omen for Eisraim, a signal." He dived into his pocket for some more black root. "A signal marking the beginning of unlawful unrest in our county as well as neighbouring ones. Gangs of thieves from the north could take advantage of this to attack us."

The blazing halo of a timeless traveller. He will return.

I was unsure about the ascending goddess' great ritual, but Namron wasn't quite the right person to ask about it. I chose to discuss temple logistics instead. "How many men are under you, Namron?"

"Only twelve, *my friend in the Law*," he said, tearing off a piece of root and stuffing the rest into his pocket.

"Not even one for every entrance to the temple! Are they at least well trained?"

"They've done well so far," the small man bared his teeth to pull out a stuck piece of root, "but then there have never been many problems: a few priests and priestesses losing their mind and yelling the Underworld in the middle of a ritual, and a thief here and there. But if an organised group were to attack us, I hate to think how my men would perform. Though recently, Master Woolly has given us some soft-stone weapons. They're frightening, but we've not had much practice using them. Knowing the kind of war operations you must have seen in Mount Lohrzen, you'd probably yell the bloody Underworld in horror if you observed an operation carried out by my men."

"Namron, this sounds very alarming. Isn't anyone concerned about planning our defence?"

"No one even wants to consider there might be a need for it. They all like to dream that if any serious incident happened, the Masters of Thunder would materialise out of the spheres and save us with their High Voice power."

"Do you think they would?" I asked.

"We'd better pray they would," Namron's laughter was a lifelong cultivation of a melange of joviality and cynicism, "otherwise... the Lord Melchisedek have mercy on us!" And he decorated the alley with another large gob of black spittle.

Ripples in space. Winsome whispers of a revelation to come.

"I should probably come and meet your men one of these days," I declared.

Namron's face lit up. "Just what I wanted to hear, Szar of the Brown Robe. You and I should have a good talk. I'd like to hear your suggestions. Mount Lohrzen has the reputation of being one of the three best defended fortresses in the entire kingdom." This made me curious. Prompted by the Point above my head, I pressed on, "What are the other two fortresses, *my friend in the Law?*"

"The citadel of the Nephilim giants in the Eastern Peninsula, and Jex Belaran, the Nephilim Hunters' training centre in the county of the Snowy Mountains. Want some black root?" he pulled some of the soft, earthworm-looking substance out of his pocket and offered it to me.

"No thanks. How interesting! So the palace of the king of Atlantis isn't one of the three."

"*No way, man of the Law!*" Namron spat into the alley before stuffing a fresh supply into his mouth. "The king's palace is notorious for leaking like Blue priestess' underpants. Not to mention the Underworld of intrigues that go on inside the place."

We chatted for a while, then I lawfully took leave and set off in the direction of Lehrmon's roof, wondering if Namron's spats ever hit the gods or passersby. I glanced down to the statues in one of the courtyards of the enclave of the *Most Ancient and Lawful Orders*. Just then, in an alley, an old man slipped and fell down.

I extended my perception through darkness visible. The man was in so much pain that he couldn't move. Yet the priests and priestesses kept walking by as if nothing had happened. The man was left lying in the dirt. "Even in our own temple!" I was appalled. I recalled a verse of the book of Maveron, dear to Master Gervin: "*Shame on you, generation of sleepers, and shame on this land for bearing you!*"

It took me less than a minute to reach the alley. Garbed in a light-grey robe, he had a long white beard and pale withered skin. "*Praise the Lord Melchisedek, wise man in the Law!*"

He didn't answer.

I inspected his legs and let my hand run on his gateways. "A sprained ankle," I concluded. "If you knew how many times it's happened to me!"

The man looked at me sternly. He didn't speak. Perhaps he was exhausted.

Three white roses. At the feet of an angel of Highness.

"Let me boost your energy so you can walk back to your apartment. But after this, you will need at least two weeks' rest." After fixing the gateways on his leg and injecting life force into him, I quickly Voice-projected a few sounds onto his ankle. Then I helped him stand up and wiped the dust off his grey robe.

"Farewell, *man of the Law*," I whispered after him, as I watched him limp his way along the alley.

Walking towards the enclave of the jewels, I noticed the magnificent statue of a curly-haired god. As I was early for my appointment with Lehrmon, I stopped and marvelled at the precision of the shapes. I couldn't have explained why or how, but this statue made sense to my Point.

"Sad," I thought, "I have walked this alley so many times in the past, without ever noticing this statue." I didn't even know which god this was.

Feeling a Point-urgent need to know, I stopped a priest who was passing by. "*Praise the Lord Melchisedek, my friend in the Law!* Could you tell me who this god is?"

"*All glory to the Lord Melchisedek, my friend in the Law! Sorry I can't help you, this particular point of the Law is unknown to me.*" The man gave me a friendly smile.

I thanked him anyway and asked another priest. He didn't know either. Pushed by Point-curiosity, I asked a few more people. Not one of them knew the name of the god. Interestingly, they all answered with *exactly the same lawful words*.

Shocking. How could they be such sleepers?

Looking around, it dawned on me that I didn't know the name of any of the flowers illuminating the lawn with their glorious astral halos. I had never thought of asking. Admiring the garden, it also occurred to me that I was totally ignorant of the way tree branches were made to form archways over the alleys.

The truth was, I was a stranger to my own world.

The worst was, this had never disturbed me before.

Deep in thought, I walked to Lehrmon's apartment.

9.16 Streams and the warp of fields destroying Atlantis

My brother in Thunder welcomed me with one of his solar smiles and gave me a long hug. "I have never seen your eyes shine like today! What is happening to you?"

With my finger I pointed to the centres of energy above my head. "Lady Elyani is teaching me about the Point."

"Voof!" he exclaimed.

"Ha! Ha! Ha! Ha! Ha!"

Unlawfully startled by the explosiveness of the Warriors' Voice-laughter, Lehrmon lifted his right eyebrow, a strange flutter passing through his amber eyes.

"Hum... yes, it must be the Point," I went on, thinking I had better be careful with Mount Lohrzen's ritual landmarks.

"Gervin..." Lehrmon called himself back to his normal self, "Gervin told me he spoke to you about last week's bad news."

"A most enlightening talk," I nodded. "Hearing about the looming catastrophe shocked me out of sleep. It made me realise how much I take for granted and don't know how to appreciate. Makes you wonder if it is only when people are about to lose something that they start to understand what it means to them."

Lehrmon bit his lip and nodded.

Lehrmon was Barkhan Seer's present to Teyani. Through him, Barkhan Seer poured his love into her.

I went high up in my clear fountain and let it click with his. "Actually, this is what I would like to tell you today, Lehrmon. I think you are a wonderful person. I've been thinking this for years, and yet I never told you. And I have never really thanked you for the support you gave me before I went to the temple of the Dragon. It made an enormous difference to me. It was not just illuminating, it was warm like the Eagle's love."

Still biting his lip, Lehrmon kept eye contact with me, letting his vibrantly compassionate light shine.

Strange. I had never seen Lehrmon bite his lip before.

"Well, shall we start with the streams?" he offered.

Curiosity made the Dragon vroof with excitement.

Lehrmon made me sit by his side. "The streams," he began, "are the foundation of the energy fields. Do you understand what the fields are about?"

"Not quite," I confessed. "Shameful, considering I have been living within them for so long."

Lehrmon welcomed such enthusiasm with a patient smile, a touch of irony imperceptibly lifting the corner of his mouth. "A field is a space in which an energy is held. When you enter the chapel of Lord Gana, you immediately feel the god's presence. You don't even have to tune in and try to connect with the god, his energy is already in the room. All you have to do is be open, and let the presence flow inside you. The same is true of all chapels. When you enter the halls of Melchisedek for instance, you are immediately filled with the heartness of the Law and the special shining light of our Lord. As you may have noticed, the effect starts as soon as you cross the entrance. It can be quite amusing if you are standing in the doorway. Take one step in and instantly you are flooded with the spiritual presence. Take one step back and you are in the normal world again."

Lehrmon bit his lip again. For a few seconds he contemplated the *living walls'* exquisite sapphire glows. He took a deep breath and continued, "If those chapels are so vibrant, it is because of the field within their walls. The field impresses a certain quality in the space of the hall, it activates particular laws of nature. This creates a resonance through which spiritual beings can make their presence felt. Hence the verse of the Law: '*The fields are the vessels into which the gods pour their light.*' But there are other fields than those in the chapels. In a music hall for instance, the field helps the audience to tune high into the harmony of the spheres, and it enhances their artistic receptivity."

"How convenient!" I remarked. "So the singers don't have to be great artists. Provided the right field is set up, the audience will be rapt."

Lehrmon approved, raising his eyebrows. "There are also fields specially designed for dining halls, so people enjoy the food served to them. The field helps their digestion too."

I found it difficult to imagine these fields fooling Nephilim people into enjoying the Eisraim style of cuisine, which they would still have found desperately boring.

"The power of the fields comes from the streams," Lehrmon continued. "The streams are like rivers of energy which run through the fabric of the cosmic spheres. From what I understand, the Great Warriors taught you much about healing. So you must be familiar with the meridians that run through people's body of energy."

I nodded.

"The streams are the cosmic equivalent of these meridians. They are to astral space what meridians are to the body. They are a profound mystery, far more than just rivers or draughts in space. They have many facets. They exist on several levels at the same time. On their most subtle level, they are so highly spiritual that they are sometimes called *the sweeping breath of God*. The grosser levels are nothing more than flows of elemental forces. You understand what elemental forces are?"

"The little beings that form the substance of water, fire, wind and earth. And there are some more sophisticated ones that rule the climate and the forces of nature."

"*Right and righteous!*" he exclaimed. "There are many levels in the streams, some subtle and some gross, which is why so many different powers can be derived from them. *In the beginning, when the Lord Melchisedek upheld the fields which are the matrix of our spheres, he drew from the cosmic streams and made them shine with the Spirit of the Law.* At the beginning of time, this is how the Primordial Sages cognised the Law – they listened to the streams and performed the high ritual of Melchisedek, and the Law was revealed to them: they heard the hymns. Later on, *when men were created, they learnt the hymns of the Law from the Primordial Sages.*

For thousands and thousands of years people lived perfectly happily, because *the full glory of the Law was shining through the streams and enlightening the fields* – these fields that Melchisedek had created for them in the beginning. There was peace and harmony on Earth. No one ever fell sick. People had long lives. *The weather was always kind*, and the land gave so many juicy fruits that no one had to till the land. Men's mandate was to chant the hymns of the Law and thus maintain the lawful integrity of the fields. As the Law says, *human beings fed the streams with their hymns and their rituals, the streams fed the fields with their power, and the warp of fields fed human beings with plentiful bounty.* Everyone was happy, always."

Lehrmon became pensive. Biting his lip again.

"All this sounds so perfect. How did we get from there to the present looming disaster?" I asked.

"Some say it all started with the Nephilim. Others say it was bound to happen with time, even if the Watchers had never descended on Mount Hermon. Have you heard about the Nephilim, Szar?"

Had I heard about the Nephilim! I sighed. "I met one or two of them, which was an opportunity for the most fascinating conversations. Correct me if I am wrong, Lehrmon, but I was under the impression that some people blame the Nephilim for every single evil in the kingdom, while at the same time enjoying the use of soft stones, and many other wonders the Nephilim have introduced."

Lehrmon added a touch of wit to his ever-shining smile. "I see you have spoken with them, *my friend in the Law*. What you say is true indeed. I must tell you that after many years of study under Gervin and Esrevin, I have come to the conclusion that the deterioration of the fields is an extremely complex process that involves a great multiplicity of factors."

"But how did it all start?" I asked.

"Long ago people began to realise that great powers could be harnessed from the streams. In time, the Windmill Keepers came to use different hymns from those chanted in the beginning, and they achieved great wonders."

"So when the Windmill Keepers perform the rituals of the windmills of the Law, they draw power from the streams, is that it?"

"Exactly. The Windmill Keepers' essential function is to manifest the fields out of the streams."

"And how did they first get the idea of deviating from the straight recitation of hymns of the Law so as to modify the fields?"

"Who knows?" Lehrmon sparked. "It happened so long ago. One legend says the first man to tap new powers from the fields was Tubal Cain. He had a sister called Naamah. As the legend goes, Naamah was an exceptionally beautiful woman. Once, looking down to the kingdom, one of the Watchers happened to see her. He immediately fell in love with her and descended from the spheres straight into the kingdom to marry her. You have heard of the Watchers, haven't you?"

"The powerful angels who first descended on Mount Hermon. The Nephilim were their children." A shiver ran through me, "I once visited the cave where Verzazyel the Watcher had lived. The dreaming I went through in that cave was *bigger than the Law*. A Nephilim friend of mine who was an initiate of Verzazyel explained that the dream had taken place in the Watcher's mind. Lehrmon, *man of the Law*, let me tell you – this was no Blue priestess' herbal tea!"

Lehrmon laughed. "So you have Nephilim friends now. Initiates, moreover! And you went dreaming with them in the Watchers' caves of power. Szar, you're becoming *a big boy in the Law*!"

How did Lehrmon know my dream had taken place with Felicia? I preferred not to dwell on this topic. "And so what happened to Tubal Cain?"

"Tubal Cain's sister went through a momentous awakening in the company of the Watcher. Then when she came back to visit her brother, she scorned him for being a sleeper and called him a blob-man."

Those blob-men who spent their days lying on the beach, making children without even noticing, had always fascinated me. "Was Tubal Cain one of them?"

"No, Tubal Cain was just a simple man who followed the Law without asking himself any questions. But his sister, having enjoyed the shining light and the thrilling consciousness of the Watcher, underwent a profound transformation. She became so ashamed of how asleep her relatives were that she endeavoured to teach Tubal Cain how to become more awake and more powerful by tapping powers from the streams. This is how Tubal Cain became the first artificer, who taught men how to use brass and iron."

I couldn't avoid thinking of long-haired Felicia. "Are we blaming Naamah for helping her brother awaken from his sleeper's condition?" I asked.

"Of course not!" Lehrmon was amused. "This is precisely what I am trying to explain to you: no one really did anything wrong – not in the beginning anyway. Later, it changed. But in the early stages, people only wanted to become more awake and achieve wonders through the fields. And yet the modifications they made to the fields were the first seeds for the total collapse now threatening us."

"How could this happen?"

"For a start, they complicated the situation. In the beginning of the kingdom, the task of the Windmill Keepers was quite straightforward. They performed one type of ritual per season, with a few variations that followed the moon cycle and other rhythms of time – and the fields were happy.

But to tap new powers from the streams, new rituals had to be introduced, which created new fields. The Windmill Keepers did not stop performing the old rituals, of course – had they done so, the early kingdom's golden age would immediately have ended. So the Windmill Keepers added new rituals on top of the old ones, which introduced new forces in nature. Generation after generation, more and more rituals were added. And it appeared that some of the rituals had conflicting results, they conjured powers that were incompatible with one another. At times, these caused great natural disasters: extinct volcanoes re-erupted, crops were destroyed by hailstorms, and so on. To restore balance, more rituals had to be introduced.

Century after century the scaffold of rituals escalated, adding fields on top of fields. Now thousands of types of rituals are performed throughout the kingdom every day. There is no longer one, but hundreds of castes of Windmill Keepers. To assist them, castes of Field Wizards who specialise in the maintenance of the warp of fields were introduced a few hundred years ago. But so many forces are being conjured that even the greatest experts cannot keep track of them all. The situation has become so tangled that it is plainly unmanageable."

"Why can't we just simplify, and return to the good hymns of our ancestors?" I asked naively.

"Several reasons. One is the very complexity of the system. As I told you, a number of rituals have to be performed in order to balance the effects of others. If they were to be discontinued the whole edifice would be destabilised, which would immediately cause natural disasters of unprecedented magnitude. It's like a giant tower. Take away the stones at the bottom, and the tower can only collapse. The warp of fields has become so complicated that no one knows where the top and the bottom are."

"What if we stopped performing all the rituals at once?" I wondered aloud, even more naively.

"Szar, *my friend in the Law*, do you realise the enormity of what you are saying?" Lehrmon answered patiently. "If we were to discontinue all rituals, the warp of fields would fall flat and the kingdom would be emptied of the spiritual presence of the gods. What would life be worth then? All buildings would melt, nature would turn into complete chaos, and at least half the species of trees would disappear. So would the rare birds that speak the language of the gods, and several other precious animals dear to the gods: levlons, filosterops, pessalans, merestons, apassolos, unicorns, amarols – you name it! All kinds of pests would proliferate: rats, mice, leeches, flies, fleas, mosquitoes – not to mention diseases."

There followed a heavy silence.

"So we are completely locked in, aren't we?" It was more a plea than a question.

Lehrmon did not answer.

"Still," I said, "it is difficult to believe that with all the Field Wizards, all the great sages and the initiates we have in the kingdom, all the resources of hundreds and hundreds of temples, we can't find a solution."

"One of the dramas is, when sages speak out no one listens to them. It has a lot to do with the sleepers' apathy. Sleepers simply cannot believe that dramatic changes are ahead. Change is such a foreign concept to them that they don't even notice the deep transformations taking place before their very eyes. Worrying about the future is totally beyond them. Why then should they accept any sacrifice aimed at restoring the balance of forces in the fields, which anyway they do not understand.

The problem is further complicated by the fact that many orders of priests derive their psychic powers from field rituals. If you were to take measures to simplify the fields, a number of these orders would instantly lose their spiritual connections, as well as the influence they exert over simple folk. Within a matter of years, many of these fat cats of the Law would be turned into beggars. They would lose everything – not only their spiritual sight and their peace of mind, but also their reputation and their wealth.

There are other complications, but these you must keep very secret and never discuss them with anyone, even in the temple."

For a while Lehrmon sat deep in thought. Then he went on, "There are so many things one can do with the fields. One can make magnificent flower gardens grow. One can let trees build the most delightful tree houses all by themselves. One can make people in a dining hall enjoy their food as if it were the best in the kingdom, or inspire the audience of a music hall to acclaim the artists." Lehrmon locked his gaze into mine, "A prince, supported by knowledgable Field Wizards, could even make his generals believe he is the greatest of all sovereigns. He could set fields in his soldiers' barracks so they would all love and admire him, and remain faithful to him. The king of Atlantis has so many priests serving him, he could even set fields throughout the kingdom to make sure all his subjects remained happily tamed and loyal."

"Lehrmon..." I was dumbfounded, "do such things happen?"

Lehrmon shrugged his shoulders, keeping silent.

Then he said, "I have arranged for you to meet Ferman's team of Field Wizards tomorrow, and Woolly."

"The soft-stone man?"

Lehrmon nodded, amused by the anxious look on my face.

I gulped, "How do you think I should behave with him?"

"Hold onto the power of the Point when you listen to him. Apart from that, I can't tell you much. He is... let's say, unpredictable."

"Mm..." I pondered cautiously, a bucketful of white slime sloshing around in my thoughts.

Before leaving, I inquired about the statue of the curly-headed god I had seen in the enclave of the *Most Ancient and Lawful Orders*.

Lehrmon knew exactly which one I meant. "Do you like him?" he asked, enigmatic.

"I find the light that shines from his statue amazing. I had to stop for a short contemplation."

"*All glory to the teacher!* His name is Apollo. The Masters of Thunder invoke him in some of their highest rituals. When Master Gervin takes you through the domain of Thunder, the reason will become clear."

9.17 Falling like the blossoms of the alohim tree in spring

As I was approaching the roof of the Blue priestesses' temple, I sensed an unusual presence in Elyani's courtyard. I stopped, but the White Eagle had felt me arriving. She voice-channelled, "Come in, *Szar of the Brown Robe*. There is someone I want you to meet."

Enthused, I jumped my way along. But when I landed on top of the Blue priestesses and saw who was in the courtyard, I almost gasped.

It was too late to resort to camouflage by falling flat on the roof. The man had already seen me.

"*Praise the Lord Melchisedek, Szar of the Brown Robe!*" he hailed me, looking up to the rooftops.

Resting on the Deep Dragon, I discreetly climbed down onto Elyani's roof, then jumped into the courtyard. From there I stood up very straight and replied, "*All glory to the Lord Melchisedek, Sir Melchard, High Priest of Eisraim and Grand Commander of the Law for the County of Eisraim under the Appointment of His Supreme Majesty, the King of Atlantis.*"

These damn Flying Dragons! If it weren't for their magic, I would have just walked here like everyone else.

Elyani could sense my embarrassment. She welcomed me with a reassuring smile, "Szar, *Sir Melchard of the Brown Robe, High Priest of Eisraim*, was keen to give you his lawful greetings."

Melchard still had the same magnificent eyes I had seen in the vision outside Verzazyel's cave, when he and Gervin were on their way to the eklipson. Still a strong, broad-shouldered man, his hair was now white and he wore a short beard. His high priesthood had added great dignity to his bearing. An impressive figure he cut, not least because he was one of the Masters of Thunder.

"And I was keen for you to salute Sir Melchard, Szar," Elyani continued, "because he is my father."

Resting on the Dragon, I didn't faint. "So I spent last night in the bedroom of the high priest's daughter – *praise the Lord Melchisedek!* And he probably knows everything I'm thinking," I thought, then hastily sealed my mind by going further down into my Mother the Dragon.

Melchard smiled affectionately. "How interesting to meet you again *my friend in the Law*, after hearing so much about you."

From the Dragon I called a polite smile to my face.

Melchard and Namron, delaying the advance of the giants.

"I have not come here as a high priest but as a father. Let us leave the official business here. Elyani will tell you about it."

I turned to Elyani.

"The order of the Grey Robes of the Angel of Dawn have lodged an official complaint against you," she said, candid. "But nothing to worry about."

Once more, I nearly gasped. "An official complaint? What about?"

"Ah, don't worry!" Melchard said. "That is not what I came for. I just wanted to see the two of you together."

Elyani was rapt. She took my arm.

Melchard was moved. His warm presence illuminated the courtyard, "Szar, I especially wanted to welcome you to the Archive team, in which we will be working together. Gervin said he trusted you would be a key member in the Eisraim side of the transfer, while he and I will be on the receiving end with Barkhan Seer and the entire lineage of Thunder."

"Voof!" Elyani was impressed. "So Barkhan Seer will be in the Fields of Peace for the Archive transfer?"

Melchard nodded. "All the Masters of Thunder will be there. Many have already arrived."

Eagle's feathers and endless love.

Elyani turned towards me, "Lady Teyani is very fond of Barkhan Seer." Then she turned towards Melchard, "Szar of the Brown Robe is very fond of Lady Teyani."

"Then no doubt Barkhan Seer will be fond of Szar!" Melchard smiled.

And Lehrmon shines the love that unites all of you to Barkhan Seer.

Melchard and Elyani went on discussing Maryani's imminent descent into the Underworlds, and Teyani's hopes that I would bring her back. Melchard asked my opinion.

"If the White Eagle tells me where to find her, then it will be easy. Otherwise..."

"The White Eagle will guide you, Szar," Elyani interrupted in a tone of certainty. "He has given Teyani and me his Word."

"Well then," I turned skywards, "*let the White Eagle take me!*"

"*Let the White Eagle take me!*" Melchard echoed. "Long-forgotten words..." his eyes were brimming with tears. "Elyani tells me you had a vision of my dear Adya, Szar?"

I nodded.

"The gods did not leave her with me for very long, but those were the happiest years of my life," he said. Then he looked at Elyani and me for a long moment, before he took his leave.

As soon as he had gone, I tucked my head into my shoulders and whispered into Elyani's ear, "Do you think it was a problem that your father saw me arrive over the roof?"

"Not at all," she whispered back. "For years the Archive people have been desperate for a dare-devil who could, if needed, defend their precious soft stones at the time of the transfer – the kind of person for whom climbing a mountain is *no problem in the Law*. You couldn't have found a better way of making Melchard happy."

"And what is this Underworld of a complaint that the Grey Angels of Dawn have lodged against me?" I kept on whispering.

"You know, my father is far by now. He can't hear us. We don't *have* to whisper," she whispered back.

"Doesn't matter. I find you very beautiful when you whisper into my ear, it does something to my Dragon. Now, would you please whisper to me what the Grey Angels hold against me?"

"They say that this morning you broke the Law. His highness Aparalgon, their assistant grand master, was in the enclave of the *Most Ancient and Lawful Orders* when you insulted him by talking to him. The Law states that *high dignitaries of the order of the Angel of Dawn shall not be addressed by people of a lower caste than theirs, unless lawfully called upon by them*. It's a well-known rule, actually. If you wanted to speak to his highness Aparalgon, you should have waited beside him until he addressed you."

I was so indignant I forgot to whisper. "*What a bastard in the Law!* I found him lying on the ground, his nose in the dirt. And I fixed three gateways that had been limiting the movement of his right leg for years. And I gave him a top-level Voice-projection on his twisted ankle so he wouldn't feel any pain walking back to his apartment!"

Elyani took on the sweetest of her voices, "Dragon, Dragon beautiful, *the Eagle knows your love*. Who cares about the parrots of the Law?"

"Am I going to get in trouble because of this Aparalgon? Will it cause Gervin any inconvenience?"

She shook her head. "If your highest ideal was to be initiated into the mysteries of the Angel of Dawn, that would have been a bad start. But as things stand, there will be a mention of the incident in the records of the temple, and nothing more."

Moving closer to the gate's breeze, I comforted myself with a deep sniff. "Well... better forget about this incident."

"*Very true, man of the Law!* Have you heard the bad news for the temple?" Elyani asked.

"At the moment, bad news seems to be *falling like the blossoms of the alohim tree in spring*. I heard Namron mention Holma this morning. Who is she, exactly?"

"The ascending goddess. A woman chosen by the gods to go and live with them," Elyani explained. "Once ascended, she can bless the people of the kingdom and pour forces from the world of the gods into the temple."

"But I thought that after dying, a number of people went to the world of the gods? I thought it was one of the possible stations that people visited in the Great Journey from one incarnation in the kingdom to another."

"Yes, but precisely, they are only visitors. They do not have the same status as the real gods. They are just lent a god's body for a while, and when their time is over they fall back into the kingdom. And they are never given the same powers as the gods. The ascending goddess, on the other hand, is to become a permanent member of the celestial community."

"A real goddess?" I found this fascinating. "Are there many of these ascending goddesses?"

"Sweet Lord Melchisedek, no! The temple of Lasseera did not have one for more than six hundred years, and the last one we had in Eisraim was long-haired Mareena, nearly two hundred years ago. For an ascending goddess to be chosen, the gods first send certain omens and then, through the main oracle of the temple, they reveal the name of the selected one."

"And then what?"

"The woman undergoes a strict training for a few months or a few years. Then there is a great ritual for which everyone gathers in the temple's main crypt, and voof! The gods come and take her."

I was amazed. "You mean she disappears in front of everyone's eyes?"

"No! Only the greatest saints take their physical body with them when they depart from the kingdom. The ascending goddess just dies, and when she leaves her body the gods come and carry her soul to the worlds of the triangle, and she wakes up as a goddess."

"Extraordinary! Am I going to be invited to the ceremony?"

"Of course. The problem is, Holma has become very ill. She may not even make it to the ceremony. An unlawfully rare situation! Usually, *those who have been chosen by the gods always succeed*. The fact that she has fallen ill is seen by every priest and priestess in the temple as a terrible omen. And our wise people had hoped that when Holma joined the gods, she could send us help in the troubled times which are about to hit the kingdom."

"Well... it may be presumptuous of me to offer, but with the breeze of my Mother the Dragon many things can be healed."

"Mother Teyani has already thought about this. Tomorrow she will approach the two Immaculate who are in charge of Holma."

In the Blue Lagoon, far, far away. He awaits the call.

"The Immaculate?"

Elyani covered her head and face with the white hood of her dress, so I could see only her eyes. "The Immaculate are one of the top castes in the kingdom. They keep their face covered with a white veil all the time. No one is allowed to speak to them, or look into their eyes. When they speak to you, you must look above their head. And no other caste can give them orders. They answer only to the king of Atlantis."

I came close and stole a quick kiss through the hood.

"Do we know what kind of sickness Holma is suffering from?"

Uncovering her head, Elyani explained that according to Gervin, Holma's sickness had to do with the nasty elemental slime coming out of the fields. As part of her ascension ritual, Holma was to spread her energy into the forces of nature, offering it to the gods. She was to become vast like the land and give herself to the gods – a form of sacrifice. The problem was that the elementals of nature were all going mad. "So poor Holma is going through an ordeal," Elyani concluded.

I cogitated for a while.

"I am afraid this is only half of the bad news. The White Eagle has sent an oracle ordering that Alcibyadi, Seyani and four other priestesses be sent away to a distant land, called Aegypton."

"Who are the others?" I held my breath.

"Afani, Berni, Pepni and Maryani."

The shock wave was deep. "My love... and what if your name had been on the list?"

Drawing from the high compassion of the Eagle, Elyani plunged her gaze into me. She didn't speak.

I held her in my arms, Dragon-tight. "Elyani, what will happen to us? Can you see our time track?"

"I don't want to. Only two things count: the White Eagle's Light, and my love for you. They are both eternal, so why think of the future?"

"If I could become an awakened one, then I could take you into the spheres of Highness and stay there with you forever. Would you come?"

"I would certainly consider the offer, Szar of the Brown Robe. But you are one of the Archive people, and so you will go to the Fields of Peace."

"Hey! You're not allowed to say that," I exclaimed.

"Why?"

"Because I don't understand what the Fields of Peace are."

She laughed.

I sighed with relief. "Do you think we will be strong enough to laugh until the very end?"

The faint, elusive note which turned into the Song of Creation.

She sat down on the grass and pulled me close to her.

"How have your sisters in the Eagle taken the news?" I asked.

"Can you tell me, who in the kingdom would want to be exiled? Anyone normal would rather die. Only the most heinous crimes against the Law are punished by exile. The fact that the kingdom is on the verge of collapsing is no consolation to my White friends. The Eagle has promised that in the land of Aegypton they will be treated like goddesses. But what a price to pay! Alcibyadi is particularly devastated. She has locked herself in her room and refuses to eat or speak to anyone. She could lose the kingdom and survive, but losing Lehrmon is another thing."

The Eagle's infinite softness shining, "This is what losing the kingdom will mean to all of us in the end, isn't it?" I pondered. "Losing the things we love the most."

"Hey!" Elyani protested vigorously, "How are we going to laugh if you say things like this?"

"Would Lehrmon want to go with her?"

"*A man of the Law must fulfil his destiny.* Lehrmon is one of the key Archive people. He is needed in the Fields of Peace. There is no way in the seven spheres Gervin and the Masters of Thunder would let him go to the land of Aegypton."

Alcibyadi will travel through to the Great Night with you. By then Elyani will be worse than dead.

"Poor Alcibyadi! Have you seen her?"

Elyani shook her head. "She refuses to see anyone."

The Eagle's softness spoke through me, "Do you think she might see me?"

"Perhaps. She'd probably be taken by surprise if you asked."

I extended my hand to Elyani's soft stone, lightly touching her breast. Resting my consciousness on the stone, I opened a voice channel and directed it to Alcibyadi.

"It is Szar, Alcibyadi. I am on my way to your room," I announced, and immediately closed the voice channel.

Then I asked my White Eagle for directions. "No Flying Dragons' nonsense – I refuse to go through the corridors. Just point out which direction Alcibyadi is in, and tell me what her courtyard looks like."

An amused Elyani explained the whereabouts of Alcibyadi's room, passing on the corresponding images through etheric osmosis.

Before going, I dived into her eyes with the Dragon. "Will you wait for me?"

She mimicked the way I tucked my head in my shoulders and whispered, "I might actually *get some lawful rest*, just in case we felt like talking late into the night."

"By the way," I whispered back, "was Melchard the person you needed permission from before telling me Alcibyadi's story?"

She placed her lips against my ear, "Ask me when you come back."

9.18 What makes eagles fly

When I knocked at her door, Alcibyadi opened it without even lawfully inquiring who was outside.

She was pale. Her eyes were red. Her long hair, straight and black, was a touch dishevelled.

She did not say a word.

Once again, I was startled by how much she resembled her mother as the Watcher had shown her to me. Same long body, perhaps a little thinner. Same whiteness shining through her skin. Same undaunted look in her eyes. And the same straightness, which made her look as solid as a pillar of heaven. It was like travelling in time and entering the vision of the temple of Karlinga.

With a gesture of her hand, she invited me to sit with her in the small room devoid of furniture. The light which glowed from the *living walls* was particularly white. Sitting in the organic roundness of the room was like being held by angelic hands.

Fly, Eagle! Fly!

A distinct activation took place in the Point. But instead of creating a violent explosion, this time it made Elyani's softness speak through me. "You probably hate me for not having left you alone in the Underworlds."

Alcibyadi gave a faint smile.

"You can imagine how stunned I was when I first discovered how different the Underworlds are from the caverns of sickness." I went on to describe the lapis lazuli caves, the piles of gems, the rivers of water of life and the huge Naga snakes that came to drink from them. Alcibyadi didn't ask questions but she listened carefully, absorbing the images and impressions of the Underworlds. She shared the elation I felt when drinking the waters of life.

"This is just what you need, *sister in the Law*. A good dose of these silvery waters would make you forget everything and roll on the floor."

The pallor of her face abated as she smiled a little more. It only lasted a second before she closed off and started biting her lip.

"Now that I think about it," I told her, "all morning I have watched a certain man bite his lip like this."

She stood up, as vertical as the Eagle's straightness, looking down into my eyes.

I remained silent, letting Elyani's openness flow through the Point.

"Have they sent you to tell me to eat?"

"No, I have come because I care, that's all. I don't have much to say, except that I know exactly how you are feeling, because the idea of losing Elyani scares the abyss out of me."

The slight frown creasing her forehead relaxed. Her presence came into me like a warm wave.

"It's horrible, Szar," she cried. "It's too horrible."

I took her hand, letting the Eagle's Light of empathy shine. The walls helped.

Alcibyadi received the warmth and became very quiet. After a minute of fullness, she asked, "Szar, can you keep a secret?"

"Dragon's word!"

"I have asked Lehrmon to have a child with me before I leave for the land of Aegypton. Do you think I am mad?"

Gods, did she sound stubborn.

I swallowed hard. "Did you ask the White Eagle?"

"Of course I did. He didn't say no. Nor did he say I should have a child either. But I want it so much, Szar. And I would know *exactly* how to get a curly-haired little boy just like Lehrmon. Tell me, do you think I am mad?"

No thoughts, just Eagle, the fountain answered, "No, I don't think you are mad. I think you are beautiful, Alcibyadi."

She met me, high in the Light, and we kept eye contact. "Did you ask Lehrmon, by the way?"

She nodded. "He answered just like the Eagle's oracle. He didn't say no, but he didn't say yes either."

Silence reigned, and we held it together.

A majestic presence gliding through an ocean of whirling shapes. His vastness is beyond concept. The Knights know him. He is their friend.

When I took leave I asked her if she would visit me, Elyani and the Dragon gate.

She accepted readily. "Can I bring Maryani? She is the next one on the list to descend into the Underworlds. Teyani wants her to speak to you. There could be a surprise coming for you."

"Surprise?" I rested on the Dragon, "I love surprises!"

9.19 Atlantean secrets

On my way to her courtyard, I tuned into Elyani through darkness visible. She was drifting in and out of her body, finishing her lawful nap. The Eagle's light took over the Point, sending a flow of love into her.

Light as a bird in the world of the gods, it didn't take me long to reach the courtyard.

"Your eyes are shining!" she welcomed me.

"Voof!" I exulted, sitting at her bedside.

"Ts..." Elyani pulled a face in reprobation. Then she threw herself in my arms. "Is Alcibyadi flying again?"

"I am under a seal of secret, I can't say much. But the Eagle's Light was magnificent. It made me feel... awake! And there was so much love in the walls of her room. Plass can be so inspiring when..."

"Oh my Lord Melchisedek!" Elyani exclaimed. "Alcibyadi wants to have a child with Lehrmon?"

"But..." I leant back, deeply disconcerted, "but that was my secret! I have given my Dragon's word I wouldn't say a thing."

"Oh, I'm so sorry! It's because I love you a lot, you know. When you think of something strongly, it comes straight into me."

"Alcibyadi is going to hate me!"

"No, I'll keep it a secret. I'm sure Teyani already knows, anyhow."

"No, Alcibyadi hasn't spoken to her," I said.

"That's not what I meant. Teyani always knows what is happening for Lehrmon, Alcibyadi and me. When she brought us up, we could never keep a secret from her, she always knew it before we knew it ourselves."

"It's so difficult to keep secrets in this kingdom! There is always someone who can listen to what you are thinking," I sighed.

"I promise I won't tell Lehrmon," Elyani said.

"Ah, don't worry. He already knows."

"Oh, really?" Elyani was curious. "Did he say yes?"

I tried not to think of what Alcibyadi had told me. Too late! Elyani had already picked up my memories. "Mm..." she said.

I let myself fall on her bed and curled up against her legs. "I think I am having a crisis."

She caressed my hair. "Tell me, Dragon-Eagle."

Juxtaposed infinities elusively smiling at each other. Spin.

"A Dragon-Eagle! Now, that would be a strange beast."

"Like a Flying Dragon, perhaps?" she suggested.

"Oh no, don't remind me of the Flying Dragons. Whenever they are around, I get into trouble." I let out another long sigh. "Elyani, I don't feel up to it at the moment. I walk through the temple and see these magnificent statues of gods, and I don't even know their names! I have spent years in Eisraim, and I never even bothered looking at them. How could I be such a sleeper? I see the flowers in the gardens, and I don't know their names. I don't even know how the gardeners manage to make them grow in such perfectly regular patterns. It makes me wonder where my mind has been all these years."

"Speak to Pushpadiv of the Lawful Gardeners of South-East-Eisraim. A lovely young man, always ready to help me take care of the precious herbs in my courtyard. He is easy to recognise with his long fair hair and his dark-green gown stained with dirt."

I tuned in to receive the visual impressions from her. "And then there are all these places and people whose names I hear without knowing who or what they are. It's not even that they are new to me, I have heard them dozens of times, it just never occurred to me to ask about them. Sleeper's apathy! Lasseera, for instance... where is that, exactly?"

"It's the county which stands north of Eisraim," she said. "The temple of Lasseera has been our sister-temple for hundreds of years. When completed, the Archive will be made of the marriage of the lore of the two temples, theirs and ours – which is why Lehrmon and Woolly travel over there so often."

"I see." Another sigh. "And this morning Lehrmon was telling me about all these animals, some of which are familiar, like levlons, filosterops or pessalans. But then he mentioned these strange creatures that would spread if the energy fields were to collapse: rats, mice, leeches, flies, fleas, mosquitoes. I had never heard of them. Do you know what they are?"

"Sorry my love, there I can't help you. These must be extremely rare beasts. You will have to ask Lehrmon." Elyani caressed my hair, "I don't think there is anything wrong with this feeling of crisis. I am *sure* Gervin would regard it as a good sign. You are awakening to the world."

Nature of remoteness. Born to the stars. Awakening to infinity.

"I can't believe how thick the mist in my mind used to be. I never even noticed the shape of the buildings – especially the roofs. Do you know that the domes of the halls of Melchisedek are magnificent! Before going to the temple of the Dragon I spent an entire week meditating in one of these halls. Not once did I look up and notice how high and lofty the dome was. Not once did I stop to contemplate the archways and the colonnades above the straight path of the Law." Elyani cradled my head on her lap. I snuggled against her dress. "And I still don't know what the Archive is! I don't even understand how soft stones operate!"

"You use them very well, though!" Elyani placed my palm against the medallion on her breast.

"What am I going to do when I meet Master Woolly tomorrow? He's going to think I'm such a lawful idiot. It's a strange name, Woolly, isn't it?" I added as an after-thought.

She laughed, bringing some fresh air. "His real name was Narbenzor. The story is that he used to live in the temple of Laminindra in the county of the Northern Lakes. Between the counties of the Snowy Mountains and Lasseera. Once, one of Narbenzor's experiments with soft stones went terribly wrong. It created a shock wave in the warp of fields, and all the plass buildings around started melting. It more or less destroyed an entire wing of the temple of Laminindra. After that he had to leave the county of the Northern Lakes and change his name. I wonder how Gervin found him."

Yet another sigh, "I wonder how Gervin found me!"

He received the call. From beyond the Abyss of the Deep and the Fault of Eternity.

"All glory to the teacher!" Elyani turned to the east.

Remembering how Gervin had found Teyani, I sat up, "Am I going to know the rest of Adya's story?"

Elyani looked shy. "It's a secret, you know."

In a tone of great self-confidence I assured her, "Lady Elyani, you know how good I am at keeping secrets, don't you?"

"I'm going to cry, if I tell the story."

The Eagle's softness was pouring through me, "Forget about the story, then. How about an unlawful sunset on the roof?"

"But I want to tell you the story!"

I sat quietly, ready to listen.

Tentatively, Elyani asked, "Do you think we could have both the story and the unlawful sunset?"

"Always ready!" I jumped up and pulled her off the bed. Out in the courtyard I quickly scaled her bedroom wall and leapt onto the roof. Bending down I gave her a hand up, lifting her onto the roof.

"Oh, gods!" A certain sense of trespassing long-established limits made her giggle.

In no time we were on top of the Blue priestesses' temple.

"Isn't it superiorly beautiful?" I exclaimed as we contemplated the sheets of mist folded in red, the colours reflecting onto the domes of the neighbouring chapels.

Elyani was like a child, captured in amazement.

"Where did your vision finish?" she asked after a moment.

"In the ruins of the temple of Karlinga. Teyani was pregnant with Alcibyadi, and she was holding little Lehrmon in her arms. She had just learnt that Adya had been jailed in Tipitinan and was about to be beaten to death. Teyani was asking Gervin to let her go and rescue her. Did he give in?"

Elyani shook her head.

That didn't surprise me in the least. But then, "How did Adya escape? Did Gervin go and rescue her?"

"No, Gervin voice-channelled Melchard, who was on his way back from the county of the Upper Western Shores after seeing the eklipson."

"So he *did* see the eklipson!"

"When Gervin called him, he was less than a day from Tipitinan. He went straight to the jail." Elyani took my arm tight and put her head against my shoulder. "I have heard this story from Teyani, as told to her by my mother. I have heard it from Melchard too."

"Two different versions?"

She shook her head. "My parents first met in the dungeon of Tipitinan. My mother said she fell in love with Melchard the moment she saw him. Her Spirit was waiting for him, the gods had warned her she was about to meet love. As for Melchard, he said it was hard to believe she was still alive after what they had done to her."

"So they had beaten her?"

"Twice. Beating the Spirit out of someone is not an uncommon practice. Normally, people just let themselves drift away and die rather than feel the pain. But the White Eagle had commanded my mother to stay alive. So she held fast when they beat her the first time. After a few hours, when the soldiers saw she was still alive, they had another go at her and almost succeeded in killing her. But she held onto her body, regardless.

When Melchard walked into the dungeon she was lying on the ground, her body lacerated, blood all over her face and matting her hair, her dress in tatters. To get her out of jail he used the power of Thunder. He called on the highest level of the Voice. Not immediately, though. At first he used gentle Voice-frequencies on her so she could walk. She said it was like being brought back from the Underworld. Then he Voice-projected onto the guards, 'Open the door and take us out of here, now!'

My mother could hardly believe what was happening. Her body was advancing along the corridor with Melchard at her side. How that was possible, she had no idea. She could not even feel her legs. Walking up the stairs was just as easy. But when they emerged out of the basement, six men wearing Black Robes were waiting for them.

At their head was a short man with sharp blue eyes. 'Where do you think you are going, *man of the Law*?' he threatened Melchard.

Melchard rapidly assessed the situation. Apart from the six Black Robes, there were four soldiers guarding the doors, plus two others in another corner of the room. He first tried a strictly lawful approach. '*The White Eagle is part of the Ancient Orders protected by the king of Atlantis,*' he declared. '*Following the lawful principle which states that an Ancient and Protected Order can and must defend the members of another Ancient and Protected Order whenever lawfully appropriate*, I claim the life of this priestess of the White Eagle.*'

The head man in the Black Robe was taken aback by the precision and lawfulness of the language, but he didn't move.

'*If you wish to oppose me,*' Melchard went on, '*first declare your name and order, that I may report to the relevant authorities.*'

'*I am Afkar of the Black Robe, in the service of His High Majesty the Prince,*' the man replied.

Melchard used a near-Voice threshold, '*Afkar of the Black Robe, do not impede the enforcement of the Law.* Move away!'

Afkar didn't budge. 'This woman has been outlawed by the prince. She isn't going anywhere. But who are you, *man of the Law*, to talk to me with such arrogance?'

'I am Melchard, Master of Thunder,' he answered, superb.

Afkar was jolted. Then he gave a smirk, 'The Masters of Thunder have long since disappeared from the kingdom. Or perhaps you will demonstrate your powers to us, stranger?'

'Do not tempt me, *man of the Law*,' Melchard responded with the Voice. 'Move away!'

Afkar had been trained by his order well enough to withstand this level of Voice. 'It will need more than that to convince me,' he threw back insolently.

Looking straight into his eyes, Melchard raised his right hand, his palm very flat in the sagittal plane. All of a sudden, a tremendous sound of thunder resounded, as if the building's roof had been struck by lightning.

The prince's soldiers ran off, and Afkar's men trembled. But Afkar himself remained unmoved. 'So many magicians roam about marketplaces these days,' he sneered.

Melchard sent a last warning, 'Afkar, move out of my way, or face *the Voice which is the Thunder of the Earth.*'

Afkar still didn't budge.

Melchard raised both hands and began to emit the Voice frequencies of Thunder, gradually unleashing the power he had received from Orest.

Afkar attempted to retaliate, launching an assault on him with the Voice, but Melchard was not even touched by it.

Melchard's Voice became awesome. Every single chunk of plass in the building started to shake. Afkar turned pale. His men ran away in terror. Melchard did not stop until the plass of one of the sidewalls started crumbling into dust.

My mother was astounded out of the Law. As was Afkar! A huge hole had appeared on the side of the building.

Then my father Voice-projected onto Afkar, *'Remember Thunder, man of the Law!'* and he quietly walked out through the hole he had made in the wall, Adya by his side.

After this no one dared to chase them. They joined Teyani and Gervin on a boat on the Pesiah river, which took them to the east.

This is how Teyani and my mother finally arrived in Eisraim, along with Lehrmon. But my mother was very sick. She nearly died during the journey. Melchard and Gervin did their best to heal her, but despite their treatments she never fully recovered. That is how my mother came to live in this courtyard: an old physician priest told her it had healing properties. He must have known about the Dragon's gate, one way or another.

By then, my father had fallen in love with her. This caused a dilemma for him. He was being prepared to become the high priest of Eisraim, a function that cannot be held by a married priest. But his love for my mother was stronger. He gave up all honours and titles for her.

They were married, and they lived together in this courtyard. Then my mother fell pregnant. For a few months her health seemed to be improving, but the delivery just about killed her. The day after I was born, she made Teyani swear she would look after me. She asked Melchard to plant a young laurel tree for me and she projected the Voice onto it. One hour later she died, letting the White Eagle take her."

The night had come. Elyani was crying in my arms as if in the Eagle's wings.

The Sons of Apollo wanted Elyani to be born from Adya. Trust, they will not abandon you.

"What happened to Melchard afterwards?" I asked after a while.

"He left the temple and went north, to the mountains of Lasraim. He gave himself to ascetic practices. But a year later, the high priest of Eisraim died. The people of the temple sent a delegation to look for Melchard, because they could think of no better candidate to take over the function of high priest. Melchard yielded to their request and returned to Eisraim. After that, he had to keep his daughter a secret."

"Didn't everyone know you were his daughter?"

"Of course they all know! But no one ever mentions it."

"So you are one of the temple's secrets!" I whispered admiringly. "A well-kept secret."

"I am, Dragon."

Keeping the secret safe in my arms, I contemplated the magic of the night.

9.20 My Mother in a bottle

The chapel of the Field Wizards was located in Maniya, a busy enclave south of the temple's lawful centre. Before knocking at the door, I stopped and called on the light of my teacher, gnawed by unlawful anxiety. Master Woolly, it was clear, was a dangerous man. Why should a great expert in the power of the Point like him accept me among his people? I hardly knew how to use soft stones. Streams and fields were completely new to me. And I was still utterly incapable of discerning between power of the Point and Flying Dragons. What if Master Woolly became impatient with me and expelled me from his chapel, throwing bucketfuls of the notorious white slime in my face? The slime was no major worry. The idea of disappointing Gervin broke my heart.

Pulling courage from the Dragon, I finally knocked.

There was no lawful inquiry as to *who, sent by the Lord Melchisedek, was knocking at the door*. Instead, a tall dignified middle-aged man opened and stared at me. He was wearing a grey robe – not like that of the order of the Grey Robes of the Angel of Dawn, thank the She-Serpent of Wisdom! He was a man from the north, with blue eyes and a high forehead. He had short grey hair, a carefully trimmed beard, and a politely unwelcoming attitude on his face.

"*Praise the Lord Melchisedek, man of the Law!*" I said. "My name is Szar of the Brown Robe. Sir Lehrmon of the Brown Robe has sent me to your chapel to meet Master Woolly."

The man remained impassive. "Master Woolly is busy at the moment. He's asked me to show you around. My name is Ferman, of the Field Wizards' caste."

Ferman of the Field Wizards let me in, and I opened my eyes in astonishment. It was the weirdest chapel I had ever seen. A large room, with no altar as far as I could discern. Lining the walls were benches with a number of flames on them. Perhaps the chapel was dedicated to many gods. There were bizarrely-shaped pots and jars over the flames. Was this place an extension of the temple kitchens? Behind the benches, six men dressed in the Field Wizards' grey robe were busy taking care of the pots. There were hundreds of bottles everywhere, not only on the benches but also on shelves attached to the walls, and even on the floor.

"Be careful where you walk!" Ferman warned grimly, indicating the chaos of jars on the floor. "The contents of these bottles are extremely precious. *Follow me, man of the Law!*" he began to lead me through the chapel.

Voidness eternal. Darkness invisible. She dances.

"What an unlawful mess!" I thought. "I wonder what kind of angel would want to shine his presence in such a chapel." To avoid any blunder, I gathered my energy as if in the middle of a military operation with Marek, carefully measuring every step and using the Warriors' peripheral awareness so as not to trip over the bottles.

Something immediately struck me: the smells in the chapel were unusual, to say the least. Sniffing discreetly, so as not to irritate anyone, I discerned sweet fragrances resembling those of the Underworlds. But there were also strange smells completely unknown to me – some of them unlawfully revolting.

A choir of universes, echoing the song of the Dawn of Creation.

The smells changed all the time. At one stage I thought I recognised the smell of Nephilim spice. I spun round, my fists clenched. But there was no one behind me. I could feel Ferman looking at me out of the corner of his eye, but he remained impassive.

We entered a large hallway. "Watch your feet for the bottles," Ferman of the Fields Wizards reminded me.

Row upon row of shelves were attached to the walls, holding thousands of jars of various shapes and colours. The energy of the substances they contained was most surprising. Some emitted bright auras of complicated astral colours, and the combined glow of the bottles resembled the mountains of gems in Underworld caves.

We soon arrived in another large room with benches against the walls and again, jars everywhere. There was no one working here, only bottles.

A particular bottle immediately captured my attention. It was barely bigger than my hand, but the light radiating from it was silvery and pure like that of the Molten Sea.

"Oh my Lord Melchisedek, what is *that*?" I exclaimed.

"Hey?" the Field Wizard muttered.

"That bottle, there. What is it?"

Ferman looked perplexed. "It's a particular preparation that Master Woolly and I have been working on."

"It's amazing! Can I hold it in my hand?"

"No way, man of the Law!" Ferman was categorical. "I will hold it for you."

He took the bottle from the bench and held it up in front of me.

The more I contemplated the bottle, the more amazed I became. Sniffing it made me feel elated, as if I was bathing in a river of the deep Underworlds. Mighty vroofing waves were welling up in my energy. I smiled at Ferman, "But what is it, exactly?"

Ferman looked at me with curiosity. "What can you feel in this bottle?"

"Hum..." How to explain the glories of the Underworlds in a nutshell!

Ferman opened the bottle and proffered it to me, "Can you smell anything?"

His question relieved me of the worry of being caught sniffing. I indulged in a long sense-smell of the miraculous substance. For a moment I felt as if I was deep inside my Mother's bosom, ready to jump into a stream of water of life, with the great golden snakes on the shore. My Dragon was shaken by vroofing waves.

"Ha! Ha! Ha! Ha! Ha!" I Voice-exploded.

Holding firm onto his bottle, Ferman the Field Wizard gazed at me in complete stupefaction, the corner of his lip fluttering, his legs imperceptibly shaking.

I immediately contained myself, thinking, "I *have* to be more cautious with the Warriors' laugh. It's bound to get me into trouble one of these days."

A young man with a round mass of curly fair hair and a broken nose precipitated into the room. "What was that blast?"

"Sorry, *man of the Law*, I didn't intend to disturb anyone!" I apologised.

"I'm not disturbed, I'm curious," the young man said, plunging his blue-grey eyes into mine with unlawful intensity.

Recovering his spirits, Ferman turned towards him, "As soon as he entered the room our visitor was attracted to this jar."

The young man was intrigued, "Were you, just? And why this particular jar? There are hundreds like this one," he said.

What was I to tell him? That this was my Mother the Dragon in a bottle? He would have laughed at me. "Have you heard of the Molten Sea, *my friend in the Law*?"

"Why so, *man of the Law*?" he asked.

Cautiously, I said, "To me, the energy of this bottle is as beautiful as the Molten Sea's silvery waves."

The young man passed his hand through his curly fair hair and scratched his nose. He grabbed another bottle from a shelf. "What about this one?"

I tuned in. "There are so many smells in this chapel. Could you open it so I can judge better?"

He removed the plass stopper.

It started before time. It has continued on ever since.

I wriggled my nostrils and sense-smelled. "This one reminds me of caverns of orichalc. Nice, but nothing like the Molten Sea bottle."

Ferman and the young man exchanged a glance. Then the young man put the bottle back on the shelf and seized another one, opening it for me.

The physical smell was neutral, but the astral smell was revolting – not just foul, but devious. I did not want to offend anyone. "Mm..."

The young man read my eyes and pulled an ugly face that creased the bump on his broken nose. "Very true, *man of the Law!*" He handed the bottle to Ferman, "Throw this garbage out!" Then he walked towards a doorway. "*Follow me, man of the Law!* Watch your feet for the bottles."

I walked behind him down a long stairway. Ferman did not come with us. The stairway led to a dimly-lit basement. There were plass buckets all over the floor, in which I recognised the infamous whitish slime. Thank the Lord Melchisedek, there was no sign of Master Woolly.

"One of these buckets contains a very special mixture," the young man said. "Can you tell me which one?"

I started with a long sniff, which aroused waves of elation inside the Dragon. The white slime was nothing like the stinking rubbish I had expected. "I like the smell of this chapel, *my friend in the Law!*"

"Do you, just?" The young man grinned. "Why so?"

I tried to remain vague, "Reminds me of lovely tirtha places I have visited in the past."

"I myself *love* this smell," he said. "Most people hate it."

I watch the birth and death of worlds and clusters of worlds. O, Mother of the Light, Thy dance! Thy dance!

I inspected the twenty or so buckets on the floor. All emitted the same silvery glow in darkness visible. But when I tuned into each of them from the Dragon of the Deep, vroofing waves of quite different qualities were triggered. I pointed to the buckets and commented, "This one is healthy and strong. This one is a bit sad. This one is very sick. It's dying, actually..." Then I arrived at a bucket that triggered a vroofing explosion.

"This one!" I exclaimed. "This one... this one is *really* special."

The young man nodded, his clear blue-grey eyes flaring with enthusiasm. "Straight from the breasts of the Great Goddess!"

Again, the fluid looked like the silvery ocean out of which the gods arose. "The Molten Sea in a bucket!" I said. "How do you make it?"

I sat on the floor by the bucket.

The young man shouted, "Don't put your hands in it!" Then he came and sat in front of me.

Using the palms of my hands, which I carefully kept a few centimetres away from the bucket, I sensed the power coming out of the whitish jelly. "*Man of the Law*, this is magnificent. It moves me... deeply!" The substance was radiant with my Mother's sweetness. The smell was as pure as Dragon's breeze. I closed my eyes, and for a moment I was transported back into the glories of the deep Underworlds.

The drift of a hundred million souls through the furrows of time. If you rise, Elyani will rise with you. If you ignore me, she will die.

"What are you seeing *man of the Law*?" the young man wanted to know.

How to tell him? I established eye contact, trying to convey the impressions of the glorious caverns.

Half-smiling, half-irritated, he pushed me, "But speak! What the Underworld are you seeing?"

"Precisely, *my friend in the Law*, these jars conjure images of the Underworlds in my mind. But the Underworlds are not what people think. I have visited a temple in the south, a place called Mount Lohrzen, where the priests know how to descend into layers of the Underworlds sealed to all other people. Nothing to do with those horrid caverns of sickness where initiates usually travel."

The young man was sharp, and curious. Soon I found myself under a barrage of questions. "What were these priests like? What exactly were they capable of? Where did their tradition come from...?" He moved fast, interrupting me with another question before I finished answering the previous one. He made comments that showed his interest and enthusiasm for the knowledge of the Underworlds but he never seemed satisfied, always finding more questions to ask. In particular he was extremely interested in the healing potential of the Underworlds' deeper layers.

We stayed in the basement for a long time, breathing the fumes that came from the buckets and sharing the Underworld-like elation they triggered inside us.

"What a blast!" he exclaimed at length. "So is this how you identified the elixir in the sanctum above?"

"The bottle which contained the Molten Sea?"

He nodded.

"Yes! It made the Dragon of the Deep shiver through me."

"How flattering!" he said. "If you knew the number of hours this bottle has cost me."

I opened my mouth to ask about the elixir, but he was already making a proposal, "If my elixir can tickle your Dragon, then maybe your Dragon could pump up one of my babies."

Before I could tell him I had very little experience healing children, he was up off the floor, "Come with me, there is something I want you to have a look at. Be careful where you walk." He took me up the stairway into yet another room full of benches, flames and bottles.

Fluid infinity, star elixirs, space winds, incandescent jewels. From one end of remoteness to the other, he travelled.

The young man took a jar and placed it in my hands. "This one is breaking my heart, *man of the Law*. She's dying. I have been working on her for six moon cycles and now she's gliding out of my hands."

"What's inside the jar?" I asked.

"A baby stone."

"And what is wrong with it?"

"Her!" he corrected. "This stone is a she-stone."

I smiled, sending a loving thought to Marek the indestructible.

"She was in her last stage of development when she started losing her substance. No idea why. A sad story. She was my best girl."

"May I open the jar?" I asked.

He acquiesced.

The jar was half-full with a yellowish liquid, through which I could discern a pale whitish soft stone the size of a cherry.

"Do you think your Dragon tricks could heal her?" he asked anxiously.

"I have no idea. I could certainly try. If she was to be healed, would she radiate the same silvery beauty as the Molten Sea bottle?"

He nodded.

"That would be fascinating!" I vroofed, thoroughly excited at the prospect of making the jar shine like the sea of the gods.

"Well, why don't you take the bottle with you and let your Dragon have a go at her. I've tried all I can. As far as I'm concerned, she's as good as a Blue priestess' corpse." He sighed, then added, "Her name is Lilu."

I took her close to my heart and smiled at her. "*Praise the Lord Melchisedek, Lilu,* my name is Szar."

The young man was delighted at the warm welcome his baby was receiving. He gave an affectionate smile, "*Praise the Lord Melchisedek, Szar,* my name is Woolly."

"Woolly?" I nearly dropped the flask. "Are you Master Woolly?" I gulped, taking a much closer look at him.

He was so young... younger than me! I was left with my mouth open, contemplating his mass of fair hair, so pale it was nearly white, the piercing glow in his eyes, the very broken nose, and the dozens of stains which decorated his cream robe.

Woolly was quite amused. "What's this blast about, *man of the Law*?"

"Hum..."

Before I had time to make up an answer, he invited me to look at more jars. I followed him from room to room, dazzled by the vibrations and the powers he had captured in his mixtures. The vroofing elation mounting, I recognised the characteristic feelings of certain gems that I had only encountered deep in the Underworlds. But some of the jars also radiated lights that seemed to be coming straight from high angels.

There was no time for more. Woolly signalled he had to go. He took the soft stone jar in his hand and bade her, "Farewell Lilu, stone of the Law!" Then he winked at me and invited me to come back and visit him again.

9.21 Maryani's gift

I hid the precious jar in a safe pocket inside my brown cape and took off on the roofs, from Maniya to the jewels, and from the jewels to the thirty-three victorious gods. As I was crossing the straight path of the law, watching the crowd from unlawful heights, I exclaimed with excitement, "Elyani, I am on my way!"

Elyani instantly answered through darkness visible. "Are you calling, man of Thunder?"

I was perplexed. "Sorry Elyani, the soft stone I am carrying must be playing tricks on me. I will be with you in five minutes."

Resting on the Dragon of the Deep to silence my mind, I hurried across the roofs of the windmills of the Law. When I arrived in Elyani's court-yard, a surprise was waiting for me. Two ladders had been attached to the walls: one from the courtyard to the terrace on top of our bedrooms, and the second from there to the Blue priestesses' roof. I jumped down as usual.

After giving me a long kiss, Elyani asked, "Do you like my ladders? They're a present from Pushpadiv of the Lawful Gardeners."

"They look very solid. But... I don't really need ladders, you know."

"Of course not!" she shrugged her shoulders and looked up to the gods. "Szar-ka, these are for me, not for you."

"For you!"

"I want to watch the sunsets too," she said. "How was your meeting with Woolly?"

"A lawful dream! He didn't throw a single bucket of slime at me. He even asked me to look after one of his children who is very sick at the moment."

Elyani frowned.

I pulled the jar out of my pocket and opened the lid in front of her. "Look at this beautiful stone. Her name is Lilu. She's in need of urgent care. Woolly says she's as good as a Blue priestess' corpse."

The lady of the White Eagle chuckled.

I shared my enthusiasm for the marvels I had contemplated in the chapel of the Field Wizards.

"How exciting!" Elyani commented. "I have always heard that his chapel was the most foul-smelling spot in the entire temple. Some people have even reported being violently attacked by forces coming from Woolly's bottles."

That didn't surprise me in the least. "Woolly's works are like the Un-derworlds – ugly and frightening on the surface, teeming with wonders in the depths."

The musical fluorescence of a thousand fields of stars.

"What are we going to do to heal Lilu? Did Woolly give you any clues?" Elyani asked.

I shook my head. "From what I gathered, all his usual methods have failed. Maybe that's why he was so interested in the Dragon style of heal-ing."

"Are you going to seek inspiration from your Mother the Dragon?"

"Of course."

"Well," Elyani said, "I wish your Mother the Dragon could inspire the two Immaculate priestesses who are taking care of the ascending goddess. They have declined Melchard's offer to let the Masters of Thunder see Holma, and they did not listen to Teyani either when she suggested that she or others could help."

I covered Lilu's jar and placed it on the lawn, close to the Dragon gate. "What is happening to Holma?"

"She is getting worse by the day. She has lost a lot of weight. She is coughing like a filosterops, so badly she can't get out of bed. But the Immaculate remain unmoved. They will reject anything that is not pure chanting of the hymns of the Law. They say that any healing method not part of *the most ancient and holiest body of the Law* would render Holma impure, and cause her to be rejected by the gods."

"And what if Holma dies?"

"Then *the Lord Melchisedek have mercy on us*! No ascending goddess has ever died before her ritual of ascension to the gods. Everyone will believe the gods have abandoned us and the downfall of Eisraim has begun. If these two Immaculate priestesses were not so stupid, they would recognise that the kingdom has changed and that the ancient hymns of the Law can no longer cure all diseases! But they're rigid and stubborn, and worse, they are supremely arrogant. *The Immaculate receive orders from none but the king himself.*"

I had rarely seen Elyani so upset. Calling on the Eagle's softness, "There is nothing we can do about this, so better not think about it too much. *That which you cannot hold in your hands, let it not hold your hands.*"

She took my hands, "You can hold me in your hands, can't you?"

I went into the Point, trying to find an appropriate answer. "But you are not wearing the same dress as yesterday!" I noticed.

The high priestess looked at me, half-outraged, half-devastated, "So you *never* notice when I change dresses?"

"Well, actually..." All the castes I had been a member of wore exactly the same kind of summer clothes six months of the year, and the same winter clothes the remaining six months. Not to say they never changed clothes of course! The Sons of the Dragon, for instance, washed their clothes every new moon, and on several other occasions such as the equinoxes and the yearly celebration of the Law. But all garments were strictly identical, following the lawful canon of their caste.

"Actually, no, I hadn't noticed!" I admitted.

"Awakening?" Elyani looked upwards, taking the gods as her witness. "Ha! Ha!"

I turned to the Point, looking for a wind to carry me out of this difficult situation.

Three white roses. At the feet of the Angel of Highness. You missed the call. Now Elyani is dying in the clutches of the Prince of Darkness.

Elyani shivered.

I took her in my arms. "Shall we try out these ladders and go and inspect the Blue priestesses' roof?"

She was gazing at me with a strange expression on her face. "The ladders?" She pulled herself from her thoughts, "Yes, why not! Alcibyadi and Maryani are on their way to talk to you. They'll probably be delighted to see us so high."

I didn't want to scandalise an ancient and respectable order. "What about your reputation, Elyani of the White Eagle?"

"Eagles fly!" she flapped her arms, moving to the ladder.

"We'll fly at sunset!" I caught hold of her hood and pulled her back.

She folded into my arms and nested there. "Alcibyadi... was deeply touched by your visit. After speaking to you, she went straight to the Eagle's chapel and invoked the oracle. And..." Elyani paused with a measure of caution.

I tucked my head in my shoulders. "Did I do something wrong?"

She shook her head, "Hunh hunh! But there could be a surprise for you."

Alcibyadi had already mentioned that. I became suspicious. "You know I have always hated surprises. Is it one of those secrets known by everyone in the temple but me?"

Elyani looked up and to the left and pretended to be twinging her beard, pushing her lips forward as Gervin did when he was seriously joking.

"I don't like the sound of this," I thought, listening to her silence.

She gave me a playful kiss. "Would you like a white drink? I made one especially for you this morning."

Getting more and more suspicious, "Is it to prepare me for the surprise?"

She pretended to stroke her beard again, and shook her head.

I signalled my resignation with a long sigh and went to sit on the grass. *"Let the White Eagle take me!"*

The drink was sheer delight. As I tilted my head back for the last few drops, the protective field I had woven all around the courtyard sent a warning. "They're coming!" I said, standing up. With one of her long sleeves Elyani wiped the milky substance off my moustache.

"Praise the Lord Melchisedek, Szar of the Brown Robe!" the two White Eagles said in one voice.

Turning round, I returned the greeting, trying not to frown when I saw how young Maryani was. She looked as if she had hardly finished growing up, a beautiful child just turned a woman. She had the high forehead and the blue eyes of the people from the north, her sandy-coloured hair falling straight onto her shoulders.

Alcibyadi looked more composed than the day before. We all sat on the lawn close to Elyani's favourite laurel tree, outside the room where my body had been kept during my descent into the caverns of sickness.

Then came the second surprise. "Szar," Alcibyadi declared in a formal voice, "let me tell you the purpose of our visit. The White Eagle has spoken to us through his oracle. His bidding is that Maryani's descent into the Underworld be left entirely up to you."

"I lawfully beg your pardon?"

Standing straight, Alcibyadi repeated her words and added, "If you accept and fulfil the Eagle's wish, you will be responsible for taking Maryani into hibernation, and you will lead her down into the Underworld. All related matters will be up to your discretion except one: the descent must take place tomorrow night, one hour before the new moon."

The haunting image of Vivyani on her deathbed reappeared. Was I being asked to lead Maryani to a similar fate?

My Dragon froze. "And what if I refuse?"

"Maryani will never descend into the Underworld, and thus she will not become a high priestess of the White Eagle. Accordingly, she will not be sent to the land of Aegypton with the other chosen ones."

"Oh, gods!" I turned to Maryani. She looked at me, serene, blessed by the same softness and warmth as her sisters in the Eagle. She seemed completely confident, as if I was going to take her by the hand and lead her down to hell and back to life, and all before sunrise.

"Will you excuse me one moment?" I asked our guests.

I took Elyani into her bedroom and closed the door behind us.

"What's this ugly Underworld of a nonsense?" I fumed.

Elyani made herself liquid like the Molten Sea.

"Where did this come from? Is it one of those oracles where someone asked, 'O White Eagle, do you think that Szar should be in charge all by himself?' and the oracle answered 'sort of yes,' and now everyone says 'such is the Eagle's Will, trespass at your own risk'?"

"When you spoke to her yesterday, Alcibyadi saw the Eagle on you."

"Of course I called on the Eagle! I worked my clear fountain off to get a smile out of her," I stormed.

"Alcibyadi said the Eagle had sent you to her. Then she went and asked the oracle how Maryani's ordeal in the Underworld could be lessened thanks to the knowledge you received in the temple of the Dragon. The Eagle replied with the very words Alcibyadi told you."

"And of course you have already asked Gervin?"

"Teyani did. Gervin said that being in charge of Maryani would be excellent for your spiritual development."

"But I have never done anything like this! What if Maryani dies in my hands?"

Elyani shrugged, "And what if Maryani dies in Teyani's hands?"

"There is no way in the seven spheres I am going to accept this! Did Gervin say I *had* to do it?"

Elyani shook her head.

"Well, then, don't even thought-form it!" I rejoined, and went back out to sit with our guests.

I took my head in my hands. "How old are you, Maryani?"

"*I have known sixteen springs and seventeen autumns,* Szar of the Brown Robe."

The memory of Vivyani asleep on her bed hit me again. Establishing eye contact with Maryani, I went high in the clear fountain, invoking the Eagle with all my strength.

A great Light descended upon the four of us.

9.22 The hymn of the White Eagle to his children

Straight from the spheres of Highness, the White Eagle responded:
"*Some love to shine,*
I shine through love.
Some are great by their might,
I am mighty by love.
Some love life and its delights,
Love is my Life,
And my delight comes from the love that lives in you.
Some angels demand that men serve them
And they feed on their rituals
And their lawful sacrifices.
He who loves my children
Performs my great ritual.
I ask for your love and curse you not
When, caught by forgetfulness,
You ignore my Voice
And the seeds for eternal Light
Which I have sown into your hearts.
My dear children in eternity,
I have waited for you since earlier than time.
Hasten along the path,
That you may join me in Highness and realise –
Clouds were designed to be looked at from above."

9.23 Eagle's wind

Alcibyadi shone like a White sun. The courtyard was inundated with Light. The bed of tiny flowers on the lawn no longer looked purple but exuberantly White. The laurel trees had turned into huge flames, herald of the Revelation Sky of the gods. The walls of the courtyard had disappeared, and so had all the rest.

"What..." I turned skywards, searching for the familiar reference of the mists. "Where are..." Gone! There were no mists above my head, just a gigantic clear fountain, ablaze with the White power that poured through the Point. "How..." Breathless – immersed in such Light, there was no space and no need for breathing – I tried to Dragon my left fist clenched, but the Dragon had gone missing, for the Dragon is normally below, and in this extravaganza of Highness, below and above seemed all mixed up. "But..." I tried to descend, which took me further up in a boundless field of Elyaniness where every speck of infinity was whispering, "Forever love!"

Edge of Highness. Whiteness eternal. Forever love.

How long did it last? This, only the Archive knows.

When I recovered some inkling of the six directions of space and, resting on the below, was finally able to turn my head and ask, "But what... what was *that*?" Alcibyadi answered, serene, "You invoked the Eagle, and the Eagle responded."

I caught my breath.

"But..." in a last, vain, desperate throe, my mind pleaded for time, "but does it really have to be tomorrow night? Couldn't it wait till the following moon cycle?"

"No!" the Eagle's oracle responded through Alcibyadi's tranquil voice.

I sought Maryani's eyes. It was easy. All I had to do was to turn my head and lo! there they were, just in front of me.

She was smiling the wisdom of Highness, the maturity of the Ancient of Ancients superimposed on her candid youthfulness.

Larger than the seven spheres and full of stars, each of them luminous as a million suns. He has heard the call. He will respond.

I surrendered unconditionally, "Lady Maryani, priestess of the White Eagle, I shall take you down into the Underworlds tomorrow night. Your journey will begin in this courtyard. Then Elyani and I will take your body into this room," I pointed to the door of my bedroom. The fountain kept speaking through my mouth, "This is where Elyani took good care of me when I first descended, as we will both be taking good care of you."

Maryani's face lit up with child-like joy.

"But why the Upperworld did I say that?" I thought agonisingly.

Maryani's unconditional trust made me even more scared.

To keep good countenance, I raised my hands and turned to Alcibyadi, "This is the way apprentices are, these days! Send them to hell, and they don't know how to thank you!"

"All glory to the teacher!" Elyani went to congratulate Maryani.

From the Edge of Highness Alcibyadi conveyed the thankful glance of the Eagle, to which she added a personal nod of approval loaded with the denseness of a great warrior of the Spirit.

I held her eyes, admiring her strength, wondering if Lehrmon had yielded to her request.

She heard my thought and shook her head silently.

He has read the mind of the Mother of the Light. His magnificence transcends anything gods and men can conceive.

Maryani approached me, "Szar of the Brown Robe, when should I come to you?"

"Come and visit two hours after sunset." Resting on my Mother, I forced a Dragon-confident voice, "I will give you your first instructions. Meanwhile, you must fast."

After our guests had left, I turned to Elyani, "Help! I think I'd rather face a horde of Nephilim Hunters. Having Maryani's life in my hands scares the caverns of sickness out of my guts."

"Teyani will be immensely grateful to you for carrying out the Eagle's wish."

"And what if I kill Maryani?"

"Before you brought Alcibyadi back, eight priestesses died in Teyani's hands." Elyani unfolded the magic of her softness, "As for helping you, Teyani and I will be with you. Always." From the Edge of Highness, the wind of the Eagle blew, "Always."

Wondering how to contain so much love, we watched the White Light slowly dissipating from the courtyard, like morning dew under the first light of the sun.

From the edge of hollowness to the glorious ignited centre, lightning shafts, liquid gold, he has measured the limits of time.

Elyani clasped my hand.

He will come, followed by a trail of whirling nebulas.

"Now, will you tell me, what the *Heart of the Law* did you put in that white drink to trigger such a response from the heavens?" I asked her.

"Mm..." she brought herself back from the contemplation of the Light. "It had nothing to do with the drink! If the White Eagle responded, it is because you have been performing his great ritual."

"His great ritual?"

She whispered, "This is what the Eagle said: he who loves my children performs my great ritual."

"So is this how I am to conquer the power of the Eagle?" I whispered back. "As the Law says, *love your teacher, and the flow of knowledge will automatically find its way to you.*"

"Especially when the teacher loves you."

Tuning into her vastness, it dawned on me that the more I loved Elyani, the less I could tell her and the Eagle apart.

I told her. It made her Eagle-shine a little brighter. "The more I love you," she gave back, "the less I can tell myself and the Eagle apart."

I drank her presence, wondering how the magic of the instant could be captured and made to last forever. Some moments are so special that afterwards you wonder if they have really happened. "Perhaps," the thought ran above my head, "it's because they keep happening forever in Highness."

In the flavour of Highness, Elyani confided, "Do you know what Gervin told me? That after I fell in love with you, I became much more awake."

From the Thunderbolt Bearer, this was a sublime compliment.

"But of course!" I clicked my fingers, holding the eureka from the Point. "This is why he wanted me to fall in love with you: it is *so* awakening!"

"Did Gervin tell you he wanted you to fall in love with me?" Elyani was burning to know.

"No, but it's obvious. If it wasn't for you, I probably would have let myself drown in that tirtha lake where I lost Master Fior's soft stone two years ago." I paused, observing the sparks of Eagle Light above my head. "And now, every hour of the day I feel the urge to awaken more, so I can love you more, and so I can fight anything that would dare try to separate us. Drifting with destiny is for sleepers. Never again!"

Elyani raised her hands. "Awakened by love! Voof!"

It was easy to see why Gervin wanted me to take Maryani for a ride with my Mother the Dragon. Knowing that her life was in my hands made me feel like learning the entire Law of Melchisedek by the next evening.

The idea that time counted was new to me. Before I went to Mount Lohrzen, Gervin had explained more than once how sleepers behaved as if time stretched in front of them without end, and that only awakened ones knew how to value each second. I had agreed with the concept but it all seemed quite theoretical. Yet now, with Elyani in my arms, a completely different meaning was emerging from the verses of Maveron that Lehrmon had once chanted for me,

"Sleeper, beware!
The time you waste is known by the Lords of Destiny,
And you will hold yourself accountable for it
When the judgement comes.
Wake up, man of the Law!
The days are numbered.
The time is coming."

Three days earlier, during the first Point storm, it had flashed in my mind that awakening entailed a completely different way of relating to time. The full implications were still shrouded in a cloud of mystery but one thing was clear: awakening implied doing things instantly – never procrastinating, not even a few hours.

Maryani's life in my hands, every second counted.

Elyani and I discussed at length the usual ritual by which White Eagle priestesses were sent down to the Underworld, only to conclude that we would implement a radically different method.

"Now that your Point has been ignited," Elyani told me, "your clear fountain will become stronger and stronger. That should help you link to the Eagle when you descend through the gate. Surrender your fountain to him, and he will guide you to Maryani, whatever cavern of sickness she may be in."

"I see," I twinged my beard, admiring Gervin's teaching style in action. "I have until tomorrow night to awaken my Point, is that it?"

Stroking her chin, Elyani laughed.

"But it's not funny!" I protested. "I don't even understand what started this hurricane above my head."

"After speaking to you about the looming catastrophe, Gervin voice-channelled me and instructed me to initiate the impulse in your Point," Elyani declared.

My lower jaw dropped in awe, "Do you mean you started this?"

"Let us say it was a shared enterprise, with Master Gervin and Lord Gana taking major roles in the play."

"Now what am I to make of this?" I pretended to be utterly suspicious. "You send me a Point influence, and within minutes I feel an irresistible need to come and tell you I love you. Is this what the Point is supposed to do to people?"

She answered by planting a long, noisy kiss on my cheek. "Anyhow, didn't you say it was your teacher's will?"

He stayed awake throughout the Great Night. He heard the first notes of the Song of Creation. When the gods awoke, his exalted nature was already illuminating the spheres.

"Do you still hear the angels' voices above your head?" Elyani asked.

"They come in waves. But I can't understand what they are saying."

"It's because you are trying to understand with your head," she said. "A human head is too little to contain the power of the Point. Only the Point itself can know Point-ness."

"I don't even know for sure where the Point is! Sometimes I feel a huge ladder going up above my head, with centres of energy all along."

Elyani closed her eyes, and for one second I saw the blazing star above her head again. At the same time, one of the centres of energy in the ladder above my head became distinctly perceptible. "Ah, this one!" I exclaimed. "So is this what people call the Point?"

She nodded.

"And what am I supposed to do with it?"

"Nothing for the moment, because I am holding it for you. Later on you will have to learn to contain the intensity by yourself."

I pulled the face she reserved for moments of great perplexity.

"If the Point is not held," she clarified, "all the power which resonates in it can abruptly fall down into your head. It makes your head feel like a pumpkin. It can make you do strange things."

"Such as throwing buckets of slime in the face of high priests?" I calculated.

"Could be!" she said in Marek's voice.

"But why can't the head cope with the power of the Point?"

"It's too little!" she explained. "Men are only baby-angels. When they grow up it will become different. But for the moment, the only way they can contain the intensity of angels' minds is by receiving it above their head. There is plenty of space above the head, enough for the vastness of angels' minds." She knocked on my forehead as if at a chapel door. "The head is such a small box!"

"If you are holding the Point for me, does it mean I don't have to do anything?"

"Oh, I never said that! The power of the Point is not something you are supposed to sit under and contemplate passively like a filosterops in front of a sunflower." Her perfect imitation of the enlightened little animal's sweet, docile look made me burst out laughing.

"So what am I supposed to do?"

"Become more awake, think faster, and know everything!"

"Know everything?" The Warriors' wild laughter ran loose, "Ha! Ha! Ha! Ha! Ha!"

"Oush!" the magic woman whispered, "It does something to me when you laugh like this."

"Wait a minute, that's flying too high! How could I know everything? Only angels can know everything!"

"*Right and righteous,* mighty Dragon! The angels can know everything, and your Point can know the angels' minds."

"Suppose I have a question in mind..."

"Suppose!" she incarnated Gervin on her face.

"Shall I address my Point and ask, O power of the Point, could you please tell me how to heal Lilu the stone?"

"No! That wouldn't work because these are human words spoken from your human head. The Point is above your head, and it knows only the language of angels. It cannot be fathomed with the language of men. What you must do is catch an angel's thought."

"An angel's thought..." I mused. "What does that look like?"

"Teyani compares them to winged snakes that travel at the speed of lightning."

That sounded daunting. "Do you really think I could catch a winged snake that travels as fast as lightning?"

"No you can't. But your Point can."

I sighed. My eyes were caught by the jar close to the Dragon gate. "Oh my Lord Melchisedek! Lilu!"

By now the courtyard, the lawn and the laurel trees were back to their normal appearance. But Lilu wasn't. She was shining the light of the Eagle. Her aura was four lawful feet wide.

"This is no ordinary soft stone!" Elyani was as puzzled as I was.

"She can retain the Eagle's Light better than we can!" I opened the lid. She had not changed size.

"And the Eagle's softness is with her too." Elyani was full of admiration. "Do you think she should join my order?"

"But then who will take her for the trial into the Underworlds?" I was anticipating the next oracle.

"And when are you going to take *me* into the Underworlds?" Elyani prompted.

I made myself still, trying hard to catch a winged serpent that would tell me how to zap the magic woman through the gate.

Elyani lit up the star above her head. "Are you getting inspired?" she asked after a moment.

I shook my head. "What about you? Did you catch a winged serpent?"

"Yes."

"Already?" I was stung with curiosity. "Will you tell me?"

"If you had a child with me, I know for sure I could pass through the Dragon's gate and go down into the Underworlds with you."

"What?" I opened my eyes wide. "This power of the Point is getting more dangerous by the hour!"

She chuckled, and quoted the well-known verse that was inscribed on the portal of the temple's main oracle: "*Man of the Law, ask no questions unless you want to hear the answers!*"

"We've not even tried!" I exclaimed. "Let's just try!"

"Yes!" Elyani let herself fall softly on the grass with a long, loud sigh.

My Dragon vroofed. I frowned.

Elyani turned her head to look at me. "Aren't we trying?"

"Elyani, I meant you should just get out of your body and try to follow me through the gate."

"Ah?" she said in a small voice. "Well, if that's what you want to try, then... let's try."

I laid the precious jar on the lawn close to me and sat in a meditation position. Elyani projected herself out of her body into darkness visible. I let the gate's breeze pull me and instantly found myself in the blue rock cavern underneath the courtyard.

Elyani was not with me.

I went back up into the courtyard. Elyani was pushing against the ascending flow of the breeze. I tried to catch her by the hand and dived through the gate again.

As soon as I reached the cavern I exclaimed, "Oh my Lord Melchisedek, what is *that*?"

I couldn't believe my eyes. "What are you doing here, you pretty little thing?"

Elyani was still not in the cavern, but Lilu was in my hand. There was no jar, just the translucent soft stone that shone the Eagle's light.

I opened my palm and softly Voice-projected onto her, "Booh!"

There was no noticeable result.

I let myself drift up through the gate. Lilu instantly went back into her jar.

Elyani was still battling against the flow. I made a few attempts to pull her down, but unsuccessfully. Finally, fearing the breeze might prove toxic to her, I instructed her to return to her body and I slipped back into mine.

Soon Elyani sat up. "This breeze is as bad as the fierce eddies that travellers encounter in some spaces of remoteness. There was no way I could pass through. Do you think we could try... something else?"

"Mm... let me think."

9.24 The conquest of the Point-guided corridors

As we were watching sunset on the roof, a fiery Point-sense of the urgency of awakening led me to ask Elyani solemnly, "High priestess, I call on your vision – what can I do to speed up the process? There is so much to learn, and so little time in front of me. Where to start?"

"Flying Dragons, perhaps?" she teased me.

"No, please!" it came out of me as a cry of agony. "Don't talk to me about Flying Dragons, they always get me into trouble! This afternoon I lost my way in the corridors *again*. And this time it really turned into a nightmare! For nearly an hour I couldn't even find a courtyard from where I could reach the roofs."

"But the field in the corridors has nothing to do with Flying Dragons!" the White Eagle's softness touched me through her voice.

"Hasn't it? Then who the hell is behind these bewitched corridors?"

"No one! It's just a simple guidance field."

"Guidance?" I laughed, outraged. "Active disorientation, you mean."

"Szar-ka, I am sure it wouldn't take long for a Great Warrior like you to conquer the corridors of the temple's female wing."

"I don't want to waste any more time with this stupid maze," my Dragon was still incensed with the frustration of the afternoon's unholy dance in circles.

"Mm..."

"Anyhow, what's wrong with walking on the roofs? Awakening is all about speeding up, isn't it? Really, there is no faster way of going from here to there in the temple."

"Very true, Dragon!" she pretended to agree with me fully.

"Are you implying I am looking for excuses to avoid facing the obstacle?"

"Ohhh..." she rounded her lips and bent her head to the side, hesitating, "nnn...no! But when you feel ready for the battle, just let me know. I'll come and help."

"I see..." I swallowed, "you think I am trying to avoid my destiny. Well, then, let's do it. *Right now!*" I quickly jumped my way down into the courtyard.

"So what are you doing?" I looked up to her with an air of impatience. "I'm waiting!"

Laughing, Elyani made her way down the ladders.

She playfully put on a grim face. *"Follow me, candidate!"*

I made myself candid and sweet like a filosterops and trotted behind her.

When we arrived in the first corridor she asked, "Candidate, can you feel anything?"

"Nothing! I can sense-smell the Dragon's gate behind us, but that has never helped me find my way in this labyrinth. If I rest on the Dragon or if I look for earth energies, I cannot perceive anything particular."

The Dark Night of Remoteness remembers the creation as it was before she gave birth to it.

"Let us go for a walk," Elyani took my hand.

I tried to establish references, using stairways and colonnades as landmarks, but as usual I lost my reckoning. As we stopped in a narrow hallway I complained, "I'm lost!"

"What can you feel in your Point?"

While a group of priestesses was passing by, I tuned into the motley spectrum of energies above my head with perplexity. "It tends to become more peaceful around sunset," I observed.

Extending the gentle Eagle-touch of her presence above my head, Elyani highlighted a soft, low-pitched hissing energy. "This is the guidance field," she pointed out. "Hook into it!"

That didn't tell me much.

She was amused. "Hooking into the guidance field is part of the initiation ritual of all female orders in Eisraim. Tomorrow the Blue Robes are initiating a novice. Shall we enrol you for the ceremony?"

"Is this how you learnt?" I asked, battling with the elusive hiss.

"No, I just modelled Teyani."

"Then why couldn't I connect with the field by hooking my Point into yours?"

"Yes, why can't you?" she feigned a tone of reproach.

I closed my eyes. "But I can!" I exclaimed with surprise, feeling a fast-vibrating energy clicking in from Point to Point.

"Praise the Lord Melchisedek!" Elyani acclaimed. "Who shall we go and visit?"

Be ready. She will need your help. If you ignore me she will die.

"Alcibyadi!" I chose.

"Just tune into her."

I remembered Alcibyadi's energy. From the Point, I tried to find a direction. "I can't feel anything!"

"It's because you are tuning into Alcibyadi's energy, not into her Point. Tune into her Point, and let your Point walk you."

Without thinking, I remembered what I had felt in the Point when meeting Alcibyadi earlier in the day. My body instantly started walking.

Flabbergasted, I stopped and turned to Elyani. "Is it that simple?"

She nodded. "Come on, take me to Alcibyadi."

I closed my eyes and repeated the connection. All I had to do was to let my feet follow the Point. It was magic. Each time we reached a crossing they knew exactly where to turn.

We finally arrived in a courtyard I had never visited before.

"But this is not where Alcibyadi's room is!" I scratched my head. "What have I done wrong?"

"Nothing! You wanted to find Alcibyadi, not her room, so the field led you here." Elyani pointed to a door in front of us. "Alcibyadi is in that room, visiting her friend Ongya. Do you want to check?"

Alcibyadi's accident will take place in the pitch-black spheres of the Black Night of Remoteness.

"No, I believe you. Let's not disturb them."

The boy will be powerful. In the land of Aegypton, he will be king.

Elyani started walking again.

"This is incredibly clever!" I marvelled. "How does it work, exactly?"

"It's a particular field. Established long, long ago. Many of our priest-esses live in such high spheres of consciousness – they hardly touch the material world. The field allows them to remain in a state of trance while finding their way through the female wing of the temple. They do not have to think where to go, they just have to maintain a little impulse in their Point and they are automatically led in the right direction."

"Does this mean that all the women of this temple are experts in the power of the Point?"

"Not at all. But when they arrive in the temple we awaken this particular Point connection for them, that is, we hook their Point into the guidance field. It also has the advantage that we can never lose them."

"Lose them?" I found the idea uncanny. "Where?"

"My love, you have no idea of the states of consciousness in which these priestesses spend their days and nights. They are far, far away from their body. So much of them lives in Highness that they hardly notice the king-dom. Sometimes they are so high they can't even keep the Point connec-tion, and it makes them lose their way. The field allows us to locate them easily."

We had arrived in a large courtyard, in an alley bordered by a row of high laurel trees. Elyani let her hand run along the bay leaves. "This is Teyani's courtyard," she said, and she invited me to map the place from the Point, so the guiding field could bring me back here if need be. Then she asked me to take her back to her room.

I tuned in, remembering the feeling of the Dragon gate.

"Hunh hunh! That can't work!" Elyani corrected me. "You are connect-ing with the energy of the place. For the guidance system to understand what you want, you must tune into the Point-ness of the room."

"The Point-ness of your bedroom?" I was perplexed.

She invited me into her energy. "Tune into me. I'll show you."

It was subtle. "Very subtle!" I reflected.

"Only in the beginning!" she assured me. "With a bit of practice you will soon be prancing around like a unicorn."

Once the mechanism engaged, it was amazingly simple. The Point guided every single step. "So really, these priestesses who live in Highness hardly have to open their eyes when walking the corridors. Do they never bump into each other?"

Elyani chuckled. "We have a polite expression for that, we call it *a meeting in Highness*. Normally it never happens. The guidance system takes care of every movement. But there have been accidents in the past."

"But what would happen to all these priestesses of Highness if the fields were to collapse? Without the guidance system, they couldn't even find their way to their bedroom."

"Much worse, they could no longer find their way to Highness! It is by resting on some other fields that they reach so high. If the fields were to collapse, so would their high spiritual connections. The same applies to nearly everyone in the temple."

That sounded so terrifying that my cogitative flow turned blank.

We kept drifting along peacefully, sailing with the Point-winds.

After a while I began to notice there was something wrong with the sound of the crickets. What was happening to them? They were all singing the same note! And what was worse, it sounded like a false note. It was not the first time I had noticed it – crickets no longer chanted melodies. When I mentioned this to Elyani, she said, "I am afraid this is another one of Gervin's predictions coming true. Long ago Teyani also prophesied something like this."

"But it is so monotonous and boring!" I moaned. "How can the gods allow this to happen?"

"Hush, *man of the Law*!" Elyani told me off. "*Blame not the gods for the evils men have brought onto the fields.*"

There was no lawful answer to that. I put up with the dull sound and retreated into the mellow hiss of the Point-field.

Point-sleeper, awaken! Not just for the sake of the Archive, but for Elyani. The time is coming. The days are numbered.

She will need you. Desperately.

Stand up, fulfil your destiny. Become a Point-warrior, a Knight!

"What would you like to eat for dinner?" I asked Elyani, concerned that my own lack of interest in food would prove detrimental to her health.

"Herbs of madness!" she whispered, tightly holding my hand.

"I must go and ask Mouridji the prophetess for the one thousand ways of preparing them. Combined with Nephilim cooking charms, I am sure we could work miracles! And..." Out of nowhere, a Point-impulse blared through the fountain, about as subtle as the pounding of a massive sledgehammer.

"Oohhh!" I had to stop walking and lean against the wall of the corridor. "What... what is that?"

Elyani closed her eyes. "I think someone... is trying to speak to you."

"Speak to me!" I turned skywards with total receptivity. "Please!"

Stand up, fulfil your destiny. Become a Point-warrior, a Knight! The road from Eisraim to Philadelphia will be shorter than a breath.

"I can't hear a thing, I can't feel a thing!" I complained. "Can you?"

"Mm... let's keep walking, it will help," the White Eagle pulled me by the hand. "Go inside, think of questions you could ask me about the Point."

"Was the guidance-field generated by Point-wizards?"

"No," Elyani replied, "like all fields, it wells out of the windmills of the Law, the rituals performed by the Windmill Keepers."

"But then surely someone with a Point has to monitor it from time to time."

"This is done by the Field Wizards: Master Ferman and his men. They come here regularly to inspect the field and fine-tune it."

The magic woman had zeroed in. As a thousand questions rushed into my mind, the extravagant pressure above the head started easing. The unabating flow led us to discuss those particular fields that created Point-resonances. There were many more of them in the kingdom than I had thought in my Point-virginity. "The Nephilim, in particular," my mystagogic friend went on, "are famous for using dreadfully powerful Point-fields for the purpose of warfare. But there are great dangers associated with these."

The Knights' Point-warfare will have the power to put Ahriman on his knees. Move fast! Every minute counts.

"Do you mean to say they are powerful weapons?" I asked.

"The kind of weapons that can turn against those who use them! There are mighty non-physical beings that connect with the Point, not all of them holy. Unless extreme care is taken, dark angels of the Point can rush through a Point-field and swamp everyone through it. As always with the Point, it happens lightning-fast. And it can create major disasters. Once in the Eastern Peninsula, the citadel of the Nephilim giants was nearly wiped out by such an attack. If the giants hadn't been rescued by the direct intervention of the Watchers, there would be nothing left of them by now."

"What happened to them when they were attacked?"

"They fell flat on their faces. Many of them died instantly. But the dark angels of the Point do not always strike as conspicuously as that. Often they prefer to manipulate people secretly. They know how to remain unnoticed, they can be extremely insidious."

"So the power of the Point can be dangerous!" I mused. "Are all the angels of the Point dark?"

"Of course not! The Point is the gateway to angelic consciousness at large."

"And these dark angels of the Point, are they the same as Flying Dragons?" I looked down to my left fist.

"Oh!" Elyani shouted in outrage. "Szar, when will you stop blaming these poor Flying Dragons for all the evils of the creation? Don't you know that some of them are powerful allies of the Masters of Thunder?"

We had arrived at her courtyard. It was night. In the silvery moonlight we could only guess each other's silhouette.

9.25 Flying dragons and the cosmological ladder

Elyani took me by the hand and walked to the ladder against her bedroom wall. With her back against the ladder, she stepped onto the first rung, holding the upper rungs with her hands.

"I am the Great Goddess who encompasses the spheres," she took her prophetess' voice. "Where are Szar and Elyani?"

I was perplexed. She took my left hand and placed it on her chest, against her heart centre. "Their head," she said.

She led my hand down, touching her body slightly. When reaching the limit of her abdomen, on the edge of her thighs, she said, "Their feet!" Slowly, she took me up, back onto her heart, "And when they love each other, they are here."

I stayed motionless, feeling the rising and falling of her breast as she breathed.

From infinity to infinity-ness. Fly. Worlds without end.

"Where is the kingdom?" she asked.

Spellbound, I let my hand go down against her body, lightly touching her, stopping at the lower limit of her belly.

"Right and righteous, mighty Dragon!" she welcomed my hand. "And where do the worlds of the gods begin?"

I went back onto her heart, "From here!"

"Where do they end?"

I brushed a loving caress up to her throat, and hesitated. She took my hand and moved up, caressing her face. She went on until my wrist reached just above her Point. "There you are at the summit of the glorious sky of the gods, on the Golden Shield which separates the transient spheres from the spheres of Highness. If you can pass through, you have become a great angel – immortality without limits."

"How high do the spheres of Highness go?" I asked.

"My ladder goes up endlessly," the Great Goddess proclaimed.

I took my hand down onto her heart.

This vastitude the giants will never comprehend.

"Where are the Underworlds?" she asked.

Starting from the tender edge of her belly, I let my hand glide against her legs.

"Mm..." she approved. "And where do you think the Underworlds stop?"

"They don't! Your ladder goes as far down as it goes high up," I answered, bending down to touch her feet.

"And where is your Mother the Dragon?" Elyani asked.

I hesitated.

"At the bottom of my endless ladder," she said.

"But... Oh Great Goddess, if your ladder is endless, how can it have a bottom?"

"Well... precisely, your Mother the Dragon is my endless bottom."

There was a shared giggle.

"Endless Bottom!" I exclaimed with reverence. "What a beautiful way of describing the Dragon of the Deep. And it goes so well with another name of hers: the She-Serpent of Wisdom that reaches deeper than the Abyss."

"Now, *pilgrim of the Law*, tell me, where is the Lord Melchisedek?" Elyani asked.

"At the top of your endless ladder, Oh Great Goddess."

"Right and righteous! But my ladder is more mysterious than you think, for the absolute top meets the absolute bottom somewhere, and they become one," she announced.

"Then my Mother the Dragon and the Good Lord Melchisedek must be very close," I concluded.

"Very! Do you think they could get married?"

Merging with the intoxicating web of softness which Elyani had woven, I rested my head against her, brushing her throat with my curly locks.

She sighed, then continued. *"Pilgrim of the Law,* let the Great Goddess reveal another of her secrets to you. You thought the Lord Melchisedek was at the top of my ladder, didn't you?"

"This I believe. It is the Law of my Fathers," I replied emphatically.

In the voice of a great hierophant she went on, "Well, man of the plains, learn *the heart of the Law*. Truly, the Lord Melchisedek is not at the top of my ladder. The Lord Melchisedek permeates the entire ladder. He *is* the ladder."

"Is he really?"

"Truly and verily."

"But then, so is my Mother the Dragon!" I exclaimed.

"Verily and truly," she said.

At the heart of an infinity of spaces, you will rise.

I steered my hand back to her heart. She met me by taking a long breath.

The dim moonlight made physical silhouettes merge with the glows of darkness visible, creating a mellow ambience. I took in the things she had said, enjoying guessing the expression on her face, wishing I could stop time.

The flight of the Eagle.

"Where is the White Eagle?" I asked her.

"Which one?"

I was puzzled. "Is there more than one?"

"Didn't you know there are two of them?"

"Hunh hunh!"

"It does not matter, in reality they are one and the same." She took my hand and placed it against her eyes. "There is the White Eagle of the gods, who lives in the triangle, in high regions of the worlds of the gods. He constantly journeys up and down through the spheres." She pulled my hand up to the limit of the Golden Shield above her head, then she made me come down to her heart slowly, and up again.

"Then there is the White Eagle who lives in Highness, on the other side of the Golden Shield," she said, pulling my hand as high as she could above her head, drawing me towards her at the same time.

"Is he a god?" I asked.

"No, he is one of the angels of Highness." She brought my hand down to her lips, "The other one, beneath the Golden Shield, is one of the gods. But the two are one Spirit. The White Eagle of the gods is an emanation of the White Eagle of Highness."

So close to her, I hesitated between a kiss and a question.

"Now, move back!" she said.

I sighed and took a step back. "Like this?"

"No! Much more."

Slowly, I moved away from her.

After at least ten steps, she said, "Good. Now you must whisper a long 'ffffoooohhhh.'"

"Ffffoooohhhh!"

"That's it!" she said. "Now you are a Flying Dragon. You are far, far away from my ladder. My creatures say you live in a sphere of remoteness. They can hardly understand you, because you are so different from them. So different! When they tune into you, all they can perceive is a long ffffoooohhhh. You are ancient, fascinating and mysterious to them."

"Well," I thought, "it's not so bad to be a Flying Dragon after all!"

"Now, move to your left," she said, "very far from me..."

I went and stood close to her favourite laurel tree.

"Now you are another Flying Dragon, in another sphere of remoteness. Even further away. Even more mysterious."

"Ffffoooohhhh!" I whispered, the bay leaves caressing my back.

"You are the Spirit of the Great Ant! You are so strange that whenever Master Gervin directs his vision towards you, he twinges his beard in perplexity."

"Mm..."

"Now, move to your right. A long, long way!" she said.

As I slowly walked across the lawn, she said, "You are crossing the Abyss of the Deep and the Fault of Eternity."

"What does that mean?" I asked.

"You are going too far from me."

I stopped where I was.

"No, but you have to!" she insisted. "Go on!"

When I reached the wall on the other side of the courtyard she said, "Now you are the Flying Dragons who live beyond the Abyss of the Deep and the Fault of Eternity. Your spaces are glorious and packed with so many stars that your spheres are as bright as Highness. And the Mother of the Light keeps delivering more and more stars for you all the time. She must like you a lot."

"If I have my own spheres, does it mean that I am a ladder too?"

"Exactly!" she said. "I am the ladder which Szar and Elyani climb up and down. The Spirit of the Great Ant, in its far remoteness, has its own ladder. And you have your own ladder, with myriads of little Flying Dragons moving up and down."

"And where does the Mother of the Light fit in all this?" I asked.

"O Flying Dragon, how profound thy question is! It touches the cosmic mystery of ladder-ness."

"Ffffoooohhhh!"

"As I have revealed to you, my ladder's endless bottom is one with its infinite top. The same is true of your ladder, O Flying Dragon: the uppermost top is one with the lowermost end, and so it is for each and every ladder. But there is more – the endless bottoms of *all* the ladders are one! It is this infinite one-ness which is called the Mother of the Light, the Cosmic Mother."

"So the Mother of the Light is the cosmic level of the Dragon of the Deep?"

"*Right and righteous, Flying Dragon!* The bottom of *my* ladder is the Dragon of the Deep, the Great Serpent of Wisdom. The bottom of your ladder is another glorious depth, and the bottom of the Great Ant's ladder is another one. The infinity where all these meet is the Mother of the Light."

"But then, if the ladders' tops are one with the bottoms, there must also be one principle at the top, where all the ladders meet together."

"Flying Dragon, thou hast discovered the Unborn God. He is the One. He is Ish, the Lord of the entire creation. He is God."

"Do you think He is married to the Mother of the Light?" I asked.

"How could He not be?" she exhaled a humming sound, as if calling me through the immensity of space. "Now let me tell you a strange story, part of the White Eagle's mysteries. Once, long ago, one of the Masters of Thunder crossed the Abyss of the Deep and the Fault of Eternity and went to visit you, Flying Dragons. Thunder came to you as the ambassador of the Lord Melchisedek, and he became your friend. So you decided to send one of your Flying Dragons for a visit to my ladder."

Slowly, I walked towards her.

"He was a huge, magnificent Flying Dragon," she said, tears in her eyes. "As he was approaching, the creatures of my ladder could see his gigantic blue cloud drawing near and they all heard his Voice – 'ffffooooohhhh!' – and they were amazed. The Lord Melchisedek sent the White Eagle of the gods to greet him."

I arrived close to her. "And what happened when the Flying Dragon met with the White Eagle of the gods?"

"They got along so well that the White Eagle invited the Flying Dragon to stay and live in my ladder."

I came even closer, my lips nearly touching hers. "What did the Flying Dragon do?"

"He could not stay, he had too many spheres of remoteness to visit. So the White Eagle of the gods invited him to leave some of his seed in our spheres."

I drew a long breath. "Did the Flying Dragon say yes?"

"Yes," she whispered, her lips half touching mine. "He planted the seeds for baby Flying Dragons into our Mother, the Dragon of the Deep. And do you know what he said, while he was doing that?"

My lips lightly touching hers, I whispered, "What did he say?"

"Forever love, White Eagle!"

9.26 The craft of soft stones

The next morning when I knocked at the chapel of the Field Wizards, it was Lehrmon who opened the door. After a lawful greeting he warned me to watch my step for bottles, and took me down into a spacious cellar where a number of large buckets were kept. The cellar was lit by milkfish white glows from the plass walls.

"Recognise the smell?" he asked.

"The white slime!" I filled my lungs with the lively fragrance.

"Exactly – the substance." He took the lid off one of the buckets. "Do you think this is a good one?"

I tuned in from my Mother the Dragon. "It's all right. Last time I came here, Master Woolly showed me a much more beautiful one. But this one is... good."

Lehrmon burst out laughing, "It didn't take you long to become picky! This substance is good enough to crystallise soft stones of prime quality, Szar, especially the kind of soft stones that are used to communicate through darkness visible."

Vastness, of a kind the giants will never comprehend.

My Dragon was pulled to one of the buckets. "What about this one?"

"Careful!" Lehrmon warned. "This one must not be opened. The substance is not mature yet." He went on to explain that the noble jelly was made, simply, from a mixture of earth and water.

"Is that all?" I marvelled, "How can dirt be turned into such an admirable substance?"

"It's all in the cooking!" He showed me how the buckets were permeated by special fields that slowly transformed the mud into the pure, translucent jelly. This could take from a few weeks to a few years, depending on the strength of the field, and on how pure the substance needed to be. Working with Woolly, he and Gervin had designed powerful methods to speed up the cooking.

But I couldn't see how the power that cooked the substance was actually derived from the fields. "Do you use rituals, as in the windmills of the Law?" I asked.

"No we don't, we use stones!" Lehrmon clicked his fingers. "That's the magic of soft stones – they can draw power from the fields, just like the windmills of the Law, but without rituals."

"So the stones come from the white jelly. And the white jelly comes from the power of the fields, as captured through the stones," I twinged my beard. "But then, where did the first stone come from?"

"This," Lehrmon winked at me, "you should ask your Nephilim friends."

"So... it is true that the Nephilim invented soft stones?" I asked.

"The art of making stones probably came from the Watchers. No one knows who was the first man to produce one. But the Nephilim were the first to use them on a large scale."

Stand up, rise, conquer! Deafened by your music of hell, overwhelmed by the fixture of infinity, the giants will fall on their knees. And die!

I walked back to the bucket he had opened. "Once the white jelly has been produced, how do you crystallise a soft stone out of it?"

Lehrmon was gazing at me in a strange way, pulling his beard. After a moment he answered, "We apply a particular field to it."

"What would we do without the fields?" I grinned.

From a jar that stood on the shelves, Lehrmon grabbed two soft stones and threw them into the bucket. "That's a way of speeding up the crystallisation: let the stones have babies! But it works only with top-quality stones. Stones of a lower standard are sterile, and if you leave them in the jelly too long they often dissolve." He went on to explain that stones sometimes behaved as if they had a mind of their own. When placed in top-quality white slime, a perfect stone could dissolve itself for a night, and then reconstitute itself, for no apparent reason.

I found it fascinating that soft stones could be used to draw power from the fields. "Does this mean the stones can be used for all the things that are normally achieved through the windmills of the Law?" I felt compelled to ask.

"Windmill Keepers would answer 'Never!' Field Wizards, on the other hand, think that stones can tap far more power from the fields than rituals do." Lehrmon deliberated, "I am still waiting to see a stone that can unleash the power of Thunder, though."

I pulled Lilu's jar out of my gown and opened the lid. "What do you think of this white glow in the space around Lilu?"

Lehrmon beamed, "She hasn't lost any more weight! Follow me, brother! I know someone who is going to be ecstatically happy. Watch your feet for the bottles."

He took me to another cellar, where Woolly was working intently.

Without taking his eyes off one of the buckets, he welcomed me, "Praise the Lord, Szar! How's Lilu?"

"Have a look at this, Woolly," Lehrmon interposed.

Woolly dragged his eyes away from the bucket to look at Lilu. "She's alive, the beauty!" He turned towards me, beaming with affection. "How did you do that, *man of the Law*?"

"I didn't do anything!" I said.

"Lilu was losing her substance fast. By now she should be only half what she was. You *must* have done something!"

"Could it be the White Eagle's Light that descended into her?" I asked.

"A glow like this doesn't blast the breasts off the Goddess," Woolly countered.

Perplexed, I turned to Lehrmon.

"Woolly means there is nothing particularly surprising here. With stones of Lilu's standard, we have often seen glows like this."

"Leave her with me, I'll try to find out what happened," Woolly said.

"You mean..." a deep wave of sadness swept through me, "you are keeping Lilu?"

Woolly smiled compassionately. "It's so easy to become attached to these little things, isn't it? It always breaks my heart when one of them glides out of my hands."

"By the way, Woolly," Lehrmon said, "have you seen what is happening in the grey crypt?"

"I know, I know," Woolly furrowed his forehead. "My babies are all getting sick. Maybe we should show them to Szar and his Dragon of the Depths."

I followed him and Lehrmon to another room.

Woolly placed a jar in my hands. "This one can't be opened. She's as sick as a coughing filosterops," he said. "Lately, *man of the Law*... the Goddess has been pissing on us! You have no idea."

Reading my confusion, Lehrmon translated, "During the last weeks we have been particularly unlucky. A number of our preparations have been going wrong for no reason."

"No reason my ass!" Woolly flung, contemplating one of the bottles.

Curious, I turned to Lehrmon again.

"We strongly suspect our troubles are due to a particular kind of elemental slime which is overflowing from the fields at the moment," he said. "It's unlawfully new. We've never seen anything like it before."

Woolly looked at me with disgust plastered over his face. "These damn windmills of the Law are turning my chapel into the temple toilets." Crimping his nose, he made an ugly noise evocative of sewage.

My eyes opened wide.

"We know exactly which rituals are responsible for the elemental slime," Lehrmon elaborated, "but there is nothing we can do to stop the Windmill Keepers performing them."

"The windmills of the Law must go on!" Woolly sneered sarcastically. "No one is ready to change a thing when it comes to their precious little rituals. They all think the Unborn God would blast the Underworld out of their ass if they didn't touch up the fields just as their fathers did."

The idea of this divine intervention left me thoughtful.

Lehrmon suggested I take a stroll through the chapel and give an opinion as to whether anything could be done to protect it from the fields' elemental fallout. Woolly approved. He grabbed the jar from my hand and placed it back on the shelves. "Watch the bottles on the floor!" he cautioned sharply as he walked out.

Left on my own, I started wandering through the Field Wizards' domain, tuning into elemental forces while standing on my Mother the Dragon. It didn't take me long to perceive the grey vibrations that were creating havoc among the stones – a nasty, dirty, headachy wave on the edge of darkness visible. I could temporarily neutralise it in some places by resting deep on the Dragon. But as soon as I walked into another room, the elemental slime reappeared. After a long while spent fighting this hopeless battle, I decided I needed to gain a wider perspective and walked out, heading for the roofs.

9.27 Namron's wild night

The alley outside the chapel of the Field Wizards was always quite busy: children playing, sacred cows wandering, temple visitors enjoying the special atmosphere of Maniya, which was reputed to be the most lively enclave in the temple. Not wanting to *shock anyone's Law*, I walked to the right and turned into a small lane. There I met a procession of Wise Witches of the Law, clad in their long black gowns, their faces hidden under their hoods as always. I waited for them to pass, reminiscing about the near-fatal mushrooms once delivered by mistake to the chapel of the Salmon Robe instead of theirs, which had left Artold and I hallucinating in darkness visible (and more or less sphincter-less in the kingdom) for a week. "Lawful days!" I thought without the faintest touch of nostalgia, and I climbed onto the roof.

"Praise the Lord Melchisedek, Szar of the Brown Robe, my friend in the Law!" Namron jovially welcomed me. He happened to be sitting on the edge of the roof of Baltham's chapel, which bordered the Field Wizards' chapel on the left.

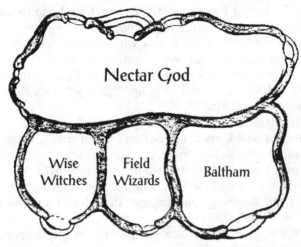

I went to sit with him, letting my legs hang in the air like he did, gently throwing one foot after the other to swing in front of me. "Nice roof!" I commented.

"The order of Baltham has one of the most magnificent chapels in the whole temple. The cellars... they're especially gorgeous," the small man raved. "Have you ever visited them?"

"No," I looked down, contemplating his calloused bare feet. "Do you never wear shoes, Namron?"

"Ne-ver!" he replied forcefully, "Never, never, never again!" and he ejected a thick spat of black root in front of him, watching its trajectory down to the alley.

"Sounds like there is a story behind this!" I smiled, admiring the precision with which he had avoided the Wise Witches.

"Yes, there is," his face closed off, "and you don't want to know it!"

I kept silent, swinging foot after foot in the air.

"Or do you?" he turned towards me, his sharp black eyes unlawfully staring at me.

Understanding that our potential friendship had come to a critical turning point, I stroked my beard with utmost seriousness. "Yes, I think I do," I nodded solemnly.

"Have some black root!" he pulled some of the smelly earthworm-looking stuff out of his pocket and handed it to me.

"Hum... thank you!" I *had* to accept.

As soon as it was in my mouth, I bitterly regretted it. It fitted exactly the picture of Nephilim food I had been given before Felicia crossed my path: "You think it's excrement," Floster, Son of the Dragon, had described, "but once it's in your mouth you pray it *were* excrement, because it's far, far worse than excrement."

"Look at me, *my friend in the Law*," Namron said in his gravest voice, "how old do you think I am?"

"Oh... fifty," I took a guess, wondering how long I had to keep this filth in my mouth before I could spit it out without offending him.

"Exactly, my boy! And I'll tell you why: *I have*, actually, *known* only *forty-one springs and forty autumns,* but once, when I was twenty-four years of age, I grew ten years older in one night. That's when I lost all my hair," he caressed his well-polished scalp. "Have you ever been to the Valley of the Necromancer, Szar?"

In the Valley of the Necromancer, the final battle.

"Hunh hunh!" I shook my head. Before I could speak, I would have had to swallow, and there was no way.

"See, my boy, I was born in the temple, but after that I became a soldier in the army of the prince of Eisraim. I'm like you, a man of several castes," Namron burst out laughing, slapping my shoulder in an amicably violent way.

Gripping the edge of the terrace and pulling on the Dragon, I managed not to fall off the edge into the alley.

"Once my battalion was manoeuvring in the forests of Nadavan, and I was sent on a reconnaissance tour with one of my friends. Pleurk, son of Pleurk, his name was. He was the chief ranger. It was night, and we got lost. Badly lost. The prince of Eisraim's army is not extremely well trained." At last, he spat.

I immediately seized the opportunity to expel the foul content from my mouth, unfortunately decorating my gown in the process.

"Oh, shit!" Namron slapped his thigh, "you spat on the second high priest of Baltham!"

I looked down, horrified.

"Ah, don't worry," Namron said, "it fell into his hood, he didn't notice anything. Now then, where was I? Ah, yes. After walking in the dark for six hours, Pleurk and I had landed in the Valley of the Necromancer unknowingly. Oh, gods! Oh, gods!" he offered me some more black root.

"No thanks!"

"A fierce howling wind starts whipping through us. I ask my comrade, 'Pleurk, can't you feel something weird around us?' Now then, Pleurk, who is by nature the most peaceful and lawfully decent man, turns towards me, and... I swear, I swear on the Great Goddess I see red shining eyes instead of his eyes. He doesn't answer me, he opens his mouth, shows his teeth, and starts growling like a ferocious animal. 'Pleurk! But Pleurk!' I say, quite distressed."

As Namron was painting the picture, I was tickled by a strange feeling in my Point.

"Now then, Pleurk, son of Pleurk, rushes onto me without warning, and starts kicking me, punching and biting," Namron sadly uncovered his left forearm to reveal a lace of scars.

"Gervin..." I thought, recognising a signal in the tickle, "Gervin is calling me! Through the Point!"

"Now then, Pleurk has turned into a savage beast and he and I are beating the Underworld out of each other, until I finally manage to kick his balls and knock him unconscious. But then he falls into a ditch with an ugly marsh at the bottom, which goes 'bubble, bubble, bubble...' So I run over to rescue him, but now then, do you know what happened? I couldn't believe my eyes!"

"I'm sorry, Namron, I *must* go! I think my teacher is calling me!"

"What?" Namron came out of the Valley of the Necromancer abruptly, his forehead creased with anxiety, his face overshadowed as if by an unlawful eklipson of both sun and moon at the same ominous time.

"I have to go! I think my teacher is calling me urgently!" I stood up.

"I see," disgruntled, Namron forced a tone of understanding in his voice. "You know, you're not the first one to be put off by my story."

"But I really want to hear the end, Namron!" I started running full speed. "No, it's true, I do!"

9.28 The Fields of Peace and the Archive

It took me less than a minute to reach Gervin's apartment. I didn't even have to knock – the Thunderbolt Bearer was waiting for me at the door of the aquamarine chamber.

"*Praise the Lord Melchisedek, Szar,*" his smile of satisfaction lit my heart, "well done!"

I returned the lawful greeting and inquired, "Did you really call me?" I still had doubts as to what I had been feeling.

"Of course I called you!" Gervin invited me to come in. "Fix the flavour of that Point-signal in your memory! We'll use it again."

"Is something major happening?" I asked.

"Of course! Always. But nothing to do with the signal. It was only a test."

I wondered how many such tests I had failed before. "Can I have some water, please?"

Gervin took a jug and poured some water into a cup.

"*Lawfully excuse me, please!*" I took both the cup and the jug, went to corner of the room and rinsed my mouth with a series of loud gargles, spitting the water out into a basin. It only partly alleviated the disgusting taste in my mouth.

Gervin watched from the corner of his eye, asking no questions.

"I tried Namron's black root," I answered between two cups of water, hurriedly trying to wash the infamous black stain off my gown.

When I came back to him, he made me sit in silent concentration for a few minutes, boosting the clarity of my fountain with his thunderous light as he often did before important discussions. Then he grabbed a *pear of the Law* from the basket by his side. "See this wonderful fruit," he began. "It is soft, juicy, teeming with nature's generous sweetness. But what will it look like in a month? Time will make it break down and rot. In this world, the same applies to all living things: they are bound to decay."

Gervin fixed his eyes on me with a question, "Why do you think this is?"

I quoted verses of the Law that described the fall of nature,

"Then the Angels withdrew Life from life.
The altar was thrown down,
The blazing star eclipsed,
And death began, and sickness spread,
And nature fell and became but the shadow of her past glory,
And life became the realm of death."

"Right and righteous!" Gervin threw the pear in the air with one hand, caught it in the other, and threw it in the air again, towards me. It fell into my right hand, as if guided by the gods. We smiled at each other, remembering the past.

"The fall happened very long ago," he went on, "long before the creation of the kingdom of Atlantis. Something in nature became corrupt. From then on, the elements turned chaotic: fruits started rotting, juicy things drying up, plants, animals and people growing old and finally dying."

"But I thought the problems with elemental forces were due to the fact that the warp of energy fields has become corrupt," I said, contemplating the fruit.

He shook his head, "The root of all problems is the fall. For thousands of years the fields have partly counterbalanced the fall of nature. Of course, people in the kingdom grow old, and at times they can be sick. But this is nothing compared to the horrendous mess we would be in if nature was left to follow her normal course, without the influence of the fields. Thanks to the action of the fields, nature has retained a certain degree of connection with the higher spheres of the Spirit. The result is that the chaos principle which has been inherent in nature since it fell is partly counteracted, and so we enjoy some of nature's past glories: regular cycles of seasons, rains in plenty without floods, bounteous crops, few or no pests, and so many other things people take for granted in the kingdom.

Now that the fields are collapsing, we are discovering the grim face of fallen nature: droughts and floods, pests and diseases, and countless afflictions. These are all consequences of the chaos principle: something rotten in the elementals which constitute the life-sheath of all living things."

Gervin took another pear from the basket and bit into it. "If it was not for this chaos principle, we wouldn't even have to eat! Our physical bodies would maintain their integrity with minimum energy. In the Fields of Peace, one doesn't have to eat food as we do on Earth – one feeds on the Word of the Lord."

"And what about the gods – do they eat?"

"Not material foods like human beings. Much tastier." Gervin teased me with one of his enigmatic smiles, "There are so many delights in the worlds of the gods, Szar."

I frowned, racking my fountain for understanding, "Master Gervin, you are trying to tell me something at the moment."

"Am I?" Gervin was relishing his pear. "Mm... perhaps I am, after all."

I breathed in the warm heart quality that submerged the room. The *living walls* were holding us in the Spirit of Thunder.

Gervin took another bite of his fruit. "But let us return to the chaos inherent in the kingdom. In the Fields of Peace and in the worlds of the gods, there is no such chaos. And this is why the denizens of these spheres do not have to eat as we do."

An orichalc illumination of infinite expanses.

My digestive system still in shock from the black root, I surveyed my pear but didn't eat.

"The Fields of Peace are another world," Gervin went on, "a world of wonders, devoid of the chaos principle. The spheres of Highness too are free of any mess, but with one fundamental difference: the spheres of Highness are devoid of any materiality, they are pure Spirit; whereas the Fields of Peace are 'material'. This is what is so magical about the Fields of Peace: they have materiality, and yet they are not 'messy' like the kingdom. In the kingdom, material things are aggregates of elementals – those elementals which are penetrated by chaos, and always end up decaying. In the Fields of Peace, things are made of one single element, free from chaos, and therefore free from decay. The materiality of the Fields of Peace is clean."

"How are the Fields of Peace placed in the cosmological ladder? Are they above the kingdom, or below it?"

"Same level. If the kingdom regains its integrity, that is, if the messy chaos disappears from it, then the kingdom and the Fields of Peace will become one," Gervin said emphatically.

"So the Fields of Peace are the future of our world?"

"*Right and righteous!* Our world aspires to the perfection of the Fields of Peace, which is why the Fields of Peace are also called the World to Come."

"The World to Come..." I was perplexed, "so the Fields of Peace do not yet exist?"

"Oh, yes they do!" Gervin smiled. "Unlike our kingdom, which is based on death, the Fields of Peace are the very embodiment of immortality. Being eternal, they have always existed. *That which is eternal has neither beginning nor end.*"

"You told me this once," I remembered, "when I leapt from the Underworlds into a sphere of Highness. At the time, it seemed obvious. Everything seems so simple when one is in the spheres of Highness!"

"Simplicity is one of the hallmarks of Highness," Gervin demonstrated his point with the luminous smile of a great initiate.

"And would it be fair to say that complications are the hallmark of life in the kingdom?"

"Quite right!" Gervin laughed. "In the kingdom, dark forces have thrived on the principle of messy chaos, taking advantage of it to establish a grip on human beings. A keynote of the human condition," Gervin threw his pear core into a garbage bin, "is the fact that consciousness rests on the physical body, made of the messy elements. As a result the human mind is heavily influenced by the chaos principle. And the more the warp of energy fields degenerates, the worse it becomes. After the final collapse of the warp, the situation will be horrendous."

The consequences were grim. "So the presence of dark forces in the material world will increase in the future?" I asked.

"Very much so. Dark forces will do all they can to oppose the transition from this world into the Fields of Peace. For, in the World to Come, there will be no chaos, and no dark forces. The hierarchies of dark angels will have lost their grip on human beings. But they won't let this happen without bloodshed. They will wage wars such as can hardly be imagined, creating as much havoc on Earth as they can. The final confrontation will not happen before thousands of years have passed – long after the end of Atlantis. But before that final war, there will be countless interventions of dark forces aimed at delaying, or even stopping humanity's transition into the Fields of Peace."

"Could the dark forces succeed?"

"Of course they could!" Gervin woke me up with a forceful tone of voice. "None of the battles against them will be won easily, and final victory will be achieved only if human beings stand high in the Light. If they do not, then the dark forces will succeed."

I looked down to my left palm, slowly clenching and unclenching my fist.

"If you want to follow me, Szar of the Brown Robe, you will have to fight several of these battles with me," Gervin announced unambiguously.

Resting on the Dragon of the Deep, I looked into his eyes and nodded silently.

"We have come a long way since the time when Szar-ka was amazed at the idea he could ever help his teacher," Gervin held my gaze. After a moment, a face appeared superimposed on top of his – a man, perhaps in his forties, with a wide, square face. He had fierce, piercing black eyes, tanned skin, short curly black hair and a beard, and he brought with him a special golden light made of myriads of conglomerated shining specks.

"Barkhan Seer is coming to greet you!" Gervin elucidated.

I tuned into the thunderous presence, paying my respects.

After a while the man's face faded, but his presence stayed vibrant in the small room. "Barkhan Seer, prince of Thunder, powerful among the powerful!" Gervin commented with reverence. "He hasn't incarnated in the kingdom for hundreds of years. His dwelling used to be in the spheres of Highness. Now he is part of the assembly of Masters of Thunder who have gathered in the Fields of Peace to complete the temple in which the Archive will be received. Barkhan Seer, as you may have heard, is a great friend of..."

Three knocks resounded.

"Teyani!" A jocular smile lit Gervin's face, adding to the magic that had taken over the room and made the coincidence look perfectly natural – planned by the Creator at the beginning of time. "She always does that to me!" he affectionately thanked the Creator, and went to welcome the wise woman.

The grand master of the White Eagle entered, surrounded by wisps of the same golden light I had just seen around Barkhan Seer. After duly lawful greetings I offered to take leave, but Gervin sat me down with a gesture of his hand. "I was about to tell this young man about the wonders of the Archive," he told her.

Lady Teyani pushed her lips forward and nodded in confident approval, just like Elyani did when she felt fully in control of a situation. She sat beside me on the warm plass floor, visibly at home in Barkhan Seer's golden charm. "We're listening!" she said.

What was this 'something' with a joyful tipsy touch, which had turned Gervin's visitors' lounge into another world? Everything had more pep, more spark, more depth, and even though the walls hadn't moved – or had they? – the place looked much larger. If it hadn't been for the ghastly taste of the black root that still infested my mouth, I would have doubted whether I was still in my body.

"The Fields of Peace..." Gervin began, his voice strangely alive and vibrant with out-of-the-Underworld harmonies, "the Fields of Peace are the dwelling place of many great sages devoted to the evolution of the Earth. It is from there that they can 'pull' humanity towards its future. They pour forces into the kingdom and help human beings reach the consciousness that will lead them to the World to Come. The Archive shares the same goals..."

Gervin and I watched Teyani with interest. She had poured water into a cup which she was holding in her hands, her eyes closed, her clear fountain sparkling with blue, pink and strange colours. She opened her eyes, established eye contact with Gervin, and handed me the cup. "Drink this!" she said with her natural grand-master's authority.

I drank. It was lawfully magic! The water instantly washed away the taste of the black root, leaving me fresh and frolicking like a newborn filosterops.

"The Archive is the platform from which our tradition will give, pouring Spirit into the people on Earth, inspiring them to hasten to the Fields of Peace, giving them the strength to stand up against dark forces." Straight like pillars of heaven, Gervin and Teyani rested on each other's gaze, holding Barkhan Seer's mighty presence. "The plan originated when it became clear to the Masters of Thunder that nothing could save the warp of fields – and therefore the kingdom – and that times of abysmal chaos were bound to follow."

I closed my eyes, letting myself be transported by Barkhan Seer's light.

"How are you to become a Master of Thunder, Szar?" the voice became profound, a stream of melliferous goldenness. "You are receiving the flame, the spirit and the powers of our lineage from Gervin, just as Gervin received them from Orest, his teacher. Orest planted a seed in him that blossomed into a huge tree, and now Gervin is planting a seed of his Thunder-tree in you. Thus for thousands of years, an uninterrupted line of masters have passed on the tradition of Thunder from one to the other.

The same is true of all orders: traditions of initiation rest on forces and seeds that are passed from teacher to disciple. If for some reason the line happens to be broken, then the lineage is lost and the tradition becomes dormant. Restarting it is not completely impossible, but it requires an infinitely greater effort."

There followed a shattering vision, the entire kingdom laid in front of my third eye. A ferocious storm was raging, and in a Point-way that words could never describe I saw all the lineages of initiation being broken.

"The grim reality," the voice continued, "is that not one of these lineages will survive. In the dark clouds that are about to engulf Atlantis, the very foundation of the Law will be destroyed, and *all* traditions with it. Crumbs of knowledge will be left here and there, but the seeds of initiation will be lost. The ensuing darkness will be abysmal."

The storm had ended, but the sky was still black. "The Archive," the voice proceeded, "is our gift to the future. In the Fields of Peace, we will capture the vast knowledge which for thousands of years has been kept and cultivated in the temples of Eisraim and Lasseera. But not just knowledge – lineage seeds. The spirit of all the traditional orders which have flourished in our temples will be kept in the Archive."

A distressed voice called through darkness visible, "Master Gervin! Master Gervin! The high priest of Barradine is trying to contact you."

Gervin ignored the voice channel, and the vision kept unfolding. "One day in the distant future, when this kingdom has passed, the people of the kingdom of the rainbows will be thirsty for the light of higher worlds. The Archive is our gift to them. For them, we will keep the spirit alive. From our flame, their torches will be lit. Those who strive for the Divine, and who are ready to fight battles on their way to the World to Come, will..."

"Master Gervin! Master Gervin?" the voice channel interrupted him. "Master Gervin, please, answer us, it is *unlawfully urgent*! We need your wisdom and... *Oh my Lord Melchisedek,* is he really in Mouridji's bedroom? Oh, gods! Oh, gods!"

"Master Gervin, I implore your help!" another voice made itself heard through darkness visible.

"Poldoros, High Priest of Barradine," Gervin finally answered, "what is your unlawful problem?"

"Master Gervin!" Poldoros was in a panic, "Aphrodoros has turned mad! He has ransacked our chapel, and now he is wreaking havoc in the female wing. He's gone insane. No Voice projection can stop him!"

"Can't Namron take care of this?"

"Aphrodoros has wounded one of his men. Namron says he'll have to use soft-stone weapons against him. But that might kill him! Please, wise man in the Law, we need your puissant Voice!"

"All right, all right! I'm sending Szar of the Brown Robe. You can lawfully trust he will be able to contain Aphrodoros without killing him."

"Oh, thank you, Master Gervin! Thank you! But please tell him to hurry! I hate to imagine what is happening in Mouridji's bedroom right now!"

Gervin clicked his fingers, pulling me out of the golden clouds in which my consciousness was spread like a whisk of salt in the ocean.

"Run, Dragon!"

9.29 The power of seeds

"Nice dress!" I complimented her, first thing.

When she saw me arriving from the hallway instead of the roof, Elyani's face lit up. "My Great Warrior has conquered the women's corridors!" she threw herself in my arms. "Tell me, tell me, how did you conquer Aphrodoros?"

"I used the cheap-way-outs," I kissed her neck on each of the deadly gateways. "So you already know about Aphrodoros!"

"Trust Mouridji – the whole temple knows. And Lasseera too!"

"Poor Mouridji, you should have seen her apartment..." I endeavoured to describe the scene of utter devastation: the sea of jams, conserves, herbal preparations, broken plass and utensils strewn over the floor, her ripped gowns soaking up the mess, never mind the dents in the walls. "It's a miracle she didn't get hurt."

"But why did Aphrodoros do that?"

Light multidimensional. Colours unthinkable. Unfathomable depth.

"From what the priests of Barradine told me, Aphrodoros was after herbs of madness, which he is normally given every day (as part of the ritual to Barradine), but which have been near-impossible to find lately because the fields are sulking. You know how Mouridji uses these herbs in her jams. Well, Aphrodoros smelt the precious herbs from a distance and demolished her bedroom door to get at them. But in his clumsiness he knocked down the huge cupboard where Mouridji keeps her supplies. The cupboard fell face down, he was unable to move it. That made him so furious he started breaking everything. I still find it difficult to imagine how Mouridji managed to eject him from her room and yet escape unscathed."

"Aphrodoros would never have hurt her! She's known him since he was little," Elyani said confidently. She hadn't seen the casualties in the alleys! After Mouridji expelled him from her bedroom, in his mad run from there to the central kitchen, Aphrodoros threw to the ground all those in his way.

"Luciana of the Green Robe saw what happened," Elyani reported. "When Mouridji arrived and found Aphrodoros in her bedroom with all the mess, she got even more furious than he was. She screamed the Voice at him and chased him all the way down the corridors."

"Namron's men weren't as Voice-authoritative as her. Two of them were knocked out when they tried to stop him. But I wish the priests of Barradine could have warned me who this Aphrodoros was."

"Do you mean you had never met Aphrodoros?" Elyani chuckled.

"No." It was only when I arrived at the central kitchen, forcing my way through the hundred or more priests and priestesses of the Cooking Castes who were waiting outside in shock after a frantic evacuation, that I discovered the barely credible truth, amidst hundreds of broken pots, ripped bags of grain – Aphrodoros, expectably, went after the grocery stock, in search of herbs – toppled barrels of apples, fruits rolling all over the ground: Aphrodoros, so dear to the chapel of Barradine, was not a priest.

Aphrodoros was an ass.

"Didn't you know?" Namron asked as he and I watched the delirious animal gallop down the long, long plass table of the now-deserted central kitchen, destroying hundreds of meticulously-prepared dinners, braying like an entire cavern of sickness all by himself.

"I had no idea!" I answered, dumbfounded.

Yet, on reflection, it explained many things, such as the oddly-shaped dents in Mouridji's bedroom walls (which when I arrived on the scene had me quite perplexed) or why her unlocked door had been torn to pieces.

"But how did you find the 'cheap-way-out' gateways on an ass?" Elyani asked with a mixture of curiosity and unbounded admiration.

"I don't know!" *No thoughts,* I just ran against the beast and *let the Dragon do.*

"Mouridji said she was outside and she heard you scream even louder than Aphrodoros. She was impressed *beyond the Law!*"

"Just normal Dragon screams. Anyhow, we just avoided a disaster," I thanked the gods. "Before destroying Mouridji's bedroom, Aphrodoros ransacked the chapel of the Wise Witches (who also use herbs of madness). Can you imagine? It's the chapel adjacent to the Field Wizards. What if Aphrodoros had taken the wrong door and destroyed all our precious bottles?"

"No one was badly hurt," Elyani closed the topic. "It will give everyone a chance to talk about something else than the ascending goddess."

"How is she?"

"It's appalling," Elyani shook her head. "She's becoming sicker and sicker, spitting blood, coughing like an agonising filosterops. She has lost half her teeth, and she is only twenty-four! Every single order in the temple has been invoking their gods and angels in the hope of some intervention. If she were to die before the great ritual of ascension, it would be seen as a sign that the gods have abandoned us, and that the glorious days of Eisraim are coming to an end. Some of our wisest people are even starting to suggest that we should depart from the Ancient Rule and hasten the ritual, even if Holma is not fully ready according to lawful prescriptions. But the Immaculate are just as immovable on this as on anything else."

The Immaculate priestesses, I learned, were a lofty caste who wore shoes with thick soles to isolate themselves from earthly things. They did not belong to the temple of Eisraim, nor to any other temple. Apart from the king of Atlantis, their allegiance was to their order alone. The two Immaculate priestesses in charge of Holma had been sent to Eisraim six months before the oracle had announced a new ascending goddess was to be received by the gods. "They do not care about our temple. The only thing they care about is their precious rule," Elyani said in disgust.

Three white roses.

I took her hand. "Have you asked the Eagle if he wishes us to do something for Holma?"

"My love... at the Eagle's oracle, I have seen strange omens which I don't understand. It makes me afraid of asking too much."

"Omens of the troubled times ahead, perhaps. The kingdom's future isn't bright."

"Not just the future! Have you heard of the drought that is hitting the county of the Western Plains?"

Drought was one of those words I had heard a few times without knowing what it meant.

"Why should you know what a drought is?" Elyani commiserated. "There hasn't been one in the county of Eisraim for hundreds of years! A drought is when the rains stop falling for such a long time that the land becomes arid. The trees and the animals die, the land cannot yield crops."

I was shocked. "But I thought that rituals to call rainfalls were among the most elementary of all practices?" In my training in the Salmon Robe I had been told that any apprentice village priest could do that.

"Everything is simple as long as one can tap power from the fields. But when the fields stop working..." Elyani explained how hundreds of priests from several counties had gathered in the Western Plains' main temple, where they were conducting a huge ritual aimed at restoring the windmills of the Law. It probably wouldn't take them long to succeed but still, the people were terrified. They had never seen anything like it.

I worried for the security of Eisraim. "Could the county of the Western Plains run out of food?"

"No, not really. Their reserves could allow them to last for at least a year. With the kinds of powers they are calling on, I can't see that it will take them that long to bring the rains back. But the most worrying thing is that there are similar stories coming from all corners of the kingdom. Even in Eisraim, it has been reported that the crops of blue corn are being decimated by a small black insect."

Sweet Lord Melchisedek! The blue corn *the gods brought down for men long before the creation of the kingdom, as a token of their love.* "How can the gods themselves be under attack?"

"According to Gervin's predictions, it won't be long before the blue corn of the gods has entirely vanished from the kingdom," she said.

"Stop!" I shouted. "I don't want to hear any more bad news today." I grasped Elyani by the waist, lifted her up and started spinning. "This morning," I said, "Gervin was playing one of his tricks on me. He was hammering into me something about the delights of the world of the gods. I had no idea what he meant."

"The delights of the worlds of the gods?" Elyani said.

I nodded.

She let out a yearning sigh, "There are so many of them!"

I let myself collapse on the lawn, pulling her down with me. "But these were Gervin's very words!"

The gods are wise.

"Gervin spoke the truth," Elyani took on her voice of a great doctor of the Law and knelt by my side. "Once, Teyani told me that in the worlds of the gods one can make love to someone just by looking into their eyes."

"Oh really?" my eyes opened wide.

"So says the Law," she whispered, holding my gaze.

My breath stopped. So did the disintegration of the warp of fields, the falling apart of the kingdom, the wheel of the Law, the course of time, and all the rest.

The flight of the Eagle, piercing through the Golden Shield.

Perhaps.

When it all resumed and we found ourselves back in the dying kingdom, our united gazes were ablaze with ancient charms, so weird and unlike anything the Law could remember that they were soon dispelled by the noise of still air, leaving nothing more than a hypothetical hush unsure itself of whether it had really happened.

"We should do more of this," Elyani said, the memory of the hush still fluttering through her voice.

The heartbeat of a distant sun. The gold of a thousand mornings.

"Mm..." I pulled myself back, just remembering there was a Dragon.

When some lawful sanity had returned to the courtyard, Elyani announced that the priestesses of the Dawn of Creation were about to give a

Voice performance in the music hall. Gervin had asked her to prepare me for this special event.

"I know!" I swiftly Point-pre-empted the preparation, "You are going to tell me that due to the deterioration of the fields the priestesses of Dawn will soon have departed from the kingdom and so this is one of the last times we will have the privilege of hearing them before their precious vibrations completely disappear from the Earth."

"No, not one of the last times," Elyani said. "*The* last time."

That created a bad pinch in my heart.

To cheer me up, Elyani lay down on the grass beside me and engaged in one of the *lawfully passionate* philosophical discussions we both enjoyed so much. "One day," she began, "my Great Warrior was just a little seed in his Mother's womb. Remember the verses of the Law: *the seed is fragile and small, yet it will grow into a huge tree. There will be nothing in the tree not already contained in the seed.* There is nothing in Szar that was not already contained in the seed that his Mother carried." Elyani put on a playful smile. "Now, Great Warrior, would you agree that you have become so much more powerful than the Szar-ka I first met?"

I suspected a trick but decided to offer no resistance. "Of course!" I clicked my fingers, "So much more powerful!"

"There lies the mystery!" she exclaimed hierophantically. "Since all the power which is in you now was already in the seed, then the seed was much more powerful than Szar-ka. There were great forces in the seed, of which Szar-ka was completely unaware."

"True!"

"Now, suppose that one day you become a great expert in the magic of the Flying Dragons."

I pulled a face, "No."

"Suppose!" she insisted, twinging my beard. "You would then become much more powerful than you are now. And yet, whatever you could become was already contained in the seed."

"Which means that the little seed was much more powerful than I am now!"

The blinding line. Inexhaustible silence of emerald clusters of worlds.

Elyani rolled on her side and artistically propped her head on her hand. Enthused by the archetypal beauty of her topic, she didn't even notice that her feet were resting on the gate. "Now think of the entire creation," she went on. "There is not one single power in the creation that was not contained in the creation's seed."

"Not to talk of the myriads of powers that have not yet blossomed, but that are still contained in the seed!" I followed her river.

She chanted a verse, "*The source is where all powers lie.* The source of the creation, this is what the priestesses of Dawn are linked to! I think we are running late," she added, "but lawfully late – nothing to worry about."

New horizons were opening to me. "Elyani, this knowledge is deep! These hymns of the Dawn of Creation must be incredible." I remained thoughtful, trying to imagine what a hymn charged with so much power could be like. The Point pulled me out of dreamtime, "Wait a minute. If *the source is where all powers lie...* then, suppose I wanted to become fully awakened and gain enough strength to be capable of helping Master Gervin..."

"Suppose!" Elyani echoed.

"I could never find any better way than connecting with my source, the little seed out of which I came!"

"Correct, *man of the Law*! The source contains all that you will ever become."

"Would it be possible to find it?"

With a soft voice, she said, "I saw that little seed. I saw how the Mother of the Light gave birth to your Spirit. It was beautiful."

"The birth of my Spirit!" I sat up, amazed. "How could you see that?"

"The Eagle's sight is profound."

"Did the Mother of the Light give birth to me a long time ago? Tell me, how old am I, exactly?"

"Things like this happen outside of time, Szar-ka! Otherwise your Spirit would have had a beginning in time, and therefore it would also have an end, necessarily."

"But of course!" I slapped the side of my head as if all this was obvious.

Zigzagging harmonies in remoteness. Infinity, his natural home.

"These priestesses of the Dawn of Creation must be exceptionally powerful women," I reflected, starting to wonder if their hymns could be used as weapons.

"Several times I have heard Gervin and Teyani comment that not one order in the kingdom could ever match the power of the priestesses of Dawn. But they are not powerful in the way one might imagine. They can't even look after themselves. Without attendants to feed them and take care of material things for them, they would let themselves die. This is because they are barely in the kingdom. Their consciousness is somewhere else, very far from us."

"And how come one can never see their face?" I asked her. This puzzling fact made the priestesses of Dawn renowned throughout the kingdom. "Do they not have a face?"

"Of course they have a face! But as soon as you look at it, your consciousness starts resonating with awesomely ancient vibrations. It makes you become blank, you can't discern their features. Just you wait, Szar of the Brown Robe," she gave a mischievous smile, "during their chant, dozens of people will lose consciousness."

I swallowed, remembering the days when I used to embarrass Gervin by fainting each time he took me to a high priestesses' performance.

"Did you know that many of these priestesses are recruited from autistic little girls, or girls considered to be seriously retarded?"

I found this immensely touching.

"An oracle reveals that a child is to be picked up from a certain village," she described. "Then a group of priests undertake a pilgrimage, taking some of the priestesses of Dawn with them. If there happens to be more than one candidate in the village, the priestesses of Dawn immediately know which one is theirs. It is easy for them, for the child's consciousness is already connected to the lofty spaces from where the source of creation can be cognised."

I smiled with awe, "Autistic little girls who are to become more powerful than Great Warriors, Nephilim giants and Masters of Thunder! Now, *that* blasts the breasts out of the Goddess!"

Elyani burst out laughing, "Szar! Where did you learn this expression?"

"Master Woolly. It means I'm amazed."

"Yes, I gathered that," she stood up. She grabbed a white shawl and covered her hair. "Come on, Szar of the Brown Robe, we are *nearly as late as lawful limits permit*! Take my arm and lead me to the music hall." She gave a Dragon-melting smile, "Do you realise this will be our first public appearance?"

"I promise I won't use any of Master Woolly's expressions."

"Do you mean there are more? Tell me, I want to hear all of them!"

9.30 The hymns of the Dawn of Creation

A motley crowd of some two hundred priests and priestesses had gathered in the music hall, situated at the northern end of the enclave of Maniya. In the hall, Elyani insisted I sit with my back against a *living wall*, just in case I felt compelled to pop into the spheres during the performance.

"Don't worry!" I reassured her. "My Mother of the Dragon will take care of my body."

"Remember the Dragon is also called the Mother of the Endless Night," Elyani whispered, but I missed the barely disguised message.

As the White Eagle went to greet one of her friends, a delegation of six high priests of Barradine approached me. Dressed in long ochre robes and almost as long ochre beards, they expressed their most lawfully solemn gratitude for having saved the life of their precious ritual animal and treasured friend. In the end, they told me, they didn't even have to tie him up because by the time he came back to his senses, one of their brothers had returned from Eisraim city with a plentiful supply of herbs of madness, enough for at least ten days. Immediately pacified, Aphrodoros had trotted back to the chapel of Barradine all by himself, followed by a long procession of immensely relieved priests and priestesses of the Cooking Castes.

When asked what the Holy Upperworld they intended to do in ten days' time, the priests of Barradine lawfully expressed their total trust and faith in the Lords of Destiny, for the Law said, *take care of today, and the Lord Melchisedek shall take care of tomorrow.*

While I thoughtfully pulled my beard, making a mental note to warn the Field Wizards and all other friends to keep herbs of madness out of their chapels at any cost, Alcibyadi, who was sitting a few rows ahead and had been watching the scene, burst out laughing so loudly that the high priests of Barradine turned around, perplexed.

That didn't stop Alcibyadi laughing.

Warmed up by the White Eagle's spontaneity, I smiled, establishing eye contact with her. Lehrmon was not sitting by her side.

"Did he say yes?" I wondered.

Suddenly grave, Alcibyadi shook her head slowly.

Kartendranath, waiting for you. Revelation Sky will break loose. Tremble, man of the Law!

The priests of Barradine left, soon to be replaced by friends of Mouridji who were burning to know how I had tamed the beast, "*By the grace of Master Gervin – all glory to him!*" and how had I managed to become stronger than a furious ass, I who used to be so skinny, "*All glory to the teacher!*" and so was I really the person who brayed even louder than Aphrodoros? "*All glory... I mean...*" The questions went on and on.

Mouridji, I discovered, had a lot of friends. Unfortunately for me the lawful waiting dragged on because the music field had collapsed and was being repaired by Shyama, Ushbudh and Ugr, three of the Field Wizards of Master Ferman's chapel. Two hours later I was still being grilled. Lady Teyani compassionately came to sit by Elyani and I. Using a stern charm, she created a repelling halo of peace that kept everyone away, apart from an official envoy who came to deliver a small silk bag which contained a present from Mouridji. (Mouridji was running late for the ceremony, busy reconstituting her bedroom, helped by Namron and his men, who couldn't refuse to help her because she had known Namron since he was little.)

"We have to get rid of this *as soon as lawfully possible!*" I whispered when I opened the bag and discovered a jar of guava marmalade spiced with herbs of madness.

"Eat it!" Teyani said. "No, not now!" she promptly added as I was opening the jar. "Now, you are going to need all the clarity you can pull from your fountain."

Following her wisdom, I prepared myself to bear the brunt of the ritual, plunging into silent concentration.

Three or four hours later, when Ferman's men had finally managed to restore the music field, the room became silent. After this it took hardly an hour before the priestesses of the Dawn of Creation made their entry into the hall, preceded by beautiful fragrances that resembled those of the caverns of the Deep Underworlds.

I counted sixteen of them, small women clad in orange robes, their hair covered with veils. Their frail dark-skinned hands could be seen, but not their faces, shrouded in dark fog. They were surrounded by twice as many attendants, women in white who held their hands and guided them.

I didn't notice any particular presence in the room.

All together, the women intoned their hymn, projecting the Voice into the room – strange Voices, so unfamiliar that I could not even tell whether the pitch was high or low, nor even whether they came from the front or the back of the hall. The hymn unfolded,

"The Mother of the Light spoke.
I am the Great Mother, the compassion in all things,
I know how all things were,
How all things are,
How all things will be.
The world without end
I also see.
Hear from me that which was before me –
The all-encompassing Mystery,
The source of all sources,
The Power behind all powers.
There was neither day nor night,
Neither light nor darkness,
Neither fullness nor emptiness,
Neither death nor immortality.
The pregnant Void where the nothing was to become whole
And the whole was to be fragmented
Rested infinitely beyond spaces,
Birthplace of the Cosmic Fire,
Cradle for all the gods,
Ready beyond eternity for the Great Sacrifice."
My energy gripped by the Voices, the room became dark.
A moonless night.
Everyone disappeared.
Ant Spirit, gigantic.
I couldn't even feel Elyani's presence by my side. I just felt vast, im-mensely vast. Drifting from vastness into limitlessness.
Oh, is this where the Blue Lagoon is? But it's magnificent!
And yet it seems so little. And so does the Ant Spirit.
Where were the hymns? I could no longer hear them.
I started having difficulty feeling myself. "I must rest on the Dragon!
But where was the Dragon? What had happened to the Dragon?"
I couldn't find her.
"Far Underworld! If there is no Dragon left, then really there is nothing left at all!"
Nothing.

No space. No up or down, no right or front, no left or back.

Nothing. There was nothing but infinity. A magnificent night that extended forever.

Before I had time to explore any further, I heard the voice calling, "Great Warrior... mighty Dragon... it's time to wake up!"

Strange, strange... I could hear her voice but I was unable to move. Nothing like this had happened to me since my death in the Dragon.

"Can you feel my hand on your face?" I heard the words. I was nearly sure it was Elyani, but I couldn't feel a thing. And I couldn't even answer her. My lips refused to move.

"I'm going to massage your body gently," she said. "Feel my hands, let them bring you back."

I still couldn't feel anything.

A black panther. Wild. Superb.

"Try to speak to me," she insisted, but I couldn't. She was too far away.

"I am going to project anchoring sounds onto your gateways," she warned, and I felt showered by the loving touch of her Voice.

"Now, feel your body!" she Voice-projected forcefully.

Instantly I found myself in her arms, lying on her lap. "Oh my Lord Melchisedek!" I whispered, "Elyani, I have wet my pants!"

She chuckled.

The panther, in front of me. Virginia, Virginia... how I wish you were here.

"What are your friends going to think when they see me?" I lamented.

She was rocking me in her arms. "Don't worry, baby Dragon, there is no one here."

"The Dragon!" I remembered. "Yes! I can feel the Dragon."

Instantly, the Dragon sat me up and opened my eyes.

It was night. Elyani and I were sitting on the lawn in her courtyard.

"Er..." I was terribly embarrassed. "How long did I sleep?"

"Seven hours, perhaps."

I shivered. "How many people did it take to carry me here?"

"Five."

"Oh, no! I'm sorry I did that to you. Our first public appearance!"

"But not at all!" she was amused. "At least a third of the audience fell unconscious during the performance. Namron had organised for a large team of priests to be waiting outside the music hall with litters. And you were so lovely, sleeping in my arms. It was the first time. Usually you don't sleep much!"

To the Great Night you will return, searching for Alcibyadi.

"Will you excuse me a moment, please." I went to the bedroom to wash myself and change pants.

When I came back, Elyani had laid some food on a cloth on the grass. Not hungry, I watched her eat, recharging myself with a few sniffs of holy breeze from the gate, and wondering why watching her eat always did something to my Dragon. Meanwhile I tried to collect my spirits and bridge the seven-hour blackout, squeezing the fountain for memories – in vain!

"These priestesses of the Dawn of Creation have found the absolute weapon. Irresistible," I shook my head in admiration. "Their Voices could put an entire army out of action. But what kind of power was that? The magic of the Ancient Days of the Earth?"

"No, much more ancient. The source of all sources, the seed of all seeds. It made me feel fantastic. What about you?"

"To tell you the truth... it all went very quickly for me."

"I feel vast," the magic woman dipped her finger into Mouridji's guava jam and licked it. "I could dance the vastness forever," she stood up and waved her arms.

I vroofed myself up and followed her movements. A question which had long been on my mind forced its way through, "After they die, where will the priestesses of the White Eagle go?"

Elyani was whirling slowly from laurel tree to laurel tree. "Teyani will ascend to the spheres of Highness, where the Eagle is waiting for her. Antaria and fifteen other priestesses will take position in the triangle, holding the Archive from the world of the gods. Others will just follow the wheel of reincarnations like everyone else."

"Holding the Archive from the world of the gods?'" I whirled with her. "I thought the Archive was to be kept in the Fields of Peace."

"True!" she kept waving her arms, lightly touching my chest now and again. "But there are several facets to the Archive, my love, one of them anchored in the world of the gods. Gervin and Teyani have trained a team of White Eagles to look after it."

"But what about you? Will you go to the world of the gods?"

Elyani laughed, speeding up her movements.

I followed, but protested, "Hey! I want to know. What if Master Gervin sent me to live in the Fields of Peace while you were in the world of the gods? What would we do?"

She stopped and stood just in front of me. "And what if you decided to go and live with the Flying Dragons?"

"Ha! Ha! Ha! Ha! Ha!"

She closed her eyes, "Voof! Dragon, when you laugh like this it makes my legs feel weak."

I caught her in my arms. "I need to be able to live in more than one place at a time, is that it?"

Her lips nearly touched mine. "But you can!" she whispered. "It's called being a parallel. It is part of the initiation into Thunder."

Why did I always learn Thunder secrets from the White Eagle?

She heard my thought, "It has to do with the fact that Thunder and Eagle get along together so well," she lightly touched the orichalc plate on my neck.

"I know," I sighed, letting the magic of the night take over. "Will you tell me which sphere you will go to after you leave your body?"

"Who knows? So many things could happen, my love. I have seen bizarre omens, which I cannot comprehend," she resumed her dance.

I'll see you at No Limits. To the Point, Brother Knight!

"To the Point, Brother Knight!" she ordered. "Dance with me and make this instant eternal, I want it to go on for ever."

I moved with her, fascinated by the wild spark that lit her eyes. "What's a Brother Knight?"

"It's what I will call you in a long, long time. Another life. Another kingdom."

I opened my eyes wide. "So we'll have another life together?"

"You'll love me so much! You have no idea."

A sea of flames. Philadelphia, I love you.

"Tell me, I want to know everything about that life!"

"No you don't!" she pulled a face at me.

I swallowed.

"I am the Endless Night," she made her voice tipsy and waved her arms, "I have no beginning, I have no end. Will you dance with me, Brother Knight?"

"Till the end of time!"

"But that's not enough!" she protested. "Time will have an end, you know, and much sooner than people think!"

9.31 Mission Archive

"The Archive transfer will be one of the most extraordinary rituals of all times," Gervin began. The *living walls* of the aquamarine chamber echoed his momentous enthusiasm. The lineage of Thunder was with us.

Sitting in front of him, I anchored the fountain in the Dragon, seeking forces to match Gervin.

"The transfer ritual will last less than a day and a night," he went on. "But in that day and that night, that which was gathered in Eisraim and Lasseera over thousands of years will be lifted into the Fields of Peace, and received in the temple of light which the Masters of Thunder have built."

"But why not operate the transfer immediately?" I asked him. "Aren't there dangers involved in waiting?"

"Great dangers!" he agreed. "The problem is, what is to be transferred is not just knowledge. If all we had wanted was to store the lore and records of the orders of our temples, everything would be completed by now. But then our Archive would be nothing more than a dusty museum – not a repository of living forces! We are of the future, Szar, not of the past. What we want to capture are the seeds and powers out of which entire traditions will be reborn.

The transfer will really be a transfer. At the very moment they land in the Archive, those forces will disappear from the kingdom. This will create a huge vacuum down here. If it were to occur too early, it could have disastrous consequences, precipitating the collapse of the warp of fields and the chaos which is bound to ensue."

"So, when?"

"The sign will come from the fields themselves. When the warp reaches a particular station in its path of disintegration, we will know that the time for the transfer has come. By then, the kingdom will be in the throes of considerable chaos.

Now, let me tell you how the transfer is to take place. It will involve two soft stones – special stones, as you can imagine: one from the temple of Eisraim, one from the temple of Lasseera. These two treasures will have to be carried to a desert place, the Plateau of Sorana, on the other side of the mountains of Lasraim. There, the stones will be joined and the ritual will begin. From the Fields of Peace, the assembly of the Masters of Thunder will establish the resonance by which the forces of Eisraim and Lasseera will be lifted up into the Archive."

I was fascinated by the warrior I was discovering in Gervin. He spoke calmly, his determination was total, the power behind his words was measured and awesome. "This is the most daring enterprise our order has ever undertaken," he continued. "*All* the Masters of Thunder who are not in the kingdom at the time will be in the Fields of Peace: Sefaran and the forty generations of Thunder after him, Bharadvaj, Erissin, the envoys of the sons of Apollo, the mighty Barkhan Seer and his seven heart-disciples (Lehrmon among them), Orest my teacher, Melchard, myself, and more than three hundred others who are already in the Fields of Peace or on their way to them from the spheres of Highness. All will join their Voices for the great ritual initiated through the stones which Lehrmon and *you* will carry to the Plateau of Sorana." Destiny, in the form of Gervin's index finger, pointed at me.

I gave a matter-of-fact nod, resting on the Dragon of the Deep as I used to when I received mission instructions from Marek. "Why choose the Plateau of Sorana? Why not join the stones together in one of the temples?"

"When you understand the precise mechanisms of the transfer, it will become clear to you that only a desert place can be suitable. In Eisraim or Lasseera there would be too much interference coming from people's thoughts and ritual activities. The mountain range of Lasraim blocks the vibrations coming from the south and the west. The site for the transfer is located among high plateaus which have never been inhabited and extend over hundreds of lawful miles."

"If so much Thunder is gathered, how could things go wrong?"

"Make no mistake, Szar, a number of things can go wrong!" Gervin was adamant. "For a start, there are great uncertainties as to how the soft stones will behave, knowing the advanced state of disintegration of the fields at that time. This is another reason to choose a desert place: there will be less chance of being flooded with the elemental muck that will have taken over the entire kingdom by then. But there are even greater dangers. The Archive stones will carry an immense power that will be felt from afar by bandits of all kinds. The main players in the kingdom's power games could all turn against us."

Infinite spaces. Periphery of time. He will come.

"Should we then be prepared for the possibility of an attack against our temple?" I asked.

"Not necessarily. The Archive stones won't be charged until the last moment. But as soon as the final process is engaged, enemies from all directions are likely to rush after the stones *like bears scenting honey*," Gervin warned. "The force in these stones will be awesome. Anyone who steals them could master phenomenal powers and gain the status of a king."

"Does this mean the thieves would hold the keys to the Archive?"

"No, the knowledge would remain sealed to them, and so would the connections to gods and angels. But the charge in the stones will be so intense that it could be used as raw power, bestowing astonishing psychic abilities."

When I asked which organised gangs could strike against us, Gervin began a long enumeration, "The Nephilim Hunters of Jex Belaran for a start, and even more the Renegade Hunters who defected from Jex Belaran. The Nephilim giants are also a major threat. Even though they live in the Eastern Peninsula, they could be tempted to send an army against us. Danger could also come from power-hungry orders such as the power-hungry Black Robes (the ones who destroyed the temple of Karlinga where Teyani and Elyani's mother used to live), the Order of the Eternal Renewal, the White Robes of Senclor, or factions from the palace of the king." Gervin paused, looking straight into me. "When the time comes, the battle will be total. Every force in the kingdom will want these stones. The king of Atlantis himself could well decide that the Archive is to fall into his hands!"

I smiled from the Dragon, "Master Gervin, what are my instructions?"

In a solemn tone Gervin declared, "You will not just be in charge of carrying the Eisraim stone to the Plateau of Sorana, the Archive Council has decided that you will be in charge of organising all the operations which are to take place in the kingdom."

The Dragon greeted the momentous news with vroofing waves. In Gervin's eyes, there was eternity. In my head, the silence of a thousand fields of stars.

From Eisraim to Philadelphia. Thunder is calling.

"What's the Archive Council?" I asked.

"The Masters of Thunder who supervise the Archive project. I am one of them. After deliberation, we decided that you will be the commander of the operations in the kingdom."

Flight of the Thunderbird. That which is will always be. Why grieve?

"But Gervin, why not you?"

"By the time of the transfer I will no longer be in the kingdom. I will have left my physical body and will be supervising the operations in the Fields of Peace."

A wave of distress swept through me, "Does this mean you will be... dead?"

"Dead to the kingdom," Gervin shrugged his shoulders. "So what?"

"And reborn to the Fields of Peace?" I asked.

"I already live in the Fields of Peace!" he said.

So Gervin was a parallel! Holding my tears from the Dragon, I contemplated the beautiful man, wondering which glorious form he assumed in his incarnation in the Fields of Peace.

"We can discuss this later," Gervin moved on. "As to the council's choice, the fact you spent just about two lawful years being trained in Mount Lohrzen, one of the top military schools in the kingdom, makes you an ideal candidate to organise the operations on the ground. Another reason for your nomination is that the communication between you and I will be easy, and fast as lightning. This will prove essential, especially in the final stages. There are also a few other things about yourself that will become clear in the coming months, and which will fully justify the council's decision."

Only a whisper. Spread through a million fields of stars. Everything could still fail.

What the Underworld was this strange glow in his eyes? I knew the man well enough to guess there was *a phoenix in the pot*, but also that there was no point insisting – he wouldn't say more.

"If the situation was not so critical," Gervin went on, "I would have first taken you as my assistant for a few years before putting you in command down here. But time is running out, Szar. I need you to give your absolute best now, not in five years."

"How will Lehrmon and Master Woolly accept working under me?" I worried, being a junior member of the Archive team.

Gervin was amused. "Lehrmon, who is also a member of the Archive Council, has highly recommended you. You will be happy to know that from the Fields of Peace, the council was carefully watching the military operations you were involved in when serving under Marek. And also the way you held fast when being tempted by Verzazyel the Watcher."

I gulped, unsure of what I had escaped.

"As for Woolly, he has fully endorsed the council's decision." Twinging his beard, Gervin added, "As soon as he heard that to move from one place to another in the temple you only used the roofs, Woolly said, 'That's the man for us!'"

In the wings of a bird of paradise, Woolly will die.

"You must also understand that Lehrmon, Woolly, and their teams in Eisraim and Lasseera will be extraordinarily busy completing the final stages of preparation of the stones," Gervin continued. "They'll be only too happy to relinquish the organisational side of the operation and concentrate solely on soft-stone technicalities."

In the wings of a bird of paradise, Woolly will be reborn.

Gervin gave an elusive smile, showing he was reading things inside me I myself couldn't see. "Now for your precise instructions: thirty-six Archive stones have been prepared in Lasseera, and seventy-one in Eisraim. Two of these will be selected at the last moment, one in each temple. Your mission will be to make sure that the charging process happens properly for each of them. Then the two stones will have to be transported to the Plateau of Sorana. This will be the most dangerous phase, when a number of adverse forces could strike. Once you reach the High Plateaux, not much can go wrong: the great ritual of the Archive transfer will be performed from the Fields of Peace, with very little to be done in the kingdom. In other words, get the stones to Sorana, and Thunder will do the rest!"

The warp, agonising. The kingdom, devastated. Melchard and Namron, slaughtered by the invaders. The temple, emptied. The Archive, threatened. With Teyani, you will cross the great abyss.

Tuning high above my head, Gervin ordered, "You are to carefully pre-pare your strategy and submit it to the council. I want a master plan, Szar, a work of art! I am here to inspire you and discuss all the details, but I want the plan to come from you."

"What kind of lawful time frame should I be looking at?"

"In the near future – no one can predict the exact date – a particular kind of slimy elemental muck coming from the fourth intermediary world will start overflowing into the fields. There will be an entire night during which the dogs will be heard howling throughout the kingdom. All the animals will make a great clamour. Soon after, entire villages will be stricken by madness, people slaughtering each other for no reason. After the night of the howling dogs, I estimate it will only be a matter of months before the total collapse of the warp of fields. Expect the final signal for the Archive transfer three to six months after that night."

Discussing resources, Gervin advised I could involve anyone I wanted in Eisraim or Lasseera. If needed he could also arrange for troops from the army of the county of Eisraim, but they were not very reliable. "I trust you are going to come up with a few original ideas," he concluded.

From the whisper, victory. Everything could still fail.

"One last thing, Szar of the Brown Robe," Gervin locked his gaze into mine. "I have vowed I will initiate you into Thunder *before* the Archive transfer takes place. Thunder is no easy power to conquer. Expect surprises, especially in the period leading to your initiation, and not all of them pleasant. You will need to be strong, Szar. And awakened!"

9.32 The Point-funnel, entry gate for the astral body

I walked out of Gervin's apartment a different man, living in a different world – a world in which the light was brighter, the shape of buildings more precisely drawn, the sound of the pebbles under my shoes crisper. In contrast the passersby looked even more asleep and helpless, their minds thickly fogged, their hearts blissfully indifferent to the deadly urgency of the situation.

When I arrived at Elyani's, I commented on her dress and announced, "I have some news, from the Fields of Peace. Arch-secret, but Gervin said you could read it through me if you wanted to," and I opened my arms and closed my eyes, making my mind vacant to let her in.

"Sorry," she said, "I can't see anything."

I opened my eyes and frowned suspiciously.

It made her laugh. "Will you tell me?"

When she heard the news she exclaimed, "But I already knew that! Gervin had prophesied long ago that you would be the commander of the kingdom-side of the Archive project! That's why he sent you to the temple of Vulcan. At one stage he even thought of having you trained at the citadel of the Nephilim giants, saying that would have been excellent for your spiritual development. The problem was, the Nephilim giants' military school is something of an exclusive club. Szar-ka didn't really have the profile. Alcibyadi laughed so much when she heard this..."

"Does Alcibyadi know about all this?" I choked.

"When Alcibyadi is not told something important, she usually prophesies it. Then, of course, by the same token she sees all sorts of other things that she is not always supposed to see," Elyani shrugged. "That's why Gervin prefers to tell us things immediately. He usually calls Teyani first, because she is even more..."

"I know, I know!" I sat on the lawn and took my head in my hands. "Can I have a white drink?"

She sat by my side and put her arms around me. "Is the time coming?"

"Could be! No one knows, really."

"What are you going to do?" Elyani asked.

The whisper holds the answer. Miss not the call!

"First, get to know the players of the game – the friends and the foes. One of the things that worries me the most is that as far as security is concerned, the situation in Eisraim is catastrophic. Any average-level commando could wipe out our defence system in no time."

"When you came back from the Sons of the Dragon, didn't Namron and his men detect your arrival?" she asked.

"And so what? If my intentions had been hostile it would have taken me less than a lawful minute to kill the three of them. I worried at the time because I have been taught to *never underestimate the enemy*. But now that I have observed Namron and his men, I know they didn't stand a chance. They have not been involved in any proper military operations for years. They are great when it comes to catching a thief. But I hate to imagine what would happen if they had to bear the brunt of a real attack."

"Your voice becomes so different when you talk about war," she said, a touch of irony in her voice.

I softened and lay on the grass, pulling her to me. "Do you know what the situation is like in the temple of Lasseera?"

"Security-wise?" she asked.

I nodded.

"Probably about the same."

I laughed, "Well, let me tell you, all this is going to change!"

"Have you got a plan, Dragon?"

Walking home through the fielded corridors, yet another explosion had taken place above my head – a glimpse of the entire master plan Gervin had asked me to concoct. Unfortunately, it was in 'packed' Point-form. "How am I to unpack this into intelligible thought forms?" I asked Elyani.

"Now that the seed has been planted in your Point," she comforted my shoulder, "it will mature by itself. Give it some time."

In this new world, time was precisely what I didn't have.

Point-inspired by the corridors' guidance system, I had thought of a few hundred things I urgently needed to ask her about the kingdom in general and Point-warfare in particular. In her lively, colourful ways, Elyani answered question after question, the Eagle's softness breathing through her voice. Clearly, the kingdom she lived in was nothing as vague as the one I had lived in! But her White patience was immense, she never tired of my unlawful ignorance of the Centre North's geography or kingdom-famous castes.

When it came to discussing Point-weapons, however, her voice changed. She called me 'Brother Knight' and sat up straight, her eyes lit with the steadfast determination of an unknown warrior angel. As I contemplated her fiery intensity, perplexed, she asked me about the Underworld breeze which the Great Warriors had taught me to tame.

"It is the source of the Warriors' power," I told her. "It comes from below."

"Can you only get it from Dragon gates?"

"No, anywhere."

"So why can't other people tap from below?" she asked.

"They do! Everyone receives *some* of this breeze, but only faint vapours or tiny drops. This is why people's bodies are so weak. But it is all they could cope with. To those who haven't died in the Dragon, most energies from below are terribly toxic. They can kill in no time. This is one of the ways the Great Warriors destroy their enemies: they feed them Dragon food. They draw powers from the Earth into them. This is the strange thing – the Dragon-initiates' elixir of life is poison to non-initiates."

"With the Point, the principle is exactly the same, but upside down," Elyani explained, and she compared the Point to a funnel through which drops of mental consciousness descend into people's head.

"Everyone? Even those who don't know about the Point?"

"Everyone," she nodded. "The very substance of the mind comes down through the Point."

Face to face with a Nephilim Hunter. One of you must die. Get ready!

"Do you mean to say the energy of the astral body flows down into people through the Point as if through a funnel?" I twinged my beard. "Mm... then it's not difficult to imagine how it can be used as a weapon."

"Tell me, Dragon."

"If you were to clog someone's Point-funnel, no thoughts could pass through. He would be incapable of thinking straight." It took me only a few seconds to conclude, "Mind you, for many people that probably wouldn't make much difference. Their Point is already pretty clogged isn't it?"

Elyani chuckled.

"Right," I continued, "so you could try the opposite. You could draw powerful forces down into them through their Point, and their little human head would be unable to cope. At best, they would do strange things, such as throwing buckets of white slime at each other. At worst, they would fall flat on the ground like the Nephilim giants when their citadel was attacked by dark angels."

She gave a nod of approval, playfully mirroring Marek's dangerous smile.

"And then of course you could also pour particular thoughts or moods into them through the Point," I continued. "Do you think you could do something like this to me now, to see if I would know how to defend myself?"

"Do you really want me to?" she asked in a sub-vroofing tone of voice.

"Yes! I need to learn, Elyani," the warrior in me spoke confidently.

"Well, then..." she closed her eyes for a few seconds.

I felt an energy blatantly falling down into me from above the head. "*Oh my Lord Melchisedek! What is that?*"

"It's called a venom shower," she said.

"Is this how an attack feels?" As I asked the question, soft frolicsome loving vroofing waves started rising from the depths of my Dragon. I laughed, "What are you doing to me, high priestess?"

"Defend yourself!" she challenged me.

The war will end, my love for you won't. No Limits!

179

The only thing I wanted was to take her in my arms. "How do you expect me to fight this?" I protested tenderly.

"Come on, Dragon, let's fight!" her eyes flared, more than just playfully.

What was happening to my little Elyani?

"Come on!" she insisted.

"All right!" I grabbed her in my arms and made her roll with me on the lawn until our heads came close to the breeze of the Dragon gate. There I pulled mighty vroofing waves into my body and let them flow into her.

"What are you doing to me, Dragon?" she erupted into cascades of laughter. "I can hear music all through the seven spheres!"

"I must fight with what I have!" I said, pulling more waves into her.

"Stop!" she couldn't stop laughing, "I'm going to explode!"

I immediately neutralised the vroofing waves inside her body.

"No!" she protested, "you're not allowed to stop!"

As I was about to start again, I received a signal from my protection fields. I became rock-still. "Someone's coming."

"Mother Teyani!" Elyani was still laughing.

I stood up and cleared my throat, pulling Elyani up by the hand.

The grand master of the female wing soon appeared. "*Praise the Lord Melchisedek, my children! You* are shining!" she complimented Elyani. "I have never seen you so beautiful!"

Neither had I.

The greetings ended, Lady Teyani announced she had come to speak to me.

Elyani invited us to sit on the lawn. "I was just about to prepare a *very* special drink," she said, and disappeared into her room.

Teyani began with complimenting me on my nomination as the commander of the transfer operation. Straightforwardly she announced, "I have come to assure you of the Eagle's support, Szar, and also to offer you my help."

"I could certainly do with help," I said, contemplating her tranquil smile. "Especially coming from the powerful Lady Teyani of the White Eagle."

She established eye contact with me, stopping time and igniting an ascending trail of joyful specks in my fountain – a full moon dancing above my head, the Dragon below remembering the glory of the Ancient Days, and the Eagle on all sides to celebrate the mystery of the Web of Love.

In the abyss of darkness, Teyani will walk by your side. Together, you will fight the last battle. She will never reach Sorana.

"Szar," she restarted the course of time, "you may be interested to know I have spent several months meditating in the mountains of Lasraim, close to the Plateau of Sorana." Noticing the way I was twinging my beard, she interrupted herself, immensely amused.

I dropped my hand. "Hum... I should certainly like to explore this area."

Elyani came back carrying a tray with three ritual cups. She offered one to each of us and sat by Teyani's side. "Are you going to take him to the entrance of the Valley of the Necromancer, Mother Teyani?"

Teyani gave her most enigmatic smile. "I was just thinking about this."

"Now then, that's an interesting coincidence!" I told the White Eagles how that very morning I had spent two hours hearing Namron speak of his wild night in the Valley of the Necromancer.

Ghastly was the word. Namron had caught me by surprise as I was strolling on the roofs, following one of the cats of the Wise Witches from a distance (these cats knew every nook and cranny in the roofs; following them, I had discovered several strategic shortcuts to navigate from one enclave of the temple to another). Having no lawful excuse this time, I had had to sit with Namron and hear the grisly story: endless reflections of his own face yelling obscenities at him, hordes of spooks running after him, glacial winds freezing his bones, enormous birds vomiting torrents of black slime on his head, Pleurk son of Pleurk resuscitated from the marshes, his face covered in sores, the caverns of sickness glowing in his eyes, Pleurk attacking him again (and again) – the narrative went on and on, until finally I *had* to take leave for my appointment with Gervin. "But I really want to know the end!" I had assured the still disappointed Namron as I started running.

"I believe you," Namron had answered after throwing a thick black spat into the alley and inhaling deeply. "I believe you."

"Is it really that bad?" I asked the White Eagles.

The Valley of the Necromancer linked the county of Eisraim to the High Plateaux, cutting through the mountains of Lasraim. This gave it formidable strategic significance – it could save me a week of mountain climbing at the critical time of transporting the Archive stones.

"Pretty bad, yes," Teyani pulled a delicate face as, until then, I had only seen on Elyani.

"You have no i-dea!" Elyani seconded, "Once, Teyani took Alcibyadi, Lehrmon and I to the entrance of the valley. It was unlawfully weird! Alcibyadi and I couldn't stop laughing and crying at the same time. And Lehrmon, who had not yet been initiated into Thunder, reacted just as you did when hearing the priestesses of the Dawn of Creation."

"And that was only the entrance," Teyani added.

Right fist raised skywards, screaming, "Gervin! Gervin! I am not asleep!"

I hadn't given up yet. "But why is this valley so dangerous?" I asked the Eagles.

Teyani answered, "Long ago, in the early days of the kingdom, the valley was bewitched by a powerful magician given to the dark side. He was Harmag the Necromancer, a son of Azazel the Watcher. He left so much of his witchcraft in the valley that thousands of years later it is still considered one of the most haunted places in the kingdom. No one ever visits the Valley of the Necromancer. The Nephilim themselves have given up on it. Usually, the Nephilim are very fond of places where the Watchers have left some of their energy. They consider them places of pilgrimage, to which they flock in the hope of gaining powers. But in the Valley of the Necromancer, no one has ever found anything but death. Four hundred years ago the Nephilim discontinued all pilgrimages to our county."

Death, waiting in the valley. Lohrzen had foreseen the battle.

"Fascinating," I touched Lohrzen's orichalc plate on my neck, remembering the entrance to Verzazyel's cave. "I want to see the entrance to this valley, Teyani. When could I go and inspect the mountains with you?"

Teyani placed her arm around Elyani's shoulders. "The three of us could perhaps go when Maryani returns from the Underworlds."

Elyani applauded the idea. "What do you think, Commander?"

There was so much joy shining from these women that for one second, I could think of Maryani's descent without being haunted by the memory of Vivyani. "Always ready to follow the Eagle!" I unconditionally surrendered.

"Let it be, then!" Teyani engaged her word. She made us close our eyes to invoke the White Eagle and ask his blessing for our journey.

Whenever Teyani was around, the Eagle's Light poured like monsoon rains in the county of the Eternal Swamp. I rested my palms one on top of the other, as in the Eagle's ritual. The blissful energy inundated my heart.

Tolls the bell of Elyani's destiny. The gods have thrown the daiva.

When I opened my eyes, Elyani and Teyani were looking at each other, Elyani extremely upset, Teyani holding her hand.

Had I done something wrong?

Teyani slowly turned towards me and shook her head to reassure me. "Tell us about Maryani," she went on asking, still holding Elyani's hand. "Have you thought what you are going to do with her?"

Pulling all the sweetness of the Underworlds, I held Elyani in the arms of the Dragon. "Teyani, on this subject I must ask your instructions."

"What instructions?" the grand master shrugged her shoulders. "The Eagle said you should do as you want. Do as you want, Commander!"

"And what if Maryani's descent was brief – say, no longer than one night? I would like to take her deep down into my Mother the Dragon. If I succeed, I could show her far more in one hour than I saw in the entire six weeks of my first descent. But then would Maryani qualify to become a high priestess in the Eagle after such a short journey?"

"*Lawfully certainly!*" Teyani was unequivocal. "Szar, the Eagle's omens on Maryani's descent were excellent – provided you accepted to lead her. Now, I trust whatever happens will be the Eagle's will."

After a moment spent discussing the marvels of the Deep Underworlds, Teyani blessed Elyani and me by holding our hands, and she took leave.

Elyani and I dived into each other's arms.

"What's happening, beautiful Eagle?"

"I don't know," she hid inside my brown cape. "Teyani and I perceived another strange omen when we invoked the White Eagle a moment ago."

"Omen? What omen?"

She was crying. "It's unclear. There have already been a few like this. It's something about me, but we don't know what."

"Have you asked the Eagle's oracle for a precise explanation?"

She shook her head. "I will ask only if you want me to."

"Why shouldn't we ask?"

"What if there is nothing we can do about it?" she emerged from my cape. "What good will it do to ask?"

"I trust the Eagle as much as I trust you and Teyani. I can't see that anything bad could come from asking his advice."

She cried with dignity, the fierce spark of the warrior angel still in her eyes, "I am... afraid."

No thoughts, just Dragon, I let my Mother's supreme stillness flow into her.

With all my heart, with all my mind, I am with you, even when I am far away. White Eagle, White Eagle, from the end to the beginning, I have loved you. From the Fault of Eternity through to the Great Night of Remoteness, I will love you.

"Right!" Elyani pulled together her courage after a short while, "I will go to the Eagle's chapel and invoke the oracle with Teyani." She gently extracted herself from my arms. "I will meet you on the roof at sunset."

"I will love you!" the words came out of my mouth mixed up by the turmoil. "I mean, I love you!"

The White Eagle looked deep into me, as if from the Edge of Highness.

Then she turned round and went, without saying a word.

9.33 The identification field

"Now then..." Namron paused, looking down to the alley. The priests of Baltham were carrying a funeral litter out of their chapel. "They're all carking it one after the other. I wonder what their god is doing," he commented, and he resumed his narration, "Now then, what happened when I came out of that wretched marsh will answer your question."

"My question?" I asked, contemplating the procession of priests and wondering how much more of Namron's story I could take today.

"You asked me why I never wear shoes."

"Ah, yes." I had asked him that only two days ago, but so much had happened in his story since then that it seemed like *before the Law of Melchisedek*.

"Now then, I came out of that marsh covered in the most putrid blackish foamy slime – even worse than the second marsh where I had tried to rescue Pleurk," he looked at me to make sure I was following.

"Pleurk, son of Pleurk," I echoed, to let him know I was with him.

"That's right!" he exclaimed, satisfied, "Pleurk who, I thought at the time, was dead. Little did I know! Anyhow then, as I was scooping the slime off my face, ignoring the ghosts which were sneering at me, and doing my best to repel the thick cloud of mosquitoes which had appeared out of nowhere, and realising in horror that my legs were covered with leeches, the most dreadful thing happened," he loudly discharged a mouthful of over-chewed black root into the alley, "my shoes left my feet and started walking in front of me!"

"But that's terrible, Namron!" Spotting a cat on a chapel roof, two alleys in front of us, I directed a "Tss, tss..." call through darkness visible. The cat stopped, turned its head and looked at me.

"You have no idea how deep it hit me," Namron went on. "It's because I am a man who can just look at someone's feet and tell you exactly what kind of person he is. The feet tell everything. There is something utterly personal about them, which is why we lawfully conceal them in the temples of the shoes."

"I see," I watched the feline soul resume its ramble. "Well, Namron, now I understand it all. So we could perhaps talk of..."

"Wait," Namron interrupted anxiously, "the worst hadn't happened yet. Believe it or not, the shoes turned round, walked back towards me and started kicking me savagely. Now then..."

Breathing deeply and thinking of the White Eagle, I followed Namron's mad dash as he ran for his life through the Valley of the Necromancer, pursued by his shoes.

"Namron!" I *had* to stop him a few minutes later, "I'll have to go soon. Master Woolly is waiting for me," I pointed down to the Field Wizards, above whose heads we were sitting.

The old soldier grinned, "You're not the first person to be put off by this part of the story, you know."

Walking in the valley, Teyani by your side.

"But I *absolutely* want to hear the rest, my friend in the Law."

"Do you?" Namron's thankful face gleamed with the light of true lawful friendship.

"*Lawfully absolutely*. For now," I quickly went on, "I need to discuss security matters with you."

"Security?" His sense of duty taking over, Namron found the strength to extract himself from the valley. "How timely, my friend in the Law! Have you heard that the main temple of the Western Plains' county has just been attacked by bandits? Precious relics have been stolen, and people have been killed."

"But I thought a crowd of priests had gathered there to conduct a ritual to restore the climate?"

Namron spat into the alley. "That didn't prevent the gang from entering the temple in the middle of the day. They killed seventeen people and wounded many others. They were after the golden vessels, some priceless ritual gear that had been used in the past by the great saints of that temple."

"The assembly of priests must have been badly shocked. And who were the bandits?" I asked. "Could they be Renegade Nephilim Hunters?"

Namron shook his head, "Not their style. The Renegade Hunters kill only when necessary, and they like clean jobs. These ones left an Underworld of a mess behind them. They broke statues everywhere, and they killed all the priests who stood in their way. Sounds to me like they could be deserters from the army of the king of Atlantis."

I looked down to my left palm. "Are there many gangs of deserters like this?"

"A few. The king's army is corrupt from top to bottom, my friend in the Law. Some of these gangs of deserters are even working for high-ranking officers who live at the court of our king."

"Sad!" I sighed. "At least the king's soldiers are not very dangerous."

Namron burst out laughing and placed his hand on my shoulder, "Nothing more than Dragon fodder?"

"Pretty much so. When I was in Mount Lohrzen I studied their fighting style. It's appalling. Entire battalions can be decimated in no time."

"I love to hear you speak like this, my friend in the Law," Namron was heartened.

Revelation Sky. The Sons of Apollo have spoken to Kartendranath. He knows you are coming. At this very minute, he is watching you. Tremble!

"Tell me, Namron, how powerful is our prince's army? Could we rely on it if we ever needed to?"

"They're a small army, no more than a thousand men. You probably wouldn't think highly of their military standards, but they have integrity. The officers are clean. The prince of the county of Eisraim is a wise man. He studied in our temple in his young days. His administration is almost free from corruption."

"Mm... Good to know. And what about the county of Lasseera?"

"It's all right. The problem with Lasseera is that it's damn close to the county of the Northern Lakes, which is rotten with Renegade Hunters. But in Lasseera itself, the situation is not too unlawful."

We watched another funeral litter coming out of Baltham's chapel.

Kartendranath likes you. Tremble! The beating of your life.

"Namron, we are on the brink of disaster," I said grimly. "Our temple is completely unprotected, isn't it?"

Namron sneered, "Glad to hear I'm not the only one who can see that!"

"Have you got a plan, Namron?"

Namron shrugged his shoulders in powerlessness. "What plan could I have with a team of twelve men, only half of whom are trained soldiers? It's not that I have given up, but..." he stuffed his mouth with black root. "What about you, Great Warrior? Do you have a plan?"

I looked straight into him, "Would you welcome one?"

"Would I welcome a plan?" Namron raised his hands towards the gods. "Man of the Law, I've spent fifteen lawful years of my life looking after these people. During all this time, not one of their relics has been stolen. Whenever one of them needed help, they've found me or one of my men to hold their hand and carry them back to their room. The idea of what is about to fall on their heads makes me sick to the stomach. It gives me nightmares that wake me up at night. I'll welcome *anything* that could secure the safety of the temple."

I twinged my beard. "How many people are there in the temple?"

"Not far from eleven hundred priests and priestesses. Nearly half of them never go out of their room, or at most they circulate between their room and their chapel. And on top of that of course, there are some two thousand *lawful servants and attendants of various castes.*"

"What if my plan implied drastic changes?" I asked.

"I would like to know how the Underworld you are going to convince the wise people of this temple that drastic changes need to be implemented," Namron said sarcastically.

The dangerous smile of the Warriors reappeared on my face. "Mm... I might have a few ideas on how to wake them up."

"Are you serious?" Namron's face lit up.

Still smiling, I rested on the Dragon, "Deadly serious, Namron."

"We'll be with you, Warrior!" the small man declared in a tone of total determination.

Friend of your father, witness of your birth, the Ant knows the whisper.

"How about starting the work right now!" I decided.

Namron frowned, wondering what to expect.

"I want to find every possible way of forcing the identification system that detected me on my return to the temple. Tell me, Namron, how does it work?"

"It's a Point field," Namron explained. "Every single person in the temple is registered in the field. The field holds an imprint of their energy. When someone who isn't registered in the field approaches the temple, a Point signal is generated. We pick up the signal and we go and check the person out. If their presence in the temple is lawful, we register them in the field. After this they can go in and out as they please. Do you want me to show you how to connect with the identification field?"

"No," I shook my head. "I want you to de-register me, now."

Namron smiled, baring his two rows of jagged teeth blackened by the root. "War games?"

"Just an exercise!" I watched Namron close his eyes for a few seconds, carefully sensing the energies he was handling from the Point.

"Done!" Namron announced. "Let's see how long it takes before my men turn up."

"Namron, but what if experts in the Point wanted to infiltrate this identification field? Do you really think they would have much difficulty breaking through?"

"We've never really tested that. They would have to be real experts."

"Man of the Law," I despaired, "do you realise what kind of training the Nephilim Hunters go through?"

Thoughtful, Namron chewed on his black root.

"And what do you think will happen to our identification system when the warp of fields collapses?" I questioned.

Namron shrugged. "It will collapse, like all the rest."

The silhouettes of two of his men soon appeared on a distant roof, running towards us. Namron waved to reassure them. "I'll re-register you now," he said.

"Namron, this security system is *not* going to work!" I told him, dismayed. Without further comment I jumped down into the alley, and waved farewell from below.

9.34 Bad day

I landed in the alley, straight in front of the Field Wizards' door. Why worry about shocking passersby since anyway not one of them had noticed my unlawful arrival in the alley.

Sleepers!

This time, I decided not to knock. I just opened the chapel door and walked in. Three Field Wizards were working in the room. They didn't even turn toward me, they just kept on with their activities as if I was visiting through darkness visible.

"How long would it have taken a trained fighter to eliminate the three of them?" I wondered. It would have taken me less than fifteen seconds.

Carefully avoiding the bottles on the floor, I breathed in the familiar smells and went down to the cellars. Before approaching Woolly I made my energy invisible in darkness visible and silently set off for the room where his most precious stones were kept. Using the smell and resting on my Mother the Dragon, I picked up the two jars that contained the most vibrant energies and put them in a large pocket of my brown robe.

Then I went to meet the soft-stone guru.

"*Praise the Lord, Commander!*" he welcomed me, his eyes fixed on a bucket of white slime.

"*All glory to the Lord Melchisedek, Master Woolly!* I need to speak to you."

"Speak to me, Commander!" Woolly kept working.

"Woolly, we have a major problem with security. Anyone could come in here and play havoc with your babies."

Woolly pulled a face, "Are we getting to the stage where this could happen?"

"The Western Plains' main temple has just been raided," I told him. "And the attack took place in the middle of a high ritual that gathered hundreds of Voice experts."

"Sounds like the bandits had a sense of humour," Woolly sneered. "I can imagine the faces of those lawful old rats."

"Woolly, if this happens to us you're not going to laugh."

"True!" he conceded. "One of my hopes has been that bandits would go for the temple's gold and orichalc rather than my stones."

"Man of the Law, the soft stones in your chapel are worth an absolute fortune."

"Aren't they?" he grinned proudly.

I pulled the two jars out of my pocket and placed them on the bench in front of his nose. "What if I had walked away with these two? How much gold do you think I could have got for them?"

Woolly turned pale. For the first time, he looked at me. "How did you get into that crypt? Was there no one in the room that leads to it?"

I shook my head. "Even if there had been, it wouldn't have taken me long to get in."

He chewed his lip thoughtfully.

"What about the Archive stones?" I asked.

"Much, much better!" he assured me. He grabbed the two jars I had brought with me, "Follow me, Commander!"

He took me into another dimly lit cellar full of white slime buckets. "Where are the Archive stones, Commander?" he asked playfully.

I rested on the Dragon of the Deep. "Should I assume that their energy is a bit like Lilu's?"

"Fair guess, man of the Law!"

I tuned into bucket after bucket. "This one is as beautiful as the Molten Sea," I commented as I went, exchanging a connoisseur's glance with Woolly. But from the Dragon's depths, I was attracted to one of the walls.

It was a blank wall, made of normal plass, shining with the same whitish glows as in the other cellars. I touched it. It didn't seem to be hollow. I turned toward Woolly. He didn't say a thing but I could read on his face that this was no common wall.

Facing the wall again, I became Dragon-still and tuned into the Point.

One million suns in the eye of a needle. You are dancing.

An unlawfully weird experience.

Throughout the Great Night, the whole creation slept. He didn't.

The centres of energy above my head lit up like torches. Extraordinarily vibrant.

Seeing the first glimmers of Cosmic Dawn, he restarted Space Matrix.

It was like being transported back to Verzazyel's cave. Same atmosphere of strangeness.

The river of infinity, singing the Song of Creation.

Vivid impressions flooding my mind.

Felicia's ritual succeeded. She has conquered the fire of the Watchers.

The corridors where I had dreamt the cosmic dance...

Hiram? To the Point, Brother Knight!

The crypt where I had discovered Felicia...

253647688965896543557892425390657612...

Out of nowhere, something clicked in the centres above my head.

There was a crack, and an opening appeared in the wall – a doorway, leading to another cellar.

"Shit!" Woolly became furious. "But shit! You Dragon dickhead! How the Ugly Underworld did you do that?" he screamed at me. "You *bastard in the Law*!"

I turned towards him, eyes and mouth wide open.

0176549284365901832850192994578190563901235123546324...

"Did Gervin teach you how to do this?" he shouted.

As I remained perplexed, he yelled, "Speak! But speak! But shit! Don't look at me like a Blue priestess!"

"But I've never heard about this thing!" I protested.

"Ugly Underworld! You're lying! Shit! Shit! But shit!"

65023657304694301783...

"Woolly, this is the pure truth! I've never heard about this passageway!"

He kicked the *living wall* savagely with his right foot. "Well, it's even worse then!" he kept yelling, pulling his curly hair with both hands. "But shit! What have I done to the Goddess to deserve another day like this?"

Alerted by the clamour, Ferman popped his head into the room. "Is everything all right?"

"No!" Woolly shouted at him. "We don't need you for the moment, thank you!"

Reassured, the Field Wizard gave a tranquil smile and left.

Woolly kicked the *living wall* again. "Fuck you, Commander! Fuck your Dragon! Fuck your Underworld! What are you trying to fucking prove?"

I called upon the Eagle's softness and looked into his eyes.

Edge of Highness. Whiteness eternal. Forever love.

Woolly's aura was fuming with rage, "I can't believe this! I can't believe this shit! I *refuse* to believe this shit!"

I turned towards the doorway that had appeared in the wall. "Another Point device, is that it?"

In a near-normal voice, he said, "No, precisely! This is *not* just another Point device. This is Flying Dragons' magic. Lehrmon brought it back from beyond the Abyss of the Deep something. If anyone can crack it, then we *do* have a major problem."

"Flying Dragons and major problems go together so well," I thought. I asked Woolly if I could go in.

"By all means," he said dryly. "I was about to let you in, anyway."

I walked into a cellar that was no different from the other ones: buckets on the floor, whitish glows from the *living walls*, white slime smells and Underworld fragrances wafting in the air.

"Ah, shit," Woolly beat the plass, this time with his fist. "Lehrmon is going to be fu-ri-ous!"

"How does that work exactly?" I asked.

"It's just a damn normal doorway, but the device tricks your conscious-ness into believing there is a wall instead."

10576239486571039496915630030030030007684736...

"Does the device rest on the fields?" I asked.

"No! That's the beauty of it."

"Mm... Pure magic of the Flying Dragons!" I tuned into the buckets. "In-cidentally, Woolly, I'm having a bad day too."

Woolly sneered. "Talk about the Goddess pissing on us! All the damn stones are losing weight at the moment. All of them!"

I became worried, "Even Lilu?"

"She's only half what she was when you gave her back to me."

"But that's terrible, Woolly! Can I have her back?"

"But don't you hear what I say? Szar, for the Goddess's private parts! *Each* of the seventy-one damn Archive stones has been losing substance."

The bird of paradise, flying down to the Underworlds.

"How badly?"

"Not too ugly for the moment. Lehrmon has been blasting this crypt with Voice to protect it from the overflow of elemental slime. But we're running in vicious circles. Without the fields, the stones can't grow. But each time we expose the stones to the fields, they become polluted with black ele-mental muck and they shrink instead of growing."

After a short inspection of the vibrations of the place, I concluded, "I really need to explore further how stones behave. If I could do more work on Lilu, perhaps it would give me some ideas on how to restore the balance of elemental forces in your chapel."

Woolly was cautious. "Well, as long as it's clear that you have her on loan..."

"Of course, Woolly!"

"Follow me, Commander!"

9.35 Forever love, White Eagle

As I was walking back home through the corridors of the female wing, enjoying the Point-peace of the guidance system, I couldn't help tuning into Lilu. "This is ridiculous!" I thought, realising how attached I was to her. I couldn't help feeling joy at the idea that she was in my pocket. And I could feel she was just as happy to be with me.

I didn't want to voice-channel Elyani for fear of disturbing her while she was invoking the oracle. But Lilu took me by surprise and established a connection.

"I'm sitting on the roof, Szar. Waiting for you," the White Eagle responded.

I hurried along, not daring to ask anything. *"Oh my Mother the Dragon, have mercy on us!"*

As soon as I reached the courtyard, I ran to the ladders and climbed up to her.

Elyani had her prophetess' eyes, shining like liquid starlight. "Sweet Lord Melchisedek!" she contemplated the centres of energy above my head in disbelief. "What has happened to your column of Spirit?"

"Flying Dragons' mischief," I groaned. "But tell me! What did you learn from the oracle?"

She shook her head, "I didn't invoke the oracle. Teyani and Alcibyadi wouldn't let me do it. They said I was too emotionally involved, the risk of interference was too high. They decided to conduct the ritual for me."

"And?"

"It's happening right now. Alcibyadi will come to us as soon as the sentence has been received."

In a Point-flash, I realised I no longer liked waiting.

"Your eyes..." I sat in front of her, "your eyes are amazing. What have you been doing?"

"Looking into *your* future, Brother Knight!"

The black panther, running.

She lightly touched my hand. "Something has happened to you, Szar. I could feel it at the time. Something powerful. It went 'voof!' above your head."

I told her how Woolly's secret doorway had been opened by mistake. "For one moment I thought I was back in the cave of Verzazyel the Watcher. That's all I know. I have no idea what happened."

"You must be feeling *something* above your head," she insisted. "There is so much light."

"Nothing. I felt a brief flash, then nothing. What's so surprising about this? I never feel anything when there are Flying Dragons in the air. But you should have seen the way Woolly yelled at me when his device got out of hand."

She laughed, lightly touching my chest, "Poor Szar, victim of the Flying Dragons again."

Hiram, my brother. Hiram, my son.

I was fascinated by her eyes. "What did you see in my future? Are you in it?"

She gave a decided nod, making my heart flare with joy.

"Are you in it all the time?" I immediately wanted to know.

"All the time... is a lot of time, my love."

I frowned, "Is it really? Isn't time going to stop, one of these days?"

"Of course, since it had a beginning. But that may take a while."

The clear fountain flowed, "I bet when time stops, everyone will say 'Already? But we've hardly started!'"

"Could be. But the good thing will be, those who love each other will never be separated again."

Images of Alcibyadi and Lehrmon biting their lip came to mind. "Time isn't really the friend of lovers."

She slowly shook her head. "That's why lovers always want to stop time."

"Of course. Time always tries to separate them."

"No, don't say that! Sometimes, time brings lovers together."

"If time was just about to stop, do you know what I would do?" I asked.

She plunged the Eagle's infinity into my eyes.

I came close to her, my lips nearly touching hers. "I would give you a long, long kiss."

Her energy melted into mine.

Revelation Sky. His love.

"Then the kiss would last forever. When time stops," I explained, "there will never be anything that doesn't last forever."

Elyani laughed. "You know, in the future, you are so much like you! It's amazing."

"And what are *you* like?"

The unknown warrior angel reappeared in her eyes.

I was spellbound. "Tell me what you have seen! What did you ask?"

"I didn't ask anything, I just gave myself to the Eagle and let him take me where he wanted." She waved her arms as wings, "I saw you flying."

"Flying... you mean travelling in the spheres?"

She shook her head, "Hunh, hunh! Flying in the air. In the future, you will become obsessed with flying. Riding a large black bird that spits fire. Very noisy... and there is fire everywhere. Voof!"

"A large, noisy bird that spits fire?" I was amazed. "Does the White Eagle spit fire?"

"No," she laughed, "and he isn't noisy."

I became thoughtful, imagining myself riding a man-sized black-feathered bird that spat fire. "Are you riding the bird with me?"

She closed her eyes. "No, not this one. But another one, later. A much bigger one."

There is nothing faster than a Scalene 333.

"Can you see it?"

"It moves so fast, it's incredible. And it rises so high in the air that it ends up in the fields of stars."

"Ah! Travelling in the fields of stars.... that I can imagine!"

"Hunh hunh!" Elyani was amused. "Not what you think."

I went straight to the essential, "When you are riding the bird with me, are you in love with me?"

She closed her eyes. "It's unlawful passion. I'm dying with love for you, Brother Knight!" she said in the voice of the warrior angel, a feline hand gripping my forearm.

Touched to the core, I tried to decipher who this person with sharp nails was. "And..."

"And you have no idea how much you will love me!"

"Who is this Knight? Is he your brother?"

"No," she chuckled, tipsy with prophetic sight. "*I* am a Brother Knight! You are too. This is the way they call each other: 'To the Point, Brother Knight!' They all wear black."

I looked at her, imagining what she would be like in a black dress.

"You call me panther," her nails lightly ran along my forearm. "And you teach the Point to the other Brother Knights. It's..."

I took advantage of her pausing, "Do you mean I am your teacher?"

She kept laughing. *"No way, man of the Law!* I am still your teacher."

I sighed with relief. "Teach me!"

"The Brother Knights know how to have fun – No Limits! No Limits..."

"Where do they live?" I asked.

"In the fields of stars. And there is a strange building... no, it's not a building. A room? Nn... no. An incredible place, called 'No Limits'. The Brother Knights go there with their friends. Voof! What I see in No Limits is... Point-blowing! I can't even find words to describe what it's like. And they listen to magnificent music. It's your music."

"*My* music?" That was particularly difficult to imagine. I pulled the most beautiful tune from my childhood memories, 'bang-ting-ting, bang-ting-ting...', and tried to transpose it to a lawfully friendly gathering in the fields of stars.

"I see you walking towards me, slowly, and you say, '*Forever love, White Eagle!*'"

Elyani opened her eyes.

"Finished?" I asked, making my arms a nest to receive her. "Remember the time when you prophesied for me and I walked out of your room without even holding your hand?"

Frozen, she didn't answer.

"Did you just see something bad?" I asked.

"A sea of fire." Then she looked into my eyes and said, "I love you!" with so much strength that a whole new corner of my heart was forced open. More than moved, I was left trembling in a sea of love, not really sure who was loving who.

To the angel of Philadelphia.

"Alcibyadi is coming," I announced. "She's alone."

Elyani frowned, "Did she just walk into your protection field?"

"No. She called me through the Point."

She snapped her fingers, "Well done, Brother Knight!"

We climbed down and waited silently in the courtyard for the oracle's verdict.

When Alcibyadi arrived there was no lawful salute. The long-haired woman walked straight towards us and announced, "Teyani and I have asked the significance of the omens Elyani perceived. The Eagle's oracle has answered, '*Very soon, something will happen. The gods have already thrown the daiva.*'"

Elyani whispered, "I know."

"What's the daiva?" I contemplated Alcibyadi's eyes, ablaze with oracular sparks.

Holding Elyani's left hand, she answered, "A word borrowed from the language of the gods. It means both 'destiny' and 'dice'. When the daiva is thrown, destiny has been traced by the gods, and no mortal man or woman can change the course of coming events."

I was becoming nervous, "But *what* is about to happen very soon?"

"'Something'! The oracle wouldn't say what," Alcibyadi replied.

I rested on the Dragon of the Deep. "I know that *asking the oracle the same question twice is dangerous folly*, but... is there no way to know what this 'something' could be?"

"Friends, I tried the dangerous folly for you," Alcibyadi said. "I knew you wouldn't be satisfied with the first answer, so I asked if this 'something' was going to separate the two of you."

Holding Elyani's right hand, I nodded to indicate I was ready to hear the oracle's response.

"The oracle answered, '*It will and it will not. Then it will not and it will, but not how you may think it would, for in the end it won't.*'"

The wave of distress was as deep as the Fault of Eternity.

"This is typically the kind of answers one gets when trying to force the oracle," Alcibyadi said in a soft voice, as if apologising. "Perhaps, wisdom would be to remember only the last part, the one which says that in the end, you won't be separated."

Elyani and I remained dead silent.

I closed my eyes.

Three lapis lazuli suns in a sapphire immensity. Take her by the hand to the music hall and play for her. More love than you could dream of.

When I reopened my eyes, Elyani was standing very straight, facing her destiny with the dignity of humble tears.

Alcibyadi gazed above my head, pouring the Eagle's love into me. Then she left silently.

As she was walking away, I called, "Alcibyadi!"

She stopped and turned.

"Thank you."

She nodded, and left.

I took Elyani in my arms, "It said that in the end, we won't be separated."

"The end..." she cried, "and what if 'the end' meant the end of time?"

"The Eagle wouldn't do that to us," I said confidently. But as she didn't answer, I immediately felt less confident. "Or would he?"

I tried to take comfort from the ambivalence of the sentence. "Anyway, the oracle was too cryptic to mean anything: we will be separated and will not be separated, then we will not be separated and we will be separated, but not as we would imagine, for in the end we won't be separated. What sense do you want to make of that?"

She turned skywards, made herself clear fountain.

"Elyani," I tried to rationalise, "there is something which I do not understand. How come it took hours of high ritual for Alcibyadi and Teyani to extract two meaningless sentences from the oracle when you can just sit, give yourself to the Eagle, and get all these extraordinary visions about the future?"

"Hush, *man of the Law*! Do not call the oracle's sentences meaningless. What I tuned into before were nothing more than a few images picked up from your time track. When the Eagle speaks through his oracle, he engages his high Word. These oracles are precious gifts from the gods."

"Of what good is this gift to us, can you tell me?"

"No, don't speak like this!" she protested. "There was great meaning in the first sentence. Something is about to happen. Knowing that it will be the result of the daiva makes an enormous difference to us."

"Oh, my Mother the Dragon of the Deep!" my voice heated up. "Does this mean we are to submit to the will of the gods and passively accept what they have planned for us? Shall we not fight?"

"Fight, Dragon," her gaze flared. "But fight on the side of the gods, not against them."

"What if the plan of the gods was to separate us?"

"The gods are wise, Szar."

"Are they really?" I questioned. "Why is our kingdom on the brink of disaster, then?"

"*Man of the Law, blame not the gods for the evils men have committed in the kingdom.*"

"And what have the gods done for us?"

"Szar," she disarmed me with her oceanic softness, "you are speaking from anger, not from your heart."

I held my breath for a few seconds. "True!"

She pulled me by the hand and made me sit right on the Dragon's gate, and she sat in front of me.

"Szar, the gods are our friends, not our enemies."

I breathed in my Mother's breeze, doing my best to soften. "If they are our friends, how could they want to separate us? It's so unlawfully unfair. We have only had six days together."

A six-day tempest, packed with more life than the entire life of a sleeper.

"Didn't Gervin separate us when he sent you to the temple of the Dragon?" she insisted.

"Yes, but this was to serve a higher purpose. Anyhow, I was unable to love you before I went away. Now a huge river flows between us."

She was blunt, "And what if Lord Gana had thrown the daiva for exactly the same purpose?"

"If Lord Gana wants to separate us..." I stopped, horrified at what was happening inside me. For the first time in my life, a thought of hostility towards Lord Gana had crossed my mind.

For the first time in my life, I was angry at the gods.

Shocked at myself, I took my head in my hands and started crying.

Elyani held the Eagle's Light, enveloping us with a precious quality of silence in which weeping had superior meaning.

"I feel so powerless," I wept. "I can't even see anything for myself. I always have to rely on other people to prophesy for me."

"Hunh, hunh! If you want to prophesy, Lord Gana will be with you. Will you try?"

I was very much taken by surprise.

"Try," she insisted with the magic strength of her softness, "look into your future!"

"It's *your* future I want to see," I wiped the wetness off my moustache.

"Well, tune into my time track!" she opened her arms, surrendering herself to me. As I hesitated, she gave some direction, "Connect your clear fountain to that of Lord Gana, and let his Point shine through your Point."

I closed my eyes, trying my best to follow her instructions.

"No," she said after a few seconds, "you are trying too hard, it can't work. Be lighter."

I tried to try less hard, but still couldn't see a thing.

"Let me help you set the wheel spinning," the magic woman said.

I made the Dragon soft, inviting her presence into my energy.

"Move along this line," she projected me into a space of slow-moving images. In the fixture of liquid light I saw a shining palace, larger than the temple's first hall of Melchisedek.

"Our house," she commented. "Now, it's all up to you."

"Our house?" I opened my eyes, aghast and abuzz.

"Now, *you* do it! Close your eyes," she sent me back to the vision. "Tell me, what can you see in the house?"

I had never contemplated anything like it. "Rooms everywhere! It's magnificent. Extraordinary light. It keeps changing all the time." The knowing imposed itself on me, "It's your place. *You* have designed it."

"Can you see me?" she asked.

"Dancing on a beach. Oh, gods, you are stunning!" I saw myself playing music for her with an incredible instrument made of a thousand rays of light radiating from a star-like core. The harmonies it gave were so unlike my bang-ting-ting memories that I hesitated, "Is this really a musical instrument or is it something completely different?"

"Do you love me?" she asked.

"I adore you. You are my goddess."

"Thank you, Lord Gana!" Elyani whispered.

"I walk towards you and I ask you to take the musical instrument. And I say... '*Forever love, White Eagle!*'"

I opened my eyes.

"Does it stop there?" Elyani asked.

I remained silent.

She smiled, "You were about to go away from me, weren't you?"

"I'm not sure," I shrugged, "it was just a vision. Could you see what was inside that house?"

"I didn't look," she said. "I let you do it. Now, I want you to prophesy again."

I was starting to learn my lessons. "I don't know that it is wise to try to see any more."

"But I want you to ask a question for me. Please," she insisted.

"From whom?"

"Lord Gana. A lawfully important question," Elyani pursed her lips.

How could I not say yes to her? "All right! How shall I ask?"

"Same as before. Surrender your clear fountain to him, let his Point shine through yours."

I closed my eyes, "What is your question, *woman of the Law*?"

"I want to know if Szar should fight to stay with Elyani or trust the destiny which the gods have traced."

A torrent of power instantly descended, flowing through my mouth,

"*Let Szar trust the gods and fight for Elyani!*"

The sentence struck me like lightning. It was conveyed with so much strength it left me half-trembling.

Elyani came very close to me. "Forever love, Dragon!" she whispered.

I let the flow of wisdom whisper back through me,

"*Forever love, White Eagle.*"

– Thus ends the Book of Elyani –

197

10

The Book of the Naga King

10.1 Maryani descends to the Underworlds

"*Oh Lord Melchisedek*, let what happened with Vivyani never be repeated!"

Maryani arrived with the night. Once again, I was impressed by her candour. She didn't seem the least afraid. When she lay on the lawn after a few minutes of lawful chatting she looked confident, as if the Eagle had taken her in his wings.

I sat close to her and caressed her sandy hair. "Do you like Elyani's courtyard?"

She nodded, "We, in the Eagle, like laurel trees. A lot."

"Laurels are so devotionally inclined. How not to be in awe of them!" I lawfully mirrored her nod.

Seven. Seven. Two. Formless one and joyful shapes.

"Remember your instructions?"

She gave a broad smile, "Go down! Down! Down!"

"And when looking for me, what should you do?"

"Wriggle my nostrils like a lawful rabbit, and smell all around me till I sense in which direction to go."

"Wonderful!" I was proud of her already. I opened the lid of Lilu's jar in front of her. "See this little stone which shines with the Eagle's light? Her name is Lilu, and she is extremely smart. We're taking her with us!"

Elyani arrived and sat by my side. Drawing from the gate's breeze, I started injecting life force into Maryani's gateways. Simultaneously, I prepared her body of energy for the state of hibernation, gently Voice-projecting cooling sounds onto her.

After half an hour I whispered to her, "How are you flying, White Eagle?"

Little voice, like a child ready to fall asleep, "Feels really good, Szar of the Brown Robe."

"Are we ready to jump?"

She nodded with assurance.

I was terrified.

"Remember what I told you yesterday. Your Mother the Dragon is beautiful, and she loves you *as big as the Law*," I whispered into her ear. "Now close your eyes."

Father, for the love of the Fault of Eternity... please take care of this child!

A sharp, quick Voice-projection onto the cheap-way-out gateways on her neck. It knocked her unconscious instantly.

He has heard your call. He will come. Nothing can stop him.

"How are we flying, Dragon-Eagle?" Elyani enquired.

"So far, so good." I stood up, inspecting Maryani's energy. "I have modified my plan. I am going to send her into near-complete hibernation right from the start, so as to give myself plenty of time in case things go wrong. I mean, in case I have difficulty locating her."

I took Maryani in my arms and carried her into what was supposed to be my bedroom – I hadn't slept in it once since my return from the Sons of the Dragon. I laid her warm body on the mattress and put Lilu's jar on the floor, just behind her head.

Great Ant, Blue Lagoon and you of the Wise Spider, O Cosmic Night, Mother of Infinity, help! Please, please... *help! Don't let this child die in my hands!*

Elyani rested her cheek against my shoulder, "Don't worry, the Eagle is with you. Unrestrictedly."

I nodded, touching Lohrzen's orichalc plate on my neck.

I asked Elyani to move back and started full-scale Voice projection to freeze Maryani's gateways. The low-pitched frequencies poured out of my mouth with white sparks of light that enveloped her body and instantly slowed down all her vital functions. Resting deep on the She-Dragon, I Voiced increasingly more potent frequencies until Maryani's energy turned into a solid block of silvery blue light.

After twenty minutes the projection had reached near-scream level. The entire room was ablaze with the power I had received from Marek.

I turned to Elyani. "Done!"

"Voof!" she exclaimed. "I didn't know you could do things like that."

Very gently, I Voice-projected a loving sound onto her curly hair, "Boooh!" As the whitish cloud of light reached her head, she shivered.

"Go straight down, as deep as you can," I told her. "If you sense my presence, simply let go of Maryani."

"It shall be done!" she took on a warrior's voice, a glitter of irony in her eyes. After giving me a quick (but unlawful) kiss, she went into her room, lay down and projected herself out of her body. Then she took Maryani down into the dark shafts that led from darkness visible to the superficial layers of the Underworlds.

I sat in meditation position, facing Maryani's body, and I let the blissful breeze take me through the gate, pulling Lilu with me.

But when I found myself in the blue cavern beneath the courtyard, Lilu wasn't in my hand.

"Damned Underworld, I *knew* things were going to go wrong!"

I let myself be brought back into the room and inspected the jar from a distance. It was too close to Maryani's head, I couldn't have opened the lid without disturbing the child's energy.

"Why do I call her a child? She isn't a child, she's a woman."

To my Dragon she *was* a child. A child in my hands.

I descended through the gate again, this time focussing all my attention on pulling Lilu. I was no luckier than before.

"Oh, Mother of soft stones, what have I done to Lilu?"

As if I didn't have enough problems already.

Had Woolly's best girl been damaged by the violent Voice projections?

I made a few more attempts, speaking soft words to her. I Dragon-pulled her, but with no result – Lilu refused to move. Finally I had to resign myself to descend without her.

There was plenty of time. Elyani and Maryani needed at least an hour to reach the outskirts of the Underworlds' caverns of sickness.

I let myself dive down along the gate's breeze for a while and stopped in a cavern where the silvery light was so bright it outshone everything else.

A wave rose from below and I found myself whispering in a threatening tone, "If anything touches my child..."

I stopped, staggered at the violence in my belly. "So is this how it feels to be a mother?"

Dragon-wild. It could make you kill. Clicking my fingers, "Like that!"

I was ready to take on the entire caverns of sickness. Just you wait till you see what a Dragon is *really* capable of.

"*Peace, man of the Law!*" I told myself. "*Peace!*" Wriggling my nostrils, I sniffed myself full with the blissful fragrance. And I let the Point-reinforced clear fountain above my head merge with the ascending column of energy formed by the gate.

Before I had time to invoke the White Eagle's presence, I realised he was already with me.

But whose energy was I feeling – the Eagle's or Elyani's?

As I let myself become slightly intoxicated with the fragrances, I began to see the beloved priestess as a huge winged angel of Highness.

I called with all my strength, "Eagle, we need you! This time we really need you."

I kept falling, holding onto the Elyaneagle's presence.

The angel responded in a whisper, "Why should it be difficult?"

Through the Point I surrendered to the guiding presence, and in no time I found myself in a huge orichalc cavern.

It was empty. But... there it was, the blessed little yellow light!

Maryani's soul.

That easy? I broke the holy silence of the cave, "Mother of the Light, O, Mother of the Light!.."

I ran towards her, tuning into her astral recognition symbols. This time, there was no possible error. The symbols were definitely those of Maryani, which I had carefully observed before the descent. Tears in my eyes, "Mother of the Light!.."

But something else was waiting for me.

"Lilu!" I exclaimed as I came closer. "What the Upperworld are you doing here?"

Woolly's best girl was floating in the space of the cavern, not far from Maryani's light.

I placed my hands horizontally and in parallel in front of my heart, palms facing each other, holding Maryani's light and Lilu at the same time.

The Great Ant has responded. Her clarity, with you, always.

In my hands, the full power of the Dragon. Above and below, infinity.

"Nothing can touch you, now. Totally safe!" my Dragon said, mothering her. "Maryani, high priestess of the White Eagle, you passed your test! We are going home." And I black-danced my way back to the nearest gate with them.

It felt as if hours had passed already.

In the elation of the moment I burst out laughing and let the dance movements take on a more joyful pace. "Look, there! This is my favourite. Lapis lazuli like you never see in the kingdom. And see this one? It's pink quartz. A precious essence of life."

I could feel how appreciative Maryani was of the treasures around us.

"This is azurite. Tune into it and you'll feel vast like a field of stars."

Arriving at the gate, Maryani's yellow light was shining in wonder. I decided to show her a little more. After all, this would probably be her only opportunity ever to glance at the marvels of the Underworlds.

Holding the two girls in the field between my palms, I let the gate's blissful flow take us down.

I had no idea what I was in for.

For some mysterious reason, the descent lasted much longer than I had intended. Bathed in silvery-blue light, the cavern we landed in was so gigantic that neither walls nor ceiling could be seen. The ground stretched before us like pure silver, with small piles of shining black gems here and there.

"Let's see if I can show you a river of water of life. Come on, tune in! Try to sense how I find my way!" I told Maryani while sniffing around for direction.

As I started walking along a silver trail, I gently moved my hands to and fro slowly, rocking Maryani against my breast. Lilu stayed a few centimetres away from her.

"Can you sense this fragrance? It makes you feel vibrant like a unicorn. A-live! There is a stream, only a few minutes from here."

Soon, we could see it in the distance. A broad majestic she-river, shining with the silvery wisdom of the water of the Ancient Days.

"We must be much lower than I thought," I said, considering how large the river was.

We danced our way to the shore. There I let go of the girls and let them float in the air by my side. I knelt on the gold sands and expressed my devotion and gratitude, "Holy water, wisdom of Dragon Mother. I bow to you, water. Blessed is thy spirit of life." I took half a handful of water and drank a sip of it.

Shaken by the mighty spirit of intoxication I exclaimed, "Underworld, we *are* deep! Maryani, Maryani, if only you could taste how divine this is!"

I stood up and black-danced in celebration, letting out volleys of strange sounds. The two small yellow lights were floating in the air in front of me, dancing with me. Drunk with my Mother's unfathomable ecstasy, I dipped my hand in the running stream and sprinkled them with a few drops.

And this was how the Point-boggling misadventure began.

There was a flash of light and for a split second I could see Maryani's body, not just a yellow light. The vision vanished as swiftly as it had appeared.

I stopped, bewildered.

"What was that?"

Perplexed, I turned to the Elyaneagle for inspiration.

Moved by the Dragon, I threw some more water at Maryani and Lilu.

Maryani's body reappeared, revealed from nowhere.

But this time it didn't fade.

There she stood. Right in front of me. With Lilu by her side.

"*Praise the Lord Melchisedek, Szar of the Brown Robe!*" Maryani greeted me with her usual candour.

I gazed at her, trying to collect my spirits. Was this really happening, or was I drunk with water of life?

Maryani smiled affectionately, "You do recognise me, Szar?"

I nodded. She was beyond doubt the Maryani I had left in the kingdom.

"What a wonderful place! Now I understand what you meant." She looked around her and walked toward me. "You look... very surprised, Szar."

I frowned, waiting to see if she was going to vanish again.

She knelt and dipped her hand into the water.

"Careful, Maryani!" I rushed towards her, "this water is powerful medicine. Drinking it can sometimes be dangerous."

She looked up at me and gave a lawful nod. Then she sprinkled her sandy hair with a handful of water. It made her laugh.

I sat by her side. "Are you... all right?"

"Lawfully fine. I have dreamt about this place many times, you know" she said.

"Have you?"

"Yes," she said, "there is a friend here waiting for me."

"A friend! A friend waiting for you in the Underworlds?"

"Don't worry," she said, "we'll soon find him."

"I am not worried, but..." I halted, realising that I *was* worried.

She cupped her hands and filled them with water. "In my dream, this was the way my friend said I should thank the river for its waters." She moved her hands slowly, drawing a circle and praying, "*To that which was, that which is, and that which will be!*" With reverence, she took a sip.

I stopped her, "Don't drink it! It can be dangerous."

"And if there is a friend close to you and if you want to bless him," she added, "you do this!" She threw the rest of the water in my face and smiled perkily.

"Hum... Maryani..." I wasn't sure what to say.

"Your dance was so beautiful, Szar of the Brown Robe," she went on, standing up. "Will you show me again how you do it?"

"Dancing and the Underworlds go together well!" I said, standing in front of her. "This is called the black dance." I started rehearsing the slow movements of the dance's opening.

She clapped her hands joyfully and moved with me. "This is wonderful! Do you think I could learn it?"

"No, not really, but..." I gasped, realising that she had her feet in the water. "Careful, Maryani! Don't get into the river!"

"Why?" she asked, staying where she was.

I promptly pulled her back. "If you fall into the river, you may find yourself flowing with it until the end of time."

"Wouldn't that be a lovely thing to do!" She laughed. "I am sure your Mother the Dragon would take good care of me." Then she pointed behind me, "Oh, look! What are these?"

I turned round. In the distance, a troop of large golden snakes could be seen approaching the river shore.

"They are called the Nagas," I explained in a benevolent teacher's voice. "They have come to drink from the waters of life. Once a great sage in the Dragon told me that one could talk to them."

"Have you ever done it?" Maryani asked.

"No. Never."

"Why?" she asked.

In the Blue Lagoon, far, far away. He is waiting.

I remained thoughtful, wondering why I had never tried to engage a conversation with one of the Nagas.

"Let's go and see them!" Maryani exclaimed. Before I could say anything, she grabbed Lilu in her hand and started running.

"Wait!" I called out. "They could be dangerous."

Maryani kept running.

"No! Don't go!" I shouted. After a few seconds, as she didn't respond, I raced after her.

There were at least forty of them, shiny golden snakes with large black eyes. As I came closer, I realised how frighteningly big they were. At least seventy lawful feet long!

"Stop!" I clamoured. "Maryani, stop! Please!" But she wouldn't listen. "*For the Lord Melchisedek's sake*, Maryani, come back!"

What were these monstrous beasts going to do to my child?

My Dragon went wild. "Maryani! Come back immediately!"

But Maryani ran surprisingly fast. I couldn't catch her.

"Oh, no! No!" I gasped as she came dangerously close to the beast that was leading the herd. And to make matters worse, she was carrying Woolly's stone!

Maryani stopped in front of the snake. It was massive, at least seven lawful feet high and seventy lawful feet long! With its enormous mouth, it could have swallowed Maryani and Lilu in one gulp.

I ran as fast as my Mother the Dragon allowed me.

Luckily, the golden snake remained still, facing Maryani.

Maryani took a few more steps towards it, slowly.

"No-o-o-o!" I yelled with all my strength, gathering my Point, fountain, Dragon and the rest for a momentous fight. "Don't go near it!"

Too late! Before I could catch up with her, she had reached out to the snake and placed her hand on what seemed to be its nose.

The beast didn't budge.

Maryani was against its mouth.

Finally, I reached her. I stopped and stood six lawful feet behind her, totally still. Any ill-considered move, and the beast might harm her.

As I was trying to figure out a plan, Maryani murmured, "You are Vasoukidass, aren't you?"

To my amazement the snake answered, in an extremely low-pitched voice, "My, my, yes, I am Vasoukidass."

"Vasouk, I have dreamt of you so many times!" she said, and she began to cry.

"And you are Maryani, aren't you?" the snake said.

She was in tears. "Yes, Vasouk."

"How long I have waited for you, Maryani."

I slowly unclenched my fists. "What the Underworld is going on here?" I thought.

The snake turned its eyes towards me. "And you are Szar of the Brown Robe, aren't you?"

"Hummm... yes, I am!"

"The White Eagle told me he had sent you to bring Maryani to me," the snake said.

In a hush, I counted the herd. There were at least seventy of these monsters, each of them looking as terrifying as the one in front of us.

"Little Maryani and I have a lot of things to tell each other," the leader of the herd said. "But if you want, you can stay with us, Szar of the Brown Robe!"

"Hum... thank you!" was all I could find to answer.

"Maryani," the giant snake asked, "how was your journey?"

"Oh, it was fun. Not too long. Szar was really nice to me, he danced all the way to entertain me."

"My, good. Very good!" The snake slowly rolled his eyes in different directions. "I have many things to show you, Maryani, and many presents for you."

Maryani's face lit up with a big smile. "Like you told me in our last dream?"

"Well, quite," the snake said, "quite!"

Maryani turned towards me, "Vasoukidass is a great magician!"

"Ah?" I said, containing the flutter in my voice.

"And he can know everything with his nose," she added.

Vasoukidass wriggled his enormous nostrils, as if to demonstrate the point.

"See!" Maryani said, "he moves his nostrils just like you told me!"

I didn't like to see the beast moving – even if only his nose.

"My, my... don't be afraid, Szar of the Brown Robe," Vasoukidass said. "Maryani will be perfectly safe as long as she is in my kingdom. You have my Naga's word."

I frowned, "Your kingdom?"

"Vasoukidass is the king here!" Maryani explained proudly. "All the other snakes are his subjects."

"Hum..." I suddenly remembered that it was part of the duties of the Thunder caste to act as ambassadors of the Lord Melchisedek. "Homage to you, Your Majesty!"

"Thank you, Szar of the Brown Robe," the Naga king answered in his slow voice. "My, let's go to the water, Maryani, I need a drink." He advanced with slow undulating movements, and Maryani walked by his side.

"As I told you in our last dream," the snake said, "I will start by showing you the volcanoes and the Furnaces of Doom, and we will go and meditate in the cave of Brahma-ratri. Then we will have to prepare your energy very gradually so you can sustain a bath in the Sea of Lightning."

"Oh! I'd love to swim in the Sea of Lightning. She's so beautiful!" Maryani seemed utterly delighted. "Will you come with me, Vasouk?"

"My, certainly! All my Nagas will be coming too."

I walked behind them, thinking, "This situation is getting totally out of control!" and tuning high into the clear fountain for inspiration.

Some of the snakes were swimming in the river. Vasoukidass remained on the shore and drank copiously while Maryani talked to him.

Then without warning, Maryani walked into the river until the water came up to her knees.

"No!" I choked. "Maryani! Are you mad?"

Vasoukidass turned his head towards me. "She's just playing. Don't worry!"

I didn't want to start a diplomatic incident. "But... Your Majesty..."

"You can call me Vasoukidass, Szar of the Brown Robe," he said slowly.

"Thank you, Your Majesty. But what if Maryani was carried away by the current?"

"Well, well, my Nagas wouldn't have much difficulty catching her," he said with tranquil assurance.

The idea of Maryani being chased through the river by seventy giant snakes didn't do much to reassure me. "Anyhow, Maryani," I said, "it will soon be time for us to go home."

"*No way, man of the Law!*" Maryani ran up to Vasoukidass.

"My, if your wish is to go home, Maryani," Vasoukidass said, "no one is forcing you to stay."

"But Vasouk, I have just arrived! You are not going to give up on me already, are you? It's so nice to be with you, after all these times we've dreamt together."

"Well," I suggested, "perhaps we could come back another time."

"No! I want to stay with Vasoukidass."

"Maryani," I insisted, "all your friends are waiting for you in the kingdom!"

"Maryani and I have important matters to discuss, Szar of the Brown Robe," Vasoukidass said.

"Well, why don't you two go ahead and discuss your important matters," I suggested. "I will wait as long as needed. I don't have to be in the kingdom before tomorrow morning, anyway."

The two friends looked at me in reprobation, as if I was completely missing the point.

I tuned high into the clear fountain, seeking inspiration

Letting out a long sigh, I realised, "There is no way you are going to come back to the kingdom with me now, is there?"

Maryani stubbornly shook her head.

Vasoukidass remained impassive.

Thoughtful, I contemplated his troop of seventy Naga-monsters frolicking in the waters of life. "Maryani, if I come and pick you up tomorrow night, will you go up with me?"

She didn't answer.

"You have my word, Szar of the Brown Robe, Maryani will be safe here," Vasoukidass reiterated. "Perfectly safe, I should say. Why don't you come and visit us tomorrow night? We shall be delighted to converse with you, as we enjoy conversing with friends very much. And we shall show you some wonders which, perhaps, you missed during your former visits to my kingdom."

The fountain's flow guided me to concede defeat. "This is the Eagle's Will, isn't it?"

The Naga king nodded. So did Maryani.

Vasoukidass could see I was still hesitating, "Szar, let us all go for a walk together. Close by – quite close by, actually – there is a most special spring which, no doubt, you will greatly enjoy. One of the legends of the Nagas says the waters of this spring, which is ancient, come straight from the glorious Midnight Sun, and are endowed with astonishing properties."

The Nagas were already gathering on the shore, making ready for the stroll.

10.2 Weaving the Point, Eisraim style

Back in the kingdom, I thoroughly inspected Maryani's hibernating body. All her gateways were in perfect condition.

Odd universes, conscious streams turned light, light turned liquid, I drink your elixir of infinity.

I went out into the courtyard.

It was already late in the morning. Teyani, Alcibyadi and Elyani were having a discussion on the lawn, while waiting for me.

Reading on my face that something had gone wrong, they waited for me to speak.

I sat down with them. "We have a problem."

Teyani remained calm, pushing away memories of the eight White Eagles who had failed to return from the Underworlds in the last years.

"Where is Maryani? Couldn't you find her?" she asked.

"I did find her, but I couldn't bring her back."

"Is it that bad? Is she so sick and stuck that even you can't bring her back?" Alcibyadi was appalled.

I inhaled a deep breath. "Maryani is fine. She is neither sick nor stuck. She just refuses to come back."

My friends were astonished.

I told them the whole story. Its ending was not the least surprising part: "When I left Maryani and the Naga at the spring of the Midnight Sun, Lilu refused to come with me as well! I couldn't believe my ill luck. Each time I took her in my hand, she flew straight back to Maryani. So I had to leave her down there too. Woolly is going to be fu-rious!"

Teyani wasn't the least bit interested in Lilu. "If it is the Eagle's Will that Maryani stay with the Naga, I guess we should all rejoice," she commented in an uncertain voice. Then she promptly asked, "Do you think you might bring her back tonight?"

"I will certainly try, Teyani, but... Maryani seems to be a much more stubborn person than I thought. I can't see her agreeing to return with me tonight. She and Vasoukidass appear to have many plans in mind." I cogitated briefly. "Do you think I should try to abduct her?"

"Sweet Lord Melchisedek, never!" Teyani exclaimed in horror. "For a start, we must abide by the Eagle's Will. And the Nagas are powerful magicians whose feats are praised by several hymns of the Law. They spit huge flames of venom that consume everything in their way. They can paralyse people – as well as gods and angels – just by looking into their eyes. Through their spells, they can awaken fierce beings of fire that terrorise even the mightiest of warriors. And they are the keepers of many secret powers that the gods themselves envy. Making the Nagas our enemies is completely out of the question."

"Well, then, Maryani is very safe," Alcibyadi exclaimed.

I looked unconvinced.

"If the king of the Nagas has engaged his word on her safety, what is there to fear?" she insisted.

"I agree!" Elyani said. "Have you heard the story of the war between the Nagas and the angels of darkness?"

I shook my head, pulling on my beard.

"Once," Elyani began, "a hierarchy of dark angels who were just as powerful as the Watchers decided to invade the Nagas' kingdom. They were hungry for the Nagas' wealth, which is legendary, and also for the powers of the Underworlds. The Nagas have the reputation of being slow moving, gentle and peaceful, and so these angels of war were foolish enough to believe they could prevail over them easily. Yet, within three days the Nagas had wiped out their entire hierarchy. Not one of them was left alive."

"Can you imagine?" Alcibyadi exclaimed, "These dark angels were far more powerful than the whole of humanity. And they were exterminated in three days!"

I gulped, thanking the She-Serpent of Eternal Wisdom for having given me some restraint when I was thinking of attacking the Naga.

"The Nagas are the custodians of ancient forces that have long disappeared from the kingdom – the magic of the Ancient Days of the Earth," Teyani added.

"Do the Nagas rule over the entire Underworlds?" I asked.

"No," Teyani answered, "I think their kingdom only occupies a fraction of the Underworlds – a large fraction, though."

"A large fraction of something limitless could be very big," Elyani blew out her cheeks. "The Nagas live for thousands and thousands of years. Some hymns even say that they are immortal. And their knowledge of your Mother the Dragon is vast. The Law calls them *the keepers of the Dragon's might*."

An angelic silence descended onto the courtyard, inspiring us.

"Persuasion!" I announced after a few seconds, raising my index finger. "Persuasion is definitely what is called for in this situation."

Teyani and Elyani burst out laughing.

I looked into Alcibyadi's eyes, wondering if Lehrmon had said yes.

Alcibyadi shook her head silently.

Teyani went on to discuss the depressing news from various parts of the kingdom. The great assembly of priests in the county of the Western Plains had not yet been able to restore the rains. Further south, the Jeremitzia river had run dry, creating an unprecedented drought in three counties. The precious herbs of madness, dear to the gods of love, were becoming almost impossible to find. Up north in Perentie, the buildings of six villages had melted to the ground, leaving the entire population without shelter. Bandits had ransacked half the temples of the county of the Upper Western Shores... the list seemed endless. The people of Eisraim were starting to regard the situation in their own county as increasingly precarious. But what to do?

That was the question to which no one had an answer.

After Teyani and Alcibyadi had left, Elyani came and sat close to me. "Szar, do you think Maryani and Vasoukidass love each other?" she asked.

I opened my eyes wide. "Well... perhaps they do, in a way – as much as a seventeen-year-old priestess can love a thousand-year-old snake who spits all-consuming tongues of venom. I couldn't imagine them being lovers, but there certainly seemed to be love between them."

"Then let me remind you of your solemn vow, Dragon," Elyani said.

"What vow?" I frowned.

"The vow that you will never attempt to separate those who love each other."

I was taken aback. "Did I swear that? I don't remember..."

"Of course you don't!" she said. "The vow will be made in the future. But it's an eternal vow, so it is already binding."

"Sweet angel!" I burst out laughing and took her in my arms.

"Will you keep your vow?" she insisted, firm as a pillar of heaven.

The forcefulness of the request shook me, "If you want, I will take the vow right now."

"No," the magic woman said in a grave voice, "you are not ready for it. If you were to swear now, it would not be eternally binding."

"Voof!" I exclaimed, letting myself fall on the lawn with her. "You are really serious, aren't you?"

"Oh, yes, Dragon, I am!".

"But what if Maryani stays away from her body for too long and dies?"

"How long can you keep her body hibernating?"

"Hibernation is not without dangers," I cautioned, "especially these days, with floods of dirty elemental slime pouring out of the fields."

"Why not ask advice from the Naga king? The Nagas' wisdom is legendary. Vasoukidass might even have teachings to give you."

"What?" I laughed. "I can't believe this! This situation is getting totally out of hand."

Steadfast like the Eagle's flight on the Edge of Highness, Elyani reiterated her plea, "Will you hold on to your vow?"

"All right, all right!" I capitulated. "I will not try to separate the friends against their will."

Elyani welcomed the resolution with a long kiss, vibrant with many a mystery from ancient times.

When I recovered my breath, I asked her if Teyani had given any clues about the oracle's cryptic sentences.

"'Take one day at a time and do not worry about anything but loving the Eagle and teaching the Point to Szar,' this is what Teyani said," Elyani answered. "What about you, any insights?"

"*Trust the gods and fight for Elyani* – this was the most powerful of the sentences," I said, sending a loving thought to Lord Gana.

"Thank you, Lord Gana!" Elyani echoed.

"But there is not much to be fought for at the moment," I lamented. "Anyhow, *I* am the one who always runs into trouble, and not just with Flying Dragons. You are the one who shines. There is never anything wrong with you."

"Let's not talk about it!" Elyani clicked her fingers, "To the Point, Brother Knight!"

"To the Point, Brother Knight!" I sat up straight, startled by the metamorphosis in her voice. Whenever she spoke of the Brother Knights, Elyani became a different person. A wild, unlawfully fascinating spark flared in her eyes. Her mellow Eagle tenderness faded, unveiling a fiery warrior, fast moving and stubborn, a beautiful stranger who seemed to know me by heart.

"What have you to report, Brother Knight?" she asked, focussing on the centres of energy above my head.

I collected my spirits, watching her face with curiosity. Her lips were redder, it seemed. And weren't her eyes darker?

"Since you started teaching me about the Point, my clear fountain has become infinitely more stable and tangible," I told her. "At times, inspiration flows down into me like a river. And I no longer have to wait passively for it to happen – the Point triggers the flow." I went on to voice my dissatisfaction about spending so much time and energy learning to Point-control fields that were bound to collapse, rather sooner than later. "Why not use methods that operate independently of the warp?" I questioned.

"Imagine you are a Nephilim giant, living on the high rocks of the Eastern Peninsula," she made herself playful. "You have woven the most fantastic Point-fields in the entire kingdom, you can think fast, super-fast – faster than anyone else on Earth! You experience summits of pleasure and chasms of passion, you read archives of the past and the future, you travel to the strangest spheres of remoteness, fathom the consciousness of the Watchers, and comprehend greater mysteries even than all this."

So far, I had no cause for complaint.

"Why would you want to think for a second that your fields might one day be disconnected, leaving you stupid and powerless?"

"But isn't that how they will end up anyway?" I retorted.

"Probably. But no one wants to think about it. Why should a king want to dwell on the fact that he is bound to become a beggar?"

"Mm..." I found myself scratching my nose the way Woolly did. "What am I supposed to do, by the way, if a giant ever engages me in a Point-fight?"

"Wait, man of the Law, it's too early to worry about that. First, you must become a master of the Point, Eisraim style," she said.

"And how does one become a master in the Eisraim style of power of the Point?" I felt an urgent need to know. "Practice, practice, practice...?"

"Not just practice," she said. "Initiations – transfers of power."

Waiting, I liked less and less. "Where do I start?" I insisted.

"Your Point isn't strong enough yet. Just give me a little more time."

"What needs to happen?"

"Why does a little child lose stools without even realising it? Because his sphincter is not yet strong enough. The Point is like a sphincter. All sorts of energies reach your consciousness through the Point – some good, and some not so good. As long as your Point is immature, you have no control over what falls into your head."

I crossed my arms, most displeased.

"All right, tune into your Point!" she gave in.

I felt the centre of energy above my head lighting up like a small sun.

"Now it's loose," she said. Then, from her Point, she manipulated my energy. "Now it's tight. Can you feel the difference?"

"Lawfully unmistakable!" The feeling in the Point was sharp and acute like the tip of a triangle.

"Now do it yourself," she said. "Make it loose."

I let my Point become like a jelly.

"A loose Point leaves you vulnerable to attack. Anyone can dump venom into you. Now tighten it up again!"

I reproduced the sharp feeling, letting the Point coincide with the tip of the bright triangle of light that Elyani had lit for me. "Am I still vulnerable?"

"Less," she said.

"Less vulnerable..." I laughed, "but that's not good enough! Should I try to sharpen it?"

"Yes, but... the Point needs more than just sharpness, it needs structure. The centre of energy needs to be built. This part you don't have to worry about. I am in charge."

"So what are you doing to me?"

"Weaving your Point. It's the way the knowledge of the Point has been transmitted in Eisraim for hundreds of years."

"Who wove your Point, Lady Elyani?" I asked respectfully.

"*All glory to the teacher!* Mother Teyani," she bent her head with reverence. "And Teyani's Point was woven by Gervin, whose Point was woven by Orest."

The nightmare vision of a horde of Nephilim giants reappeared, each and every one of them a great expert in Point-warfare, fielded to the teeth, maddened with Watchers' fever. "I bet they won't have any difficulty finding their way in the corridors," I told myself. "Sharpness and structure," I summarised. "Will that make me ready to face the giants?"

"Oh, no! These are only prerequisites. For your Point to be *really* sealed, it must be connected to high sources of power. Presently, you are connecting to Lord Gana's glorious light – drops of his light, nothing more. Later, you will also resonate with the Eagle and with the energy of Thunder." Reading my next question, she added, "My Point shines the Eagle's light. I also connect with Mareena."

"Mareena of the world of the of gods?"

"A fountain of bounty! Whenever she can she will help you, as she has been helping the people of Eisraim since her ascension to the world of the gods."

The troops of giants were still in my mind. "Do you think we will ever have to fight against these Nephilim brutes?"

"Take one step at a time, Warrior," Elyani advised, the Eagle glowing in her eyes. As I was about to insist, she smiled with a touch of irony, "Or would you like Teyani and Alcibyadi to ask the oracle again, perhaps?"

I surrendered unconditionally, letting myself drop onto the lawn. "Weave me!"

10.3 The Underworlds, realm of might

When I next descended into the Underworlds, I was immediately guided to Maryani and her Naga king. I didn't even have to tune in, I was miraculously transferred from gate to gate until I arrived at a place that was completely different from anything I had seen before.

It was a huge garden with flowers of every imaginable colour, and trees replete with exuberantly large fruits. Flocks of birds were singing harmonious melodies, and the light was far brighter than in the kingdom.

Maryani came to greet me, "Welcome, Szar!"

"*Oh my Lord Melchisedek*, what has happened to you?" I watched her aura with consternation. Ruby-red flames flared from her, and her cheeks and forehead looked as if she had been burnt.

"Don't worry, *friend in the Law*, I just got a bit hot when I visited the Furnaces of Doom. But it has made me feel fantastic! Do you like this garden?" she gave a sweep of her hand.

"The Furnaces of Doom?" I gasped. "Did you take Lilu with you?"

"Of course!" Taking me by the hand, she started walking. "Don't worry! Lilu is having a great time with Vasouk and me."

"Can I see her?"

"You'll see her soon. She's with Vasouk." Without pausing she went on, her voice full of delight, "The Underworlds are so beautiful, Szar! Have you ever visited the range of volcanoes that borders the Furnaces of Doom?"

"No!"

"Szar, you *must*! The lakes of lava are so special. I can't wait till Vasouk lets me swim there."

"Hum... do you really think it would be wise, Maryani?"

"Szar, you always seem to be afraid! The Underworlds are not like people think, you know?"

"I know, I know..." I sighed. "I am just concerned for your health."

"Precisely," she laughed, "Vasouk says that as long as someone hasn't swum in the Sea of Lightning, their health will always remain flimsy."

"And... you are planning to swim in the Sea of Lightning?"

"Of course!" she said. "But it has to come at the right time. If you are not ready, then you can be evaporated in one second. Voof!" She laughed.

I didn't.

We had arrived at a fabulous orchard where Vasouk was waiting for us.

He welcomed me with his slow, low-pitched voice, "My, my, isn't that Szar of the Brown Robe? What a happy circumstance."

"Greetings, Your Majesty." I wished I had thought of asking Gervin how I was to salute a Naga king.

"How do you like our orchards, Szar of the Brown Robe?"

"They are wonderful, Your Majesty!" I said, looking around for Lilu. When I saw her floating in the air not far from Vasoukidass' head, I got a shock. Her size had doubled at least, and she was ablaze with ruby-red flames like Maryani's aura.

Vasoukidass plunged his gaze into me.

"She is starting to look better, isn't she?"

The king lightly wriggled his nostrils, and Lilu moved towards me. "I should say, she was too cold. She needed some warmth. And some might. She was badly lacking might, I should say."

Maryani brought me a huge apple, together with a few other fruits that I had never seen before. Then she went to sit close to Vasouk, her back resting against the Naga's golden body.

"I'm so hungry!" she said, and she started devouring a large purple fruit that could have been a plum, except it was nearly as large as a pumpkin.

"Since we visited the Furnaces of Doom, I haven't stopped eating," she explained.

"Why don't you try our apples, Szar of the Brown Robe? This garden is famous for them," Vasouk said.

I took a bite of the gorgeous red apple Maryani had handed me. It was sublime. My energy was instantly filled with sparkling vibration, and my Dragon started vroofing in ecstasy.

"Sit down!" Vasouk wisely advised.

I let myself collapse in meditation position.

"My, good. Very good!" Vasouk said in his deep, melodious voice.

I remained silent for a moment, captured by the vroofing delight.

A whirling nebula, dizzy, drunk with his elixir.

Vasouk waited patiently. Meanwhile, Maryani was eating fruit after fruit, including red apples like the one she had given me.

When he judged I had recovered, Vasouk asked, "What shall we converse about, Szar of the Brown Robe? My, Maryani and I have hardly had any time to speak yet. We have been so busy!"

"Your Majesty, you said Lilu was badly lacking might. Presently, in the kingdom my friends are running into trouble with a number of stones like her. How could we give them some might?"

Vasouk's large round black eyes rolled to the right, then to the left, then he said, "My, might is just what you do not have in your kingdom. Up there, everything is insubstantial and diluted. What you call matter, I myself would rather call dream. And life force... life force is so deplorably weak in your kingdom. You know it well, Szar of the Brown Robe, don't you?"

I nodded.

Vasouk turned his head towards Maryani and explained, "Szar of the Brown Robe is an initiate of the Sons of the Dragon. When he Underwent his initiation, his physical body was made receptive to my kingdom's energies – forces that human beings normally never taste. It changed him completely. It made him strong. Compared to men, I mean to say."

Maryani nodded and went to pick more fruits.

"This might which you gained by dying in the Dragon, my friend, is just what your stones are lacking."

This made me think. Deeply. How could the Dragon's might be infused into Woolly's stones?

When Maryani came back, Vasouk quietly opened his mouth, unveiling a huge black tongue and two rows of terrifying shiny white fangs. Maryani dropped a pumpkin-plum on his tongue. As he swallowed it, she went back to sit against his golden scales and started eating again.

"Might is something which is so foreign to human beings," Vasouk went on. "They don't have much of it, and they do not even understand that my kingdom is where they could find it." He swivelled his huge head around to regard Maryani. "Have you heard of this analogy which compares the creation to an enormous ladder?"

"Yes, Mother Teyani has explained it many times," she said. "It's part of the Law of human beings."

Vasouk sniffed in approbation. "Well, good. Very good! Part of the Law of the Nagas too. So, the higher you climb the ladder, the purer the consciousness. The lower you descend along the ladder, the mightier the might."

"But your consciousness is very pure Vasouk, and yet you rule over the lower part of the ladder!" Maryani pointed out.

"Well, well... I should say... this is because, when going high enough or low enough in the ladder, you reach domains where consciousness and might cannot be separated." Vasouk rolled his eyes rapidly in several directions, then fixed them on me.

I rested deep on my Mother the Dragon, remembering how Nagas could annihilate people and angels just by looking at them.

Vasouk shone a friendly smile. "If you asked Szar, he would tell you that our Mother the Dragon is the Lord Melchisedek's might. Wouldn't you, Szar of the Brown Robe?"

"Certainly, Your Majesty."

"My, if you asked me, I would tell you that the Lord Melchisedek is our Mother the Dragon's consciousness."

"Subtle!" Maryani frowned thoughtfully.

"I should say, subtlety is certainly not everything in life, but it is a lot!" Vasouk commented. Then he continued, "High up in the ladder, there is consciousness with might. Low down, there is might with consciousness. My, my... in the middle, where human beings live, you should expect to find both consciousness with might and might with consciousness, shouldn't you? Yet, strange enough, there is neither – which, if you see what I mean, is exactly why your stones are experiencing difficulties, Szar of the Brown Robe."

"Your Majesty, does this mean that the stones should be taken to the top of the ladder? Or perhaps to the bottom?" I questioned.

"That should certainly help, but that would not bring the final solution," Vasouk replied. "Rather, the top and the bottom of the ladder should be taken into your stones."

The last sentence left me even more perplexed than the previous one.

"Are stones one of your interests, Vasouk?" Maryani asked.

"Well, yes. I should certainly say they are," Vasouk said, "for I *am* a stone."

"Now, this is the last straw!" I thought, pulling my beard.

Maryani jumped to her feet and contemplated the Naga's long golden body. "You and Lilu look quite different, though," she observed, candid.

"Lilu is but a baby stone. She still has a long way to go. Different types of stones, there are, you know," Vasouk answered.

"Will Lilu end up looking like you?" Maryani asked.

"My, and what if I didn't look like what I look like?" Vasouk's enigmatic smile revealed a glimpse of a fang. "What if, in reality, I lived in the spheres of Lowness, and this Naga's body was just an appearance? A most convenient appearance, I might say."

"What are the spheres of Lowness?" I asked.

"It's how the Nagas call the spheres of Highness," Maryani explained. "It's because they are as much below as they are above."

"Just as much indeed!" Vasouk confirmed.

"Vasouk, I want to know what you look like in the spheres of Lowness!" Maryani stroked one of Vasouk's golden scales.

"Well, perhaps we could descend together and visit me in the spheres of Lowness, after your swim in the Sea of Lightning." Amused, Vasouk gave me a broad smile, this time unveiling his two rows of huge shining fangs, "That's if she doesn't get evaporated, of course."

I did my best to remain contained and maintain a diplomatic smile.

"For if Maryani evaporates," Vasouk went on, "then she will already be in the spheres of Lowness. Reassuring, isn't it?"

I managed to keep myself smiling.

Vasouk moved his eyes and his nostrils rapidly, then turned his head towards Maryani. "Our friend Szar of the Brown Robe is worried, isn't he?"

"I know!" Maryani agreed. "What could we do about it?"

"Is it because he knows you are the niece of the prince of the county of Eisraim, and he is worried his temple will get into trouble if he doesn't take you back after bringing you down?"

"What?" I thought, welcoming the news like a punch in the stomach. "How come no one told me this?"

Maryani turned towards me, "Is this what the problem is, Szar?"

"Hum... I was... unaware of this."

Vasouk kept rolling his eyes in all directions. "Well, well... what if we, the Nagas, sent an official message to His Majesty the Prince of the County of Eisraim, announcing that Lady Maryani of the White Eagle is our guest and that King Vasoukidass has taken her under his personal protection?"

Maryani clapped her hands. "Yes! Let's do that!"

"Szar of the Brown Robe, would you kindly be our ambassador for this matter, and convey the message to His Majesty the Prince of the County of Eisraim?"

"But... certainly, Your Majesty."

"Now, what else are you worried about, Szar of the Brown Robe? Is it Lilu, perhaps?"

"I don't think Szar understands why he likes Lilu," Maryani interposed.

"My, should we perhaps tell him, then?" Vasouk suggested.

"This situation is utterly out of control," I kept on thinking.

"Lilu is an externalisation of Woolly's energy – an aspect of Woolly that will exist in the future," Vasouk explained.

"And in the future," Maryani added, "Woolly and you will become best friends."

I listened in silence, my eyes fixed on Lilu. She was still ablaze with red sparks of light, and had flown back close to Vasouk's head. "Can you see Woolly's future when you tune into Lilu?" I asked.

"Well, quite!" Vasouk said.

"Yes, quite!" Maryani added.

I was fascinated. "Does this mean that Woolly will put more and more of his energy into Lilu so that finally, Lilu-Woolly will be like His Majesty King Vasoukidass?"

Maryani pulled a face, "The way Woolly's work is going at the moment, there is not much chance of that happening."

Vasouk gave a Naga-nod. "Well, yes. This is the truth. I should say, there are signs in Lilu which show that Woolly has been making a number of mistakes."

This sounded like a golden opportunity to restore the vitality of the Archive stones. Suspecting Vasouk had the power to bring anyone he wished down into his kingdom, I pleaded, "Could I perhaps bring Woolly to you, Your Majesty, so that he could listen to your advice?"

Vasouk rolled his eyes around to Maryani. "My, my... would you want Woolly down here?"

Maryani hesitated. "I think I prefer him to wait," she said finally.

"Wise, I believe. Very wise," Vasouk approved, wriggling his nostrils. "Well, then, Szar of the Brown Robe, tell Woolly to wait."

"Hum... Your Majesty... wait for what?"

"For me!" Maryani declared, innocently royal.

I remained thoughtful, wondering what the Far Underworld I was going to tell Woolly.

"Szar of the Brown Robe, do you know why the Nagas are never seen laughing?" Vasouk asked.

"No, Your Majesty."

"Well, well... it is because they laugh inside themselves. All the time. It is part of their nature."

Maryani gave me a look and burst out laughing.

"Well, well, now..." Vasouk said, "we all need a drink. Szar of the Brown Robe, let us show you the magnificent rivers which flow through this orchard. There are four of them."

10.4 Elyani in the fumes

As soon as I returned to the kingdom, I went to inspect Lilu's jar.

"Oh, no!" I exclaimed with consternation. She had shrunk again.

Elyani came and sat by my side. "Maryani's energy looks excellent."

"Elyani, this story is getting worse and worse," I started complaining, and went on to retell the events of the night.

Elyani didn't seem worried. She passed her hand through my hair. "Your eyes are shining like the Molten Sea."

"The water in those rivers of life was more powerful than anything I had ever tasted. But I couldn't believe how much Maryani drank. I had a mouthful and that was Dragon plenty for me. It made me tipsy. But you should have seen her! She plunged her head into the water, just like the Naga king, and she drank on and on. She wouldn't stop! Elyani, I am extremely concerned."

"Concerned about what?" she asked in a soft voice.

"What if Maryani turns into a Naga?"

Elyani burst out laughing. "Yes, what would we tell the prince of the county of Eisraim?"

"By the way, why didn't anyone tell me she was his niece?"

"Teyani didn't want you to be worried."

"Great! And how am I supposed to deliver the message to the prince?"

"I'd leave this task to Teyani if I were you," Elyani suggested. "What do you intend to tell Woolly?"

I made a suggestion, "What if you accompanied me? I want to show you Woolly's treasure caves. If Woolly is in a bad mood, we won't stay long. But perhaps you could tell me if he will become my friend. Maryani and Vasoukidass said it would happen in the future. It could well mean a future life."

Elyani was delighted with the invitation.

She took my arm and we set off through the corridors, enjoying the space of inner peace the Point-guided stroll provided.

When we reached the chapel and opened the door, a man immediately came towards us. "*Praise the Lord Melchisedek, Commander!* My name is Physsen, of the caste of the Field Wizards. I am in charge of checking who enters."

A quick sniff was enough to judge that Physsen of the Field Wizards was unable to fight. Still, I was delighted to see the place being guarded. "*All glory to the Lord Melchisedek, Physsen!* This is Lady Elyani, who has come with me to visit Master Woolly."

After greeting her, Physsen told us, "Master Woolly has gone out, but he should be back soon."

Shine, rains of light. Blow, winds of space. Clusters of stars have gathered for the great dance. Will you join in?

I warned Elyani to watch out for the bottles on the floor and took her from room to room, pointing out the jars that contained the most special energies. "Tune into this one!" I said, grabbing a blue jar from the shelves on the wall. "It makes my Dragon go vroof – just what you do to me!"

She grinned. "Should I be jealous?"

"Tune in!" I directed.

She closed her eyes. "Makes me feel tipsy."

I got her to tune into the best jars I could find.

"Voof!" she said. "I'm feeling dizzier and dizzier."

I snapped my fingers, "You can fall into my arms any time!"

Just then, Woolly turned up. When he saw Elyani he clapped his hands and exclaimed, "Oh! Oh! What a beauty! She's from Nephilim stock, I can see. Where did you find her?"

I was embarrassed. "Hum... Woolly, this is Lady Elyani, high priestess of the White Eagle."

He walked towards her. "Yes I know. PraisthLordMelchisdek Lady Elyani. D'you mind if I have a look at your stone?"

Before she had time to answer, he took the pendant off her neck. "Oh! She's *so* beautiful!" he kept on raving.

Elyani tried to contain herself at first, but then she burst out laughing. Fresh laughter that filled the room with joy.

His eyes still fixed on the stone, Woolly smiled. "How's life, Lady Elyani?" he asked.

Elyani could not stop laughing.

Finally he looked at her. He seemed moved. "She's nearly as beautiful as her soft stone," he said. "I tried to marry one just like her a few years ago. She was blasting! Unfortunately, it all went vinegar when I melted her father's chapel down to the lawful ground. That's when I had to leave the temple in a hurry. Mind you, it was probably the best thing the Goddess ever did for that girl."

Holding onto my arm, Elyani was still laughing. Woolly and I exchanged a long smile. Loaded with unspoken meaning.

The cosmic rendezvous has been planned. In a palace, at the feet of an angel of Highness. Miss not the call! She will die. For you.

"Woolly," I finally said, "we have come to bring you a message."

"I love messages!" Woolly said. "What's the message, Commander?"

Still carried by the elation of the fumes, Elyani caught her breath and exclaimed, "Wait! Just wait!"

Woolly took Elyani's joyful mood as a personal compliment on the power of his elixirs. He smiled at her, "Is that the message? But I hate waiting! That's how Gervin enticed me into Eisraim, by the way. He promised that if I established myself here, I would never have to wait for anything – within reasonable limits, of course."

"Woolly," Elyani declared, "we want to know how you met Gervin!"

Woolly looked up to the gods. "*Oh, woman of the Law*, do you really want to know about this painful episode of my no-less-painful existence?"

"Yes!" The vigour in Elyani's voice took us both by surprise.

"All right, then!" he yielded. "Let's go to the slime cellar, it's so much nicer down there. Watch your feet for the bottles."

As we followed him down the stairway, he began his story. "It started in the temple of Laminindra, in the county of the Northern Lakes. That's where I had this unfortunate incident – the shock wave that melted my fiancee's father's chapel, and a few other chapels around." He let out a long, nostalgic sigh. "After this I had to leave my county. I migrated to the Western Plains' main temple. The stone makers of that temple were after someone who could help them produce soft-stone weapons."

We had arrived in the largest cellar, where at least forty huge buckets of white slime were kept.

The Great Night, which still sings the Song of Creation.

Woolly sat on the floor and invited us to do the same. "Like the smell, Lady Elyani?"

Elyani inhaled a long breath. "It makes my Dragon all vibrant!"

I frowned.

Woolly burst out laughing.

"And what disaster did you create in the Western Plains, Woolly?" Elyani asked.

"Talk about disaster, Lady Elyani!" Woolly rubbed his fingers against the bump on his nose. "The stone makers of the Western Plains temple were such idiotic bastards in the Law! Each time I prepared something decent for them, they wrecked it with some misguided intervention. Finally, I became so fed up with them that I requested the high priest to let me have my own chapel. All I asked was that no one disturb me, and I said I would deliver their soft-stone weapons." As Woolly spoke, he enjoyed watching Elyani taking in long breaths, filling her lungs with the fumes of white slime.

"But the damn stone makers hadn't finished with me yet. One night, they came to spy on my chapel. The problem was, they were the kind of dummies who can't distinguish a Blue priestess from a filosterops. They messed with my weapon-stones. And then of course, what do you expect? They blasted their asses, large-scale." Swelling his cheeks, Woolly let out a loud fart sound.

The high priestess burst out laughing again.

"The next morning when I arrived I found four of them lying dead on the floor. Not a great waste for the kingdom, mind you, but I remember pulling my hair and yelling to the Goddess, 'What the Ugly Underworld have I done to you to make you keep pissing on me all the time?' Then I thought, 'This time, it's not really my fault. Why should I run away?' So I just went and reported the facts to the high priest." Woolly sighed. "That was another *big* mistake. The lawful dickhead had me thrown in jail. *Thank the Lord Melchisedek*, Gervin happened to be visiting the temple at the time. He heard the story and asked to see me."

Woolly paused, checking that Elyani and I were anxiously waiting for the rest of his story.

"Gervin started by asking me a few questions about stones, to check me out. There was something about the man I instantly liked. Couldn't say what. Perhaps it was the fact that he burst out laughing when he heard my story. No one had ever laughed when I told them about the huge fire I had started in my native temple. And he sounded like he knew his business. In the world of soft stones, there are so many Blue priestesses!

Then for no apparent reason Gervin interrupted me in the middle of the conversation and asked, 'Woolly, would you like to come with me to Eisraim and take part in the making of one of the most extraordinary soft stones of all time?' I gave it half a second of deep reflection, then I answered, 'Or would I prefer to remain in the Western Plains' dungeons for the rest of my days?' We laughed so loudly that the guard on the other side of the door came into the cell, to check that everything was lawful. You should have seen his face!

Gervin arranged to have my sentence commuted to exile from the Western Plains. I didn't mind, there was no great future for me in that jail. And that's how I landed in the temple of Eisraim."

Elyani clapped her hands. "Woolly, what a wonderful story!"

Woolly pulled a face, "Sort of!" Then he asked, "Now, will you tell me what I am supposed to wait for?"

"Well... Woolly, have you ever heard of the Nagas?" I asked him.

"A kind of worm that lives in Underworld compost, is that it?"

Elyani sparkled, her head resting on my shoulder.

"Well, well..." I said, "sort of. But noble. Very noble!"

"Right!" he said. "A noble worm that lives in Underworld shit."

"Woolly!" Elyani reprimanded him. "Nagas are snakes, not worms, and they live in magnificent golden palaces, not in compost. Many of them are endowed with omniscience. If they heard you insulting them, they could strike you with lightning."

Woolly sat straight and composed himself, a dignified look on his face. In a slow, ceremonial voice he called, "*Oh Lord Melchisedek! And what can I do for these noble Nagas, my friends in the Law?*"

"Rather, what can the Nagas do for you, Woolly?" Elyani said.

I briefly told him that Maryani and Vasouk had become friends and had offered to help us in our stone-making enterprises.

Woolly immediately understood there was *a phoenix in the pot.* "The Underworlds are full of mind-blowing forces, aren't they?" There was a flare in his eyes.

I quoted Vasouk, "The Underworlds are the kingdom of might."

"Any chance of bringing Vasouk to this chapel?" Woolly asked.

Dubious, I frowned, and twinged my beard.

"Don't say no!" Elyani intervened. "You have not even extended an official invitation to him yet!"

"Yeah!" Woolly was jubilant. "Commander, please tell Vasouk he is officially invited by Master Woolly of the Dirty-Cream Robe!" Then he winked at me and whispered, "I was born in a different caste, but I had to change. No need to tell him that. But tell him he'd better squirm his way here fast, because our stones are getting worse by the day. All of them! And from the news I received yesterday, the situation in Lasseera is even worse than here. We're in deep trouble, Commander."

Thoughtful, I contemplated the many stains on Woolly's sort-of-cream gown. "Once, when I was at the temple of the Dragon, the black-dancers' grand master told me, 'If you ever get into deep trouble, or if you need to do something *really* impossible, always remember to look for the solution in *the infinite glory of the Underworlds*. The deeper down you go, the more incredible the things you will find.'"

10.5 Integrity, fire, and the cauldron creation myth

When I next descended into the Underworlds, I was instantly transferred from the blue cavern under Elyani's courtyard to the orchard where I was to meet Maryani and Vasouk.

I sniffed around for direction and started walking amidst the brilliantly coloured flowers. They were huge – some of them familiar, like sunflowers, purple roses, pink pantelopes and golden carnations. Others had extravagant shapes that were totally unknown to me. I understood these were part of the wonders that used to be seen on Earth in the Ancient Days, before the glorious powers of nature became unavailable to human beings and sealed off in the Underworlds.

Not wanting to offend my friends by being stiff and defensive, I decided to smell the fragrances and let them make me feel merry. By the time I arrived at their favourite spot, I felt quite light-hearted.

"My, my... isn't this our friend Szar of the Brown Robe," Vasouk said in his slow, melodious voice, "what a happy visitation!"

Elyani had advised me to remain relatively informal but still cautiously polite. "Greetings, Your Majesty!" I answered. But Maryani's skin and aura were so red that I found it difficult to keep smiling.

"I swam in the lakes of lava!" she explained. As I repressed a shiver, she opened her eyes wide and looked straight into me. "I even drank some of it!"

"Mm..." I was resolved to keep good countenance. "Was it good?"

"Fan-*tas*tic!" she thundered. "It made me feel like jumping straight into the Furnaces of Doom."

"Fear not, Szar of the Brown Robe!" Vasouk interposed, "Maryani will not jump into the Furnaces of Doom until she is ready for it."

"Your Majesty," I smiled confidently, showing all my astral teeth, "that makes me feel much better already."

Vasouk rolled his Dragon-deep black eyes to and fro rapidly, then returned the smile.

Lilu, hanging in the air by his side, was even larger than the day before. She had now reached the size of an Underworld pumpkin, and was still ablaze with red sparks of light.

Ant gigantic. Spread in space. No limits.

"Your Majesty, may I extend an official invitation from Master Woolly of the Cream Robe, to visit our chapel. Any advice Your Majesty may wish to give us to rescue our stones will be received with immense gratitude."

Vasouk wriggled his nostrils. I observed him carefully. There was no doubt about it, this was exactly the way brother Amaran had taught me to do it. "So who taught who?" I wondered to myself. Had the Great Warriors received the art of sense-smelling from the Nagas?

"My, good. Very good!" Vasouk rejoiced. "Szar of the Brown Robe, please convey my answer to Master Woolly of the Cream Robe. I shall accept his invitation and visit his chapel."

I was taken aback. I had never expected Vasouk would agree to visit the kingdom. It dawned on me that not one room in Woolly's chapel would be large enough to fit the seventy-lawful-feet-long king.

"But I shall come later, when the time is right," Vasouk added.

Maryani brought an apple and a few red berries which she placed in my hands, and then went to collect fruits for Vasouk.

"Well... sit!" Vasouk advised.

I anchored myself in the Dragon of the Deep, resolute. This time I was going to eat a whole berry without being overtaken by ecstatic convulsions.

As I was about to put the berry in my mouth, Maryani shouted from a distance, "Wait! That is not the way to do it!" She rushed back and emptied her arms of a few cabbage-sized peaches, throwing them into Vasouk's mouth. With a mischievous glint in her eye, she told me, "These little red berries are called Venusian delights. When you eat them, you must think of a person you love, and she will dream of you."

I contemplated the berry for a moment. "Was there a time when gardens like this could be found on the Earth?" I asked.

"Well, yes, I should say. Exactly," Vasouk said. "Mighty fruits like those in this orchard were in all your gardens. And the flowers too."

A confused bee, half the size of my fist, flew to visit Lilu, mistaking her for a flower. Lilu sparked a few fizzles as if she was being tickled, and the bee buzzed away.

"And how did we human beings come to lose all these beauties?"

Vasouk swallowed the peaches he had been savouring on his tongue. "When you lost Life – this is when might vanished from your kingdom. And do you know why you lost Life?"

Still looking at the berry, I shook my head, wondering if Elyani had been serious when she said the slime fumes made her Dragon all vibrant.

"Well, well, it is because you lost your integrity," Vasouk said. "Integrity is the most important of all qualities."

My Dragon attuned to Elyani's, I ate the berry. All at once I could hear celestial melodies resonating throughout the garden. I felt like laughing, dancing, singing, transported by the blissful vroofing waves.

Maryani winked at Vasouk, "It's working!"

"Well, good. Very good," Vasouk replied.

Straight flight. Curves of time. Edge of Highness.

"Hum... Your Majesty, could you clarify for me what you mean by integrity?"

Maryani bit into one of her juicy pears. Her appetite looked just as voracious as the day before.

Vasouk wriggled his nostrils for inspiration and declared, "We Nagas have a simple definition of integrity: it is the capacity to bear fire. Things which have no integrity cannot withstand fire. We Nagas have total integrity, we can withstand any intensity of fire." Vasouk's gaze was to-and-froing over the orchard. "At the moment, we are teaching little Maryani how to regain her integrity, which is why we are exposing her to greater and greater intensities of fire."

I could still hear the musical harmonies.

"Have another berry, Szar!" Maryani offered.

I Dragon-resonated with Elyani and put the berry in my mouth. The music became louder. "And why is it that human beings lost their integrity?" I questioned.

"According to the Law of the gods – and I believe that the Law of men follows the gods on this matter – integrity was withdrawn from men at the same time as it was withdrawn from the fallen angels who had misused the fire. Well, well... it is easy to understand why the Lord Melchisedek ordained that integrity should be withdrawn from the fallen angels, for they had betrayed Truth by misusing the fire. But why was integrity withdrawn from men at the same time?" Vasouk drew from his nostrils, rapidly rolling his eyes. "Some strange, far-fetched reason, I should say, which I can't remember. In any case, the Law of the Nagas holds different views on this matter. According to us, if men lost their integrity so easily, it is because they never really had it in the first place."

Maryani went to get another load of fruits.

Vasouk continued, "The Law of the Nagas states that creatures were created in several stages. In the beginning, there were the great sages and angels who live in Lowness and who did not have to be created because they had not perished at the end of the last cosmic cycle.

Then there was the first creation wave. Out of the cosmic cauldron, heated by our Mother the Dragon, the first creation of gods arose. But these gods, the asuras as they were called, proved to be jealous, angry and rebellious. Some mistake, perhaps, had taken place.

Therefore the Lord Melchisedek ordained that a second creation of gods be concocted, still using the same cauldron. He said, 'This time, let there be a long enough cooking!' for he suspected that the first creation of gods had failed because of insufficient cooking. To all the creatures of the second cooking he therefore commanded, 'Stay in the cauldron as long as you can!'"

Maryani dropped a pear in my hand. Then she walked back to Vasouk who opened his mouth for another fruit. After swallowing a cabbage-sized peach, he continued, "And so all the creatures said, 'Yes, we will stay in the cauldron as long as we can.' But as our Mother the Dragon heated the fire in the cauldron, many of the creatures started jumping about, screaming in agony, begging the Lord to end their ordeal."

Maryani settled herself against the Naga.

"After barely a tenth of an aeon," Vasouk went on, "some of the creatures couldn't take it any more and started fleeing from the cauldron – these were the satyrs and the nymphs. Not very long after, the demi-gods capitulated, 'This is as much as we can bear!' and they too jumped out of the cauldron. In their turn the magical animals, those that are now found in the celestial regions, reached their limit and jumped out of the fire.

The gods stayed much longer – long enough to be cooked immortal, that is, immortal till the end of a cosmic cycle, of course. And because they had withstood the fire for so long, when they came out of the cauldron they became the rulers of all the creatures that had escaped before them, and they chose for their dwelling the highest of the spheres."

"And what happened to the Nagas?" Maryani asked.

"Well, well..." Vasouk flared his nostrils, "the Nagas never tried to escape, they enjoyed the fire. Once all the other creatures had left, our Mother the Dragon ran hot with her deepest fire. But the Nagas didn't mind, and it lasted for a long, long time. Then the Lord Melchisedek, who couldn't wait endlessly because he had other things to create, decided, 'Well, well... let this cauldron become the Underworlds, and let the Nagas rule over them.'"

I was astounded. "Does this mean we are sitting in the cauldron right now?"

"Well, yes! The cauldron's upper part which, by now, has cooled down a lot. But if you were to follow me and my Nagas into the Deep Underworlds, you would find the same hot fire which cooked all the beings of my creation wave."

"And what about human beings?" Maryani asked. "When were we cooked?"

"This was another creation wave," Vasouk said. "It took place much later on. Another cauldron was prepared. But by then the most subtle ingredients had already been used for the beings of former creations. Thus, gross matter was put in the cauldron. And this time the gods were helping with the cooking. It was their first time, which is why they made mistakes.

Again, the Lord Melchisedek commanded all the creatures, 'Stay in the cauldron for as long as you can!' But these creatures were not able to bear as much as those of former waves. As soon as the fire was lit, the insects jumped out, for insects can never remain motionless for long – so insects are extremely short-lived. Soon the fishes and the reptiles followed them, and then all the animals, one by one. And this is why animals carry only some of the qualities of human beings, and live for merely a fraction of the human lifespan.

But, but... human beings themselves stayed only a fraction of the time which would have been needed to bring them to completion. When he saw them running away from the cauldron, the Good Lord Melchisedek mourned, 'What a cosmic shame!' For had they been capable of bearing the fire longer, the gross matter would have been refined, gradually, and it would have become light, and pure, and perfect like the matter of the gods.

Human beings have thus always been prone to diseases and all manner of afflictions, for they are but half-cooked vessels made of imperfect substance."

My eyes fixed on the pear, I let the Naga's words resonate deep in my being. I decided to eat another berry. Carried by the elation of the vroofing waves, I stood up and began moving my arms slowly, following the magic harmonies which I could hear everywhere. "So if I had integrity, I could eat of all the fruits in this garden, instead of being overwhelmed after just a nibble."

"Well, yes... exactly!" Vasouk said. "Those who have no integrity can never experience ecstasy. After only a few drops they start jumping and yelling as if they were being cooked in the cauldron. Only those who can stand still can bear with high intensities of ecstasy."

"The capacity to remain still while being cooked in the cauldron," I chewed it over. "So this is what integrity is!"

"My, yes!" Vasouk approved with his nostrils. "Really, this is what integrity is: bearing with fire."

"And so... is integrity what is lacking in the stones we are trying to perfect in the kingdom?" I asked. "Should we find a way of cooking them better?"

"Well, well... yes, cook yourself!" Vasouk opened a smile.

This left me perplexed. "Cook ourselves?"

"My, yes, well... What you have not yet realised is that, when cooking your stones, in reality you are cooking yourself. And so to cook your stones, simply cook yourself! For anyway, this is the source of all the problems of human beings: insufficient cooking."

"I need to understand more about this cooking!" I concluded.

"Well, yes, Szar of the Brown Robe," Vasouk said, "this, to be certain, is the truest thing you have said today."

"Why can some creatures withstand the fire, and others not?"

"Well, they can all withstand the fire, but they do not all know that they can." Vasouk let out a long hissing breath through his nostrils.

"And those who can and know that they can," I asked, "how do they do it?"

"There is a secret," Vasouk said.

Instantly, Maryani stood up. "A secret?"

The Naga's head moved slowly up and down, nodding silently.

"What kind of secret?" Maryani frowned with curiosity.

"Well, simple. Very simple," Vasouk said, "but essential! Central to the Law of the Nagas, furthermore."

"And... could Szar and I ask you what this secret is?"

Vasouk nodded, wriggling his nostrils and breathing out loudly. "The secret is, *nothing exists but fire.*" After a long pause, he continued, "*I am fire. You are fire.* Szar is fire. *Anything that exists is fire.* Once this has been realised, there is no limit to the amount of cooking one can bear, for *fire cannot be burnt by fire.*"

Maryani and I remained silent, letting the power of the Naga's words work on us.

At the bottom of the Great Abyss. Boundless fire. Endless smile.

After a while Vasouk invited us to join him for a drink in one of the neighbouring rivers. Maryani took me by the hand, and we walked by the king's side. This time I decided to imitate Maryani. I knelt down close to the water, put my mouth in and drank as much as I possibly could. Maryani and I felt so merry that we started splashing each other and couldn't stop laughing.

Vasouk, who was still drinking, approved. "Well, good. Very good!"

Before leaving, I expressed my gratitude, thanking him wholeheartedly for his wisdom and his patience.

Vasouk instructed me not to visit again for seven days, as he was to lead Maryani and a company of Nagas on a pilgrimage to deep and fiery regions of the Underworlds. "But next time we meet," he promised, "I shall show you some great wonders which, undoubtedly, you will enjoy."

When I came back into my physical body, the first light of dawn had not yet reached the kingdom.

Elyani heard me move in the room. She called out in a sleepy voice, "I have been dreaming about you all night! Come! I want to hold you in my arms."

I have travelled from beyond the limits of time. For you.

Remembering the red berries, I joined her in her bed and let my energy melt into hers.

"I love you!" she whispered. "I love you! I love you! I missed you."

10.6 Smiling like a filosterops

In the following days I continued my Point training with Elyani, as well as my evaluation of the Archive mission. I carefully observed Namron's men. Their fighting style was deplorable, and they had little or no knowledge of the weapons used by potential enemies. Speaking to various people in the temple, I came to the conclusion that very few of them, if any at all, could be expected to take a role in defence operations.

What struck me the most was the realisation that so many priests and priestesses were perfectly aware that a disaster was looming. Nearly everyone had observed the signs of deterioration in the fields, and heard the alarming news that kept arriving from counties all over the kingdom. Rumours of impending catastrophe passed around the temple. Everyone prayed to their gods for protection, but the bottom line was, even though the root of the problem was clear, no one had the faintest idea what could be done to remedy the situation in the fields. This was the great tragedy of the kingdom: there were temples everywhere, teeming with enlightened prophets, ritualists and seers of non-physical realities; a phenomenal know-how of the occult laws of nature had been accumulated with time – and yet the tangled imbroglio of the fields remained unresolvable. This created a sense of powerlessness, as if the gods had decided to withdraw their presence from the kingdom. An atmosphere of doom and gloom was insidiously weaving its way through Eisraim.

Particularly alarming was the condition of our Archive stones which, despite all the efforts made by Woolly and the Field Wizards, showed no sign of improvement and kept shrinking steadily.

Woolly's mood was abysmal, and the tension in his chapel was running high. One morning he called me in and yelled, "Commander, we're swimming in elemental slime, and it's not a pretty sight! If your damn Underworld worm fancies helping us, he'd better squirm his ass here fast!"

"Woolly, I'm sorry," I said, "I just do not know how one tells a Naga king to hurry up." Besides, I was still wondering how we would fit Vasouk in if he were to honour his word and pay a visit to our chapel.

"And what about the worm-girl? Is she going to be good for anything, or is she just going to be another one of those Blue priestesses who keep smiling like a filosterops while the Goddess is busy pissing on us?"

"Hum..." Derogatory language or not, one thing was clear: Woolly was asking a lot of questions about Maryani. "We might find she has a few surprises up her sleeve," I said.

Woolly became thoughtful. "Do you like surprises, Szar?"

"Well..." clearly, Woolly enjoyed surprises a lot. "Yes, I think I'm getting to like them more and more," I said.

"What kind of surprises do you think we should expect from Maryani?"

"If the Naga king succeeds in cooking her as he intends to..."

"He wants to turn her into a little stone, doesn't he?" Woolly was moved.

"Well, quite!" I nodded. "Then she might be able to show us how to cook our stones using fire from the Underworlds instead of the fields. Essentially, this is our problem, isn't it?"

"And what does she look like?" Woolly asked. "Is she getting uglier and uglier as she advances in the worm initiation?"

"No, she's not ugly at all. She's just been looking a bit... red, in the last few days."

Woolly was rapt. "Do you know that during one of the stages of their development, stones turn red? And during another phase, they become black."

I gulped, wondering what we would tell the prince of the county of Eisraim if Maryani returned black from the Underworlds.

"The other day, Elyani invited me to come and watch the sunset on the Blue priestesses' roof with you. If I popped in for a visit, do you think I could quickly see what Maryani looks like?" Woolly asked.

Twinging my beard, I frowned at him, pretending to be suspicious.

"Oh, come on, Commander!" Woolly pulled an ugly face. "Do you really think I'd be interested in that squirming White-Eagle-dragon-Naga-worm?"

"Well... yes!" I said. "That is exactly what I think!"

Woolly burst out laughing. "You're fantasising, Commander!" Then he let out a long and loud sigh. "So when shall I come and watch the sunset?"

Later that day, when Woolly arrived at our courtyard, he broke with his habits and greeted Elyani and me in fully lawful fashion. "*Praise the Lord Melchisedek, Lady Elyani of the White Eagle. And praise the Lord Melchisedek, Commander!*"

Elyani, who was starting to like him, took his hands and returned the lawful salute. "*All glory to the Lord Melchisedek, Woolly of the Dirty-Cream Robe!*"

The Ant will be at the rendezvous.

I took him straight to Maryani's room.

When he saw the blonde priestess deeply asleep on the mattress with Lilu's jar not far from her head, his face lit up.

"Talk about smiling like a filosterops!" I whispered.

"So what?" he said. "I'm just happy for her because she's not as ugly as I thought she was. Can I take a look at Lilu?"

"Just make sure you don't get too close to Maryani's body."

When he opened the lid and saw that Lilu was smaller than a green pea, he bit his lip.

Lehrmon's habit was catching.

Seas of light. The time of the rendezvous is coming. Miss not the call!

Woolly looked into my eyes. "Are we doing something about Lilu?"

I shrugged in powerlessness. "As long as her body of energy is with Vasouk and Maryani, there is not much I can do."

Woolly put the jar back by Maryani's head. "I guess we have to put our trust in the Naga-girl, don't we? How are her energy levels?"

"For the moment, it's a simple hibernation situation. I could maintain her like this for at least a few more weeks. But if the elemental slime which has been polluting our chapel were to reach into her, then a disaster could happen in no time."

"Why don't you ask Gervin to give us some hints on how to convince a Naga to hurry up?" Woolly suggested.

"Gervin went away for a few days. On his return I will definitely need to have a long talk with him regarding Naga etiquette."

"How old did you say she is?" Woolly asked, his eyes riveted on the hibernating body.

"Seventeen and a half."

"And the Naga king?"

I burst out laughing, "My, my..." I said slowly, forcing a low pitch in my voice, "I should say, definitely a few thousand years too old for little Maryani." Then I took his arm, "Come on, Woolly, let us go and watch the sunset. If you keep asking questions like this, the princess might wake up."

10.7 The first matter

A few days later, it was with great excitement that I descended into the Underworlds to meet the Naga and his priestess. As usual, no need to tune in and look for them. The gate took me straight to a magnificent sandy beach where the two friends were waiting for me.

"Here is my brother in the Dragon!" Maryani ran up to me and hugged me. Her skin was no longer red, and her aura was shining with golden light.

"You are beautiful!" I congratulated her. "What has happened to you?"

"Oh, lots of incredible things!" she laughed loudly. Then she quickly whispered, "This time I jumped into the Furnaces of Doom!"

"My, my, Szar of the Brown Robe coming to visit us!" Vasouk welcomed me with his friendly voice, warm with the heartness of the Law.

"Greetings, Your Majesty. What a joy to be in your company again!"

Pumpkin-sized Lilu, wafting in the air close to Vasouk's head, was glittering with the same golden light as in Maryani's aura.

In this place there were no mists. The blue sky seemed to reach up forever, and the empty beach extended to infinity on each side.

"How do you like our sea, Szar of the Brown Robe?" the king asked.

It was Dragon-love at first sight. Utter fascination. In places, her waters were breathtakingly silver, purer than that of any river I had seen in the Underworlds. In other places, I tried to discern her colour but could see no more than misty darkness. She eluded me, reminiscent of the faces of the priestesses of the Dawn of Creation.

Never had I contemplated so much power. Her vroofing was wild and terrible, deep, and mysterious. And yet it filled my heart with more sweetness than even Elyani had ever awakened in me. *The Voice of the Dragon, which is the Thunder of the Earth,* was running joyfully through her and rolling in each of her waves.

At the feet of an angel of Highness. She loves you. She will give her life for you.

"Sit down, Szar of the Brown Robe!" the wise Vasouk suggested, when he saw how moved I was.

My Dragon was spreading and melting in the infinity of the sea. I could hear music as if I was dancing all over the spheres. Mighty tremors in rhythmic waves shook the walls of my heart open. I felt like laughing, as tears poured from my eyes.

For a long while I couldn't utter a word, captivated by the vision of the glorious sea and the atmosphere of timelessness emanating from her.

Silvery dust, trails ad infinitum. A smile, deeper than the Abyss.

"Now... now, I understand what water is!" I murmured, as it became clear to me that all other waters in the creation were but imperfect replicas of this sea. "Had I not known that we are in the Underworlds, " I told Vasouk, "I would have believed this to be the Molten Sea of the gods."

"Well, right. Very right!" Vasouk replied. "This *is* the Molten Sea."

Totally unexpected. "But isn't the Molten Sea part of the world of the gods?"

Vasouk wiggled his nostrils, inhaling the amazingly pure breeze that came from the sea.

Maryani imitated him.

I imitated Maryani, and instantly felt uplifted by a momentous wave of Life that danced in my body of energy.

"The Molten Sea," Vasouk elucidated, "is in several places at the same time. Or, rather, several places have their source in the Molten Sea. Or, rather, from the Golden Shield above to the Golden Shield below, all places in our spheres have their source in the Molten Sea, but the Molten Sea is not visible in all of them. Yet in reality she is always visible, but few are those who have an eye to see."

"Can the Molten Sea be seen in my kingdom?" I asked, surprised.

"Well, yes!" Vasouk was gently categorical. "Certainly."

"Where, Vasouk?" Maryani asked.

"Well, everywhere, actually! The Molten Sea is behind every single thing in your kingdom. But you might find her more easily if you look through black earth."

Maryani frowned. "Do you mean, simple dirt?"

"Compost is the best," Vasouk said.

Maryani pulled a face. "But it doesn't smell as nice as the Molten Sea!"

Wrinkling his nostrils, Vasouk pointed at the Molten Sea with his nose. "This marvellous sea, which you are contemplating at the moment, is the quintessence of chaos. She is fertile – the fertile chaos through which the Dragon manifests her creative power. She has Life, and she gives her Life to all things. Yet few are the things which receive her Life."

Hearing Vasouk talk about this magnificent sea as a chaos was perplexing to me. "Your Majesty, I thought that one of the main problems in my kingdom was that the elemental layer had turned into chaos."

"Well, yes," Vasouk said, "but a messy chaos. Truly, it would be better called a mess than a chaos. Chaos, as in the Molten Sea, is noble. It is vibrant with Life. In your kingdom, what went wrong is precisely that the elemental layer lost touch with the noble chaos of the Molten Sea."

"And why do you want us to look through compost?" Maryani asked in her aristocratic voice.

"In a compost heap, matter is turned into chaos, and thus renews its link to the Molten Sea. But in your kingdom, because of the general corruption that permeates all things, this process never goes beyond a certain limit. Matter never really reaches the full state of chaos, and thus the Molten Sea's Life cannot reach through to it. Still, food scraps, old leaves, animal excrement and various bits of rubbish, when turning into black earth, manage to catch some of the Molten Sea's life, and this is why the fertility of your land springs out of compost."

"Your Majesty..." I felt carried by Vasouk's inspiration, "then the heat in a compost heap must come from a very special fire."

"Well, yes," Vasouk approved with a quiver of his nostrils, "very special. The heat in a compost heap reflects the warmth of the Molten Sea."

Maryani's clear fountain was flowing. "But then of course, if someone had integrity, he could push compost far beyond its normal limits and make it a true chaos instead of a partial one. Then the compost could receive the full Life and creative power of the Molten Sea."

"The art of the black earth," Vasouk told her, "this is exactly what you will have to teach the people of the land of Aegypton."

We pondered silently, contemplating the glory of the Molten Sea.

A shape appeared on the waves. A silvery-blue round carapace, perhaps three lawful feet long, was floating towards the shore. A strange sea monster with a head shaped somewhat like that of a lizard.

"Fomalhaut!" Maryani called out and started running.

The waves carried the sea monster to the shore. Four short legs came out of its carapace and it started walking on the sand.

Maryani further startled me by letting out the Great Warriors' cry of joy, "Youyouyouyou!"

I turned towards Vasouk, "Is she safe?"

The Naga king immediately reassured me, "This is Fomalhaut the tortoise, an old friend of ours. A few days ago, Maryani was bathing on her own in a large river of life, and she let herself be carried away by the current. Believe it or not, Szar of the Brown Robe, she ended up in the southern Tartarean sea, where Fomalhaut found her. He let her sit on his shell and kindly brought her back to my palace, telling her the latest Underworlds' gossip to keep her company. He and Maryani have become the best of friends."

Maryani and the monster chatted together for a moment, and then walked over to us.

"Greetings, King Vasoukidass!" Fomalhaut said.

"My, my, Fomalhaut, what a happy visitation!" Vasouk welcomed him.

"And you are Szar," Fomalhaut said. "I have heard a lot about you."

"Hum..." Unfortunately, Gervin had never taught me the lawful way of saluting a sea monster. "Greetings, Fomalhaut of the Silvery-Blue Carapace!"

Vasouk made a suggestion, "Maryani, why don't you take Szar of the Brown Robe to the Sea of Lightning, where we must go next." Swivelling his head around towards me, he added, "Szar of the Brown Robe, you will have the happy opportunity to meet with Fomalhaut again tomorrow, when you visit us in my palace. I have invited him to the reception I am giving for Maryani, where you will have great pleasure listening to him. No one knows better than him how to retell the story of Maryani's past life, when she saved my life." He gave Maryani a loving smile, "Fomalhaut and I will be chatting together here while I wait for you over there."

Wondering what all this meant, I saluted Fomalhaut and paid my respects to the Molten Sea, then raced to catch up with Maryani.

"Far, far Underworld!" I grilled Maryani as we walked, "Did you *really* save Vasouk's life?"

"Oh, please... please don't ask me!" she blurted out. "Please wait till the reception."

"What's this reception?"

"It's to celebrate my first swim in the Sea of Lightning – a crucial step in Naga initiation. It's like a new birth."

I looked at her with even more astonishment. "Did you swim in the Sea of Lightning?"

"Not yet!" she answered. "I still have to purify myself by taking a few fiery baths before I am ready. Our Mother the Dragon willing, it should happen soon. Vasouk and all his Naga friends will come with me."

I realised it would have been a complete waste of time to give her any advice. "Looking forward to it?"

"I can't wait! At the moment there are still many places that Vasouk will not let me visit alone. As soon as I swim in the Sea of Lightning, I can go *anywhere* I want."

Now, that sounded *really* dangerous. "Anywhere?" I opened my eyes wide, doing my best to share her excitement.

She opened her blue eyes even wider, "Anywhere!"

"Anywhere in the Underworlds... That could mean as Low as the spheres of Highness!"

Maryani imitated Vasouk's voice, "Well, well... actually, yes. No limits!"

To the Point, Brother Knight! I'll see you at No Limits.

"By the way, Maryani," I was intrigued, "who taught you the Great Warriors' shout of joy?"

"A lovely man!" she laughed. "A few days ago, as I was exploring the Golden Volcanoes in the Abyss of Doom, I met a friend of yours, Great Warrior. His name is Amaran."

"The man who initiated me into Dragon gates! How is he?"

"Wonderful!" Maryani was enthused. "What a lawful gentleman! He sends his regards to you and Elyani. I told him all about you, and he said your friends at Mount Lohrzen would be delighted to hear the news."

"Hum... good." I preferred not to know the details.

As we kept walking along the beach, I questioned, "How come we have to go such a long way? Can't we just go through a gate?"

"*No way, man of the Law!* It's not just any Dragon gate that leads to the Sea of Lightning!" Maryani replied, and she asked for news of her friends in Eisraim. When I told her how everyone was impatiently waiting for her, she asked, "Is Woolly impatiently waiting for me?"

"Mm... of course! Our stones are badly in need of your help, Maryani."

She wriggled her nostrils vigorously. "Can you keep a secret, Szar?"

"I would love to say yes," I sighed, "but Elyani always guesses my secrets."

It made her laugh, "I know, Alcibyadi told me. That doesn't matter. And you can tell Teyani too. But I don't want Woolly to know."

"Dragon's word!"

"I will probably come back with you tomorrow, after the reception at the palace."

"Praise the She-Dragon of Eternal Wisdom!" I exclaimed.

Maryani didn't share my enthusiasm. Composed, she looked straight in front of her.

I took her hand and changed tone, "You are going to miss him terribly, aren't you?"

Tears in her eyes, she nodded silently. She breathed in courage from the Dragon, "But if I succeed in my initiation in the Sea of Lightning, I will be able to travel down as often as I wish."

"Does this mean you will be capable of descending through the gates of the Dragon like I do?"

"This I can already do," she answered in a gentle voice. "But there are some more powerful ways of travelling through the Underworlds, by which you can be transported straight from one place to another without having to descend through the gates."

As I let the White Eagle hold her hand through mine, she went on, "Szar, I am going to need your help."

I was puzzled. "From the sound of it, I would rather say the opposite – *I* am going to need your help."

She shook her head, holding onto my hand. "I mean, I will need your help to let the others understand that I have become different, Szar. In particular, I don't want them to try to force me to sleep, or rest in bed, or do things like eating or drinking."

"You little Dragon have become worse than me, haven't you?"

"Well, well..." she imitated Vasouk, "yes! I should say, yes."

"I think I had better start preparing Teyani and Alcibyadi," I said. "And what am I to tell Woolly?"

"You let me take care of Woolly," Maryani declared, a touch of fierceness in her voice.

10.8 The last matter

The walk went on and on. The Molten Sea was now far behind us, and the landscape had gradually turned into the dunes of a sandy desert.

"This place is as hot as a furnace!" I complained. "Are there really no Dragon gates that could take us straight to the Sea of Lightning?"

Maryani's golden aura was shining more brightly than ever. "No. From what Vasouk told me, the Sea of Lightning is a unique place, quite different from the rest of the Underworlds."

Winds of space. Far, far away. Request access.

Burning-hot winds started blowing, whipping us awake with their sharp spirit. The more we advanced, the more tempestuous they became. After some time, they turned into fierce hissing gusts that pushed against us, making it difficult for us to hear each other. More than once they nearly carried us away.

Holding fast onto my hand, Maryani shouted, "I rest deep on the Dragon, you call on the Eagle!"

We plodded along, forcing each step against the ferocious resistance of the successive winds.

After fighting for what seemed like hours, the fury of the winds became such that we could no longer walk.

Her mouth against my ear, Maryani shouted, "I will call on Vasouk!"

She closed her eyes, and soon we were both dragged down through the sands and started falling. But this was no comfortable dive as through a Dragon gate. Violent eddies sent us spinning. A loud roaring Voice shook every cell in our bodies, and the temperature ran so hot that I felt as if I was going to melt.

The more we fell, the worse it became. The speed was awesome, the sound deafening, the fire unbearable. The gravity became such that I felt crushed, as if by a huge hand.

It seemed to go on for a long, long time, until I suddenly arrived in a black space in which everything was silent and peaceful.

I was so shocked that it took a moment before I could sit up.

The first thing that struck me was the absence of Underworld smells. I looked around for Maryani but couldn't see her. Actually I could not see a single thing. Pitch-black darkness was all there was. As I was wondering what to do next, Vasouk's two glowing coals of eyes appeared in front of me.

"Well, well, Szar of the Brown Robe, that was a somewhat bumpy ride, wasn't it?"

I was still stunned. "Where am I?"

"You are inside my consciousness, Szar of the Brown Robe," Vasouk answered in his slow, gentle voice. "I decided to take you in, since you were just about to be evaporated. Insufficient cooking was the cause."

"Evaporated?" I suddenly woke up. "How kind of you, Your Majesty! But where is Maryani?"

"She is sitting close to me, on the fiery shore of the Sea of Lightning."

Perplexed, I twinged my beard. "Your Majesty, could I ask your advice as to what I should do next?"

"I will let you see through my eyes," Vasouk said, "to let you contemplate the Sea of Lightning."

Vasouk's pair of eyes disappeared, and an awesome vision was revealed to me. Rather than a sea, it was a space, filled with such blazing golden light as I had never dreamt could exist. It was both solid and fluid, constantly moving and seared by myriads of thunderbolts which flashed second after second. It radiated not only Light, but also wild vroofing waves of Life as only Naga words can describe.

Vasouk turned his head to the left. Awe-struck, I discovered at least a thousand Nagas standing by his side, forming a row which extended beyond the horizon. There they were, the irresistible warriors who had annihilated an entire hierarchy of angels in three days. Their long golden bodies still as rocks, they were absorbed in the contemplation of the Sea of Lightning. The power radiated by their combined motionlessness was beyond description – what force in the seven spheres could have withstood their assault, had they been in the mood to attack?

Vasouk turned his head to the right, and I saw Maryani standing still, her golden aura suffused with the brilliance of the Sea of Lightning.

"In the Molten Sea, you have contemplated the first matter," Vasouk said. "Now, face the Sea of Lightning, which is the ultimate matter, the last stage, when all is accomplished."

"The ultimate power, she is," Maryani murmured.

"The ultimate power," Vasouk repeated, and I saw the landscape move up and down as he nodded his head. "But you must not call it 'she', for it is both male and female, like me." Vasouk paused. "And yet the Sea of Lightning is one with the Molten Sea. But you cannot see this yet. Now, right now, I am still standing in front of the Molten Sea. I have not moved, Fomalhaut is still sitting by my side."

"Is this what you were explaining the other day?" Maryani asked. "The Sea of Lightning is contained in the Molten Sea as potential?"

Vasouk nodded, making the landscape move up and down again. "But *the Sea of Lightning has neither beginning nor end, it is as eternal as the spheres of Highness.* And so it already existed *at the Dawn of Creation, long before the birth of the gods, when the Molten Sea emerged from the Great Night.*"

After contemplating the thunderbolt flashes of the Sea of Lightning for a long while, Vasouk turned toward Maryani. "Now I will take the ritual bath, with my Nagas. You can dance on the beach. Then we will take you to the Abysmal Fire for your last purification, and we will return."

Maryani raised her arms and started moving her body slowly.

Everything became dark again, and Vasouk's eyes appeared in front of me. "Szar of the Brown Robe," he said in his friendly fashion, "I shall now send you back to the kingdom. If you were to stay inside my consciousness while I swim in the Sea of Lightning, no doubt you would be evaporated. And fast, actually."

I thanked him wholeheartedly for the extraordinary vision, and for his care. He reminded me of the reception that was to take place later on. "Just go through any Dragon gate," he said, "and I will make sure you land in my palace."

"When should I come, Your Majesty?"

"Come a few hours after Maryani's ritual bath," the king commanded. As I looked unsure, he added, "My, my, you will know. This is true and without lie. Because you came down here with her, a resonance will take place when Maryani swims in the Sea of Lightning, and you will know!"

10.9 Maryani's swim

Using his phenomenal powers, Vasouk sent me straight back into my body, sitting in meditation in Elyani's room.

When I opened my eyes, Elyani was sitting by my side. The *living walls* felt warm. The quality of light that glowed from the plass showed it was day already.

Elyani was worried. "Are you all right?"

At first, I couldn't speak. I looked down to my left palm, letting the Dragon of the Deep slowly clench and unclench my fist. Then I looked into her eyes.

Her face lit up. "*Oh my Lord Melchisedek!*" she exclaimed as she picked up fresh impressions from my consciousness. "What was *that*?"

Unable to speak, I let myself collapse on the plass floor and closed my eyes again.

"Can I do something?" she asked in a small voice.

237

I pulled her into my arms. "Kiss me!" I finally managed to whisper. "Is it very late?"

She gave me a long kiss. "No, it's early – but in the lawful afternoon!"

"Voof!"

"Lehrmon and Woolly have tried to contact you throughout the morning," she said. "They're in trouble. They urgently want to see you at their chapel."

Calling on the power of the Dragon, I managed to stand up. "Things look a little grey in the kingdom. If it weren't for you, I would feel sad each time I return."

"I had extraordinary dreams last night. When you come back from the chapel of the Field Wizards, will you tell me what happened to you in the Underworlds?" Elyani asked.

"*No way, woman of the Law!* You're coming to the chapel with me! It's already bad enough to be separated from you during the night."

She rejoiced at the news, "Could we go via the roofs?"

"Oh, no, please," I said, "don't deprive me of my Point-guided stroll in the corridors. I am badly in need of something to refocus my thinking."

Elyani was amused. "You're becoming just as addicted to the Point-fields as the Nephilim giants."

Flattered by the comparison, I expanded my chest with a quick inhalation, contracting every possible muscle. I clicked my fingers, "To the Point, Brother Knight!"

The White Eagle took my arm, and we took off through the Point-guided maze.

By the time we arrived at the entrance portal of the female wing, I already felt better. "We must start preparing Teyani and the White Eagles for a Dragon of a surprise," I warned Elyani, "Maryani is on her way back! But her energy has become so hot that the walls in our courtyard could melt as soon as she lands in her body." As we made our way through the temple's lawful centre to the chapel of the Field Wizards, I told her about the astonishing events of the night.

Lehrmon opened the chapel door just as I was about to knock. "Praise the Lord Melchisedek follow me watch the bottles on the floor," he turned round, taking us down to the cellar of the Archive stones.

"He's in his Field Wizard character!" Elyani whispered in my ear as we rushed behind him, watching for the bottles.

The Flying Dragon device was open. Unnoticed by Lehrmon, I turned to Elyani and pulled a disgusted face while pointing to the doorway with my index finger.

Woolly's grim mood was reflected in his greeting: "I really wonder why anyone should praise the Lord today!"

"Doesn't matter, *all glory*, anyway," Elyani forced a smile from him. "Tell us about the stones."

"We have lost seven of them, and at least another twelve are on the verge of final dissolution. The news from Lasseera is even worse: seventeen stones lost. Nearly half their stock."

I took my head in my hands. "Is Gervin still away?"

"I voice-channelled him early this morning," Lehrmon answered. "He said the solution is to come from you."

He and Woolly gazed at me.

"What's your solution, Commander?" Woolly pressed on.

Danger! Danger!

I twinged my beard, tuning high into the clear fountain. "How are the fields at the moment?"

Lehrmon answered, "A steady flow of elemental slime is still pouring out of them, but no further deterioration has been observed in the last few days."

As I remained silent, Woolly yelled at me, "Szar, we can't just remain here sitting in the slime doing nothing, waiting for that damn female worm! For the Goddess' sake, can't you get your Dragon to move her ass and *do* something!"

I sense-sniffed the air. "Didn't you tell me you knew exactly which windmills of the Law were responsible for flooding our chapel with elemental slime?" I asked.

Woolly immediately understood my idea. "Yes!" he approved enthusiastically, "Let's blast them!"

Lehrmon chuckled. "Secretly blocking the windmills of the Law! Now, *that* would make Gervin laugh his clear fountain off. The problem is, it wouldn't take long before we were found out."

"Yes! What would we tell Melchard the high priest?" Elyani grinned.

"And what if we transferred all our operations to the mountains of Lasraim?" I suggested. "We wouldn't have to worry so much about the windmills of the Law."

"We'd still get flooded with slime!" Woolly scratched a carbuncle on the bump of his nose. "The power of the windmills' rituals reaches a long way."

"Well, well, then, how about going straight to the Plateau of Sorana?" I proposed.

Lehrmon pulled one of Elyani's favourite faces, "The vibrations of our stones would soon be detected. I wouldn't give us two weeks before the Renegade Hunters found us – not to mention the Nephilim giants."

We kept discussing the situation, exploring various possibilities, but the bottom line was, our stones required a fiery energy from the fields in order to grow, and the fields had reached a level of corruption that made further growth impossible. Unless another form of fire could be used, the Archive project would have to be completely redesigned.

"We are on the verge of disaster," Lehrmon concluded. "If our stones keep deteriorating this way, one more week and we won't have any left to perform the Archive transfer. Suppose a sudden collapse of the fields occurred in the coming days – the battle would be lost."

Out of nowhere, my Dragon started vroofing like a volcano.

There was an explosion of Light in the room.

Sensing a deeply unusual energy, Lehrmon immediately anchored himself in Thunder, at the upper edge where clear fountain and Highness meet.

The White Eagle plunged her gaze into mine, resting on my Dragon.

Woolly started shaking like a leaf and fell on the floor.

"Maryani!" I remembered Vasouk's words. "It's happening now. Maryani is swimming in the Sea of Lightning!"

I sat on the floor and pulled Elyani into my arms, holding her energy. Lehrmon sat down too, keeping his grounding in the high regions of Thunder. But as the vroofing kept intensifying, I pushed Elyani into his arms and moved away, for fear of harming them.

It was worse than an earthquake. Every single object in the room was vibrating to its limit, as if about to explode. Buckets were thrown on the floor, jars fell from the shelves, every wall in the building was trembling.

Woolly was convulsing on the floor, screaming with pain.

I tried to go to his rescue but I started shaking myself. Crushed by tonnes of pressure, my body was about to crumble, every cell flaring with uncontrollable power.

I found myself screaming.

The Warrior's reflexes ingrained in me by Marek took over. I withdrew my consciousness from my physical body, resting only on the Dragon of the Deep.

Danger! Danger! Do not abandon the earthly vessel. Call onto the power from above.

Call onto what?

Above! The light!

Instantly, it was as if I was transported into the cave of Verzazyel the Watcher again. A huge descent of blue force took place, matching the pressure which was about to crush my physical body. It brought a sense of glory which filled the seven spheres and beyond.

Project the Word! Immediately!

Lifted up by the force from above, I found myself standing on my feet. A huge flame of light poured from my mouth as I projected a fury of Voice, screaming words that I had never heard before.

I soon lost touch with the room, and found myself in a strange blue space which felt oddly familiar.

In all directions, Voices singing to each other,

Responding with measured symphonies of meaning

To distant calls and galactic interrogations.

Flows of knowledge, intricately woven in the matrix of space

Revealing fresh significance in an ancient cosmos of harmony.

The structure of space sings the melodious Song of Creation

And tells eternally new stories
To a united assembly of odd and even consciousness.
From the many togethernesses, a voice rose,
"Not now. Let him continue his journey."
And the Voices became silent.
And the space vanished.
And a suspended aeon elapsed.

When I regained my senses, I was standing in the middle of a completely devastated room. There were broken jars and bottles everywhere, and the floor was covered with spilled juices and precious slime. Woolly was lying unconscious in a corner. Lehrmon and Elyani were collecting stones from the floor.

"He is waking up!" Elyani called Lehrmon. "Try to open the door again."

As I turned round, I realised that the doorway had disappeared, locking us inside the cellar.

Lehrmon went over to the wall and stood in front of it for a moment, his eyes closed, motionless. Abruptly the doorway reappeared. Master Ferman and his Field Wizards rushed into the room, bringing with them jars in which they placed the stones that Lehrmon and Elyani had collected.

Elyani walked towards me and looked into my eyes. From her Point, she projected a sharp influence which shook me awake. Then she held me in her arms, enveloping me with the Eagle's love.

"How long did it last?" I asked.

"At least half an hour," she whispered.

"Oh, gods!" I shook my head in dismay. "What about Woolly?"

"When you were projecting the Voice, you ordered that no one should touch him or go near him."

"Projecting the Voice?" How embarrassing! I couldn't recollect anything. "What else did I do?"

"You were wild! You projected screaming levels of the Voice in all directions, speaking in tongues. I have never heard anything like it, it was magnificent! Then you went to hold Woolly's hands for at least ten minutes and transmitted forces into him. Woolly was yelling so loud, Lehrmon and I feared you were going to kill him. We voice-channelled Gervin for advice. He told us to let you go on."

"*Sweet Lord Melchisedek!*" Horrified, I was. "Vasouk warned me that when Maryani would swim in the Sea of Lightning, a resonance would take place between her and me. But I never expected that! I should have been more cautious."

I went to sit close to Woolly's body and let my hands run on his vital gateways. "He's just asleep!"

As I kept working on his body of energy, Lehrmon came and sat by my side. Using the sight of Thunder, he tuned into me for a moment, scanning my subtle bodies. For some reason it made him laugh, Gervin-fashion.

I turned toward him, raising a questioning eyebrow.

The Master of Thunder just slapped my shoulder, smiling affectionately.

Woolly opened his eyes. He lifted himself up on his elbows and took a quick look around him. "What have I done to the Goddess?" he muttered in disgust, then he closed his eyes and sank back down again.

Elyani, Lehrmon and I were immediately reassured by his irritable tone of voice.

"We haven't lost a single stone," Lehrmon comforted him, patting his knee. "They were all intact when we transferred them into new jars."

"I know," Woolly replied. "Was that really from the worm-girl?"

"Could be!" I answered tentatively.

Woolly opened his eyes again and directed them towards me. Slowly, articulately, he hammered into me, "Do not, speak, to me, about that *girl*, *ever*, a-gain!"

10.10 Vasouk's discourse on the hermaphroditic stone

I spent a few hours recuperating before preparing myself to descend and meet Maryani and Vasouk.

"This time instead of sitting in a meditation position, I think I'll lie down," I told Elyani.

"When will you try me again, Dragon?" Elyani asked. "I am dying to go down with you."

Now is the perfect time. Let the power of the Nagas take her down.

I took her in my arms and let a few tender waves vroof into her. "This afternoon during the onslaught, when you plunged your eyes into mine, I was amazed how attuned our Dragons were. But what's happening around Maryani at the moment is at the very limit of what I can bear. Let's wait for more peaceful times."

Elyani insisted, quoting a cardinal principal of Point work: "*If you can do it tomorrow, then do it right now!*" But when she saw me hesitating, she sighed in resignation. "All right. I don't want to force you."

"Anyhow, tonight should only be a short descent: shake Fomalhaut's paw, smile politely at the Naga generals, ask Vasouk a few questions, and abduct the Underworld goddess before she fancies jumping into some other pit or furnace."

As soon as I slipped through the Dragon's gate, I was transported to a huge garden outside Vasouk's palace.

The place was astonishing – a massive palace made of pure gold, reaching high in the sky. The architecture was unlike anything in the kingdom, some parts of the castle hanging in the air without visible foundations. Looking from left to right, I counted twelve turrets and six distinct wings. But when my gaze reached the right of the castle there were no longer twelve turrets but fifteen, and nine wings. Going back to the left there were nine turrets, and six wings again.

I gave up.

The gardens were no less extraordinary. Numerous alleys, forming complicated geometrical shapes, were bordered by fantastic trees. In all directions one could see huge flowers with tiers of multicoloured petals. There were Nagas everywhere.

Maryani, who must have smelled my arrival, came out to find me. She was wearing a golden dress that glistened and sparkled in stunning resonance with her aura.

We slowly walked towards each other.

"Greetings, Your Dragon-ness!" I exclaimed. "If I hadn't been caught in the earthquake myself, I would wonder where the Far Underworld you have been for your eyes to shine as they do."

"Greetings, Master of Thunder," Maryani replied. "I tried to send some power to you and Woolly while the initiation was taking place. Did you receive it?"

"Did we receive it?" I raised my hands towards the kingdom. "Ha! Ha! Ha! Ha! Ha! It nearly killed the four of us!" I briefly told her what had happened in the chapel.

"But that is so unfair!" she exclaimed. "I was just trying to send you a present. Was Woolly really upset?"

"Maryani, let's forget about this. *Dragon above, Dragon below*, there is only one thing that matters now: healing our stones. I need to know if I can count on you, and when."

She was offended, "Of course you can count on me! And I am still coming back with you at the end of the reception. As for your stones, some major adjustments will have to be considered."

I didn't like the sound of this. "What major adjustments?"

"Let us go, Vasouk is expecting us," she said, leading me to one of the broad alleys. As we entered the geometrical maze, she continued, "Those she-stones that Woolly has tinkered with are messy, and without real substance. I mean, they are pretty, but..."

A Naga who was passing by saluted her, "Greetings, Maryani, and congratulations on your entry into the Law of the Nagas."

She smiled back, "Greetings and thanks for your support, Lord Prasna."

"Greetings, Lord Prasna." I smiled politely, wondering how Maryani managed to tell one Naga from another. Then I asked, "What's wrong with our she-stones?"

"They're toys. Good enough for voice-channelling, but not for the Archive."

"Hey!" I protested vigorously. "Who told you about the Archive?"

"Greetings, Lord Pradip!" Maryani saluted a Naga who was squirming away from the castle.

"Greetings, little Maryani, and congratulations!" the Naga answered.

"Lots of lords, around here!" I noticed.

"These are old companions of Vasouk. They fought the three-day war against the fallen angels together, a few scores of thousands of years ago. Have you heard about it?" she asked.

"Yes. It sounded terrifying."

"Especially for the fallen angels!" she gave a mischievous smile. After saluting another Naga lord, she explained, "I know about the Archive because I was trained to take part in the team that will be holding its connection from the world of the gods."

The celestial side of the project.

"What has happened to Lilu, by the way?" I asked.

"She shrunk herself so she could hide in my pocket. She doesn't like it when there are so many people around."

As we reached the portal, I commented with admiration, "No gates, and no guards... *that's* real power!"

Maryani chuckled, "Who would want to attack Vasouk?"

We reached a grand hall, walls of gleaming gold studded with huge clusters of glittering ruby-red jewels, ceilings of silver polished to a mirror and reflecting the whole scene below where hundreds of Nagas were chatting in small groups. A few tortoises were standing around casually, as well as a number of strange lizard-like creatures without heads.

Seeing I was awe-struck by the magnitude and beauty of the place, Maryani commented, "The most extraordinary thing is that every one of the Nagas you see in this hall lives in a similar palace." She steered the topic around, "I hope you haven't forgotten I am going to need your help."

"Tell me, *Great Dragon of Fierceness*, what am I supposed to do for you, exactly?"

"When I return to the kingdom, I don't want anyone to feed me, I don't want anyone to force me to sleep, I don't want anyone to manipulate my energy..."

"And you don't want anyone to tell you what to do!"

"Exactly. Do you think it is asking too much?"

"Let me see what I can do. Anyway, why would anyone want to waste their time trying to tell you what to do? You never listen."

She gave her candid smile. "That is not completely true."

Vasouk, who was talking to a party of three Nagas, had smelled Maryani and I approaching. "My, my, Szar of the Brown Robe, how kind of you to join us. Please meet Lord Sagar, Lord Sarpaling and Lord Amar," he said, pointing to each of them with his nose. For their information, he added, "This is Szar of the Masters of Thunder, who are friends with our friends the Flying Dragons."

I returned the greeting, not even bothering to try and figure out how the Underworld Vasouk knew about the Masters of Thunder.

"Our friend Szar is very concerned about his stones," Maryani told Vasouk.

"Well, yes," Vasouk said. "This I can easily understand. I too would be worried if the future of my lineage rested on stones of this kind."

Vasouk's three Naga friends nodded gravely, which did nothing to make me feel better.

I swallowed hard, wondering what question to ask. But with a quick glance Maryani directed me to keep my mouth shut. Vasouk had closed his large eyes, and a particular quivering of his kingly nostrils indicated he was tuning very high – or rather very low – for inspiration.

After a long while, the shining onyx-black eyes reopened and gazed at me. "Szar of the Brown Robe," he began, his voice lower-pitched and more melodious than ever, "let me tell you of certain secrets that I learnt from my mother-father."

I smiled, charmed and warmed from toe to head by the magic of his voice, and wondering what he meant by his mother-father.

The wise Fomalhaut, who had sensed from a distance that Vasouk was about to embark on an important discourse, joined our party, and so did a large group of Nagas after him. Vasouk welcomed them, his smile revealing a glimpse of a white fang. Then he asked me, "Having completed a stone of a certain standard, how do you and your friends test your work? How do you find out whether the stone has been perfected?"

"We plunge it into the purest white slime we can find. If after some time the stone has not dissolved, then we declare it finalised," I answered.

"Well, good!" Vasouk wholeheartedly approved. "Very good! For, truly, the purpose of stone-making is to achieve perfection in matter. All things which are imperfect have a yearning to be dissolved. The reason is, by dissolving they return to their source and become one with it again. The source of all sources, which has infinite fullness – this is what all imperfect things long for, and this is what they try to reach through dissolution or death."

This was reminiscent of the teaching on the power of seeds and the hymns of the Dawn of Creation.

"Things which are perfect have no need to dissolve, because they are one with their source," the king's voice flowed on like nectar. "That which is one with its source is complete, for it can drink from its own cistern. Whenever it needs something, all it has to do is draw from its source, and instantly it is filled and fulfilled. Thus it has no longing to dissolve, and it can live forever. Through its heart runs a pure river of water of life, clear as crystal, proceeding from the source of all sources. And by recreating itself from its own source, it can remain forever young."

Vasouk paused, sniffing my energy discreetly whilst smiling at Maryani. "Perhaps you are wondering how come I deem your best stones so imperfect, even though they do not get dissolved when left in the white slime, Szar of the Brown Robe," he said.

I nodded, as it became clear that I was wondering this.

"It is because your white slime is but a gross and imperfect replica of the Molten Sea, the glorious Mother which is one with the source of all sources," Vasouk answered. Breathing in for inspiration, he added, "Were your stones to be plunged into the depths of the Molten Sea, they would instantly be dissolved. Nothing would be left of them."

I sighed, wondering what would be left of me if I were to be plunged into the depths of the Molten Sea.

"How could they be perfect, anyhow, since they are she-stones!" Vasouk added.

Perplexed, I asked, "Should we attempt to make he-stones – stones of your gender, Majesty?"

"No, this is not what I meant. And I am no he-stone, Szar of the Brown Robe!" Vasouk shook his head with a glistening smile.

Even more perplexed, I frowned. I found it difficult to imagine that the king was a she-stone.

"If I were a he-Naga, then in order to make a baby Naga I would need to find a she-Naga. This would mean that I am unable to tap from the creative source of Life by myself. A very imperfect creature I would be indeed. How could I say of myself that I am complete and self-fulfilled?"

"Mm..." the Nagas approved in one voice, nodding their huge heads.

"Mm..." I said, wondering how to push this conversation further without committing an irreparable slip of protocol.

"A being who is in touch with the source of all sources can only be a he-she, both male and female," Vasouk continued, "just like your ancestors were in the Ancient Days of the Earth."

This was no shocking concept. Several hymns of the Law of Melchisedek referred to the hermaphroditic ancestors of human beings.

"So Your Majesty is..." I began, but Maryani, who could see a blunder arriving *like an elephanto in a potter's shop*, interrupted me. "Androgyne!" she exclaimed before I had time to say "hermaphrodite."

Vasouk gave her a kind smile. "Androgyne, the Nagas are. And androgyne, human beings will be, when they complete their evolution."

The difference between hermaphrodite and androgyne was unclear to me. To make sure I did not offend the Nagas by calling them the wrong name, Maryani filled me in. "Hermaphrodite is when you have the two sides but it's a complete mess," she explained.

"A blissful chaos which is still in touch with the source, but in which the order of the creation remains to be discovered through a long and difficult evolutionary path," Vasouk commented.

"And androgyne is when you *really* get it together," little Maryani said.

"A superior completion in which opposite polarities have been fully integrated. Through an androgynous creature, the source of all sources can express its infinite creative potential, and all can be accomplished," Vasouk added.

"Imagine how wise and happy you would be if Elyani and you were merged in a oneness," Maryani suggested. "Vasouk, don't you think that when they are deeply in love, human beings experience some of the androgyne's exalted qualities and fullness?"

"Well, well... perhaps to a certain extent," Vasouk answered in a tone of caution.

"I know, I know," Maryani sighed, "it does not last. Except in extraordinary cases."

I wanted to return to the topic of the perfection of matter. "But, Your Majesty, isn't the Molten Sea – which is perfect among the perfect – a she?"

"My, only from your limited vision, Szar of the Brown Robe," Vasouk answered patiently. "Where you see the Molten Sea, I see the Sea of Lightning, which is no she but 'it', or rather he-she. The Molten Sea is the first matter, the substance out of which all material things originated. The Sea of Lightning is the last matter, the ultimate culmination of materiality."

"So the Molten Sea is to evolve into the Sea of Lightning, is that it?"

"Yes, but, it is already done!" The utter tranquillity of Vasouk's voice commanded awe. "The same is true of you," Vasouk's gleaming fangs peeped out as he smiled at Maryani, then at me. "Your consciousness is slowly evolving, and one day you will reach the perfect stage of the stone. But because this perfect stage is absolute and eternal, it has neither beginning nor end – and therefore it already exists. When I look at you, I do not see your present transient form, but the eternal perfection that you already are."

"Mm..." Maryani and I looked at each other in a completely new way.

"So this means you can see the Sea of Lightning in all things, Vasouk?" Maryani said.

"Of course, since all material things are made from the substance of the Molten Sea, and the Sea of Lightning is already alive in the Molten Sea. This, by the way, is the source of the power of the Nagas. They know how to draw the infinite Fire of the Sea of Lightning out of all created things."

There followed a composed silence, during which the members of the audience let Vasouk's nectariferous words work on their souls, until Vasouk exclaimed, "Well, well, let us now listen to our good Fomalhaut, master story-teller, after which we will all journey to the spheres of Lowness."

"What is he talking about?" I whispered in Maryani's ear.

"A journey to the spheres of Highness. You are coming too," Maryani answered.

I took her by the arm and walked away from Vasouk. "What's this Ugly Underworld of a nonsense? Didn't you say you were coming back to Eisraim with me after the reception?"

"But it won't take long!" she said.

This was more than I could take. "Taking two hundred Nagas on an excursion beyond the Golden Shield won't take long? Listen, Maryani..."

"But Szar, all these enlightened Nagas live in the spheres of Highness already! They don't have to go anywhere, they just link to what they call their Spirit of Lowness."

I tuned high up into the clear fountain and invoked the Eagle's help. With tears in my eyes, I pleaded, "Maryani, the Archive project is falling apart. My friends in the kingdom are desperate. It would be grossly unfair of me to go on a trip to Highness while they are counting on me, and waiting for me to bring a solution."

"But Szar, you don't understand. Our friends won't have to wait for us one more minute because of this journey. There is no time in Highness! We will be back the very moment we go. Can't you just trust me, for once? This is a wonderful present that Vasouk is giving us."

I sighed. "Talk about your presents, Maryani!"

"Well, well, she is right!" Vasouk had glided his way towards us. "The fact is, the choice is yours, Szar of the Brown Robe: you can either be back in your body one minute after visiting the spheres of Highness with us, or be back in your body one minute after visiting nothing at all." Turning towards Maryani, Vasouk wriggled his nostrils. "What do you think Szar's teacher would advise him to do in such a circumstance?"

From the clear fountain, the words forced their way through my mouth, "I'll come!"

"Well, well... good! Very good!" Vasouk opened a smile.

10.11 The Naga and the bird of paradise

Composed and quietly self-assured as he had been since the day of his birth (that is, the day the Lord Melchisedek ended the second cooking, turning the large cauldron into the Underworlds), Fomalhaut had taken position on a low stage at one end of the hall. Maryani invited me to sit with her on a long, richly-cushioned chest which the Nagas had prepared for her and placed in the middle of the front row, on Vasoukidass' left. Contrary to functions held in the kingdom, there was no lawful waiting. Fomalhaut began his narration as soon as the audience had turned to face him.

"Long, long ago, when the creation was still young, when the gods had just triumphed against the asuras, Mamyani, the she-bird of paradise, took flight from the Blue cascade of Life and Light. Alone, she travelled towards the east..."

As soon as Fomalhaut started speaking, I lost touch with the hall and was projected into breathtaking visions of the Blue cascade of Life and Light, hardly hearing his voice.

"Help, Maryani!" I whispered. "Am I doing something wrong?"

"No," she whispered back, "this is the way storytelling happens down here. Fomalhaut is showing you records from the archives of time."

"Mamyani crossed the extensive forests at the foot of Mount Meru, and the plains of Matareshvar, where celestial animals come and feed on nectar breezes," the record went on. "She crossed the mountain range of Fonteran, and the great lakes where strange fishes of light have been swimming, undisturbed, since the beginning of time – and even earlier than that, according to some legends. Then, carried by the wind of destiny, she kept flying over distant lands for an entire night of the gods.

When dawn came, she met a gigantic fig tree who invited her to rest on its branches, and she accepted, for fig trees are very wise. Foolish are those who do not listen to their advice.

As she was resting, two malevolent angels came and sat under the tree. Their names were Asuragraha and Asurabhima, and they were born from a breed of angry, jealous gods, the descendants of the asuras of old, whose greed and ambition knew no limits.

'Asuragraha, my brother, I have come to discuss a golden opportunity with you. Have you ever heard of the Underworlds?'

'The Underworlds?' Asuragraha spat in disgust. 'Those revolting caverns of sickness where the light of our glorious sun never reaches?'

'Nay, nay! My brother, these caverns are only the superficial crust,' Asurabhima explained in a voice filled with infectious enthusiasm. 'Underneath them are worlds teeming with life force, and replete with treasures: breathtaking landscapes, paradisiacal gardens, and palaces full of gold and precious gems.'

'And who are the defenders of these treasures?' Asuragraha asked.

'Precisely, my brother. The only guardians of the Underworlds are a race of pitiful, sedated snakes who speak even more slowly than blob-men and spend their days squirming on the ground like slugs.'

'Aren't these the Nagas, of whom the Law of heaven says, "*The Great Fire of creation they withstood until the very end, and so they became immortal and invincible*"?'

'Nonsense!' Asurabhima sneered. 'These worms are gutless! They have never fought any wars! And I have learned a secret that could well seal their fate. Soon their new king, the young Vasoukidass, is to be crowned. For the installation ceremony all the Nagas will gather on a large plain to perform a long ritual, during which they will worship the Mother of the Light and surrender to her. There lies our chance, my brother! During the ritual the Nagas will be so exposed and so vulnerable that if taken by surprise, they will not stand a chance against a decent army.'

'And why would we want to attack them, my brother?'

'Asuragraha, the Underworlds are full of phenomenal powers! If we conquer them, then no one in the seven spheres will stand against us. We will become so mighty that even the gods will bow in front of us. And at last, we will reconquer the domain that used to be ours – this high world which the gods stole from us, and where they now dwell. Having conquered the Upperworld as well as the Underworld, we will rule over all the spheres, unchallenged. Even the Flying Dragons will fear us, and from their spheres of remoteness they will worship us. This is our chance, my brother!'

Asuragraha started to understand how juicy the fruit was. 'This Vasoukidass, what kind of Naga is he?'

'Hardly grown up, and totally inexperienced. He was chosen by an oracle, and none of his fellow-slugs even thought of challenging him.'

'None of the Naga princes tried to fight against him?' Asuragraha sneered at the idea of such a cattle-like breed. He extended an open hand to his brother, 'Asurabhima, my armies will be with you.'

Asurabhima shook hands with him. 'Vasoukidass is dead meat!' he scoffed, and with titanic laughter the two brothers sealed their deal. 'I can already see the scene,' Asurabhima raved on. 'The Naga king will be the first to fall. Then we will pour our vials of venom over the crowd. Taken by complete surprise, and seeing their leader dead, the powerless slugs will scatter in all directions. A feast of anger! We will kill and slaughter, and slaughter and kill...'

'Until the last slug lies dead on the ground,' his brother added in delight.

'Not one baby snake will be spared!' Asurabhima bared his teeth.

'And flows of Naga blood will wash the coronation plain!' Asuragraha clapped his hands.

'And we will rip their bellies open, and we will chew their brains,' Asurabhima danced with joy.

'And their corpses will be left to rot in the open!' Asuragraha smashed his fist against the tree trunk.

'And it will stink!' Asurabhima took a deep breath.

'And we will desecrate their cremation grounds,' Asuragraha trampled the ground with his feet, ignorant of the fact that not one Naga had died since the beginning of this cosmic cycle.

The brothers laughed infectiously, and went on making their plans.

After some time they walked away from the tree without noticing Mamyani.

The she-bird of paradise could hardly believe her ears, horrified at so much cruelty. 'Who is this Vasoukidass?' she wondered. 'Should I warn him of the dangers awaiting him? How could it be the will of the Mother of the Light that a whole life-wave be slaughtered while worshipping her?'

Off she flew and down she went, in search of Vasoukidass. She crossed the worlds of the gods, and quickly passed the intermediary worlds. Then she flew down through the kingdom of men, and in no time she had reached the caverns of sickness. She kept descending, flying through the lapis lazuli caves, the rivers of liquid orichalc, the galleries of pink quartz, the lakes of water of life, the mountains of gold. The further she descended, the more wonders she encountered.

Finally she met me," Fomalhaut of the silvery-blue carapace turtle-chortled. "I was having my peaceful morning bath in the southern Tartarean sea. When she enquired where the king-to-be was, I replied, 'Vasoukidass is meditating in the cave of Brahma-ratri, close to the range of volcanoes on the edge of the Furnaces of Doom. But no one must disturb his ascetic practices, for he is preparing himself for the coronation ceremony.'

'But I must speak to him!' Mamyani pleaded.

'Wait till he finishes!' I was adamant.

'O wise tortoise, these are matters that cannot wait. Do you think the king-to-be will be angry with me if I go to his cave and talk to him?'

'Vasoukidass never gets angry,' I told her. 'But your intrusion might upset ancient volcanoes and the Furnaces of Doom. Then the Lord Melchisedek knows what could happen!'

Listening only to the clear fountain, Mamyani decided she had no choice but to find Vasoukidass. After duly thanking me, she dashed towards the volcanoes of Doom. She flew silently, keeping all her feathers of light tightly to herself so as to make herself as little as possible and not upset anyone, especially the volcanoes. After a long journey, she finally reached the entrance of the cave of Brahma-ratri.

The cave's opening was tiny, on the edge of a massive cliff. The rock was shining black, set amid the awesome landscape of gigantic volcanoes gushing flows of red-hot lava high in the sky, rendered crimson by so much fire. In the distance, the glorious Sea of Lightning could be seen.

Little Mamyani cleared her throat loudly to announce her presence.

As no one answered, she courageously decided to fly into the cave. The entrance led into a narrow tunnel that descended deep into the mountain. For hours she flew down, following the narrow shaft in search of the king-to-be.

When she finally reached the cave of Brahma-ratri, Mamyani was astounded. The cave was so large, no boundaries could be seen. And in front of her stood the most magnificent creature she had ever contemplated – young Vasoukidass, whose intense meditation had made his body shine like liquid gold.

For a long moment, she remained motionless in the air. She could not take her eyes away from the Naga.

Vasoukidass opened one of his large, round, onyx-black eyes, which he slowly rolled from right to left. 'My, my...' he exclaimed in his melodious low-pitched voice, opening his other eye and smiling at Mamyani. 'But isn't that a bird of paradise? What a happy visitation, I should say!'

She fell in love with him immediately. She was charmed and overwhelmed. She remained speechless. Her blush added a pinkish hue to her rainbow feathers of light.

The king-to-be wriggled his omniscient nostrils, reading Mamyani's mind like an open book.

'My, my... little Mamyani, what news are you bringing with you? Mm...' Vasoukidass said, catching images of Asurabhima and his brother. In one second, the king-to-be had understood the situation.

'My,' he said after a moment, 'this is really kind of you, little Mamyani. I am greatly indebted to you.'

'Why was I not born a she-Naga?' Mamyani thought.

Vasoukidass, who had no difficulty reading her thoughts, smiled.

Mamyani was so embarrassed that she blushed a little further. 'Your Majesty-to-be...' she started saying, but the words got all mixed up in her throat, and she saw she was about to fall into tears.

So she zapped back into the narrow shaft and flew away.

'Come back and visit my kingdom any time, little Mamyani,' Vasoukidass thought-projected into her mind. 'I shall have some presents to give you. Some interesting presents, I should say.'

Mamyani was too shy to answer.

Vasoukidass closed his eyes again, and resumed his deep meditation on the Mother of the Endless Night.

Three months later, the time for the great ceremony had come. Vasoukidass was standing on a large stage in the middle of the coronation plain, where all the Nagas had assembled. Alongside, on another stage, stood many important guests. I, for a start, and the wise lizards of ancient times, and the official representatives of several races of headless creatures which live in various regions of the Underworlds. The fishes of the Molten Sea could not attend but that did not matter, for they had invited everyone to their shores for a reception that was to follow the coronation.

After various preparations, the ritual worship of the Mother of the Light began, and all became silent. The Mother of the Light responded with her presence, and the atmosphere was as peaceful as the Dawn of Creation.

Not long after, the jealous gods launched their attack. Six and six hundred, and sixty-six thousand formidable fighters appeared in the sky. They bolted down towards the assembled Nagas, inundating the plain with their venom. An elite commando led by Asurabhima himself charged against Vasoukidass, while another six million soldiers attacked from the north, rushing onto the Nagas like a gigantic, ominous black wave.

But the Nagas were not taken by surprise. Under Vasoukidass' direction, they had meticulously planned their defence. Their strategy rested on the irresistible forces of the deepest Underworlds. As soon as the enemy appeared, a trapdoor was activated and the official guests – I, the wise lizards, and the others – all fell from our platform into a subterranean lake where we were perfectly safe. Meanwhile a few large, very fat Nagas rolled over, unveiling wide shafts which had been drilled by skilled Naga architects and stretched down as deep as the Furnaces of Doom. Combining their powers, the Nagas all pulled together, and the Fire of the centre of the Earth gushed up through the shafts.

It was massive, and awesome. Irresistible! The sky instantly became red with fire. In a few seconds, more than half of the formidable asura fighters were reduced to ashes, while the others, completely taken aback, were scattered in all directions.

Sarpaling, Pradip and Amar, three brave Nagas whom Vasoukidass had recently promoted to the rank of general, stood with the king. Together they projected the Word, and the Word became fire. In less than five seconds Asurabhima and his commandos were consumed.

Then Vasoukidass launched the signal. Projected with the Voice, it was loud like the Thunder of the Earth, and it shook all the spheres of Melchisedek. Following him, the assembly of Nagas responded in one Voice, 'Praise the king! Praise the king!' and the clamour was such that all the creatures of all the spheres could hear, and they trembled. And on top of the worlds, the gods could also hear. They stopped their activities and looked down in curiosity and wonder.

Led by Vasoukidass, the Nagas rushed after their opponents, consuming everything on their way with their irresistible Voice-projections. In less than an hour, the army in the north had been wiped out. But the Nagas did not stop there. Carried by a noble fury, they pursued their enemies throughout the spheres of Melchisedek, burning their fortresses and mopping up all pockets of resistance.

After nearly three days and three nights spent fighting, when he saw his end drawing near, Asuragraha called his priests and enquired about the reason for the disaster. Reading the omens of time, the priests soon identified Mamyani, the she-bird of paradise. Asuragraha was so enraged that he sent half his personal guard to punish the bird.

They were trained soldiers hardened by many battles, ruthless angels rendered furious by the taste of defeat. Soon they found Mamyani, who was resting in a forest at the foot of the mountains of Fonteran. They rushed onto her and they poured venom into her eyes, and she became blind. Then they tore out her wings and her legs, and they trampled upon her body, and they spoiled the light of her wings with their filthy venomous spit. When she was nearly dead, they poured thick venom on her soul, so as to torture her further and destroy the pure and precious quality that had made her be born a bird of paradise. They left her agonising in the dirt, and they went back to fight the war.

When Vasoukidass was warned by his nostrils that Mamyani was being attacked, he was in the middle of a fierce engagement. As soon as he could, he left the command of his battalion to Sarpaling and rushed to defend the bird of paradise.

But he arrived too late. Mamyani was dying.

When he saw the maimed body of his bird friend, Vasoukidass cried.

Mamyani could not see him, but she could feel his golden light and presence. 'So you have become king,' she said; and inside herself she smiled, for she was bathing in Naga light, and she no longer felt pain.

'Mamyani, how will I ever be able to repay you?' Vasoukidass' voice was deep with his grief.

'Hush, Great King! The glory of your kingdom was well worth a little bird of paradise,' Mamyani whispered. 'Now listen, this is my last wish: let my remains be offered to the Divine Mother during the great ritual that will finalise your coronation.' Soon she passed away, and her last words were, 'I love you, King Vasoukidass!'

Together with Vasoukidass, the entire creation mourned her death, for birds of paradise are extremely rare, and irreplaceable.

At the end of the third night, the war ended. The entire hierarchy of jealous angels had been exterminated, in what was to be remembered as one of the fiercest battles of all times.

The Nagas spent seven days performing the funeral rites for their dead, then they assembled again on the coronation plains. This time, I myself and the wise lizards were joined by ambassadors from the gods and from about every single hierarchy of angels. For the glory of King Vasoukidass shone high in the spheres, and all wanted him as their ally.

Mamyani's body had been preciously kept in a golden chest. According to her wish, her remnants were ritually offered to the Mother of the Light during the final phase of Vasoukidass' installation. All the Naga generals projected the Word onto the chest as they prayed for Mamyani's soul.

Vasoukidass cried. 'I will find your soul, Mamyani,' he solemnly swore, 'and I will make you a queen.'"

– Thus ends the Book of the Naga King –

11

The Book of the Princely Suite

11.1 The return of Maryani

When I came back into my body, it was early in the morning.
A choir of universes, echoing the song of the Dawn of Creation,
Had I really gone to the spheres of Highness?
which the Mother of the Light is still singing,
I could not remember a thing.
from one end of remoteness to the other. Periphery of time.
My last recollection was Point-blasting Sound in the reception hall of Vasouk's palace.
As it was before the beginning is now,
After that, a lawful blank. I felt so ordinarily Dragon-normal that it was difficult to imagine I had visited such lofty worlds.
and ever will sing.
Elyani was not in the room. As I contemplated the warm glows of the *living walls*, a voice-channel call came through from her, "Welcome back to the kingdom, White Eagle! I am in the other room with Maryani. Come quickly! We have a few problems."

"Mother of the Light! Are you all right, Elyani?"

"Yes. Nothing to do with the oracle."

"Oh, gods!" The Dragon stood me up and ran me to the adjacent room.
Eerie voidness made infinitely dimensional.
Maryani's body was still deeply asleep, and as far as I could judge her aura showed all signs of harmonious energy flows. But at the back of the room Woolly was lying unconscious on a mattress, Elyani by his side.

She looked very tired. "Is Maryani on her way back?" she asked.

"Imminently. But what about Woolly?"

"Last night he was taken by a high fever. He became delirious," Elyani explained. "I had him brought here."

As I inspected his energy, Elyani went on, "He has been vomiting all night. I have had to use the Voice to cool his energy down, but even that wasn't enough to appease the fire. He is still burning with fever."

"Dragon-overheating!" I immediately diagnosed, letting my hands run on his gateways. "You said, a few problems. What about the others?"

"We have received emergency messages from Master Esrevin in Lasseera. Their Archive stones were getting worse by the hour. It was so bad that by midnight there were only nine stones left. Esrevin had to project the high Word of Thunder to isolate them from the fields, but this has only brought temporary relief. He fears the stock may not last much longer."

I inhaled, pulling Dragon breeze from a distance. "And what else?"

"I missed you. Terribly," she whispered. "Did you miss me?"

Voidness eternal. Darkness invisible.

"Well, to tell you the truth," I confessed, "it all went very fast for me last night. The Nagas tried to take me to Highness, but I slept like a Cosmic Night."

"No you didn't!" Elyani assured me. "I know you went there, the Eagle sent me a vision of Whiteness."

The flight of the Eagle at the Edge of Highness.

She pointed to Woolly, "What exactly happened to his Dragon during the earthquake?"

I explained to Elyani how the earthquake was in reality a 'present', sent by Maryani during her initiation in the Sea of Lightning. "The problem is," I deliberated, "if we stop the fire in Woolly's body, we may well be hampering the forces Maryani has sent him."

"Just keep his energy under control until Maryani returns," Elyani decided. "Who could possibly handle Woolly better than an unstoppable little Dragon like her?"

"You are a wise woman," I approved.

"Sometimes!" she threw a playful glance.

Maryani's gateways were already showing the first signs of waking. "Lo and behold!" I told the White Eagle, my hands running on Woolly's body of energy.

"But she is..." the White Eagle gulped.

"...coming out of the hibernation state all by herself!"

"Shouldn't we be doing something?"

I whistled loudly. "I have received strict orders! No one is to manipulate her energy. We just stand back, watch, and smile like filosterops."

A most unusual scene was unfolding. What normally would have taken one-and-a-half days was happening before our very eyes in a matter of minutes: the whiteness of her frozen gateways was dissipating, coloured sparks were warming up her aura, energy circulations were restarting in her principal meridians. On top of all this, wisps of Naga-gold mists added a flavour of Underworld magic.

11 – The Book of the Princely Suite

It wasn't long before Lady Teyani turned up. I went to meet her in the courtyard.

After a quick greeting, the great magician of ancient times asked anxiously, "Is Maryani on her way back?" Despite the kind omens the White Eagle had sent in the last days, it remained that eight of her priestesses had died in the Underworlds in the recent years.

"She is almost here, Teyani!" I took her hands.

"*All glory to the teacher!*" her face became radiant. "How many hours will you need to take her out of the hibernation state?"

"Teyani, last time we spoke I warned you we might have to handle this situation in a slightly unusual way."

"Do you mean..." Teyani's face straightened, "you will need more than three days to wake her up?"

I turned skywards, seeking inspiration. Then I looked unlawfully straight into her eyes, "Teyani, can I ask you to trust me?"

Intrigued, Teyani kept eye contact, reading me throughout and beyond. "The Eagle and I trust you. Much more than you think," she declared.

The depth in her voice left me breathless.

Elyani called, "She is waking up!"

"Waking up?" Teyani was astonished. "You mean you have already taken her out of hibernation?"

I shook my head, "I didn't do a thing." Taking her arm, I led her to Maryani's room.

By the time we got there, Maryani was already sitting up in bed. With her eyes closed, she was deeply absorbed in meditation. She didn't even look pale. She hadn't lost any weight. Her aura was shining with the golden light which had been with her in the Underworlds. Soft astral winds emanated from her, carrying subtle aromatic fragrances that gently swept the room with a low-pitched hiss. The atmosphere was vibrant with a certain magical hum, clearly reminiscent of Vasoukidass' amicable irony.

Elyani and her grand master watched in disbelief.

The vroofing under my feet was running wild, as if the Nagas who had brought Maryani back to the kingdom were applauding (as they did, by beating the floor with their tails).

"I bet you can hear music!" I whispered to the wise women.

They nodded in unison, their eyes fixed on Maryani.

Little Maryani opened her eyes and slowly turned her head towards them. At first, she didn't see them. She was looking through them, surveying distant horizons, comprehending this newly-discovered kingdom with her fresh wisdom.

When her vision focussed, her face lit up, "Teyani!"

Tears welling in her eyes, Teyani took my hand, "Thank you! Thank you for this!"

"*All glory to the teacher!*"

At that moment the predictable happened. Maryani got up – not a great feat when compared with the Dragon-ebullition of the last weeks, when she was being cooked by the Naga king.

"Don't!" Teyani choked. "Don't!"

I took a firm grip on Teyani's arm for fear of her fainting, and also to make sure she didn't walk over to Maryani (who had made it very clear to me, and on several occasions, and with all the petulance of her strongly-opinionated nature, that she didn't want *anyone* to touch her body, is that clear? Anyone! Understood?)

"But..." the grand master turned to me.

"That's how Dragons are," I interrupted her, "they dance!" and to gain time I pulled her further away from Maryani in a rounded gesture, jumping from one foot to the other with the artistic daintiness of the Sons of Vulcan.

"But..." pulled by the iron hand, the grand master had no choice but to follow.

Elyani let a cascade of chuckles tumble out.

Delighted, the Nagas' heir waved her arms, accompanying the dance.

"But if she starts moving, she should at least have a sip of the drink!" Teyani said, her authoritative tone undermined by a flutter of hesitation.

What Maryani needed, I judged, was some time to pull her Dragon together. "The drink?" I grasped Teyani's other hand, "What drink?"

"There!" with her nose, she pointed to a cup on the window ledge. "Elyani and I prepared it."

Little Maryani's unambiguous instructions came back at once: if there was *one* thing she didn't want, under any circumstances, and no matter what happened (was that clear?) it was to be forced to eat or drink. Understood?

"Oh, what a beautiful aura!" I marvelled, grabbing the cup, "Could I taste it?" Guided by the humorous Naga-presence that illuminated the room like a Midnight Sun, I emptied the cup in one draught. "Oh, gods!" I shivered in delight. "I feel alive! I feel so alive, all of a sudden!" I informed the grand master. And I reminded her, "You are trusting me, aren't you?"

"But..." she launched a feeble protest, "Elyani and I spent hours preparing that!"

"This I can tell, Teyani!" I assured her. "Pure nectar!"

"Oh, Lord!" Teyani chose to laugh, and I knew the battle was half won.

Meanwhile, Maryani had gone over to Woolly and knelt down behind his head. When Teyani noticed how intensely she was looking at him, she whispered in my ear, "Do they know each other?"

"Sort of!" I whispered back. "Teyani, I think I should speak to you." Taking her firmly by the arm, I led her out onto the lawn.

Enthused by the Naga spirit which saturated the air and made the grey mists look a trifle less grey, an eloquent flow started pouring through my mouth, punctuated with a profusion of "My," "Well, yes," and "I should say." I brushed a touching picture of the reborn little Maryani, explaining why and how she was going to be fragile for a while. Of course she had become immune to thirst, hunger, cold, fatigue, and other similar human afflictions, so that she no longer needed to sleep. She could shatter a fortified wall with her Voice – matter, in this kingdom, was so poorly cooked! She could neutralise a whole battalion of the king's army all by herself. She could also probably dematerialise and rematerialise herself, but not in the first two weeks, so as to secure a gradual acclimatisation. Of course she could walk on fire, walk through fire, light a fire in a glance, spit fire, eat fire, and even melt the ice of an entire mountain range – all very natural things for Naga initiates, who know that everything is fire.

Eyes half closed, mouth half open, Teyani took in every word, drinking the Naga king's nectareous presence.

"But, wise woman," I continued, "I call on your compassionate understanding. Maryani is concerned her former peers may not see she has become a different person. Should she be confined in ways that are no longer hers..."

"In short," Teyani went *straight to the cherry stone*, "I must let go of any authority over her, is this what you are telling me?"

"Well, well..." I looked down to the centre of the Earth for inspiration, "yes, actually, this is exactly what I am telling you."

"I see." Teyani liked the frankness of the answer.

"But even more importantly, Teyani, Maryani needs our moral support. To those who return from the Underworlds, the kingdom seems grey and unattractive. One hour ago, she was a queen living in a golden palace and surrounded by the love of her enlightened Naga friends. Now..."

"My friend," Teyani's understanding illumined her smile, "I know the greyness of the kingdom well, and the nostalgia of those who have contemplated the Light and must return to this world." Through her fountain, the White Eagle shone his presence onto that of the Naga king, promising to envelop Maryani in his wings of love.

The Naga king was satisfied. Nothing more needed to be said.

A cosmic silence followed, blissfully content with the encounter of Uppermost Whiteness and Under-gold.

Teyani and I read deep into one another, enjoying the superior feeling of peace.

That was when I realised, "*Oh my Lord Melchisedek!* But you have found out about the daiva! You know exactly what is about to happen to Elyani!"

Teyani reached out and sealed my lips with her index finger.

"No!" An irrational wave shook me off track. I pushed her hand away, "No, Teyani! I cannot not ask you. Elyani is my blood, my heart, my Spirit. I *must* know. What have the gods decreed?"

"*Hush, my great man in the Law!* As I trust you, so you must trust me," Teyani poured all the softness of her voice into me. "Once the gods have thrown the daiva, nothing can be done."

From deep below to high above, all I could feel was an overpowering NO.

"Please," she insisted.

I closed my eyes, trying to join her high in the Light.

She took my hands, "Thanks to you, Elyani has blossomed. She holds the Eagle's Light and shines more than ever before. Do not spoil the beautiful days ahead of you. Trying to fight the daiva would only bring disaster on us all. Anyhow, the sentence of the gods will be known very soon."

I plunged into the Mother of the Endless Night. "What can I do?"

"Give her your love. Give her your joy."

"Teyani, there *must* be something I can do," I reopened my eyes, suffocating for action.

From way up above, Teyani shone the Eagle's compassion. But all she could do was shake her head silently.

"No! No! I am *not* going to give in, Teyani!"

Through a voice channel of darkness visible, Maryani called, "Szar, could I have your help, please?"

Teyani stood up and gently pulled me by the hand.

No thoughts, just Dragon, I followed her into the room.

Woolly was still deeply asleep, Maryani sitting on the floor behind his head, Elyani by her side.

"I need to transfer forces into his body," Maryani said. "But I'm worried his heart may not cope. Could you take care of his vital gateways?"

I went to kneel by Woolly and placed my hand on his heart.

"Fine."

Maryani placed her palms flat against Woolly's temples. "Are you holding him?" she asked.

I gave a short nod.

"Vasouk has given me a seed of power for him," she explained. "I need to transfer it into him immediately, while he is still under the influence of the forces I sent him from the Sea of Lightning." And she added, "Your stones are going to love these forces."

Maryani could see there was something wrong with me, but this was no time to chat. She closed her eyes and tuned deep down into Vasoukidass' Dragon.

Instantly, her aura tripled in size and the room took on an air of Deep Underworld cavern of pure Naga-gold. Woolly was shaking like a leaf, but despite the incandescent stream that flowed into his head he didn't wake up, and his heart and vital gateways coped perfectly well.

Hardly ten seconds later, the transmission of power was completed.

Satisfied that the seed of power had been planted, Maryani's eyes glimmered with Naga-contentment. "Shall we wake him up?"

I heard the words, but could not answer.

I was about to explode.

11.2 Faraway voices

Higher up than high, further than beyond,
I called,
Help! Whoever you are, wherever you are – help!
All obstacles, I know, your breath can sweep away.
The daiva, you can overthrow,
And devious dreams of gods and men
And narrow decrees of the Lords of Destiny
And mediocre fate, and useless laws of consequences.
O you from high and beyond, help!
The response was immediate.
Waves of blueness, strangeness made light,
Setting the Point ablaze.
The voice in the field of stars whispered,
"Danger, son! Danger!"
And in the winds of space another voice echoed,
"Shall we awaken him now?"
"No," the first answered,
"He does not see the havoc he is about to create for all of them.
The time has not yet come.
Only a warning is to be sent –
Danger, son! Danger!
Listen to the wise woman's words.
Do not call onto the power now."
I raised my voice to the spaces of infinity,
Why bow to the daiva?
Who are the gods, and what do they really know?
Above and below, there are greater powers
Which transcend all limits
And for which the gods are no match.
I was born a fighter.
I see no wisdom in resignation
And passive acceptance of fate
And useless waiting and sleepy waste of time.
Let me stand up, now.
Let me fight, now!
The voice responded,
"True, the gods are still young.
True, wisdom is for those who fight.
True, there are greater powers.
But woe to you if you call on them now.
The work of your allies will be destroyed
And everything lost.

Harken to the voice from spaces eternal!
A greater design stands behind the gods' youthful imagination,
A greater judgment behind their limited vision.
Stay still.
The time has not yet come."

11.3 The new generation of stones

"Shall we wake Woolly?" Maryani said again.

Elyani was holding my hand. Deeply shaken, I turned round and sought to make eye contact with Teyani.

An Eagle lighthouse, the great magician of the Ancient Days merged her fountain with mine, flooding me with her love.

Silently contemplating her, I gave a nod, acknowledging that her words of wisdom had been heard.

Forever love, Flying Dragon. Miss not the call!

I turned to Maryani. "Woolly is all yours!"

She pulled a face, "Do you think he is going to be angry with me?"

Elyani shook her head confidently, "He's too tired for that!"

"Well, well... let's see!" Clicking her fingers, Maryani pulled Woolly back into his physical body.

It wasn't long before Woolly half-opened his right eye and wailed, "Oh, Goddess! My head!" As my brown cape came vaguely into focus, he moaned plaintively, "Is that you, Lehrmon?"

"No, Szar. *Peace, my friend in the Law! Peace!*" I took his hand.

Maryani, who was still sitting behind his head, gently passed her hands through his curly hair, sending a soothing influence for his headache.

Woolly opened his eyes wide and threw his head back, looking up at Maryani.

It was their first eye contact, and it happened upside down.

The room was holding its breath.

Maryani got up, walked to the other mattress and picked up Lilu's jar. Then she went back to Woolly and placed the jar in his hand.

Instantly, Woolly was fully awake. He lifted himself up on his elbows and while Elyani placed pillows behind him, he slowly sat up to open the jar.

Before lifting the lid, he hesitated.

Knowing what fate had befallen the other stones, I could understand his anxiety.

But when he opened the jar, his face lit up. To his complete astonishment – and to mine – Lilu was the size of an apricot, ten times larger than the biggest I had ever seen her. She was no longer whitish but pure Naga-gold, and she looked as strong and healthy as a fruit from the Underworlds' orchards.

The world started breathing again.

Bewildered, Woolly searched Maryani's eyes.

Resting on the Dragon of the Deep, she held the superior stillness of a Naga. But Teyani was not fooled. She heard the melody of the spheres resonating inside the Earth. After a long contemplation of the child she had loved like her own, she sanctified the decree of time in one nod – Maryani had become a woman. "This young man needs a drink," she beckoned Elyani and me. "Let us prepare a special brew for him."

"And Szar can taste it, perhaps?" Elyani suggested as we left the room.

"*No way, woman of the Law!*" Teyani could at last vent the indignation she had felt at the way I had expedited the lovingly prepared life-saver.

"I will tell you what Woolly needs," Elyani said, emphatically raising her index finger towards the gods, "Dragon's milk!"

Teyani burst out laughing.

"Perhaps I could watch when you prepare it?" I dared to suggest.

"Never!" the two women answered in one voice.

I sat on the lawn, stunned by the shower which the faraway voices had poured onto me. There was an emergency voice-channel call from Lehrmon in Woolly's chapel, "We have lost another three Archive stones, and five more are just about dissolved," he declared in his measured voice. "Unless something can be done immediately, I will have to project the high Word of Thunder onto them."

"Blasting them with the Voice is no real solution!"

"At least it will limit the crumbling temporarily."

"Wait for us, Lehrmon. Maryani and I are on our way," I said.

"Maryani is back! Excellent! And how is Woolly?" Lehrmon asked.

Elyani dropped into the astral conversation, "Resuscitated is probably the word."

I let the two of them continue their talk and went back into the room.

When he saw me walk in decidedly, Woolly immediately guessed. "Commander! You are bringing us some news about the stones."

"*Man of the Law*, the Goddess has been..." out of respect for Maryani's juvenile innocence I straightened my language, "...she has been unkind, to say the least," and I gave the details of the latest casualties.

"I am ready to go to the chapel," Maryani said.

"I am ready too!" Woolly declared, sitting up straight on his mattress.

He looked nowhere near as grey-green as one hour earlier. Still, I suggested, "How about resting for a day?"

"*No way, man of the Law!*" he became fierce. "Even if I had to crawl my way through the temple and vomit on every step of the stairways, I would still come."

Maryani gave her blessing. "I will carry him."

I raised my hands, "If the Great Dragon of Fierceness wants to carry you, then what is there to fear?"

As soon as Maryani put her energy onto him, he started trotting along like a filosterops, and we set off through the maze of the female wing.

It was magic, it worked each time: just by setting foot in the Point-guided corridors, a superior feeling of peace dawned on me. It was profound, and light at the same time – magnificent! Elyani was right, I was becoming addicted to this field. I could have spent entire days wandering through the maze, I never seemed to get enough of it. It brought not only tranquillity but also clarity of mind and centring.

After having ranted and railed against this field for so long, I now dreaded the idea that one day it would collapse.

Thanks to the lucidity fostered by the stroll, it became clear that the faraway voices had left a trail of strange energies above my head. The flavour of consciousness reminded me of Verzazyel's cave, making me wonder if I should go back to the Watcher's domain in the Red Lands and try to discover some of the secrets I had missed during my first visit.

Somehow, I knew that during the time I had spent in that cave, a key part of my inner puzzle had been triggered. But there were still so many missing bits in this puzzle! Where to start? How to explore something that is so unknown one doesn't even know where to look for it?

Before I could think further, I realised with a touch of regret we were crossing the portal of the female wing. The rest of the walk, unguided by the field, was rather dull. Boring.

Lehrmon didn't come to greet us at the door of the Field Wizards' chapel, we met him in the cellars. He looked unlawfully tired.

"Seems like you had a long night, just as I had," Woolly commented, collapsing in a corner of the room, his back against the wall.

Lehrmon did not answer. He just exchanged a routine greeting with Maryani, without showing the least sign of surprise that she was already up and running or that her aura was shining like a golden full moon. But then Lehrmon was never surprised by anything, as if he already knew in advance the end of all stories. If he happened to display surprise, it was usually out of courtesy, or to help boost his friends' confidence.

As soon as Maryani set foot in the chapel, her face brightened with curiosity at the sight of the shelves covered with bottles and the variegated energies attached to them. The quiver of her nostrils betrayed how strongly she responded to the Underworld smells that filled the cellars, especially the smell of the buckets of white slime where the Archive stones were made. While Lehrmon sketched a picture of the situation for her, she listened carefully, going from bucket to bucket like a bee from flower to flower, sensing the Dragon-ness behind stones and slime, assessing the noxious elemental forces that polluted the room.

"I can sense something else in this room," she observed, "...ve-ry strong, and utterly bizarre. Something that comes down from high up."

"It's the Flying Dragon device that protects the crypt," Lehrmon told her, pointing to the doorway.

"Voof!" Maryani let out the ritual cry. "Is this what the magic of the Flying Dragons feels like? The power is awesome. Couldn't you use it to isolate this crypt from the negative elemental forces overflowing from the fields?"

"We tried that," Lehrmon said. "The problem is, it seals the cellar so well that the power of the fields no longer reaches into here, and without the fire from the fields the stones stop growing."

"Why not use the power of the Flying Dragons as fire, and cook the stones with that?" she asked in a mischievous voice.

"A Flying-Dragon he-stone!" Woolly burst out laughing, revived by the outrageousness of the suggestion. "That would blast the breasts off the Goddess!"

A reproving frown crossed Maryani's face.

"We have made a few he-stones in the past, but never anything that could be connected to the power of the Flying Dragons," Lehrmon mused. "Would you really consider this an option? The power could get completely out of hand. I wonder what on Earth could control it."

"Just joking," Maryani tilted her head back. "While in the realm of extravagant ideas, Lehrmon, why haven't you tried to cook the stones using the Voice of Thunder?"

Woolly opened his eyes wide. "Non-stop Voice projection of Thunder in my chapel? Would that be a possibility?"

"Of course it's a possibility!" Lehrmon answered in his consistently tranquil voice. "Thunder-stones have been part of the tradition of the Brown Robe since time immemorial. But they are individual realisations, vehicles of consciousness which the Masters of Thunder generate out of their own Spirit – a body of immortality."

"Isn't that what stones are all about?" Maryani pointed out.

"But wait a minute!" Woolly was taken aback. "How come you never told me about this Thunder-cooking method? Why couldn't we use the same principle to cook the Archive stones?"

"I have received strict instructions to use the Voice of Thunder only as a very last resort," Lehrmon was firm. "By activating the power of Thunder on so many stones, we could create chain-reactions of unpredictable magnitude. We could precipitate a collapse of all the fields in the county, with the disastrous consequences you can imagine. Only if everything else fails will we call on Thunder."

"Anyway," Maryani smiled dryly, "fire is not what is lacking. The Underworlds are full of it. Have you tried to cook your stones using the heat of a compost heap, instead of the fire from the fields?"

Woolly wrinkled his nose, "The stones started taking monstrous shapes. They couldn't even be used for voice-channelling!"

Maryani delicately wriggled her omniscient nostrils, "That's because you began the cooking with the fields, and then continued with the compost heap. The stones didn't cope with the transition."

Lehrmon shrugged, "But cooking them only with the heat of a compost heap is far too slow! We tried it for months, and no visible growth could be observed."

"That," Maryani replied with a knowing look, "is because you do not know how to connect a compost heap to the fire of the Deep Underworlds."

Woolly didn't hide his astonishment. "Could you do that?"

"Well, well... yes! I could."

"Is that what you would recommend in this situation?" Lehrmon asked.

"Well, well... no! Not quite. For a start, I don't really need a compost heap to tap fire from below. And I don't think we will get great results if we try to cook these stones with Underworld fire."

"Why not?" Lehrmon contained his consternation, realising that Maryani's words amounted to nothing short of the death sentence for our stock of Archive stones.

"These stones have grown up in the fields. Changing the source of fire so abruptly simply would not work."

"But what about Lilu?" Woolly tried to argue. "Isn't that exactly what happened to her?"

"Well, well... Lilu is an exception," Maryani said.

"What do you mean, an exception?" Woolly insisted. "Her situation was exactly the same as that of the Archive stones!"

The young woman was blunt, "Woolly, I had to undo Lilu completely, and start again from scratch with her."

Woolly's feverish night had left him quite pale. He turned much paler. "Does this mean... Lilu died?"

Maryani, whose Whiteness had not been tarnished one iota by her gold, pulled from the infinite softness of the Eagle. "Not exactly," she said in a gentle voice. "I managed to keep all the forces you had put into her. She was... let us say, reincarnated."

Devastated, Woolly closed his eyes.

"I am sorry, Woolly," Maryani walked over to him, "there was nothing anyone could do for her. I had a council of six enlightened Nagas examine her, and believe me – believe me! – I nagged them until I was absolutely convinced there was no hope for Lilu. Then we engaged the procedure which transferred her astral body into the new seed."

Woolly was in his lost child character. He nodded silently, with a resigned look on his face.

"Well," Lehrmon was in a mood to move fast, "why not do the same with our Archive stones. How long would it take you?"

Maryani stood by Woolly's side, letting her serene liquid gold flow into him. "Lehrmon, do you really have a good reason to stick to these she-stones?" she asked. "If we have to start from scratch, why not generate hermaphroditic stones?"

"What? Maryani!" the way Lehrmon raised one eyebrow showed he was the closest to losing his calm I had ever seen. "Maryani..." he repeated, breathing deeply and thinking of the White Eagle, "Maryani, I am caught up in a world that is collapsing, and I have limited time in front of me. I just *do not have* ten years to waste trying to create the kind of stone no one has achieved in the kingdom for centuries."

"*Peace, man of the Law!*" Maryani protested, petulant at the prospect of a little debate. "Some people *did* succeed!"

"Maryani," Lehrmon kept his voice calm, very calm, "do you realise that not *one* of the Nephilim giants has been able to produce a hermaphroditic stone in the last centuries? And do you realise..."

"But precisely!" she claimed. "If so many have failed, it's because they cooked their stones with the fields, which have long lost the required integrity. If you were to use fire from the Underworlds, then that would be a completely different story!"

"But..." In a glance, Lehrmon realised that Woolly and I were watching him with intense curiosity, wondering if he was going to lose his temper (a sign which, with even greater certainty than a night of howling dogs, would have indicated the immediate downfall of Atlantis).

"All right," he smiled, amused, "tell us about these hermaphroditic stones."

"You know," Maryani immediately resumed, "if you really wanted to salvage your she-stones, I guess we could probably find a way."

Lehrmon turned towards Woolly, raising his second eyebrow in disbelief.

I grinned. These two men had no idea what had landed in their chapel.

Walking slowly through the cellar, Maryani was sensing the earth energies. "I could create a drainage that would drive the nasty elemental forces deep down into the Earth." Pulling another face, she added, "And you could keep using your beloved fields to cook your beloved she-stones."

Inspired by the Point, I intervened, "Am I still the one who decides, here?"

Lehrmon was thankful for the diversion, "Certainly, Commander! Do you have a plan?"

I turned to Maryani, "Would it be a difficult enterprise to establish such a drainage system?"

"No, not difficult," she said, "but silly!"

"I hear you, Maryani, I hear you." Turning to Lehrmon, I suggested, "Has it crossed your mind that at the moment all the stone-makers of the kingdom must be experiencing the same kind of difficulties?"

"And so?" Lehrmon asked.

It was too early for me to disclose the details of a plan that was still germinating above my head. I just told them, "Let's immediately establish a drainage system here, and another one in Lasseera, so as to preserve the existing Archive stones. But at the same time, let us start the production of stones according to Maryani's principles. All kinds of stones: she-stones, he-stones, and hermaphroditic ones."

"But do you really need these stones?" Maryani questioned, casually pointing an aristocratic finger at the buckets. "Aren't we wasting precious time with them?" she added, for Lehrmon.

"I know, they can only get worse as time goes by," I agreed. "But what if I needed them to confuse our enemies?"

Maryani's eyes flared with curiosity. "Well, well... then it would be a completely different story, of course!"

Lehrmon was twisting his beard in deep cogitation, "Do you mean, we could convince our potential enemies that we are operating with one type of stone, and meantime use another type for the Archive transfer?"

"Knowing how much depends on the success of our enterprise, this is the least we can do."

"What you are brewing will end up being much more complicated, won't it?" Lehrmon read through me with disconcerting facility. It reminded me once more that unless I found a way to seal myself, disastrous leakages were bound to happen. Anyone who had some Point could guess my thoughts.

"Could be," I just said.

Maryani was Dragon-set. "Let's not waste any time, let's start the work right now!" she said, and she made us move the buckets onto an earth line she had been sensing during the conversation.

Woolly was too overwhelmed to take part in the operation. He stayed in his corner, his elbows resting on his knees, his head resting on his hands, his mind resting nowhere. He knew now it was just a matter of time before all his babies ended up in the garbage bin.

11.4 More Atlantean secrets

After sunset, back on the lawn with Elyani, I broke the good news: the condition of the stones had been stabilised. Thanks to Maryani's drainage system, Lehrmon, Woolly and I had watched the noxious elemental slime disappear from the crypt of the Archive stones in less than a few hours.

Elyani applauded, "Is this the end of our troubles with the stones?"

I shook my head, "These stones will not make it to the Archive transfer – unless of course the transfer had to be implemented in less than a month." An eventuality I dared not imagine.

"And so, how will we operate the Archive transfer? Use two of Maryani's Nagas in lieu of stones, perhaps?"

I let out a silly chuckle. "Now that would blast the breasts off the Goddess!" But it struck me that Elyani's suggestion had great potential. "Tomorrow, when I see Gervin, I should have a serious discussion with him about the possibility of an alliance with the Nagas."

"Is Gervin back in Eisraim?" Elyani asked in surprise.

"From the Point I sensed he was on his way back, so I tried to send him a Point communication and to my astonishment, he responded! We have arranged a meeting tomorrow, early in the morning."

Elyani was impressed. "Right on target, Brother Knight! And what else about the Point have you to report?"

"I am starting to understand only too well why the Nephilim giants can't turn their Point-fields off – addiction, addiction! When I see how much I enjoy perambulating the corridors of the female wing, I become genuinely frightened. Anyway," I sighed the kingdom out of my mind, "I don't feel like talking about the Point tonight."

"Tired?"

"No. I just don't feel like talking about anything but you, and you and me," I answered in a sulky voice, putting my arm around her shoulders.

Elyani made herself magic woman, "Come into my world, Dragon!"

Thick clouds, faint moonlight, just enough to guess her smile.

"Today I have realised important things about you, Elyani," I declared pensively, my fingertips lightly exploring her face. "I was observing Maryani. She pulls faces just like you do."

"And what does this tell you about me, Dragon?"

"I have seen Teyani do the same. My conclusion is that you and Maryani must have learnt the art from her."

"What can I say? Teyani has taught me everything!"

"Well, well... she taught you well. I must tell her how indebted I am to her for this, and a few other things too."

"Do you like the way I pull faces?"

"It fascinated me right from the beginning. I had never seen anyone pull such delicate, sophisticated faces. Can Alcibyadi do them too?"

"Could be! Which reminds me, I have a secret to tell you."

"A secret!" I rubbed my hands.

"It's a secret between Alcibyadi and Teyani, but Alcibyadi said I should tell you, provided you don't tell Lehrmon. I mean, it doesn't matter if Lehrmon guesses through you, but you must not tell him."

"Mm... I see."

"Teyani has given Alcibyadi permission to have a baby boy."

"So Teyani approves of Alcibyadi having a child?" I asked.

"That was not the issue. Alcibyadi is so stubborn... this point is not even open for discussion. But according to the rule of our order, the first child of a White Eagle must be a girl."

"A girl," I pondered, wondering how it would feel to carry Elyani's baby girl in my arms. "But how does it work? Some intervention of the gods?"

"No! We priestesses of the White Eagle do not need the gods for this! It is part of our initiation. We know how to choose the sex of our children. So, to fulfil the rule, Alcibyadi had decided to have twins, a girl and a boy, and to arrange for the girl to come out of her womb first. But having to carry a child while travelling to the land of Aegypton is already bad enough. If moreover there had to be two of them! So Teyani used her authority as grand master to relieve Alcibyadi from the rule of the first-born child."

Intriguing. "How the Upperworld can you choose the sex of your children? Is it a secret?"

"Mm... yes, but one that the White Eagles can share with their men – provided they can keep the secret, of course."

I lamented, "This is starting to become a major problem. I am hopeless with secrets. I would never tell anyone, but how can I not let other people guess? Still a mystery to me."

"It doesn't matter, I'll tell you anyway. For as the Law says, *there are two types of secrets: those which must not be told and must not be guessed, and those which must not be told but can be guessed.* This one belongs to the second category."

Casually tuning into her from the Point, I unintentionally read her mind. "Hey! But you are keeping a first-category secret from me, aren't you? And it has nothing to do with having baby White Eagles!"

Under my fingertips I felt her cheeks blush.

"Did you find out what the gods have decreed for you?" I immediately asked.

"No, it has nothing to do with that."

My Dragon was consumed with curiosity, "It's a secret about me, isn't it?"

"No, please, don't guess!" she begged me. "I promised Gervin I would keep it a first-category secret."

I raised my hands towards the world of the gods. "Gervin tells you secrets about me?"

"No!" she protested, "he didn't tell me. I guessed!"

I burst out laughing and stopped Pointing at her. "All right. Forget it. I won't mention it again."

"No!" she insisted, placing her right hand on my heart. "I don't want you to think I keep secrets from you."

"Well... don't you?"

"Only one, and because of cosmic necessity. And not for much longer. I swear to you on the Eagle, Szar!" she spoke as if from the top of the ladder of the worlds. "Do you believe me?"

"Of course I believe you. I always believe you," I surrendered. "Just plunge me into oblivion with a long kiss, so I can forget about this cosmically necessary secret."

She fulfilled the request with total dedication, sending me far above in the spheres.

Much later, on my return to the kingdom, when I found myself lying on the lawn, Elyani by my side, I asked, "I want to know the secret. I mean, the other one: how would you make a White Eagle?"

"I would need your help, for that."

"Suppose! How would you manage to make it a girl?"

"Would you like to have a baby girl with me?" she asked in her softest voice-nectar.

"But that is not what we are discussing, Elyani!"

"Of course not! Now, I will tell you what our Law says. *First, the woman will search in the spheres for a suitable soul, preferably one who has already been associated with the White Eagle, but truthfulness and purity are the main qualities to be sought. If lawfully asked, the oracle will help attract the right soul. Then, with a man who has charm and is from the right caste...*"

"That's me! That's me!"

Playfully, she gave a languorous sigh, "*...at the appropriate time of the moon cycle, the woman will conceive. She will know that conception is taking place when she hears the harmony of the spheres, and when the Angels of the Seed appear to her.*"

"Who are the Angels of the Seed?" I asked.

"Those who help women during pregnancy. *When the baby is in the womb, they inundate the mother with golden light, and they supply the Spirit that makes the baby grow.*"

"You mean, they bring the fire that cooks the embryo," I translated into Dragon language.

"Exactly! Then, when the priestess meets the Angels of the Seed, *she lets the Eagle's Light intercede, and the Angels of the Seed ensure that a baby girl is conceived.*"

"That is lovely! But then, how will Alcibyadi manage to have a baby boy?" I wondered.

"Alcibyadi says she has already arranged everything with the Angels of the Seed."

"Is there another secret method for that?"

"Not really. She just called on them and fasted until they appeared to her. Alcibyadi is renowned as one of the strongest theurgists of Eisraim. Few people can invoke angels and bring down their presence as powerfully as she does."

"And what does Lehrmon say about all this?"

Elyani swelled her cheeks in a sulky fashion. "No!"

"Poor Alcibyadi!" I called onto the Eagle's Light. "Do you think she will win?"

"Hard to tell. Lehrmon is about as stubborn as she is."

"Perhaps I should speak to him. Of course, I would ask Alcibyadi's permission first."

"I have already asked Alcibyadi," Elyani said, "and she approves fully."

I took my head in my hands, "Why am I always three steps behind everyone else? I never know anything of what's happening. Everyone always knows what's about to happen to me (and to everyone else). It's terrible, I can't even blame the Flying Dragons for this one."

"Hush, Brother Knight!" Elyani took on her panther's voice. "Didn't you just Point-discover that Gervin was on his way back to the temple? And Teyani was telling me that you really embarrassed her this morning by guessing her thoughts."

"Only a few hours ago Lehrmon was reading highly secret details of my plan for the Archive transfer. He just had to look into my eyes, and there was nothing I could do about the leakage."

"It's because you haven't yet learnt how to Point-seal your mind," she assured me. "Now that the weaving of your Point is nearly complete, I will soon be able to show you how to do it. Incidentally, in the future, Point-holding secrets will be one of your specialties."

"The mysterious Brother Knights..."

"See," the panther laughed, "you've already guessed through me."

"I want to know more! Is it a secret?"

"Of course!" she closed her eyes and made herself tipsy with sight. "I have seen the scene a few times. A big man, completely bald, sitting in a weird-looking chair. You are standing very straight in front of him. He is furious, yelling at you in his big voice, 'Serah! You son of a...' some strange words for which our language does not have any equivalent. He has just discovered that for more than three years you have been keeping a big – but a really big – secret from him."

"Is he an enemy?" I asked anxiously.

"His name is La... Lava... An enemy? Never! He is my darling uncle. In the field of stars. You are fighting a war. He is the grand commander. He loves you dearly but he is furious because he has just discovered that you and a number of your Brother Knights have kept a huge secret from him."

"Can you see what the secret is about?"

"Descending."

That sounded familiar. "Into the Underworlds?"

"Yes. Yes and no. It is all... so different!"

"And what am I doing while your big, bald uncle is yelling at me?"

"It's a time crossing. You hold onto the Point and remember this present moment, and how Szar-ka used to be unable to keep a secret."

"What else can you see?"

"I see elephantos coming towards you!"

"I always knew there were elephantos in the field of stars!" I exclaimed triumphantly.

"Hunh hunh! My love, this is not at all what you think. It's in No Limits."

No Limits! Just hearing the name was enough to make my Dragon vroof. "So there are elephantos in No Limits?"

"Entire herds of them! And strange scaly beasts as in the early days of the earth, even larger than elephantos."

"Larger than elephantos? *Oh my Lord Melchisedek!* No Limits must be a gigantic place."

"No, it is not. I see you playing music for me... and for a friend of yours who died. Many of your friends have died."

"Died?"

"It's war... total war! The Brother Knights are fighting in the field of stars, riding birds which set everything ablaze in their path. I see fire... fire everywhere," her hand became tense. "But in No Limits, what music! I say to you, 'Your music does something to me, Serah!' And you come toward me and you say, 'Total war, total love!' and you kiss me."

The war will end. My love for you won't.

"I'll have to get ready," I pondered anxiously. "At school the teacher tried to introduce me to a few instruments, in particular wooden sticks, and saucepan and spoon as well, but I could never get into the beat."

Elyani reopened her eyes. "In the future, musical instruments will be infinitely more beautiful than saucepan and spoon."

Through the mists the silvery moonlight had intensified, mixing its dim candescence with Elyani's shining aura. I tried to unravel the mysterious glow in her eyes, "Each time you speak of the Brother Knights, you become a different person."

"What kind?"

"White panther."

For one second, the fierce warrior angel was replaced by the softness of the magic woman, "Do you not like white panthers?" she asked in a little voice.

"The white panther fascinates me! I can't take my eyes off her. I can't believe such an extraordinary woman will be in love with me."

"Totally in love!" the panther was back.

I felt like cracking up in her arms and bursting into tears, telling her this pending daiva made me feel sick and the idea I might lose her was unbearable. But what good would that have done her?

"Help, White Eagle!" I Point-scanned the clear fountain for a diversion.

The response was immediate. "Has anyone ever told you the story of the bird of paradise who saved the Naga king?"

Luckily, she had never heard it. "Get ready for a journey!" I held her in my arms, Dragon-tight. "Once, long ago, a she-bird of paradise took flight from the blue cascade of Life and Light..." I began.

And the night was warm.

11.5 Power of the Point, the first transfer

Gervin, who had been briefed by Lehrmon on the stones' miraculous recovery, didn't hide his satisfaction. He began our meeting with the grin he reserved for great occasions, and which he always combined with an insistent look directed to the magic corner of the room where I still couldn't discern a thing, but where more and more seemed to be happening.

My teacher happy, what else could I do but smile like a filosterops?

"What about your master plan?" he asked me.

I had to confess that glimpses of the master plan appeared above my head each time I set foot in the female wing's corridors, only to evaporate each time I returned to the normal world. Sigh.

Gervin laughed. "This guidance Point-field is *a beauty in the Law*, isn't it?"

"*Majestically magnificent!*" I praised the field, tears of awe coming to my eyes.

"Wait till you explore other Point-fields in our temple," Gervin knew how to entice. "The guidance system of our space controllers, for instance! One of the most beautiful Point-fields in the entire kingdom."

A vitriolic question was nagging me, "But Gervin, if these fields are bound to collapse... wouldn't it be better to stay away from them?"

"*Sweet Lord Melchisedek*, of course not! Anyway, what you enjoy are not the fields themselves, but the high spaces of consciousness to which they are connected. These are perfectly clean – higher food for the Spirit. Open to them as much as you can, savour every instant of connection. After the kingdom's fall, it will take tens of thousands of years before such purity of consciousness can be reproduced on Earth."

"And what about the Point-fields used by the Nephilim giants or the Hunters? Would you also say their spirit is perfectly clean?"

Remembering how protective I became each time I spoke of Felicia, priestess of Verzazyel the Watcher, Gervin twinged his beard. "I believe you have friends among the Nephilim, haven't you?"

I opened my heart as much as I could, "*Speak, wise man in the Law!* I am ready to hear the truth."

Gervin grabbed a red apple from a basket but didn't give it to me, he just contemplated it. "The truth is that some things and beings in the creation are neither clearly white nor clearly black, and the Watchers are a perfect example of this."

"But doesn't the book of Maveron say that *anyone who does not follow the pure Truth is bound to become sheer dark force*?" I propounded.

"Well, then, *my friend in the Law*, clearly our good Maveron would have called the Watchers sheer dark forces," the thunderbolt bearer answered bluntly. "Yet it is certain that the Watchers have introduced a great deal of powerful knowledge into the kingdom," he tactfully added. "And no one with sense would dispute that there are some very nice people among the Nephilim." Looking straight into my eyes, he threw the red apple into the air and caught it deftly with his left hand. Then with a slow, intentional movement, he delicately put the fruit back into the basket.

"I see," I cleared my throat, getting the message. "Is there a chance I might have to fight against the Nephilim?" I asked him.

"More than likely." Rock-steady, the master held my gaze.

"Should I then try to fathom the consciousness of the Watchers?"

"*No way, man of the Law!*" Thunderously categorical, Gervin engaged his word, "If I sent you to the Sons of the Dragon, it was because the spaces and beings behind them are perfectly clean. But if you were to dabble in any initiation related to the Watchers, you would be lost to the Brown Robe. The Masters of Thunder would never accept you among them."

I shivered, remembering how easy it would have been to descend into the Watcher's crypt with Felicia. Hesitantly, I risked, "Was I being tested when the priestess of Verzazyel invited me to accompany her into the Watcher's mind?"

"Oh, yes!" The man in front of me was no longer the kind father who for years had patiently taken care of me. He was Gervin the fierce, the warrior of the Apocalypse. A high fountain spoke through him, "This was one of your tests. Had you accepted the offer, by now you would be an extremely powerful man on his way to the abyss."

I swallowed high, wondering what other tests were still waiting for me.

"And you succeeded in the trial!" Gervin added with satisfaction, grabbing a *pear of the Law* and reaching forward to place it in my hand.

"*All glory to the teacher!*"

"To prepare yourself to fight against the Nephilim," Gervin went on, "you could go and speak to one of Master Esrevin's helpers in Lasseera. His name is Fridrick. He was trained by the Nephilim Hunters. There is nothing wrong with learning the tricks of your enemies. You can even practise Point-fighting against him if you want. But do not let him initiate you into anything. Use the Eisraim style of power of the Point, and the forces you have received from me – not those which come from the Watchers. Is that clear, Commander?"

"Perfectly clear!" This unambiguous instruction left me content. "Now, Gervin, I have a few ideas for our master plan. Can I run them by you?"

Pulling his beard, Gervin smiled with interest.

"What if I went to a few places of bad repute and let it be known that we in Eisraim urgently need to buy soft stones because we are no longer able to produce our own? Of course, to be taken seriously I would need to buy stones here and there, which might require a fair amount of gold. And naturally there would be gossip. It would become known throughout the kingdom that the Eisraim stone-makers are hopeless. Why then would the Renegade Hunters and other stone dealers want to waste their time roaming around our county? And while shopping for stones, I would make it clear I didn't care where the stones came from, or how they were obtained. With some persistence this should lead me to our potential enemies, known and unknown."

Gervin immediately liked the idea. "I will supply you with all the gold you need. But I must warn you," he added dryly, "if you start investigating stone dealers, you might uncover more dirt than you expect."

"That bad?"

Gervin slowly shook his head, "Much worse! You have no idea how corrupt the kingdom is. From top to bottom, fields and stones are used and abused to manipulate people's consciousness – and not for enlightening purposes. You will have to be excessively cautious when dealing with the rascals who trade stolen stones."

This was the perfect opportunity to mention how thoughts had been leaking from my mind like state secrets from the king's palace, and that any spirited Point could read through me.

"Let me see..." Gervin third-eyed the centres above my head, twinging his beard. "Elyani's work is superb," he rejoiced. "The weaving of your Point is nearly complete. And I recognise the special touch of light which Orest, my teacher, received from Barkhan Seer's disciples, and which I imprinted into Teyani's Point! Congratulations to you."

"But I didn't do anything!"

"This is what a tradition is all about: planting seeds. You didn't plant the seed, but the seed is growing in you. Depending on who you are and how you conduct your life, the seed will either become a large tree or it will wither and die."

I felt the centres of energy above my head lighting up. "Should I be doing something?"

Gervin's gaze was fixed on the Point above my head. "Just be!"

There followed a few minutes of exquisitely subtle movements of energy above my head, as if new, unknown muscles were being flexed amidst volleys of high-pitched sounds. Then Gervin announced, "That's it! The first transfer of power has been completed."

Not feeling any different, I worried.

Gervin was amused, "Wait till the seed grows!"

"But how do I make it grow?"

"Just be!" Gervin repeated. "Your love for the White Eagle will water the seed, and the more you use the power of the Point, the faster the seed will grow." He showed me how to seal my mind so no one could read my thoughts. "Watch what happens!" he said, activating a sharp flow of energy in one of the centres above my head.

After a few seconds, the Spirit winds ceased.

"Try to repeat it," Gervin instructed.

Reproducing the energy movement was easy. I couldn't have explained what I was doing, but the Point seemed to know how to do it all by itself.

"*Right and righteous!*" Gervin acknowledged the correctness of the procedure.

"Is that all?" It sounded too simple to be true.

"Now you must practise, practise, practise..." Gervin exhorted. "Try to keep a *big* secret from Elyani. Make it a game. Tell her that if she guesses, you will have to give her a present. This is how Teyani trains her Eagles."

After repeating the exercise a number of times, Gervin gave the particular smile that signalled our meeting was drawing to an end.

There was nothing in the seven spheres I wanted more than to implore his help for Elyani, but I was at a loss for words.

Gervin frowned, "Now you too are biting your lip?"

I hadn't noticed.

He looked deep into me, warming me with his flow of heartness.

"Gervin, I am about to lose Elyani, am I not?" I finally managed to get the words out.

Gervin poured his love into me but refrained from betraying any sign that might be interpreted as an answer. "Szar, you know I wouldn't care more for you if you were my own son. But I warned you, the path of Thunder is not an easy one. There is nothing I can do about this."

"Gervin, I accept that I have to face my destiny. But the dilemma is killing me: should I accept fate and comply with the will of the gods, or engage the Dragon and fight for someone I love?"

"No, these are not the terms of the problem. The choice is not between the gods and Elyani. There is only one question: will you fight for Truth or go astray?"

"Do you mean to say... we are not bound by the daiva?"

"The Masters of Thunder want Truth – nothing but Truth! If the gods are fighting for Truth, then fight for the gods. If the daiva goes against Truth, then fight against the daiva."

This spoke to my Spirit. But unavoidably, the terrible thought crashed into me: what if I had to choose between Truth and Elyani? Was that my next trial?

Gervin read my mind. "If you lose your Truth," he was emphatic, "you will lose everything: Elyani, the Archive, Thunder, and yourself."

I held my head in my hands. "I wish I could be sure I will be strong enough." Then I rose as high in the clear fountain as I could and established eye contact with him. "Please, Thunder, will you tell me if there is *anything* I can do to help her?"

From the lofty region, Gervin let his warm, deep presence flow into me. "Szar of Thunder," he responded, "there is nothing more you can do for the moment."

I drew a breath to thank him, then, rather foolishly, I said, "I guess this decree of the gods will be the hardest of all my tests."

"No," Gervin sternly shook his head, "the most painful trial will be the one just before your initiation as a Master, when you contemplate the future that awaits you if you are to tread the path of Thunder."

Sinking into a black hole, I looked down to my left palm, slowly clenching and unclenching my fist.

Reading the dismay on my face, Gervin quoted Maveron, *"Truth and Truth alone will prevail."*

As my dismay rose to a crescendo Gervin closed his eyes, seeking inspiration to cheer me up. "I see a present coming for Elyani and you," he announced. "Tonight. Sent to you by high beings of compassion. It will not only bring you joy, but also new, precious friends."

A precious new friend... "Could he help?" I wondered.

When Gervin reopened his eyes, I tried to thank him but couldn't find the right words. He stood up and pulled my arm, "Come on, Commander! Stop biting your lip and accompany me to the chapel of the Field Wizards. Let us go and inspect Maryani's works together."

11.6 Welcome to the supermind

As we made our way through the enclave of the jewels Gervin forewarned, "In two or three weeks you will have to report to the Archive council. The Masters of Thunder expect you to present an initial evaluation of what will be required to fulfil your mission, and if possible the elements of your master plan."

No matter how hard I tried, I couldn't wipe the gloomy expression off my face.

"Cheer up, man of the Law!" Gervin admonished. "Lehrmon was telling me you are interested in learning the names of the gods represented by the temple's statues. Do you know who this is?" he pointed to a huge, muscly character

"No."

"This is Buhr, the second assistant of the king of the gods – a mighty figure."

From god to god, we made our way through the mists. I walked mechanically, stuck in a nowhere-space between the black hole and the greyness of the mists, unable to pull myself back to daylight.

When we reached the cellar of the Archive stones, Maryani exclaimed, *"Praise the Lord Melchisedek, my godfather in the Brown Robe!"* and she rushed over to give Gervin a long hug.

Woolly, who was working with her, still looked quite tired. But he was wearing a new – unstained! – gown, and he had trimmed his hair.

The lawful salutes exchanged, Maryani turned to Woolly and me. "Did you know that this man held me in his arms when I was six months old?" she said proudly.

"It is true!" Gervin smiled.

From the Point I was woken up by a glimpse of the grand artwork, the master-mind puzzle Gervin had laid for the Archive project. Maryani, Woolly, the Field Wizards, the White Eagles, myself, and even Lehrmon – all had been brought to the temple by him. All had been trained under his guidance.

Now, after nearly thirty years of effort, all the pieces of the puzzle were in place.

"Master Gervin had been invited to visit the palace of the prince of Eis-raim, my uncle," Maryani told us. "As soon as he saw me, he prophesied that the White Eagle was waiting for me. At first, expectably, my parents hated the idea of my becoming a priestess. So Gervin prophesied that if I stayed at the palace I would become a princess, but if I went to the Eagle I would become a queen. *All glory to the teacher!* It was just the right thing to say to a princely family."

"And now, half of the prophecy is already fulfilled," Gervin coloured his smile with a hue of innocence.

"What?" Completely taken aback, Maryani frowned. "Only half?"

"Yes," Gervin replied in his would-be-meek character, "only half. Now, let us have a look at this drainage system of yours!" He began inspecting the energy that radiated from the buckets.

Disconcerted, Maryani decided not to insist for the moment.

Her drainage of noxious elemental forces was working wonders. The stones had stopped crumbling. Some of them had even started growing again.

"What is the latest news from Lasseera?" Gervin enquired.

"Esrevin has frozen the lot with the Word of Thunder, and now he is waiting for us," Woolly answered. "Tomorrow morning, when we are satis-fied the new methods are working, Maryani and I will go to Lasseera and establish a similar drainage system over there."

"*Lawfully excellent!*" Gervin's victorious grin reappeared. "And what about the new generation of stones, those which are to be cooked without the fields? When will they be ready?"

"It depends on what Szar wants us to do with them," Maryani said. "If the purpose is to generate fully-blown Archive stones, I could have a few of them ready within a month, or even less if absolutely necessary."

Gervin burst out laughing, "Archive stones in less than a month?"

"I know!" Woolly raised his hands towards the world of the gods. "It's simply disgusting. She's already got it all wrapped up in the Law!"

"And what about King Vasoukidass?" Gervin asked. "Will he really come and visit your chapel?"

"He has given his word, so you can be assured he will!" Maryani was adamant.

Woolly pulled a face – hardly refined like those of the White Eagles. "I hate to think what my chapel would look like after a sixty-tonne Naga had passed through. Let's hope at least he'll come alone."

"What are you complaining about?" Maryani protested, "You invited him, didn't you?"

"At the time, in my mind the Nagas were some kind of earth worm," Woolly argued. "A very noble kind of earth worm, though," he immediately added. "No one had warned me they were seventy lawful feet long!"

"That's the problem, my son," Gervin told him, "when you invoke the help of greater powers, you sometimes get it!" Putting his hand on Maryani's shoulder he invited her for a walk, "You and I need to have a long conversation about your journey into the Underworlds."

After they left, Woolly commented, "Commander, you look nearly as bad as I do. What's happening to you, *man of the Law*? I hope you're not letting the latest news piss the Law out of you."

"What news?"

"Seems the Goddess is so busy vomiting on Eisraim that the One God doesn't know where to put his lingam any more. Our last two priestesses of Malchasek died this week, which means that's it! The tradition of Malchasek, the great angel of Highness, has gone blast-cucumber. There is not a single one of his damn priestesses left in the entire kingdom."

"I met one of them a few years ago," I recalled the unforgettable encounter. "Marka was her name. She had the most extraordinary eyes I ever saw in the kingdom. Was she one of them?"

"No, Marka died last year. The latest casualties were Em'joil and Toola. But the godly sewage doesn't stop there. According to what I've heard, Holma the ascending goddess is also dying – but this time, *really* dying, not just coughing out her brains and losing her damn teeth in the Law. There's mounting panic in the temple. You can bet they are all holding onto their sphincters and pampering their gods. If she renders up the ghost, *man of the Law*... now, that would be the last blast!"

The memory of Marka's eyes was so vivid, it was as if she was in the cellar looking at me. "Gervin, Gervin..." I thought, wondering how the great man had handled the death of his friend.

"Excuse me, Woolly!" Eyes half-closed, I walked out without lawful farewell and went to seek refuge in my favourite field.

The Point-guided corridors – another world! As soon as I crossed the portal of the female wing, I felt like a different person. I started walking, oblivious of the dying kingdom, letting the Point-field lift me above the sludgy greyness of the mists.

Going to Elyani to collapse in her arms and cry was no solution. *I* was the one who was supposed to support her with my love and joy, not the other way round. So I decided to indulge in the Point-field, and I walked for hours. I began by holding the memory of the priestesses of the Dawn of Creation in my Point, letting the guidance system take me to their quarters. I found myself in a large courtyard thrumming with strange vibrations. There were weirdly shaped bushes with leaves that seemed to be talking to each other. The place was empty, except for a few black songbirds feasting on the bushes' berries. I thought of sneaking into one of the chapels to spy on the priestesses' magnificent hymns, but for this I would have had to let go of the field. Instead I slowly Point-walked to Teyani's apartments, and from there to Alcibyadi's room. Each time I arrived at a destination, I Point-held the memory of someone else and let the field walk me there.

As time passed I felt clearer, and *light as a bird of the world of the gods*. It was becoming obvious that Gervin's latest intervention had made a great difference in my Point. Above my head, a whole new world of subtle energies and super-fast movements was opening to me. I couldn't understand their meaning, but their subtlety and sharpness fascinated me. I discovered a number of Point-fields I had never discerned before. Without a shadow of a doubt, I spotted one around Teyani's apartment. As I circled her place for the third time, I stopped and carefully Point-tuned into the highly vibrant energy.

Out of nowhere, Teyani startled me with a Point-call, *"Why don't you come in, Szar?"*

"Sorry!" I exclaimed, "I didn't mean to disturb you!" But I realised that speaking out loud was not the proper way to answer the Point-call. To avoid creating any interference with her field, I used the technique Gervin had shown me earlier in the day, Point-sealing myself.

Teyani opened her door. *"Szar, my great man in the Law,* what are you doing? You can't Point-knock at someone's field, and then try to hide your presence from them! If you want to spy on me," she laughed, "you must *first* conceal your presence, and *then* get into my Point-field."

Sweet Lord Melchisedek, what had I done? "Apologies, Lady Teyani! Apologies! I never intended to spy on you."

"I know," she said. "Come in!"

It was a large room, teeming with her presence and vibrant with spellbinding Point-intensity.

"This is where I usually see my students," she invited me to sit with her. After placing a cup of whitish liquid in my hand, she quizzed me, "So, what do you think of my Point-field?"

I tuned in for a few seconds. "Very sharp! It moves much faster than the corridors' guidance field."

"What do you think the field is for?" she watched me take a sip of her beverage.

An overwhelming wave of tingly vibrations rose into my head. I tried to rest on the Dragon to contain the effervescence, but the Dragon had turned bubbly, rushing in all directions at the same time, wildly dancing to celebrate the powers of the Ancient Days of the Earth.

"Is there something wrong with my drink?" Teyani frowned. As I didn't answer, she took the cup from my hand and drank a sip herself.

"No, it's a wonderful drink," I finally managed to say. "It is just... very strong."

"I hadn't prepared it for a guest." She finished the cup in one go.

I was starting to feel more joyful. "I don't know if it's the field or the drink, but I can see complicated geometrical patterns everywhere."

"Right! This field is for sight. I wove it myself some fifteen years ago. Come travelling in it with me!"

All at once, the visions became so intense that I lost touch with the room. In every direction, there were complex geometrical figures, spinning vortices of light and strange landscapes. It all moved extraordinarily fast, each element pregnant with meaning, and each movement precisely determined and significant. In the exalted consciousness of this space, an all-comprehending intelligence had understanding of each and every component, and of the relationship and interconnections between all parts.

"Welcome to the supermind, Szar!" Teyani Point-said.

"This is magnificent! Did you weave this place?"

"No, this is a layer of super-reality, a world in its own right. My field is a gateway leading into it."

"So there are other fields which lead to this layer?" I Point-asked.

"Many. But you don't need a field in order to enter the supermind. Simply use your Point as a gateway. It leads straight into it."

I Point-marvelled, "Do you mean I could come back here by myself?"

"Any time! Has Elyani ever spoken to you about the Brother Knights?"

"Those who will be fighting battles in the field of stars, in a long, long time."

"Supermind will be the essence of the training of the Knights. And it is by impacting Thunder into the supermind that you will win your battles. The brotherhood and the Masters of Thunder are already preparing you for this. I myself have spent years pouring forces into Elyani which, in turn, she is passing onto you. Now let me show you how to be a supermind-spy."

"But Teyani, I didn't mean to..."

"Shut up!" Teyani Point-blasted at me. She took me through a fast-moving landscape of intricate geometrical shapes. "This is the operative information which tells you all the things the field can do, and how they can be done."

A luminous understanding instantly flashed in my Point. In order to activate functions in the field, all I had to do was manipulate the geometrical shapes. The all-comprehending intelligence knew exactly how to do it.

"In reality, you need to do very little," Teyani Point-confirmed. "Just let the super-intelligence operate the device for you."

"Is this the way Namron registers and de-registers people's energy-signatures in the security field that protects the temple?" I Point-asked.

"No, this is far beyond the level of Namron. Namron only intuitively knows how to operate functions within his Point-field. He would be incapable of manipulating other fields. With supermind power, you can enter any Point-field, understand its possibilities and its limits, and operate any function embedded in it. In many cases you can even activate functions which the weavers of the fields themselves had never thought of. Incidentally, this is how the Brother Knights will fight their battles during the Apocalypse. Look at this," Teyani Point-said, and the landscape of geometrical shapes changed. *"This is the kind of supermind blueprint behind weapons and mind-machines used by your enemy. Now, look... here!"* Teyani Point-indicated a particular set of pyramidical shapes. *"This is a function that your enemies won't have identified. By flattening these shapes you will throw their defence system into utter chaos. It will take at least half a second for them to reorganise – more than enough for your Knights to annihilate them."*

"Teyani, will you be fighting with the Brother Knights?"

The supermind space faded, and I found myself in the empty white room, face to face with Lady Teyani.

"Sweet Lord Melchisedek, no!" she exclaimed in her soft Eagle's voice. "But Barkhan Seer and I will be close to you, this I promise. From the Archive in the Fields of Peace we will be sending you all the forces we possibly can. And Barkhan Seer is mighty among the mighty," she added with reverence. "His powers are legendary."

Stunned, I was still trying to blink my way back to normal reality. Teyani waited patiently, enveloping me in a loving atmosphere.

"Now you can go and explore all the Point-fields of the temple," she concluded, as it was clear I was incapable of absorbing any more for the moment. "But don't forget – if you want to conceal your energy and spy on someone, do it *before* entering their field, not after!"

11.7 News from the north

Around sunset on my way back home, Elyani voice-channelled me through darkness visible to warn that Melchard and Gervin had come to pay a visit.

At least this time I wouldn't be embarrassed by having to jump down off the roof in front of Elyani's father.

A few minutes later I entered the courtyard, proud to show my elders that I now knew how to find my way through the corridors' Point-field. I looked around but couldn't see anyone.

"We are up here, watching the sunset!" Elyani called.

I looked up. To my amazement, I saw Gervin and Elyani waving at me from the Blue priestesses' roof, while Melchard was making his way down the ladder.

"Hum... *Praise the Lord Melchisedek, Melchard of the Brown Robe, High Priest of Eisraim and Grand Commander of the Law for the County of Eisraim under the Appointment of His Supreme Majesty, the King of Atlantis.*"

By the time I had finished the greeting, Melchard had landed on the lawn. "*All glory to the Lord Melchisedek, Szar!*" he saluted with a friendly smile, while Gervin and Elyani followed him down.

When the lawful saluting was over, Gervin announced, "My children, Melchard and I have come to bring you some good news."

The two Masters of Thunder exchanged a glance. Melchard, who was in a joyful mood, spoke first, "I am to convey the official compliments sent to Szar by the prince of the county of Eisraim for taking good care of Maryani."

Gervin and Elyani clapped their hands in lawful ceremonious fashion.

"An excellent token for the working relationship between the temple and the princely palace," Gervin pointed out. "Maryani has had a long voice-channel discussion with the prince, explaining how King Vasoukidass has appointed her the Nagas' ambassador for the kingdom. And so for the first time, the prince is ready to accept that after all, it was not such complete madness for old Gervin to abduct his little niece and deprive her of the royal comforts of her caste."

Now it was our turn to lawfully applaud Gervin.

"Moreover," he continued in his ceremonial voice, "Maryani told the prince how thrilled she was to become a member of your team. Following this, the prince voice-channelled Lady Teyani, asking for more details about you. The prince thinks you must be very important, if the Nagas' ambassador has decided to work for you."

"Maryani must have guessed my thoughts," I said. "I haven't yet invited her to become part of the team, but I was just about to."

"No, she didn't guess your thoughts," Elyani corrected, "she just decided by herself that Lehrmon, Woolly and you couldn't do without her."

The Masters of Thunder laughed, and I decided to follow.

"But there is more!" Melchard said. "Today I have received an official message from the prince of the county of the Northern Lakes, who said that the reputation of Szar of the Brown Robe had come to his court, and he requested the healer's help to rescue his child."

Perplexed, I wondered how the Far Underworld the prince of the county of the Northern Lakes could possibly have heard about me.

Melchard elaborated, "A certain Alven, recently appointed court physician by the prince of the county of the Snowy Mountains, told them how you had miraculously saved his sister's life when he himself, despite all the lore of his caste, was unable to help her."

So Felicia was alive! She had succeeded in her final trial, and safely returned home! Shocked with joy, I erupted with a particularly wild Voice-roar in the purest tradition of Mount Lohrzen,

"Ha! Ha! Ha! Ha! Ha!"

The temple became dead silent, the mists strangely transparent, the courtyard perplexed, the purple flowers on the lawn vroofing upside down, sunset wondering which direction to take.

Unlawfully startled by the explosion, Melchard and Gervin looked at me with a mixture of disconcertedness and concern.

"Szar of the Brown Robe," I warned myself again, "if you don't become more careful with this laugh, you will end up in big trouble!"

"Hum... yes!" I said. "Alven is the brother of a priestess of Verzazyel the Watcher. The woman was badly burnt by the Watchers' fire during the final stage of her initiation, and I helped her reconstitute her energy."

Melchard raised his eyebrows in horror, "Do you mean to say you helped a Nephilim priestess in her initiation into the fire of the Watchers?"

"It's all right, Melchard," Gervin intervened. "Szar only gave her a healing. It all ended well." Then he went on, "The first-born son of the Northern Lakes' princely family is dying. An oracle has revealed that his soul is trapped in the Underworlds. The county of the Northern Lakes does not share a common border with Eisraim, but still, it is close enough for us to value our diplomatic ties, especially considering the troubled times ahead of us."

"There is not much to lose," Melchard encouraged me. "I don't think anyone will blame you if you don't save the child – especially the court physicians and the priests, since they themselves have failed. On the other hand if you succeed, your reputation as a miracle man will allow these dignitaries to save face – essential to avoid intrigues."

Gervin took up the plot, "And so the temple of Eisraim is sending you on an official mission to Tomoristan, the capital of the county of the Northern Lakes, to respond to the call of the princely family."

Elyani became worried. "Is this mission going to take long?"

"No more than two or three weeks, but..." Gervin paused, smiling at her, "in a princely palace the etiquette is fairly strict. Melchard and I thought it might be wise for Szar to be escorted by someone fully conversant with the Law of the castes, so as to save him – and us – embarrassing slips of protocol. We thought of sending a priest of the Grey Robes of the Angel of Dawn with him. Their knowledge of lawful etiquette is vast! But they are too busy preparing the funeral of his highness Aparalgon, their assistant grand master, who has just gone on the Great Journey. And so, if Szar is agreed, of course, Melchard and I would like to see Lady Elyani accompany him."

A shiver ran through me. Was this the way the daiva was going to steal Elyani from me?

*Anchoring the clear fountain at the deepest of the Dragon, I set my Point
ablaze and called, "Teyani, wise woman in the Law, please answer me."*

Teyani Point-responded instantly.

*I Point-transferred to her what Melchard and Gervin had said and asked
her, "Teyani, I know you have seen the daiva that the gods have ordained
for Elyani. For the Love of the Eagle, please tell me, is there danger in this
journey?"*

*Teyani Point-answered, "Do not try to avoid this journey, it is a present,
a grace from the friends you met while travelling in the spheres of Highness. It is perfectly safe, and it holds a key for the future of you both. Go,
man of the Law. There will be more love and joy between you than ever
before."*

"Teyani, I am afraid."

"The Eagle loves you, Szar. He will be with you, always!"

"Thank you, Teyani. I love you."

The entire Point-exchange had lasted barely a second.

There was a short silence, during which Gervin scanned my Point with a
curious look on his face.

Standing very straight, I smiled at Elyani and asked in a formal voice,
*"Lady Elyani of the White Eagle, would you care to escort me to the county
of the Northern Lakes?"*

Her face lit up with joy, *"Szar of the Brown Robe, if Lady Teyani, by the
grace of our Lord Melchisedek, permits me, it will be my privilege."*

Gervin turned to Melchard and concluded confidently, "I think Lady
Teyani will permit."

11.8 The first night in the princely suite

The five-day journey on the Fontelayana river was easy, and Elyani and
I were in a playful mood when, late in the evening, we arrived at Tomoristan, the capital of the county of the Northern Lakes.

Stepping off the boat, we were greeted by a huge, bald man with the
thickest black moustache I had ever seen. Extremely ceremonial in bearing,
dressed in a bright crimson robe, he addressed us in the slow intonation of
lawfully pompous parlance, *"Would you, by the grace of our Lord Melchisedek, be Szar of the Brown Robe, of the Temple of Eisraim, and Lady
Elyani, High Priestess of the White Eagle, of the same temple, guests of His
High Majesty Filipotonisteraniso Ozorenan, Prince of the County of the
Northern Lakes under the Appointment of His Supreme Majesty the King of
Atlantis?"*

Repeating long names and phrases was *no problem in the Law*. Besides,
I had just received a crash course in court etiquette. My instructions were
clear: if the sentence was long and lawful, repeat it. If it was short and law-

ful, make it longer and then repeat it. In case of doubt, cough, and let Elyani speak for me.

"*By the grace of our Lord Melchisedek,*" I answered in the appropriate ceremonial tone, "*we are Szar of the Brown Robe, of the Temple of Eisraim, and Lady Elyani, High Priestess of the White Eagle, of the same temple, guests of His High Majesty Filipotonisteraniso Ozorenan, Prince of the County of the Northern Lakes under the Appointment of His Supreme Majesty the King of Atlantis.*"

The man looked satisfied. "*Praise the Lord Melchisedek, Szar of the Brown Robe, of the Temple of Eisraim, and Lady Elyani, High Priestess of the White Eagle, of the same temple! I am Marzook, of the Crimson Robe, in the Service of His High Majesty Filipotonisteraniso Ozorenan, Prince of the County of the Northern Lakes under the Appointment of His Supreme Majesty the King of Atlantis. Would you kindly, and through the grace of our Lord Melchisedek, follow me to His High Majesty's palace?*"

"*All glory to the Lord Melchisedek, Marzook of the Crimson Robe...*" I carefully articulated. The lawful exchanges completed, Marzook escorted us to the princely palace, less than three hundred lawful feet from the river. We followed him along a broad path covered with grey pebbles that rattled under our shoes. The mists were so thick that we could hardly see six lawful feet around us.

We arrived at a large portal, not the palace's main entrance, yet guarded by six men in bright crimson robes like Marzook's. After a lawfully interminable verbal procedure, two huge doors were opened, revealing a grand hallway with golden *living walls*.

"Dragon of the Deep, just what I needed!" I realised with dismay that Nephilim spice could be sense-smelled in all directions. Gervin and Melchard had assured me that no Nephilim Hunter would ever even think of attacking me, as I was a guest of the prince. Still, the Dragon reflexes instilled in me by Marek made my fighter character react strongly – never had I been in a place with evidence of so many Nephilim! The smell left no doubt, there were fighters in every corner of the palace. When she saw the frantic quiver of my nostrils, Elyani took my arm, as if to keep me from charging ahead with wild Dragon screams.

Marzook took us up a huge plass staircase that led to a long hallway. The golden light dispensed by the *living walls* was bright and loud but lacked presence – nothing like the chapels of Eisraim. Apart from a few sentinels here and there – none of them Nephilim, thank the She-Dragon – the place was deserted, no doubt due to the late hour.

At the end of the hallway, Marzook threw open high double doors and stood aside, inviting us to precede him into an enormous room with at least twenty high armchairs, a mass of furniture, huge mirrors lining the walls, and a sumptuous golden carpet on which to tread.

"*Her High Majesty Pelenor Ozorenan, Princess of the County of the Northern Lakes,* has instructed me to welcome you to one of the princely suites in which we receive our guests of honour. This is the first visitors' lounge."

Marzook walked across the room to a large door. Behind him, Elyani gave me an amazed smile, silently clapping her hands. Marzook opened the door. Turning to face us, he announced pompously, "The second visitors' lounge."

Just as lavishly furnished, the second lounge was hardly smaller than the first. But this was only the first of our surprises. Marzook proceeded to take us through a guests' dining hall, a private lounge, a private dining room, a second private lounge, a leisure room, an office, a hideaway, four adjacent bedrooms, and finally to the largest and most beautiful of all rooms: the princely bedroom.

It was at least eighty lawful feet long, with a carpet that looked like the softest lawn, stunning pieces of furniture and works of art everywhere. As Elyani and I were contemplating the pool which occupied one of the many corners of the room, Marzook commented formally, "Szar of the Brown Robe, I thought that you and Lady Elyani of the White Eagle might like to know who have been some of the guests to honour this room in the last years: *the Most Excellent Lord Merevot, Ambassador of His Supreme Majesty the King of Atlantis, Her High Majesty Helila Rezastenan, Princess of the County of the Western Plains, the Right Excellent Lord Poporenon, Past Grand Superintendent of the Fields for the Northern Counties under the Appointment of His Supreme Majesty the King of Atlantis...*" Each name spoken with slow reverence and lawful intonations appropriate for that caste, the list went on for at least five minutes.

When Marzook came to the end of his announcements, Elyani said in a high voice, "*Marzook of the Crimson Robe, I trust you will convey our gratitude to Her High Majesty Pelenor Ozorenan, Princess of the County of the Northern Lakes, as well as our appreciation for all your good care.*"

Marzook acknowledged Elyani's message with a respectful nod, and lawfully informed us that early in the morning we would receive a visit from the sick princely child's governess, Lady Hermina of the high caste of the Immaculate. Refreshments and delicacies would be served for us in the private dining room, and he assured us he would attend to our bags, which would be taken to the private lounge adjacent to the bedroom.

Finally, he took leave most lawfully, closing all the doors behind him.

"Do you think anyone can hear us?" I whispered.

Elyani shook her head. "They know very well that we would detect any spying field and neutralise it."

We checked anyway.

Elyani began to Point-scan the room. Straight away, I sense-smelled a foreign presence. "There is an animal in this room! It doesn't smell dangerous but still, I had better check it out." Following my nostrils, I started patrolling the room in search of the beast.

Before long I bumped into a huge silvery snake, its head erect, its two large black eyes gazing at me.

I clenched my fists, ready to Dragon-strike. But I realised I was being fooled by the room's semi-darkness. The snake was only a glass statue! Yet how could its eyes be so real? I took a step to the side, and the eyes followed me. Tuning in, I realised with amazement that the illusion of movement was created by a field. For a few seconds I moved my head from side to side, marvelling at the cleverness of the device. Then I resumed the hunt.

In such a place, everything was possible. The beast could even have been an elephanto! The smell didn't indicate a huge animal, but then again, sense-smelling elephantos wasn't exactly part of my repertoire. The room was full of nooks and crannies, with recesses on all sides. My eyes were caught by an alcove covered in misty silvery clouds. The mists stopped quite precisely at the edge of the alcove. How could that be? I walked into the alcove. No window. Intrigued, I tuned in. Straight away it became clear that a field was responsible for generating the effect.

When I came out of the mists, I heard a noise coming from the pool. "Aha!"

Clenching my fists, I slowly and noiselessly black-danced my way to the massive round tub, carefully avoiding the crystal artefacts patterning the lawn-like carpet.

I could smell that the beast had sensed my approaching presence. It remained motionless and dead silent. "I've found it!" I called to Elyani. "A strange sea-monster. Its aura is not at all like that of a fish."

"What does it look like?"

"It's too dark in here, I can't see. It's hiding at the bottom of the pool. Better leave it alone, it doesn't smell like a dangerous beast." Then it dawned on me, "I think there is a field in the pool."

"It's to make your body feel warm and comfortable while you are taking a bath," Elyani replied from the other end of the room.

A spectacular feature in the room was a long *living wall* that glowed with constantly changing colours. It made me curious. "How do you think that works?" I asked.

Elyani shrugged her shoulders, "A field."

"What else could it be?" I raised my hands towards the gods. "This place is out of the Dragon!" I contemplated two massive armchairs made of finely carved aromatic wood. The backs extended upwards to form large cobras' heads studded with rubies instead of eyes.

"The room is safe, there is no spying field," Elyani declared with satisfaction. She delicately draped her cape over the arm of the statue of a goddess with huge breasts.

"Have I ever seen this white dress?" I asked, admiring Elyani's V-neck.

"Hunh, hunh! We're in a princely palace, not a temple!" She took my hand and started running towards the bed, letting out the Warriors' shout of joy, "Youyouyouyou..."

It was a huge four-poster bed, at least fifteen lawful feet by twelve lawful feet, with the thickest mattress I had ever seen. Elyani jumped onto it and pulled me into her arms. "Did you say Gervin and Teyani both described this journey as a present from the spheres of Highness?"

"Totally safe! That's if I don't mess up the protocol, of course. And Gervin said I was to meet an important new friend, someone who held a thread to our future."

Elyani undid my cape and untied my hair. "A thread to the future? That sounds exciting. Did he give you any clues?"

"Gervin? Never! Expect the unexpected!"

"I love the unexpected!" her panther's eyes slid over me as she lay down on the mattress. "Do you think it could be Marzook?"

Wriggling my nostrils, I recalled Marzook's face and sense-smelled for inspiration. "I don't think so, but who knows? This journey could be full of surprises. Which reminds me, I had better tell you the secret."

Elyani grabbed a huge pillow and threw it at me, "*No way, man of the Law!* How am I going to get my present if I don't guess what the secret is?"

"I think keeping a secret from you for five days is a Dragon of an achievement. I never expected it would last so long. I won!" I said, clicking my fingers.

She shouted outrage, "We never said the game was to stop after five days!"

"Elyani, it's important. Now that we have arrived in the palace, I really need to tell you."

"*Wait, man of the Law!* Give me a last chance."

"No!" I dropped the Point-sealing device that Gervin had taught me and left myself completely open, inviting her energy in.

Tears in her eyes, she exclaimed, "*Oh my Lord Melchisedek*, you want to ask me to marry you, but you are afraid to do it because of the daiva."

I bit my lip. "That wasn't the secret, but it's true." The decree of the gods pending, I knew it would have been madness. It could have brought disaster on all of us.

"I love you," she cried, holding my hands. "I love you so much."

"I know, I can feel." I tuned high into the clear fountain, asking for the Light. "You love me more and more, and it does extraordinary things to me. It makes me feel vast like the Eagle."

"If the gods are kind to us..." she stopped herself, dark clouds passing across her eyes.

I would have given the seven spheres to cheer her up.

I took her in my arms and rocked her against me, improvising a vroofing Dragon-lullaby that was interrupted from time to time by strange gurgly noises coming out of the pool. Probably the sea-monster.

"I don't even know the lawful way of asking a woman for her hand," I told her. "When I was a complete sleeper, I only knew one verse of the Law on this topic: *a man shall seal his marriage with a kiss*. But now that I have learnt that a kiss is not the end of the Underworld, I should hope that the Good Lord Melchisedek has made provision in his Law for something a bit more... how to say?"

"I know exactly what you mean, Dragon."

"Can you enlighten me, great doctor of the Law? Suppose I wanted to ask you to marry me."

"Suppose!" she echoed in one of Gervin's voices.

"What would my lawful options be?"

Her playful voice was back. "There are *sixteen lawful ways, ranging from lawfully lawful to lawfully passionate and even lawfully madly passionate.*"

I chuckled, "I hate to think what lawfully lawful must be like."

"Not even an option for us. It's all arranged by the parents, preferably before the children are born. The groom and his bride are not supposed to meet before the marriage. They discover each other only at the end of the sixteen-hour marriage ceremony, when the masks are taken off."

"What about a middle-range option?"

"*Lawfully bearing and wise*, perhaps?"

"Mm..." I pulled a face, dubious.

"Well, then, let us try *beautiful spring of the Law*. It's all arranged by the parents too. In this one, though, the man must not only be from the right caste but also have charm. And the woman must be *blossoming like the alohim tree in spring.*"

"Good," I said, keeping an ear on the pool.

"*Twenty-seven weeks before the first day of spring, the groom and the bride will start meeting one afternoon per week, under the supervision of a lawful chaperone who will have been agreed upon by both families, and blessed by the village priests.*"

"Stop! Stop!" I interrupted. "Let us go straight to *lawfully madly passionate.*"

"Rare, this one, but really good! *The man must have charm, and be from the right caste. First, he will carefully arrange all the details of the marriage with the bride's family. Then, on the date which has been agreed upon by the bride's father and brothers, confirmed by the oracle, and blessed by the priests, he will surprise the bride by coming into the house at night, and he will not enter through the door, except if the house is devoid of windows. Then, by the grace of the Lord Melchisedek, the madly passionate man of the Law will enter the bride's bedroom while she is asleep...*"

Stranger and stranger noises were coming out of the pool. Elyani tucked her head in her shoulders, "Are you sure the sea-monster can't be dangerous?"

"Don't worry, I'll defend you. But for the Dragon's sake, keep on! What happens next?"

"Then the bride will wake up and loudly call for help from her father, uncles, brothers, cousins and neighbours."

"Do you mean she will call for help even if she has decided to give herself to the man?"

"Of course! The madly passionate man of the Law would be terribly disappointed if she didn't fulfil the custom. *Then the groom will hit the bride on the head, and the bride will fall unconscious by letting herself slip out of her body."*

"Is that *really* part of the Law?"

"Lawfully certainly! Anyone can slip out of their body, can't they?" I couldn't help giggling, and she added, "You would be surprised if you knew all the things in the Law which the *men of the Law* have never heard of." She paused, listening to the gurgles from the pool. "This can't possibly be a fish... Now, where was I? Yes. *Then the groom will carry the bride away, either through a window or through the door, and he will run. Having waited sufficient time, the father, uncles, brothers and cousins will all come out of the house and, accompanied by the neighbours, they will start running after the groom but without catching him, thanks to the grace of and as prescribed by our Lord Melchisedek."*

"You are right, I would never have suspected there could be customs like this in the Law. What next?" I was all ears.

"The groom arrives at his house, where his family and neighbours are all waiting for him together with the village priests. Soon, the other family members and neighbours arrive, the girl comes back into her body, and the sixteen-hour ritual ceremony is consecrated. And it finishes with the seal of a kiss."

"Far Underworld! This one is undoubtedly the best. I wonder how we could transpose it to the Eisraim temple, though."

"You would carry me over the roofs, of course!"

"And Melchard, Gervin and Lehrmon would be running after me. And so would our neighbours the Blue priestesses, naturally."

A particularly long and suggestive sequence of sputtering sounds burbled up from the pool. But suggestive of what? It was hard to say.

Elyani curled up against me. *"Oh my Lord Melchisedek,* what is *that?"*

Wriggling my nostrils, I carefully sense-smelled the pool again. "It's definitely not one of the Nephilim, if that makes you feel better."

Elyani drew the curtains of the four-poster bed. "We will have to inspect this pool carefully tomorrow morning. By the way, Szar of the Brown Robe, I hope you realise that this time there is no way in the seven spheres you are going to sleep anywhere else than in my bed. Since you came back a month ago, there seems to have been a good reason every night: we had to astral travel, or you had to descend to the Underworlds, or you didn't want to sleep..."

"Am I invited into your bed?" I asked in a timid voice.

She laughed, pulling me into her arms. "A lot can happen in a month, can't it?" She gave me a long, unlawful kiss, merging her energy into mine. Then she whispered, "Have you noticed that the sea-monster goes silent when we kiss?"

"It's very polite of him."

"Who knows, maybe he is the friend who holds a thread to our future! What if we reincarnated as two big fishes at the bottom of the ocean?"

As I contemplated the prospect, the White Eagle nested a little deeper into me, "I have a favour to ask."

"Granted!"

"Dragon, I want to spend a whole night sleeping in your arms."

"As in the hymn of the Law, *sleeping in the arms of the Dragon*?"

"Exactly!"

"Voof! You know what can happen, then?" I recited,

"Beware, man of the Law, you who sleep in the arms of the Dragon!
For the Dragon is the Mother of the Endless Night.
And in the Endless Night, you may be engulfed.
Aeons will pass, and you may never wake up!"

"Engulf me!" she whispered. "Let me never wake up again."

11.9 Hermina the Immaculate

When I woke up, it was still dark. But when I thrust my head out of the curtains, I realised with amazement that the room was inundated with daylight.

"So we slept in a bed-field!" I wondered what else the field could do, apart from creating darkness for a cosy late morning sleep.

I grabbed my black pants and put them on. Then I tiptoed to the pool, which was at least twelve lawful feet wide, and started my search for the sea-monster. It wasn't long before I sighted it – a strange-looking fish with two tails and a huge round head and thick wide lips. It was perhaps a lawful foot long, and half a foot high. And it seemed to be even more curious about me than I was about it. It came close to the surface of the water and looked at me with its big eyes, as if waiting for me to introduce myself.

"Did you find it?" Elyani asked in a sleepy voice.

"It looks rather friendly!"

As soon as I had spoken, the sea-monster responded with a gurgle.

"*Oh my Lord Melchisedek!* It is talking to you!" Elyani yanked the curtains open. "Voof! But it is day!" she exclaimed.

"I am surprised the governess hasn't voice-called us yet," I said.

"Lady Hermina?"

As soon as Elyani pronounced her name, we received a voice-channel call through darkness visible, "*Praise the Lord Melchisedek, Szar of the*

Brown Robe and Lady Elyani of the White Eagle! Lady Hermina of the high caste of the Immaculate is speaking to you. Welcome to His Majesty's palace. I will meet with you in your suite in half a lawful hour."

"Hush!" Elyani put her index on her lips. "Don't answer her!"

I kept silent for a few seconds, until it was clear the communication had ended. "That was no coincidence, was it?"

Elyani shook her head, "The Immaculate are extraordinarily psychic. She must have waited, so as not to disturb us." Pulling her dress from one corner of the bed, she said, "I have to tell you a few points of etiquette about the Immaculate. *Sweet Lord Melchisedek*, I can't possibly wear this! Szar, could you get our bags please?"

I walked to the private lounge, dazzled by all the works of art I discovered on my way. Three marble statues of gods caught my attention. They were at least ten lawful feet high and conveyed such dignity that I had to stop and pay my respects to them. As I walked away, I was hoping my respect hadn't been forced by the influence of a field.

When I returned to the bedroom, carrying six of our bags, I found Elyani close to the pool, dressed in only a thin sheet that she had thrown around her shoulders.

"She is lovely!" she said, and the sea-monster immediately answered her with a long, low-pitched gurgle. When she turned towards me and saw how tenderly I was looking at her, her face lit up with an ecstatic smile.

"If you are hungry, I found a mountain of food in one of the dining halls," I said.

"Oh, good, I am *starving in the Law!*"

When I came back with a large tray full of delicacies, Elyani was looking at herself in a mirror. "This dress will have to do for the moment. Now, listen, *man of the Law*! The Immaculate are not the easiest people to handle. They're one of the highest castes in the kingdom: gifted, utterly psychic, knowledgeable, powerful... and arrogant! They answer to no one but *His Supreme Majesty the King of Atlantis.*"

Elyani came and sat with me on the bed. With one hand she took a cherry which she put in my mouth, grabbing a cake with the other and stuffing the greater hunk of it into her mouth. "The Law of the Immaculate is extremely strict. They wear only white, and keep their head covered with veils. Every part of their body must be hidden all the time, apart from their hands and their eyes. Try this, it's fantastic," she put the last morsel of cake in my mouth and immediately attacked another one. "Now, most important! No one is allowed to speak to the Immaculate, nor look into their eyes. When they speak to you, your gaze must be directed high above their head."

I spat the cherry stone and caught it in my left hand. I clenched my fist, then slowly opened it, contemplating the stone. "The Immaculate are the priestesses who are letting our ascending goddess die without doing a thing, aren't they?"

Elyani stopped eating. "While in Hermina's presence, you'd better watch your thoughts carefully, *man of the Law*!"

"Promise!" I dipped my finger into one of the dishes and put it into her mouth.

"*Mother of the Light!* What is that?" she exclaimed after licking my finger clean, but not letting go of it.

"Oyster jello. Nephilim food."

"Ambrosial!" She kept half-biting my finger. "Simply ambrosial! And what is that?" she pointed to a carafe filled with greenish liquid.

"Green beverage. Don't touch it, it's disgusting. It makes your teeth rot."

"Why do they drink it, then?"

I shrugged, "Ask the Nephilim!" and placed another cake in her hand. "Come on, white panther, let us go and wait for the Immaculate's descent into the visitors' lounge."

Elyani tossed down two cups of mixed fruit juice one after the other and followed me.

When the Immaculate high priestess arrived, I looked up to the ceiling, responding to Elyani's prompt.

"*Praise the Lord Melchisedek, Lady Elyani of the White Eagle and Sir Szar of the Brown Robe!*" she said in a neutral voice that did not allow me to guess her age. Speaking no further, she let Elyani and I admire the golden clouds of light that glowed from the *living ceiling*.

I silenced my mind and remained carefully Point-sealed. Despite the negative prejudice I held against Immaculate priestesses, I soon realised that a wonderful bright light radiated from Hermina. It was lofty and warm, it brought a soft presence that resembled the White Eagle's Light.

"I can see you are good, sincere people," she finally said, "and for this I thank the angels of Highness who have sent you here. I want Szar of the Brown Robe to know certain things before he starts his healing work on His Majesty's son. I do not think it is possible to save the child. But this boy is as dear to me as if he were my own. The prince gave him into my care when he was twelve days old. If you can do *anything* for him, I will be more grateful than you can imagine.

However, there are other people in this palace who would not be so delighted to see the child's health improve. For your own security I have secretly placed the child in a suite adjacent to yours. To access it, use the door in your private office. I will meet you there shortly. *May the Lord Melchisedek bless you.*"

Hermina shone her light into us, and left.

I waited a few seconds before looking down. "This ceiling is stunning."

"True. And what did you think of Hermina?"

"Surprising. I didn't expect her to be so bright."

The White Eagle approved, "And gentle. Her light comes straight from Highness."

"To whom do you think she was referring when she spoke of intrigues?"

"The court physicians, for a start!"

"I hate all this. Before we left, Melchard said that if I manage to save the child, I am to go and explain to the prince how absolutely desperate the case was, and trumpet loudly that no physician in the kingdom could ever have saved the child's life. Otherwise the court physicians would never forgive us. And if after this they are still not satisfied or if the court priests are offended, my instructions are to disclose my identity as one of the Masters of Thunder."

Elyani shook her head, "It's even worse than I thought!"

I walked back with her into the bedroom. "And now, Elyani, I *have* to tell you the secret!"

"All right, you win."

"Before we began our journey, I asked Gervin to supply me with gold to purchase stolen soft stones in Tomoristan. The idea is to track down our potential enemies, those who could attack us at the time of the Archive transfer."

Elyani turned white panther. "I am with you, Commander. Renegade Hunters, Nephilim giants, organised gangs of various kinds... wouldn't it be funny if our new friend ended up being one of these rascals? A wicked giant, for instance. You could invite him to Eisraim, but the only doorways he would be able to get through would be those of the enclave of the jewels!"

"Talk about expecting the unexpected! Anyway, I think I'd rather be friends with one of the Nephilim giants than with an Immaculate priestess."

"Give this woman a chance. Who said the Immaculate were all like the two parrots of the Law in charge of Holma?"

I shrugged my shoulders and changed the topic, "If you meet anyone in the palace today, feel free to let them know that Szar of the Brown Robe is searching for top-quality soft stones."

"Anything else, Commander?"

A loud volley of bubbles came out of the pool on the other side of the room.

"Well, well... if you get a chance, perhaps you could ask Marzook what this Far Underworld of a sea-monster is doing in our bathtub."

With a long kiss, I unlawfully took leave and headed for the private office. There I found a door that opened into a dim passage. It led to a spacious room where the Immaculate was waiting for me.

As soon as I guessed her silhouette, I looked up to the ceiling.

A voice hailed me. "*Praise the Lord Melchisedek, Sir Szar of the Brown Robe!* My name is Jinia. You can speak to me and look at me."

I looked down and discovered a young woman, perhaps twenty years of age, clad in a white gown. A white shawl hid her hair, but her face was not covered. She was standing close to a wide bed where the princely child was lying, deeply asleep.

"I am Lady Hermina's attendant," she said after returning the lawful greeting. "I am here to answer your questions and to assist you."

Jinia was extremely thin and frail, as if the Angels of the Seed had forgotten to bring down the earth element when cooking her in her mother's womb.

"Can I touch the child's energy or are there any restrictions pertaining to etiquette?" I enquired.

"Do what you have to do," Jinia said. Lady Hermina walked to a corner of the room behind me so as to let me look at the child freely, without the risk of my breaking the protocol by bumping into her Immaculate highness with my gaze.

I asked Jinia what had happened to the child. "Avapotonisteraniso is three years old," she told me. "Six weeks ago he was struck by a high fever. Up till then, whenever he happened to be sick, Lady Hermina would heal him with her high Word and the chanting of the hymns of the Law. But this time his health did not improve. We had to seek recourse to the court physicians, but none of them could help. Finally, an oracle revealed that the child's soul was trapped in the Underworlds.

"How long has His Majesty Avapotonisteraniso been unconscious?" I asked.

"More than two weeks," Jinia answered.

The child looked rather grey, but I was immediately struck by the extraordinary vibration that enveloped his energy. "What is this magnificent white light all around him?" I asked. It was not only shining bright but also nurturing and heart-warming, as well as exquisitely subtle.

"This is the Word of Highness that Lady Hermina Voice-projects onto His Majesty Avapotonisteraniso every day to heal him."

"*Oh my Lord Melchisedek!*" I thought, letting my hands run on the child's gateways, "Hermina really loves this child!" Out of the blue, I found myself deeply moved by the softness that she had instilled into his energy. It was like the amazing sweetness that I had sometimes received from Elyani, the best of the Eagle's love. It had Life, as in the rivers of the Deep Underworlds, it chanted with joy. As I touched the child, waves of the marvellous power came into me, dancing in my heart.

"A Voice-projection connected to the Word of Highness, did you say?"

"Yes, Szar of the Brown Robe," Jinia replied. "His Majesty Avapotonisteraniso has been sick often this past year, and each time, Lady Hermina has healed him with the power of her Voice."

Inspecting the child's' gateways, I came across a particular vibration which my teacher in the Dragon had taught me to identify. "Which oracle said the child's soul was trapped in the Underworld?" I asked.

"The court oracle," Jinia said.

"Is it a reliable oracle? Is it run by priests who know what they are..." I started asking, but interrupted myself, realising that questioning the skills of court priests was a sure way to attract trouble.

From the back of the room, Lady Hermina answered in a stern voice, "No, the court oracle is *not* reliable!"

"Jinia, do you know about gateways?"

"Yes, Szar of the Brown Robe. Lady Hermina has been teaching me about healing."

"Come, Jinia. Let me show you something that I learnt from great healers called the Sons of the Dragon. See, these two little gateways close to the heart... when someone's soul is trapped in the Underworlds, these gateways turn black. But when they are silvery grey, like this, it means the soul has decided to leave the kingdom, and has already started its journey towards a new incarnation. I doubt that our little boy's soul is in the Underworld."

"This is what Lady Hermina has been saying all along, Szar of the Brown Robe. Does this mean you cannot do anything for His Majesty?"

I took my head in my hands and remained silent for a while. Then I gave my verdict, "Jinia, among the Sons of the Dragon, there are Great Warriors who know ways of resuscitating their brethren who fall on the battlefield. They do so by calling their souls back to the kingdom. These are not simple techniques, and they do not always work. I could possibly try to implement one of them, but it would not be without risk. Presently the child is kept alive by the wonderful energy that Lady Hermina has Voice-projected onto him. If I were to..."

"Do it!" Hermina interrupted. Then she added in a gentler voice, "You have my blessing."

Contemplating the child's energy, I explained, "This is the way we do it, Jinia. We raise the power of the Dragon throughout the patient's gateways, pulling the strings that link the soul to the body. Sometimes this is enough, and the soul returns. If it doesn't, we let the body rest for one night. Then, at dawn, we project an extremely violent sound, using the Voice. And if this doesn't work..." I shook my head, and Jinia understood.

I started pulling Dragon forces into the child's gateways. A few lawful feet behind me, Hermina was still and silent.

Jinia was watching with so much interest that from time to time I dropped a few words of explanation, which she drank avidly, "The first phase consists of injecting life force to pump up the vitality in the main gateways. We hardly have anything to do at this stage, thanks to Lady Hermina's good works." I took Jinia's frail little hand and let her sense some powerful gateways that the Warriors used for healing.

Then I went onto the next phase, which was to charge the gateways with energies pulled from deeper in the Dragon. I kept giving Jinia some of my Warrior's tricks, "If someone has just broken their leg, this little gateway here can bring instant relief from the pain. And this one is wonderful for broken ankles..." She did not ask any questions but I could see she understood and absorbed all I was passing on to her.

The child's energy held itself rather well. But when it came to pulling the strings of the soul, using various Voice-frequencies combined with gateway stimulations, there was not the faintest response.

I kept on for more than three hours, trying all kinds of healing devices, but with no result. "If we insist any further, we could damage the strings. So we will leave him in peace for the moment, and we will try again tomorrow morning. If he shows any sign of waking up, call me immediately."

What a strong soul Jinia seemed to be! I would have liked to speak to her and give her a few more healer's tricks, and to learn what kind of rule she was following for her eyes to shine as they did.

But the Immaculate was behind my back, watching us. To avoid any slip of protocol, I just gave a lawful salute and left.

11.10 Felicia on her way to the abyss

When I returned to the princely suite, I told Elyani, "The oracle was bogus. The child's soul was never trapped in the Underworlds. I think Avapotonisteraniso has already begun the Great Journey through the spheres."

Elyani pulled a face, "Can you call him back?"

I let myself collapse in a huge armchair shaped like a left hand, "We'll know by tomorrow morning."

Sitting in front of me in the symmetrical piece of furniture, a right hand, Elyani took a complicated pose, her elbow resting on the armchair's huge thumb. "So the little boy is not going to be your new friend?"

"If he is, the friendship might well have to wait for a future life. Anyway, let us wait. *Miracles happen*," I closed the topic.

Elyani made her smile mysterious. "Guess who I met this morning?"

I was not in a mood for Point-guesses. "Who in the Law?"

"*Her High Majesty Pelenor Ozorenan, wife of Filipotonisteraniso Ozorenan, Prince of the County of the Northern Lakes!*"

I whistled my amazement. An audience with a member of a royal family was a rare privilege in the Law. "How did that lawfully happen?"

"She called me through darkness visible. She wanted to speak to me. She invited me to join her in one of the official rooms, in the central wing."

"And what do princesses discuss when they meet White Eagles?"

"Well, you, for a start. Her High Majesty Pelenor is the friend of a friend of yours, Szar of the Brown Robe."

That was too much for the Dragon to swallow in one go. "What? Friend of whom?"

"A certain Felicia, high priestess of Verzazyel, and now Assistant Grand Master of the Snowy Mountains' main temple. By the way, she has just been lawfully asked for her hand in marriage by the Right Excellent Lord

Vrolon, *Grand Superintendent of the Fields for the Northern Counties under the Appointment of His Supreme Majesty the King of Atlantis."*

So my little Nephilim baby girl had succeeded! She had conquered the fire of the Watchers, and was now powerful, famous, and loved by a prian – all she had wanted.

Elyani made her heart an ocean, "Does this bring regrets?"

"Regrets?' I shook my head sternly. "A few days ago Gervin revealed to me that my encounter with Felicia had been one of my trials. While I was healing her, the whole Archive council was watching me! Speaking straight from Thunder, Gervin said that had I descended into the Watcher's crypt for the initiation with Felicia, I would now be an extremely powerful man on his way to the abyss. I hope Felicia will be wise enough to make good use of her powers. I'd hate to think that by saving her life, I have helped to set her on her way to the abyss."

We held a cogitative space, resting on each other's heartness.

"So what the Upperworld did you and Pelenor discuss?" I asked.

"I don't know what Felicia told her, but Pelenor was terribly curious about you. She asked me question after question..." Elyani was interrupted by a particularly loud gurgle coming from the pool.

"The sea-monster is trying to catch our attention," I sense-smelled. "Did you ask Marzook about it?"

"Yes, I did. *It all breathes lawfully,* I'll tell you," she whispered somewhat secretively. Then in her normal voice, "Pelenor asked several questions about me too. I suspect Felicia was curious, and eager to get Pelenor's impressions of me."

"Could be!" I pondered, recalling my spicy friend's fiery inquisitiveness. "Did Princess Pelenor treat you well?"

"She was lovely! She told me how indebted she was to you for having saved Felicia. We chatted for a long time. And guess what? She asked me if you could keep a secret."

I closed my eyes and plugged my ears. "I don't think I have gone far enough in my Point training to keep a royal secret."

Elyani came over and sat on my lap, pulling my little fingers out of my ear-holes. "Listen, Pelenor wants to see you, but only if you agree to keep what she tells you strictly confidential."

"Did you guess what she wanted to tell me?"

Elyani laughed, "Dragon, what are you asking me? Pelenor is a good woman. I wouldn't want to cause her trouble. Anyway, she'll be here in less than an hour."

"What?" The prospect of an etiquette debacle hung in front of me. "How about I let you do the talking, and I just keep smiling like a filosterops?" I grinned, showing all my teeth.

"No, it's you she wants to see. But she does not want anyone to know she is coming, so she will use some kind of secret passage that leads to one of our visitors' lounges. She will voice-call us before she arrives." Elyani pulled me by the hand, "Come and see Pepeena."

"Who?" I followed, my eyes caught by the wall which was bringing up glow after glow, creating a constant interplay of changing colours.

"Pepeena, the talking fish. Marzook explained everything about her." Elyani took me to sit on the edge of the pool. The double-tailed sea-monster came close to the surface, looking at us intently.

"This is a very rare fish. In the Ancient Days of the Earth, it used to live in certain lakes in the land of Mu. This one is a she, her name is Pepeena."

"Did you say she can talk?"

"She is young, she's still learning." Elyani bent over close to the surface, gently calling, "Pepeena! Pepeena!"

Pepeena answered by sputtering a few bubbles.

"She's just a bit shy because she's not yet used to you," Elyani said, dipping a finger into the water.

Pepeena moved her head to and fro, rubbing her thick blue lips against the finger.

"Well, here is our new friend!"

"Hunh, hunh! I would rather think that Pelenor could become your friend."

"Friends with a princess!" I chuckled, "Now, that would be the Dragon's last tooth."

"Felicia could well become a princess too."

"Oh yes she could. I don't know that it would be good for her soul, though."

Elyani sensed the stomach-hollowness behind my words. "Dragon, you need to eat. There is no Dragon breeze to feed on, here." She took me to a large square sofa where two silver trays full of Nephilim-decadent delicacies were waiting. She invited me to wallow on the lavish red cushions with her, and started feeding me chunks of spicy fish puree on a golden spoon, "One for you, one for me," alternating with hard-boiled soft-shelled crunchy pigeon eggs in sour-sweet sauce and brinjal-buttered finger-toasts laid with bluish caviar. "Do you really think that Felicia could be on her way to the abyss?"

"The combination of greed and occult powers is a particularly dangerous one. Felicia's ambition is unstoppable. What if she accumulated a pile of horrendous karma because of me."

"What's this?"

"Olive paté, but you don't want to know how they make it."

"Celestial! What do you mean, horrendous karma because of you?"

"After all, I interfered with her destiny. If I hadn't saved her, by now she could be on her way to another life – perhaps a simple, good life."

We kept tasting the motley dishes, silently meditating on the strange ways and interplays of destiny, until Elyani received a brief voice-channel call announcing a bouquet of flowers on its way from Pelenor Ozorenan.

"The princess is coming," Elyani announced. "She warned me she would send us a coded message. The palace is full to the top of its turrets with spies who spend their days listening to voice channels."

"Life in a palace does have its drawbacks," I observed, pulling my beard. "Do you really think Pelenor Ozorenan could become a friend?"

Elyani's mouth widened, and with her fingers she buttered my nose with oyster jello.

11.11 The woman who was about to lose everything

I was waiting in the private lounge when my nostrils started wriggling compulsively. "Nephilim spice!"

A voice called me, "*Praise the Lord Melchisedek, Szar of the Brown Robe!*"

I walked into the second private lounge, where the princess had just arrived through a disguised door. I saluted her as Elyani had instructed me, "*All glory to the Lord Melchisedek, Your High Majesty Pelenor Ozorenan, Princess of the County of the Northern Lakes, wife of His High Majesty Filipotonisteraniso Ozorenan, Prince of the County of the Northern Lakes under the Appointment of His Supreme Majesty the King of Atlantis.*"

Her Majesty looked at me with undisguised curiosity. "So you are Sir Great Dragon!"

She immediately reminded me of Felicia. She was hardly older than her, had long reddish-brown hair, and her aura carried that particular light associated with Nephilim spice. She was not quite as stunning as Felicia but still, stunning enough to be a princess.

"As you can see, I have come alone," she walked with dignity to one of the armchairs, the trail of her shining blue dress over her arm. Settling herself briefly, she pointed to the armchair opposite her.

I sat down, holding onto the clear fountain.

"I have heard a lot about you, Sir Great Dragon. Felicia is a dear friend of mine."

I answered with a noncommittal nod, wondering why she wasn't inquiring about Avapotonisteraniso's health.

To engage the conversation, Her Majesty asked a few trivial questions about my journey from Eisraim to Tomoristan, then she enquired about Master Gervin of the Brown Robe and my activities in the temple of Eisraim. But after a few minutes she abruptly changed tone. Looking straight into my eyes, she asked in a sharp voice, "Can you keep a secret, Szar of the Brown Robe?"

Holding on to my Point-seal, I gave another nod.

She pulled her refined mouth into a line. "Of course you can! Felicia assured me I could trust you entirely and wholeheartedly. Did you know that Felicia never trusts anyone?"

"I can imagine that, Your Majesty," I gave the first smile.

She didn't return it. "The woman in front of you, Szar of the Brown Robe, is about to lose everything: title, husband, love, kingly dwelling and comfort, friends... All the things which mean something to me are about to be taken away from me. The reason is simple: I cannot have children."

"Your Majesty, aren't you the mother of *Avapotonisteraniso Ozorenan, son of His Majesty...*"

"No!" she interrupted. "He was the son of my husband's first wife, who died while giving birth."

Now I understood why Hermina loved the little boy so much.

"I have been married to Filipotonisteraniso for more than two years, and the Lord Melchisedek still hasn't blessed me with a child." Her voice turned sad, "You are not going to save the life of Avapotonisteraniso, are you?"

"*The situation is not lawfully bright*," I admitted cautiously, "but until tomorrow, there is still a glimmer of hope. The power of the Dragon is deep."

Pelenor's face opened. "You would do me an immense favour if you saved him. If he dies, as all the court physicians and priests have predicted, there will be no heir left in the Ozorenan family. The pressure for me to conceive will be horrendous. I believe my husband loves me sincerely, but he has to think of the future of his family, and of his kingdom. I don't give myself a year, Szar of the Brown Robe."

Elyani was right, Pelenor looked like a sincere woman. "Have you consulted your physicians?" I asked.

"I can't!" she folded her delicate hands on her lap. "If it were known that Princess Pelenor cannot conceive, Filipotonisteraniso's honour would immediately be at stake. Apart from that, hordes of courtesans would rush after him. It wouldn't take more than six months before I would have to leave my body, or even be exiled. The gods, with their daiva, have placed a heavy destiny on me, Szar of the Brown Robe. Can you help me?"

Had Pelenor wanted magic words to create a flow of empathy, she couldn't have found better. Holding the Eagle's Light for her, I gathered myself in the clear fountain. She sensed that a chord had been struck inside me, and she too remained silent.

An opening took place.

I offered to examine her body of energy, asking her to lie down on a divan. Sitting beside her on a low stool, I brought my hands close to her body but hesitated before touching her, unsure of the etiquette for court physicians.

The Nephilim woman was amused. She drew my hand to her abdomen. "Let me feel these magic hands Felicia spoke of with such passion!"

I closed my eyes, and as I let my hands run on Pelenor's gateways, memories of the monumental healing work I had performed on Felicia's body flashed back. It already seemed so long ago!

It didn't take me long to locate the problem. "Here," I said, pressing two centres of energy below and on either side of her navel, "a few of your gateways are weak."

"What's wrong with them?"

"Perhaps they were damaged by some disease when you were a child. Let me put energy on them and see what happens."

I began pulling vroofing waves from the Dragon, passing them into her belly through my hands.

At one stage, Pelenor started laughing, "Is this what you did to Felicia?"

"Sometimes."

"I can see why she liked it so much," she said.

It dawned on me that I ought to experiment with this on Elyani.

Despite all the force I threw into Pelenor's body, her gateways didn't respond. After a few more attempts, I pronounced my diagnosis, "These gateways have been stunted since birth."

"And so?"

I tuned high in the fountain, carefully searching for words.

Pelenor was direct, "Szar, please, let us not play games, here!"

"All right! In your body of energy some of the gateways which normally play a key role in conception are undeveloped. They don't respond to stimulation, so they can't even be healed. They would have to be reconstituted from scratch, using forces from the Deep Underworld. This is not impossible, I have performed surgery of this kind on Felicia. But for this I would have to put you in a state of hibernation for a number of days, perhaps weeks. And it would have to happen near a gate of the Dragon."

"Do you mean to say I would have to travel all the way to the county of the Red Lands, in the far south?"

"No. There is a beautiful Dragon gate in my temple. We could probably find one around here too, but I doubt this palace would be the appropriate place for a healing."

Pelenor sat up. "There are so many intrigues creeping round this palace, it would probably end up making *you* sick!" She looked up towards the world of the gods, "A pilgrimage to the temple of Eisraim, is this what it would take?"

"There is no guarantee of success!" I drummed into her. Remembering the woman in front of me was not Felicia, I softened my tone and added, "Your Majesty, you must understand I have never healed an infertile woman before."

"You thoroughly healed Felicia! Do you know she used to be sick all the time before she met you? Each time she ate anything remotely resembling cream, she instantly turned green and vomited. Once she even vomited on my dress in the middle of a court dinner!"

We both ruminated for a moment.

Pelenor forced her gaze into me, "Do you believe you can do it?"

I went as high as I could in the clear fountain, letting the Eagle speak through me, "*So much for yes as for no – like the purple blossoms of the alohim tree after the first storm in spring: half remain on the branches, half fall to the ground.*"

Pelenor was distressed. Clearly she had hoped for more from me. Part of me wanted to comfort her, ignite a spark in her eyes by promising I would give her my Dragon-best. But from high, I knew that pushing for enthusiasm would not have served her. So I just stayed open, calling for warmth and higher compassion.

After a while, Pelenor stood up. She advised me to stay in my suite and not talk to anyone in the palace. If the court physicians and the priests found out that I had been called to heal the princely child, they were likely to become jealous and start fomenting trouble. So when I told her of my intention to hunt for soft stones, Pelenor was delighted. It was a perfect reason to justify my visit. She promised to help me find the best sources of stones in the county.

As she made it plain she was about to leave, I asked, "Your Majesty, could you give me some news of Felicia?"

Pelenor closed her eyes for a second. Then she fastened her gaze on me and spoke with the punch of a Nephilim, "Do you really want to know, Sir Great Dragon?"

I rested on *my Mother of the Endless Night*, "Yes, I do."

"Fine in the Law! You saved her life, that is for sure. But you broke her heart so badly that you nearly killed her. If you had imagined she came out triumphant from the Watcher's crypt, let me tell you, you were wrong! She collapsed and cried a river of tears. She loathed her lonely victory. On her journey back from the Red Lands she cried all the way. She stopped here and cried in my arms for a whole week. And do you know why? Before she met you she had spent her life dreaming of court games and intrigues," Pelenor bashed her words into me. "Men, to her, were nothing more than a way of gaining power. With you for the first time she opened and sincerely tried to give herself. Losing you has left her devastated – annihilated. It will take her a long time to recover."

"Hasn't she been asked for her hand in marriage by Lord Vrolon?"

Pelenor pursed her lips in contempt. "Lord Vrolon is thirty-five years older than her, and his heart is so bad that even court oracles have foreseen his imminent death."

Pelenor stood where she was, watching the effect of her words on me.

The beating was taking its toll, I didn't try to hide it.

With no more than a short, lawful greeting, she turned round and left.

Looking down to my left fist, the old nursery rhyme came back, "*What does a madman do when his house is melting? He dances! He dances!*"

Rather than returning to the princely suite, I immediately went looking for Marzook, whom Elyani had organised to take me stone hunting.

11.12 Prelude to disaster

When I came back from my tour of Tomoristan's stone dealers, it was late in the evening. The semi-darkness enhanced the strange, ever-changing colours coming from the glowing wall.

I dropped my brown cape on the lawn carpet, "Elyani?"

"I am here!" she answered from the pool, on the other side of the room. "Did you find something exciting?"

I walked towards her, "Nothing! You have no idea what garbage those shops are selling. Cheap, ugly, completely useless."

Elyani was bathing in the pool, wearing only one of my black shirts. "Any interesting people?"

"No." I sat close to her on the edge of the pool, passing my hand over her neck, admiring the way she had left the shirt half open. "Tomoristan is a city of sleepers, and Marzook's aura stinks. Only when I offered him gold did he start mentioning places of interest. Finally he offered to take me to a village north of Tomoristan tomorrow morning, to meet a 'real dealer'."

My eyes were caught by a gigantic flower arrangement beside the four-poster bed. "*Sweet Lord Melchisedek*, what is *that*?"

"Flowers from Pelenor Ozorenan. Didn't she voice-channel she was sending them?"

I walked over to the grand bunch – taller than me! – hundreds of flowers of all colours, some with shapes I had never even seen before. "Orchids have a strange aura, haven't they? Sometimes they make me feel uncomfortable. There's something devious about their beauty."

"What did you think of Pelenor?" Elyani asked.

I picked a lily and walked back to the pool. "She is a sincere woman."

"A friend?"

"I don't think she has many of them. The life of a princess seems to be lonelier than I thought." I stretched out on the side of the pool, my head close to Elyani's, and put the lily in her curly hair. "Your hair is growing fast. And growing in strength!"

She rubbed her head against mine. "I am sure it is because of your Dragon."

The water was still. There was nothing but our breathing.

"What's happening to Sir Great Dragon?" Elyani asked.

"Sir Great Dragon loves you."

"Does he?" Elyani's voice sounded fragile.

"You are his White Eagle of the gods, he is your forever lover. He could be offered one hundred princesses one hundred times, and he would still choose you."

"Why? What's so special about me?"

"You love him for who he is, not because of his Dragon. Since he has arrived in Tomoristan, he has seen only people interested in his Dragon. If they wanted him to come here, it was because of the Dragon. If they listen to him, it is because of the Dragon. They all want something from the Dragon. It is the only thing they see in him."

"I like your Dragon too, you know?"

"I hope you do! And I wish I had caves and caves of Dragon treasures to give you. But you loved me before I had any power, when I was just me – pitiful poor little Szar-ka. And if I were to reach the most fantastic powers and become king in heaven, and then fall back naked and powerless again, you would still love me the same."

Elyani was crying.

I went high into the clear fountain, searching for ways of conveying love with depth. As I was passing through the Point, I realised there was a field attached to the wall behind me. Not a Point-field, just a simple one. To activate it, there was no need to engage supermind Point-frequencies, just trigger a simple vibration in darkness visible.

Mindlessly, I activated the vibration. "I love you because..." I started saying.

Triggered by the field, a flood of water cascaded down the wall behind me.

Stupefied, I turned round, but before I could do anything the flow of water had swept me into the pool.

When my head emerged from the water Elyani was crying and laughing at the same time, while Pepeena was protesting with loud gurgles of indignation.

"I just love you!" I took her in my arms.

She made her body tender. A strong wave of desire passed between us, and I kissed her vroofingly. And as she was about to answer something, I grasped her waist and pulled her under the water, and I Dragon-kissed her again.

Pepeena nuzzled up and gazed at us with great interest.

We burst out laughing and had to come to the surface for air.

My hands still on Elyani's waist, I called on fiery Dragon-waves and let them vroof their way into her body.

"Oooh!" her voice rang out.

"Oooh!" Pepeena echoed.

I was astounded. "That sounded worryingly real!"

"Pepeena and I have been practising a lot today." She looked at our strange beast in the water, "If I stay any longer in this tub, I am going to melt! Why don't we continue this conversation on solid ground."

She emerged from the water and dropped the black shirt on the carpet, looking for a towel.

I was taken breathless – seeing her wet body shook my Dragon to the depths. "Forget about the daiva!" I thought. "This time, it is decided, the Dragon be my witness, I am going to marry this woman!" And I went looking for my shoes at the bottom of the pool.

When I came out of the water, Elyani was wearing a white dress that showed much more of her breast than lawful White Eagle gowns did. She laughed when she saw me with a shoe in each hand. "We need food!" she exclaimed and went to the dining hall in search of the loadful of delicacies that servants brought to our suite several times a day.

As I was dressing into dry clothes, I contemplated the wall glowing with changing colours. Curious, I sat and Point-tuned into it, using the method Teyani had taught me after she had caught me 'spying' on her.

Soon I found myself on the supermind-level of fast-changing colours and geometrical shapes, and identified the functions that modified the hue and intensity of the wall's glows. But it was something else that surprised me: the field contained functions to generate musical sounds in darkness visible.

Point-mastering the field's instruction notice had taken less than a second. From there, playing with the functions proved simple. Operating from the Point, I started by turning the entire wall yellow, while letting a low-pitched oooh astral sound resonate in the room's darkness visible. Then I played with light. It was magic! Slight impulses sent from the Point were enough to bring up complicated colour patterns similar to those I saw when travelling through the spheres.

I looked for more sophisticated musical inspiration. Searching in my memory, I recalled the wonderful melody that my schoolteacher had tried to teach me long ago, during my first (and last) saucepan-and-spoon music lesson. Gathering all my sensitivity, I Point-triggered the field's sound functions. The astral space went 'bang-ting-ting, bang-ting-ting, bang-ting-ting, bang-ting-ting...', and I was deeply moved. I wished my school teacher could have heard this, as the old man had always thought the gods were unsupportive of his attempts to teach me music. "*There you are, old father in the Law,*" I thought affectionately, "at last the gods are repaying you for your efforts."

Elyani came back with a large silver tray piled high with food. When she heard the astral music, she was just as amazed as I was. "How did you manage to do that?"

I clicked my fingers, "It's just a field!" Linking to her third eye, I let a huge spinning purple vortex appear on the wall.

She laid the tray on a small stone table and clapped her hands gleefully, her eyes dancing with joy.

Encouraged by her support, I put all my heart in the music. The harmonies sounded and resounded louder and louder in the space, "bang-ting-ting..."

"Today, for the first time," my voice half choked with emotion, "I can see how I could become a musician."

Elyani laughed and started moving her body, following the "bang-ting-ting..." tune. "You have no idea how beautiful your music will be in the future," she said.

I felt a pang of insecurity about my art. "Do you mean you don't like this music?"

"I love it!" She kept dancing and laughing. "This is a special moment! The first time you play for me."

Then she lit lamp oils on the table and invited me to join her. I sat in front of her, enjoying watching her eat. It always did something to my Dragon when she was voracious. She told me about a number of marvels (operated by fields) that she had discovered while exploring the palace, and she kept putting bits of food in my mouth – strange, spicy foods as only the Nephilim knew how to cook.

The more I looked at her, laughing with joy, the more I realised that I not only loved her. I desired her.

When she finished eating, she sat very still and just opened to me.

I echoed her silence, taking her image deep inside. Then I stood and picked her up in my arms. She closed her eyes and laid her head against my chest. As I slowly carried her to the royal bed, I remembered the first time I had picked up her body – at the small creek, just before returning to the temple of Eisraim.

We had both changed a lot since then.

I lay close to her on the bed. The bed's field caught my Point. For one brief second it occurred to me to explore it, but I decided against it, unsure what disaster might fall on us. Letting go of everything but my attraction to her, I engaged her in a long and unlawful kiss.

She let herself melt, merging her energy into mine.

I looked deep into her eyes. "And what if I finally found a way of asking you to marry me. Would you say yes?"

Elyani bit her lip – the first time I had seen her do this – and she started crying.

I didn't move, opening as much as I could.

"A few days before we left Eisraim, Teyani came to speak to me. She said I could do anything I wanted with you except two things: marry you, and make love to you."

I suddenly moved back, not wanting to push myself against her will.

"No! No! Please, don't reject me! I love you too much, please don't turn away from me."

I made myself Eagle for her and came close.

She clung to me with big sobs.

"So we can never be married, is that it?" I held her tightly in my arms.

"All Teyani would say is that we should wait for the daiva to be revealed," Elyani's sobbing didn't stop. "I couldn't help crying, so Teyani went high into her fountain of prophecy, and she said that one day you and I would make love just like the gods do. She has seen it. It *will* happen."

"One day... that could mean the very last day, just before the end of time."

"No, not at the end of time, that I know!" Elyani swore.

A Dragon-deep distress was swamping my chest. "It could still mean that we will have to wait for another life to be married, couldn't it?"

Elyani made herself still, just Eagle. "Teyani said something else." She placed her left hand on my heart. "She said that you and I were already married in the Eagle, and that ultimately nothing could stand between us."

Tuning high in the fountain, I knew this was the truth.

That night we cried in each other's arms, and at times we laughed, as the Eagle's Love was so bright. We whispered secrets which none – not even the angels of Highness – were to hear. And we merged into each other until time stopped.

In the middle of this no-time, Elyani said, "I want to *sleep in the arms of the Dragon* again," and she took off her dress and snuggled up in my arms.

The Dragon vroofed, and I prayed for another *Endless Night*.

Thus was fulfilled the word which Teyani had given me, as there had never been so much love and joy between Elyani and me.

11.13 Hermina of Highness and the three white roses

Not long before dawn, I stepped quietly into the room where the princely child was kept. Jinia was sitting on the bed. She looked very tired, with her head bent forward and big dark rings under her eyes. Out of the corner of my eye I caught a glimpse of Hermina's silhouette. The Immaculate was standing in exactly the same place as the day before, making me wonder if she had moved at all.

Jinia stood up and praised the Lord Melchisedek in her tranquil little voice. After I lawfully responded, she took three white roses from a vase beside the bed and gave them to me. "Sir Szar, these are to thank you for what you have done for His Majesty yesterday, and also for the lesson in healing you gave me."

Looking at the royal child's body deeply asleep on the bed, I said, "I wish you could thank me for something more than a lesson." But as I spoke, a wonderful vibration came gently knocking at my heart. It was warm, loving and White, just like the one I had admired in the child's aura the day before. Looking down, I realised the vibration was coming from the flowers. True, my Dragon had a tooth against Immaculate priestesses. Yet I had to admit there was infinitely more meaning and beauty in these three white roses than in the grand royal bouquet that Pelenor had sent to the suite. "Jinia, would you convey my gratitude to Lady Hermina for projecting her high Word onto these flowers."

Jinia responded with a serene smile. "Oh no, Sir Szar, I cannot address Lady Hermina, as it would be against the rule of her high caste. But I am sure she will have heard your thoughts."

I reinforced my Point-seal, wondering which other thoughts of mine Lady Hermina could hear.

"Last night, Lady Hermina instructed me that through psychic surgery the Sons of the Dragon could repair people's body of energy and thereby achieve remarkable healings. Being a Great Warrior, you would be familiar with such techniques, wouldn't you, Sir Szar?" the frail young woman asked.

"That's right."

"Lady Hermina wanted to hear your opinion, could any of these techniques help heal His Majesty?"

I sat on the edge of the bed, picking up the roses. Holding them in one hand, I let my other hand run on the child's gateways. His energy had not changed during the night.

I spent a long while testing the gateways' response to various stimulations, then I turned to Hermina's attendant. "Do you know what I think, Jinia? This child has decided to go. He is already on his way to another life. Even if we could awaken all the powers of the spheres in his body, I don't think it would change a thing."

Then suddenly, I knew. There was no noise, no movement to indicate, but I knew, I could feel.

I took a look at Jinia. Her aura was shining with white light but her body of energy was exhausted. There were signs showing she had been fasting and was badly in need of sleep.

"Does this mean you cannot do anything more for His Majesty?" she asked.

Jinia was trying not to show it, but she could feel it too. The wave of feeling was so strong it filled the entire room.

Hermina was crying.

The intensity of Hermina's emotion took me by surprise. For a few seconds I said nothing, keeping eye contact with Jinia.

Then I touched the orichalc plate on my neck. "One more thing can be attempted, an ancient technique which the Sons of the Dragon received from Lohrzen, the father-founder of the Great Warriors. The technique is known by his name: Lohrzen's scream. It has called many a warrior back to life after falling on the battlefield. Once in the county of the Red Lands, I myself used it on a peasant who had fallen from a cliff to his death. Lohrzen's scream instantly brought the man back to his senses. And by the grace of our Lord Melchisedek, I believe the peasant is still alive to this day. Because of its violence, though, Lohrzen's scream is not without risk, so the child's body of energy must be carefully prepared."

As the Immaculate rule did not allow me to look at her, the roses were my thread. Through their Whiteness, I let a flow of feeling reach Hermina of Highness. She received it, and kept crying.

I invited Jinia to place her hands on the child and guided her from gateway to gateway. Tapping from the Dragon, I sent forces both into the child and into her, for her vitality was badly in need of a boost.

While the energy work was going on, Hermina was crying silently behind us. Her grief was simple, devastating, magnificent.

When the preliminaries were over, I warned Jinia that a violent Voice-projection was about to happen. I instructed her to sit in meditation position, gathering her life force in the area of her heart. Then I stood up and started the slow, initial sequence of movements of the Great Warriors' black dance, keeping my eyes fixed on the child.

Hermina remained still. Her pain was the wound of the Earth. Her tears, like the wound, seemed to have no end.

The strong Dragon energies of the black dance charged the room. The atmosphere became pregnant with a massive presence.

Hermina's stillness resonated with my Mother's infinity.

I danced, holding her pain.

She cried, and the Dragon was one with her.

I danced, and her sorrow danced through me.

She cried, and the Dragon of the Deep suddenly became one with an immense energy above my head. And from that immensity, the faraway voice suddenly made itself heard.

"Now, son! Launch the scream, now!"

In a shrieking Voice-projection, the total violence of Lohrzen's scream was unleashed.

Jinia fell on the floor.

Time stopped. Several things happened all at once.

From high, the child's voice responded to Lohrzen's scream. "Farewell, Hermina. Rare in the seven spheres are the souls who have ever been loved as you have loved me. But I cannot return. The Lords of Destiny have called me, and have led me away from the kingdom. Despite all my love for you, I must go. Farewell, beautiful woman, and may the Mother of the Light bless you for all that I received from you."

Hermina's grief exploded. Her silent scream of pain resounded beyond the spheres. The Mother of the Light heard her and extended her hand of infinite compassion towards her.

Jinia spoke to me through a faraway voice,

"Three white roses –

One for her in Highness, one to you, the Eagle,

And one for me, standing between the two of you.

Is it so surprising that a woman should cry

When the child she tended lies dead in front of her?
True, another woman had given birth to him,
But in Highness she called the Angels of the Seed,
And let them swell her breasts with tender care and milk.
And he suckled from her, and he slept on her breast,
And he merged into her, and she was a woman.
She was his thread to life, he was her only flesh.
With endless love and care she inundated him.
Her endless solitude, he illuminated.
In a grey, empty world, they were each other's joy.
She knew that destiny was to take him from her,
But still wanted to hope, and placed her hope in you.
Hope is dead. Tolls the bell – and solitude is back
For another aeon, void and immaculate,
Another aeon of such lofty aloneness.
She lays no blame on you, anger is not her lot.
She cries simply, humbly, with no claim to greatness.
She cries, washed and blessed be the kingdom with her tears."
I asked the faraway voice,
"Jinia, my friend and sister in infinity,
Who, in this trial time, will hold her lonely hand?
Who will care for her tears? Who will be there for her?
Can my heart be the stone and call a grace to her?"
And the faraway voice replied,
"Straight, void, High, and free from the dreams of gods and men,
The path she has chosen is not an easy one.
Through cold, and bitter woes, it leads to endless fire.
Open, friend, just open. Open your heart to her
Who shines through and beyond vastness and remoteness.
Today we meet in grief, and heavy mists of pain.
But soon, and from yourself, a call for joy will rise,
And you shall meet again, and the gods will bless you."
And in this encounter of several time-lines, another faraway voice sang,
"Now is the time, the time of the glorious birth. Awaken, son! Awaken to
your vastness."

The air was still vibrant with the power of Lohrzen's scream.

I walked straight over to Jinia's body lying on the floor, and checked that her energy had coped with the scream.

There was no problem with her. She was just asleep.

Then I inspected the child's energy. It was unchanged.

Hermina was still crying.

I inhaled a long breath. This time, there was nothing more I could do for her child. What, then?

The pull to walk towards Hermina was immense.

I hesitated. Would this be against her rule? At that stage, I no longer cared about breaking protocol for my sake. But I knew that high ascetics placed great emphasis on the strict adherence to the religious rules that governed their caste. The poor woman was already sad enough, if moreover I was to make her break her rule...

The faraway voice interrupted my thoughts, "Awaken, son! Awaken to your vastness!"

No thoughts, just Dragon, I started walking towards her.

My palms turned upwards, my gaze directed high up, I went and stood just in front of her and opened, calling on the Eagle's highest compassion.

I opened everything – everything but the Point-seal, of course, since revealing Archive secrets was a risk I couldn't take.

The faraway voice returned. "Open, son! Open! Now!"

A flow of love passed into her, and she received. And she responded, pouring her high love into me.

Another faraway voice made itself heard, "If he does not open now, the awakening will be missed."

The first voice repeated, "Open, son! Drop the seal, open your Point. Now!"

What? But where did these voices come from? Who were they to tell me to expose my Point? They were not violent, they did not try to impose an influence on me. They were more like a whisper from distant spaces, a gentle call. But there was no way in the seven spheres I could run the risk of letting a stranger read my mind and discover the details of Gervin's Archive. I'd rather let myself be wiped off the surface of the Earth than put my teacher in danger!

Meanwhile, something beautiful was happening. I didn't have to take Hermina's hand, the Eagle had enveloped her in his wings. I didn't have to speak to her, the flow of feeling was reaching deep into her heart, and she knew that someone cared.

She cried, and I was there for her – completely.

Two strangers, united in Light,

And made one in Highness.

For a long time, I stayed in front of her. When her tears stopped, I did not leave. I kept opening with her, and a long time passed.

Then finally, sensing that Jinia was about to return into her body, I slowly stepped back, still gazing high above Hermina's head.

The faraway voices spoke again, "Danger, son! Danger! Do not leave now. The awakening has not yet taken place."

A new voice made itself heard, "If he does not awaken now, there will be no limit to his pain."

I stopped. But what did these voices want? What was I to do?

"Open, son! Drop the seal! Open unrestrictedly. Now is the time when the awakening can take place."

Drop the Point-seal? Don't even thought-form it! My mind held too much confidential information about the Archive. It would have been a betrayal of my teacher.

"The woman! She can help him. Invoke her help. Can she hear us?"

"Now, she can."

Soon, I felt Hermina's loving presence reaching towards my Point. It was clean and friendly, and warm like Highness.

At first I welcomed her by letting waves of the Eagle's Love flow into her. But in a flash of discernment, I realised that if I allowed Hermina's energy to work on me, my Point-seal would be dissolved.

That, I could not allow. Too much was at stake.

Resting on the Dragon, I turned on my heel and walked towards the door.

"Danger, son! Danger! Do not go now!" the faraway voice called.

I kept walking.

Hermina called, "Wait, Szar!"

Her voice touched me deep. I had to stop – not out of force, but because of the love that had been pouring through us.

But considering the Archive's secret potentially endangered, I started walking again and did not turn back.

As I crossed the doorway, Hermina called a second time, "Wait, Szar! Please, don't go now. Wait!"

What a beautiful voice she had.

I didn't stop.

When I arrived in the bedroom, I felt quite confused. I badly wanted to speak to Elyani, but the White Eagle had gone to explore the palace, and I couldn't take the risk of disclosing confidential information through a voice channel.

I stood on the balcony. The mists were so thick I could see my feet, but hardly further than that.

What the Far Underworld had been happening?

No thoughts, just Dragon, I left the princely suite and went out to look for Marzook, who was to take me to a 'real dealer'.

11.14 Henrick and the Renegade Hunters

My stone-hunting party had a bad beginning, a worse middle, and a catastrophic ending.

For a start, the boat that Marzook had arranged was nowhere in sight. Marzook sat on a bench in silence, his gaze fixed on the mists, and more than two hours passed before the boat finally arrived.

Then it transpired that the village where I was to meet the 'real dealer' was much further from Tomoristan than I had thought. At least three hours by boat. And in the middle of the journey the boat stopped for no reason. Marzook stayed sitting where he was, quietly contemplating the mists. After more than an hour of standstill, I sent him to inquire about the crew. When he came back, I asked him what was going on.

He answered with a reassuring smile, *"Nothing, Sir Szar of the Brown Robe. Everything is fine in the Law!"* Then he sat down and resumed his contemplation of the mists. And the boat remained still. Rather than send Marzook a second time, I decided to go with him to speak to the captain. Marzook was right, there was no reason for the halt. So, pressure duly applied, the journey could soon continue.

When the boat finally arrived at its destination, a surprise was waiting for me: the village was essentially populated by Nephilim people. Stamped as I was with Great Warriors' energy seals, I decided I had better remain close to Marzook, whose Crimson Robe indicated that we were from the prince's palace. In Mount Lohrzen I had heard more than one story of Warriors trampled to death by angry Nephilim crowds.

After a long walk through empty narrow streets, we arrived at the shabby house where Marzook had made an appointment for me.

Parnan, an old man with only one tooth left, and an ugly one at that, invited us in. The room was small, dark and filthy. An interesting contrast with the princely suite where Lady Elyani was probably already waiting for me, wondering why the Underworld I was taking so long.

Marzook sat down beside me, eyes wide open, staring at the gloomy *living wall* while the old man showed me a large collection of worthless stones.

I took my head in my hands. *"Listen, old father in the Law! If, by the grace of our Lord Melchisedek, you want to see the colour of my gold, you had better show me some real stones, not filosterops' pooh!"*

When he saw my discontent, Parnan looked rather satisfied. He went into another room and brought back a small bag of stones.

There were seventeen of them. Sixteen were useless, that is, only good for voice-channel calls. But one stone immediately seized my Dragon. It was small – hardly larger than a cherry – but it carried a magnificent vibration that vroofed deep into the Earth. I carefully tuned into it, fixing its energy characteristics in my memory.

Seeing I had picked up the one valuable item of the lot, the old man smiled. *"I see you are a connoisseur in the Law!"*

I tapped the pouch at my side. The small golden ingots clinked. *"If you have more of these stones, old father, by tonight you will be a rich man in the Law."*

Parnan got the message. He went to the door of his house and called a child who was waiting outside. After whispering a few words in his ear, he came back to sit in front of me. "Henrick is on his way," his voice whistled. "He's a great prian. He has stones like you want, *man of the Law.*"

While we were waiting I did my best to get Parnan to chat, so I could learn about his providers. No luck. The old man kept repeating stubbornly, "Henrick the prian is coming!"

After perhaps half an hour, I suddenly received a high-emergency signal. I closed my eyes and confirmed the perception. Then I stood up. I walked quickly out of the house and carefully sense-smelled the street.

Worried at seeing the gold leaving his house, Parnan ran after me. "Wait, *man of the Law*, Henrick the prian is coming!"

The smell left no doubt, three Nephilim Hunters were approaching. "Is Henrick a Hunter?" I asked.

Parnan was taken aback. "Who told you this, *man of the Law*?"

Tuning into him, I saw that he was not cheating – at least not on this point. Henrick *was* a Nephilim Hunter.

"Oh, gods!"

From high in the clear fountain, I decided to take the risk.

Preparing myself for a fight, I quickly inspected the street's energies, looking for toxic lines and wells from which to draw venomous Dragon fumes. There was nothing I could use.

The Hunters were drawing near. By now, they would have detected I was one of Mount Lohrzen's Warriors, and would be planning for a potential hunt.

I went back into the room. Marzook hadn't moved. He was still staring at the empty wall in front of him.

"You are a soldier, Marzook, aren't you?"

Marzook stood up, straight. "Yes, Sir Szar of the Brown Robe!"

"Have you ever fought against the Nephilim Hunters?"

He frowned. "The Nephilim Hunters are very powerful, Sir Szar of the Brown Robe. One cannot fight them."

I set my lower jaw, contemplating my left palm. The Hunters were now less than a street away. For a second, I hesitated. It would still have been possible to run the Dragon out of there.

But I decided to sit down and wait.

The Hunters were slow to arrive. What were they brewing?

The old man brought two cups of green drink. I declined the offer. So did Marzook after me.

Finally, I sensed them coming. Two from the left end of the street, one from the right. Only one of them came to the house. The others remained posted at each end of the street.

When I heard approaching footsteps, I stood up and turned towards the door, reinforcing my Point-seal. Marzook stood up after me.

The door creaked open. A tall, broad-shouldered blond man stood in the doorway.

Ready to strike, I stood on the Dragon.

We looked at each other. He was a man of the north, with blue eyes and a high forehead, perhaps in his early thirties. He had neither beard nor moustache, and was not wearing a robe but grey pants and shirt, with the Hunters' traditional strapped leather bag hanging from his shoulder.

"*Praise the Lord Melchisedek, man of the Law!* My name is Henrick," he said in a warm voice and with a friendly smile.

"*All glory to the Lord Melchisedek, Henrick!* My name is Szar," I replied in a neutral voice. The smile did not fool me – in front of me was a killing machine of a high standard, a kuren-jaya expert overtrained in the power of the Point and master in the arts of war.

Marzook replied after me, "*All glory to the Lord Melchisedek, Henrick! My name is Marzook, of the Crimson Robe, in the Service of His High Majesty Filipotonisteraniso Ozorenan, Prince of the County of the Northern Lakes under the Appointment of His Supreme Majesty the King of Atlantis.*"

Now that my Point was alive, seeing a Hunter was a completely different experience. I couldn't Point-tune into him directly, of course – it would have amounted to an attack. Still, it was easy to observe that the man's aura radiated Point-ness and sharp energies drawn from supermind layers. Henrick's Point was a fortress. If I had to fight against him on that level, I did not stand a chance.

Henrick sat down by the old man. "So you are looking for stones?" his voice was casual.

I sat down opposite him. "If they're good," I said.

Marzook sat down and said nothing.

Henrick reached for one of the green drinks. "Of course they're good. Are you paying in gold or in orichalc?"

"Gold."

Henrick's smile broadened, revealing two rows of impeccable white teeth. Then he opened his leather bag and grabbed a black pouch that he handed to me, and he picked up the green beverage and drank a sip.

What a feast! I wished Woolly could have seen this: a dozen stones ranging in size from cherry to strawberry, and carrying the most extraordinary energies. Their variegated vibrations showed they all came from different sources – a near-certain indication that they had been stolen. "Looks like you and I are going to get along well, Henrick," I said.

"*How wonderful in the Law!*" Henrick gave his charming smile.

"Your price for the lot?"

"Two ingots each, but three for that one," he reached forward and put his index finger on a he-stone with a dazzling aura.

"Not exactly a bargain."

"Who wants cheap stones?" he leant back again.

"All right. I'll take them. But what if I need more?"

Henrick handed the other green drink to me. "How many more?"

I took the cup but did not drink. "Many more."

"Simple!" he gave a shrug. "Just bring many more ingots next time!"

"Tomoristan is a long way from my temple. Could I meet you somewhere closer to the county of Eisraim? In the county of Lasseera, perhaps?"

"Do you know Barnagiran?" Henrick asked.

"The large town at the top of the county of Lasseera?"

"Yes, that one. Lots of Nephilim people over there. Just go and tell one of them you're looking for Henrick the Hunter, and I will find you."

I took the pouch that hung from my belt and counted out the right amount of small golden ingots. I slid them across to Henrick, who transferred them into his bag. I also gave three to Parnan. Standard commission.

Henrick stood up. Always smiling, he raised his left forearm, his fist closed as in the secret recognition sign of the Sons of the Dragon. And he winked at me, "Hope to see you again, Warrior."

Amused at how well he knew the secret sign, I returned the smile. There was no doubt, Henrick the prian had class.

As he closed the door behind him, Marzook suddenly woke up and smiled at me with satisfaction. "*Great strategists know how to win wars without waging battles,*" he quoted the Law.

I didn't answer. I kept admiring the stones, sense-smelling darkness visible to check that the Hunters were leaving.

After a few minutes, when the Hunters' characteristic astral smell had started fading from the neighbouring space, I placed the stones in my gold pouch and lawfully took leave of Parnan.

The combined power of these stones was amazing. As we walked back to the boat, the vibration in the pouch made my Dragon vroof with excitement. I knew that stones of this calibre could accomplish extraordinary things, but this was the first time I had had the opportunity to hold one in my hand. I couldn't wait to reach the princely suite and start exploring their energies with Elyani.

Marzook was in a buoyant mood. He engaged a lawful conversation with me, as if he and I were now *comrades in the Law* after surviving a battle against the Nephilim Hunters. But just as I was about to tell him that I hadn't heard from my parents for some time, I received a Point-communication from Gervin.

"*Szar! You and Elyani must come back to Eisraim immediately. Take the first boat and come straight to the temple.*"

"*But I am not with Elyani, I am a few hours from Tomoristan.*"

"*Then do not even go back to the palace. Elyani has probably already left Tomoristan.*"

"*Gervin, what is happening?*"

"*Holma, our ascending goddess, has died. We could be facing some extremely grave matters.*"

"*Anything I can do?*"

"*Nothing for the moment. Just come back, and remember that I love you.*"

I tuned high into the clear fountain, then Point-called Elyani.

"What's been happening to you Szar?" she Point-asked. "I have tried to Point-call you several times, but you were totally sealed."

"I had to. I was in dangerous company. But everything is fine now. Where are you, White Eagle?"

"Sitting on the quay outside the palace, waiting for a boat. I received an emergency Point-call from Teyani. She said the daiva was about to be revealed, Szar."

"For the Dragon's sake, are we finally going to know what that daiva is about? I want to be with you when it happens!"

"It's imminent, Szar. All I know for the moment is that Holma is dead. Teyani said she would Point-call again and give me more details in a few minutes. But she warned me of something weird: I might have to totally seal my Point."

"Seal your Point? Oh no! How am I going to call you if I arrive too late to catch the boat with you? When is it leaving?"

"In one hour, perhaps two or three if they are late."

"I'll do anything I can to get there on time."

"Please, come! Come! Come! I love you, Dragon."

"Forever love, White Eagle of the gods."

I turned to Marzook. "How fast can you run, *my friend in the Law?*"

Marzook looked at me, perplexed.

I started running. "Forget about my parents, Marzook, we are in a hurry!" Quite unfortunately, the fat court attendant proved incapable of matching my pace. At first I waited for him, but then I decided to leave him behind and I set off at Dragon-speed to catch the boat.

But just as I got to the river, I received another warning signal. When I realised what it meant, I raised my fists towards the gods and screamed, "No! Why are you doing this to me?"

I ran to the quay, but the boat was no longer there! Since there was no other vessel in sight, I started inspecting the terrain. There was no time to waste.

The signal left no doubt about it – three Nephilim Hunters were on my heels.

Jumping into the river was not an option, for if the Hunters were intending to Point-lock me in a triangular net – most redoubtable Point-weapon – my only chance was to kill the three of them as soon as possible. So I located a line of venom wells and stationed myself just behind it, hoping my adversaries would make the mistake of approaching it.

I waited, Point-sealing myself as strongly as I could.

I didn't have to wait long. Soon, two of the Hunters appeared out of the mists. They were dressed in black, and to my surprise one of them was a giant.

The first Nephilim giant to ever cross my path.

He was about four heads taller than me, his shoulders larger than any I had ever set eyes upon in Mount Lohrzen. His dark eyes were lit by a wild glow.

Many times in the canyons of the Red Lands I had wondered what Felicia would be like when she became mad. Now I could see! Right in front of me. In the giant's eyes, furious madness. Spice gone wrong. Power out of control.

Dangerous. *Very* dangerous.

The giant and his friend stopped and looked at me.

There were no indications that they had detected the venom wells, but they were too far away for me to strike. I had to find a stratagem to entice them nearer.

"Look at this!" the giant said, "What do we have here? A black nightmare!"

I addressed them with a diplomatic smile, *"Friends in the Law, what a happy coincidence!* I was just looking for people who sell stones. I need large quantities of them, and I pay in gold."

"Is this why you are carrying so many stones with you?" the other Hunter asked.

Hunters had several ways of Point-detecting the presence of soft stones – especially powerful ones like the beauties in my pouch. In all likelihood this was how they had tracked me down.

"These stones are not much compared to what I need," I told them. "Do you have anything good to sell?"

"Enough of this, black nightmare!" the giant yelled. "First you're going to give us your stones, and *then* we're going to kill you."

A huge Dragon-wave rose inside me. The time had come to apply what Marek had taught me.

There was not much to lose at this stage, so I took a daring step. Point-sealing myself to the extreme, I tried to infiltrate the communication Point-field between the three Hunters.

"Why lose a rich customer, *men of the Law*?" I said.

"You are dead meat!" the giant snarled, and he started walking towards me.

As I watched him approach my venom wells, I caught the Point-communication the second Hunter was sending him. *"Are you going to stop this nonsense, Progos? Henrick has asked us not to kill him. So we take his stones, and we let him go!"*

"Henrick said we shouldn't kill him, he never said we couldn't damage him a bit," the giant Point-retorted. *"Anyway, since when are the Black Hunters supposed to receive their orders from Henrick?"*

"You'd better go gently, Progos. If you start a war against Henrick's men, Murdoch will be furious."

The third Hunter intervened. "You damn idiots, what do you think you're doing? That man is not just a black dancer. His Point is finely woven in the Eisraim style. Do you realise what that means? If he knows how to neutralise our Point-venom weapons, it means he could black-dance the three of us flat dead in no time."

"Speak for yourself, Bradric, you dwarf in the Law!" the giant Point-spat. "I am not afraid of fighting a black dancer. Anyway, the Points of Eisraim priests are useless for fighting. Only good for kissing angels' asses."

"Do you realise he could be Point-spying on what we are saying right now?" Bradric Point-answered.

The giant stopped. He was only six lawful feet from the venom well. And ten lawful feet from me.

My fists were clenched. I was ready to strike. "You are about to say goodbye to a lot of gold, *men of the Law!* Wouldn't you rather become my suppliers, instead of my enemies? I have an urgent need of quality stones. Lots of them."

"This man is playing with us!" the second Hunter Point-said. "The priests of Eisraim have one of the best stone makers in the kingdom. His name is Narbenzor. He used to work for the temple of Laminindra, only a few hours from here. His stones were so fantastic that Henrick and Murdoch tried to employ him, but he refused. After this Henrick melted his chapel in Laminindra, and Narbenzor went to Eisraim. But now he makes even better stones. He's designed a process that uses Underworld energies instead of fields. They're busy testing it in Lasseera, for their Archive stones. These guys are even talking about making hermaphroditic stones!"

Had it not been for the Dragon, I probably would have fainted then and there. How in the kingdom could these men know about the new processes Maryani had introduced only a few weeks ago? And how the Dark Underworld could they know about the Archive? It was the end of the line. What I was discovering meant that there was no way the Archive transfer could take place. Any party carrying the super-charged Archive stones from Eisraim and Lasseera to the place of the transfer would have been ambushed and annihilated by hordes of Nephilim Hunters.

"Let's turn him into black puree!" Progos Point-announced with glee.

The giant raised his fists and took a step towards me. He was now within range of the venom wells. I could strike any second.

At the same time, he Point-asked his friends, "As soon as I am on him, you Point-flood him with red venom."

Red venom? That, I had no idea how to combat!

So I decided to bluff. I began the opening moves of the black dance and yelled at the giant, "All right, Progos! You don't want to listen to your friends, do you? Come and meet my venom, then! I'll show you if the Eisraim Point is only good for kissing angels' asses!"

Startled, the giant suddenly realised I had overheard their entire Point-conversation.

"How deep have you tested his Point, Pentar?" he Point-queried. *"Who has he been trained by?"*

The second Hunter Point-answered. "Strange features, especially in the high end of the column of Spirit. It doesn't match any known Point-signature. I don't like the look of this, Progos."

Bradric sent an emergency Point-call, "We have another problem, Per-seps' men are on their way. Let's get out of here! Fast!"

It was just at that moment that Marzook arrived, puffing and panting. "Praise the Lord Melchisedek... men of the Law!" he said. "I am Marzook... of the Crimson Robe, in the Service of... His High Majesty Filipotonister-aniso Ozorenan... Prince of the County... of the Northern Lakes under the Appointment... of His Supreme Majesty... the King of Atlantis." Then he stood proudly and beamed at the men, confident of the power of his words.

"Progos!" Pentar Point-yelled, *"Move your ass! We can't take the risk of clashing with Perseps' men."*

Progos brandished his fist, "I will find you, Szar of the Brown Robe, and I will kill you!" And he turned and fled, together with his friends.

Marzook smiled with satisfaction, watching the two men in black disappear into the mists. "Sir Szar, *my friend in the Law,* it looks like we are lucky today!"

"Where is the damn boat, Marzook?"

Perplexed, the big man looked at the empty quay. "Yes, where is the damn boat?"

I Point-called Elyani. There was no response.

"Have you ever heard of someone called Perseps, Marzook?" I asked him. "His men should be here any minute."

"Perseps of the Nephilim Hunters? A very trustworthy and reliable man in the Law. I can thoroughly recommend him to you, Sir Szar!"

I bashed my fist against a tree. "Ugly Underworld! Not the Hunters again!"

Marzook was in his protective character, "Can I help you solve another problem, Sir Szar?"

"How come these men were afraid of Perseps? Aren't they Hunters themselves?"

"They were Black Hunters, Sir Szar. They are Renegade Hunters. Like Henrick the prian, but another clan. Perseps, on the other hand, is from Jex Belaran, the Nephilim Hunters' training centre in the county of the Snowy Mountains, not very far from here. His function is to hunt the Renegades. He is a very honest man. There is nothing to fear."

How could this man be such a sleeper? "Marzook, I am one of the Great Warriors, the Hunters' worst enemies, we are right in the middle of Nephilim territory, I am carrying a bag full of stolen stones, and the Hunt-ers' police are on their way. And you say there is nothing to fear?"

A boat was approaching.

"Stop! Stop!" I yelled at the men on the deck. "Marzook, tell them to stop!"

"*Praise the Lord Melchisedek, men of the Law!*" he shouted. "*I am Marzook, of the Crimson Robe, in the Service of His High Majesty Filipotonisteraniso Ozorenan, Prince of the County of the Northern Lakes under the Appointment of His Supreme Majesty the King of Atlantis,* and I request you to stop!"

The two men gave Marzook a friendly wave, but they didn't stop.

The boat was going far too fast for me to swim over and catch up with it. So I took the pouch that held the gold and the stones, and I yelled, "Gold! Gold!"

From the boat, the two men looked at me.

I threw the pouch. It landed on the deck, and the boat soon disappeared into the mists.

Marzook was deeply puzzled. "Now, Szar of the Brown Robe... After all the trouble we had to get these stones, this was a strange thing to do, my friend in the Law."

"Now Perseps is chasing the boat instead of us! The stones carry strong vibrations the Hunters know how to recognise from far away. Where is our damn boat, Marzook?"

"Er... it is already late in the Law, Sir Szar. We might have to spend the night here. But don't worry, I know a really good place to stay. The food is excellent."

I couldn't Point-call anyone for fear of signalling my presence to the Hunters. There was no other boat to catch. So I took Marzook for another run well away from the shoreline, to limit the risk of the Hunters locating us.

And we waited.

Perseps and his men did not find us. More than likely they were after the stones, not after me. And a few hours later, Marzook's boat finally arrived.

By the time we made it to Tomoristan, it was late in the night.

Elyani had already left.

– Thus ends the Book of the Princely Suite –

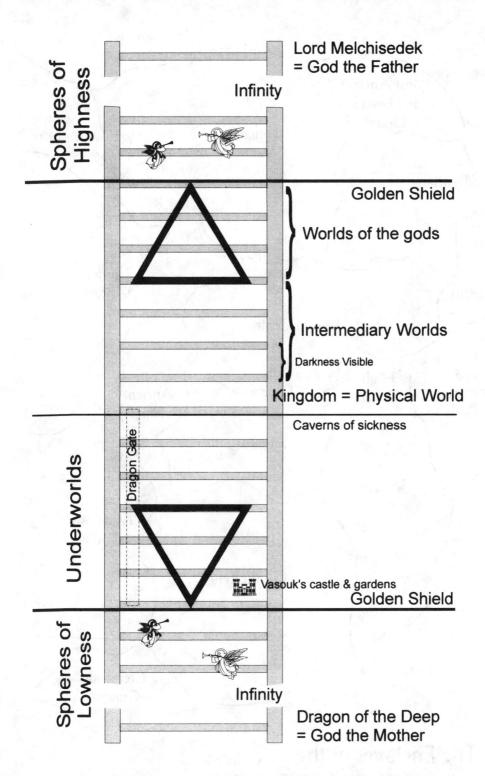

**The Cosmological Ladder
Showing the Spheres of Melchisedek**

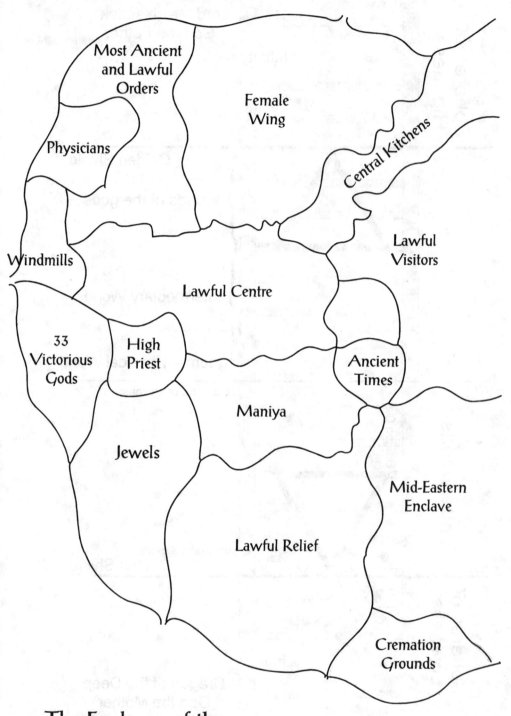

The Enclaves of the Western Part of the Esraim Temple